THE MISSING TWIN

Alex Day is a writer, teacher, parent and dreamer who has been putting pen to paper to weave stories for as long as she can remember. *The Missing Twin* is her first psychological thriller but she is a bestselling author of fiction under the name Rose Alexander.

Inspired by a real pair of identical twin girls, *The Missing Twin* also draws on Alex's experience of teaching newly arrived refugees, migrants and asylum seekers in a London comprehensive school.

🐦 @alexdaywriter

The Missing Twin

ALEX DAY

A division of HarperCollins*Publishers*
www.harpercollins.co.uk

KillerReads
an imprint of HarperCollins*Publishers* Ltd
1 London Bridge Street
London SE1 9GF

www.harpercollins.co.uk

This paperback edition 2017

First published in Great Britain in ebook format by HarperCollins*Publishers* 2017

A catalogue record for this book
is available from the British Library

ISBN: 978-0-00-827129-9

This novel is entirely a work of fiction.
The names, characters and incidents portrayed in it are
the work of the author's imagination. Any resemblance to
actual persons, living or dead, events or localities is
entirely coincidental.

Set in Minion by
Palimpsest Book Production Limited, Falkirk, Stirlingshire

Printed and bound in the UK

A little water clears us of this deed.

Macbeth; William Shakespeare

It was a dry cold night, and the wind blew keenly, and the frost was white and hard. A man would die tonight of lying out on the marshes, I thought. And then I looked at the stars, and considered how awful it would be for a man to turn his face up to them as he froze to death, and see no help or pity in all the glittering multitude.

Great Expectations; Charles Dickens

SUMMER, 2015

Edie

A shaft of bright sunlight found the gap between the misaligned wooden screen and the window frame and lanced across the room. The girl in the bed groaned, shifted onto her stomach and buried her face in her pillow. Moments later, she turned back onto her side, clutching her stomach as she fought back the nausea. Tentatively, she opened her eyes, feeling her pupils contract painfully against the light and becoming aware of a dull, persistent pounding in her head and a thumping at her temples.

Little by little, Edie Marsh woke up enough to sincerely regret the amount she had drunk the night before, and to chastise herself, as she had many times before, for not knowing when to stop. Hauling herself into an upright position, she reached out for the glass on the floor by her bed and drank, finishing it all even as she screwed up her face at the water's stale taste and tepid temperature. Holding her hands to her head in an attempt to calm the throbbing, she shut her eyes and tried to concentrate. Something was wrong.

She dropped her hands to her lap and forced her eyes open

again, head still drooping down with the effort of it all. Gazing around the room from corner to corner, scouring all pathetic three square metres of it, she did not see what she was expecting to. There was no one there.

No one but her.

The door was firmly closed – no sign that anyone had got up early for a swim or gone out in search of hangover-curing coffee and paracetamol. Even so, in case her eyes could not be trusted, Edie got up and investigated a couple of piles of discarded clothes, picking garments up and immediately throwing them back down again. She even looked under the bed. Then she slumped down onto the single plastic chair, the pulsing in her head suddenly overwhelming and uncontrollable. Massaging her eyelids with her thumbs, she searched her memory. What had happened last night? Hazy snapshots drifted through her mind but the details were sunk in alcohol and wouldn't surface.

They had planned to sleep squashed into the single bed together, something that they were used to, that they'd grown up doing, of that she was sure. 'They' being her and her adored identical twin sister, Laura, whose unexpected arrival at the holiday resort on the shores of the Adriatic sea where Edie was working at midday the day before had filled Edie's heart with happiness. They'd gone out on the town that evening, for sure. But right at this moment, Edie couldn't remember how or when they'd got home or anything much of what had gone on at all, during their night out or afterwards.

And the bed, now that she, Edie, had got out of it, was completely empty.

Where the hell was Laura?

Fatima

The sea looked flat and calm. Benign. Perhaps it always did from the shore, with the lazy ripples of tideless waves lapping the fringes of golden sand that gleamed in the heat. Fatima didn't know as she'd never been to the seaside before. She wasn't exactly here for the beach, anyway. Screwing up her eyes against the sun she could see, hazily in the distance, the outline of what she supposed must be the island they would be heading for.

It wasn't far. Really not far at all. Just a little water in-between. Compared to the distance she had already travelled it barely registered. You could almost swim there.

But she had never learnt to swim and neither had her children. She was sure that Ehsan didn't know, either, nor his son Youssef. Despair threatened to engulf her, together with an utter weariness that suffused her body and made her bones feel liquid, no longer able to support her weight. She sank to the ground, right there on the seafront promenade, crouching into the scanty shade offered by the low beach wall whilst tourists strolled past, all wobbly pink skin and red noses. They were so well fed and rested, so *oblivious*. But that was to be expected – they were on their holidays, after all.

A sudden, searing jealousy made Fatima want to stop them, to tear their expensive clothes from their backs, grab their over-priced ice-creams and throw them into the sea. *Look at me*, she would say to them. *This is what it's like to have nothing.* But the problem was that wasn't what it was like. Having no property, no income, no possessions, was not the problem.

The problem was having no hope.

The sun beat down on her head. She wanted to lie down and rest, regardless of the passers-by, heedless of the noise and bustle. She felt she could sleep for a hundred years. Perhaps if she looked pitiful enough, someone would save her. But she knew they wouldn't. The more needy you were, the more they ignored you. The more woeful, the more uncomfortable for others. Few, if any, wanted to get involved and who could blame them? There had been kindness amidst the devastation in her home country, people sharing their shelter and what little food they had. But Fatima wasn't stupid and not ignorant, either. She knew how she and her compatriots were viewed, talked about, written about.

As 'swarms' and 'floods' and 'marauding invaders'. Or, possibly even worse, as piteous and desperate, each pair of pleading eyes or outreached arms diminished by the sheer number of them, dehumanised and depersonalised by being one face amongst so very many.

In deciding to leave her country – although was it a decision when there seemed to be no other option? – she had taken on inconceivable, unimagined challenges. There was nothing to do but pull herself together and face those challenges. To get on with it. Think about Marwa and Maryam. She closed her hand around the warm, metal object in her pocket and squeezed it tight. It was the key to her house that no longer existed in her city that had been razed to the ground. She

4

should throw it away and would have already done so but for the fact that it was all that was left of her old life, the only thing to remind her.

Getting up off the pavement and dusting herself down she defiantly tucked in her headscarf where it had come loose. Some women had stopped wearing a scarf so as not to stand out, to avoid being noticed. But Fatima would no more go out with an uncovered head as with uncovered breasts. They had not taken everything away from her yet, not reduced her to being ashamed of her culture, her identity.

Setting off along the busy promenade, she held her head high and tried to look purposeful. She had a list of things she must buy, but it meant spending money and she needed to protect every cent because there were so many things to be paid for. She must choose wisely and purchase only what was absolutely necessary for the next stage of their odyssey.

Perhaps the saddest fact of all, the most depressing, she thought as she handed over the precious notes for the life-jackets, the plastic wallets for the mobile phones, water for the journey, was that if it wasn't her and her fellow citizens fleeing for a better life, it would be other people from other countries. There would always be another war, another catastrophe whether man-made or natural, to cause the human tide to swell and surge. This was a fact that would never change.

ONE

Edie

'Service!'

The cry rang out as it did endlessly during the lunchtime shift. Edie seized the large platter of mixed seafood from the counter and walked to table ten, as quickly as she could without looking too deferential. It might be her job to serve but there was no need to look servile in the process. She passed Milan, one of the other restaurant staff, on the way there.

'How's it going?' he asked, grinning cheerily. He was always inexplicably jolly.

'Not bad,' replied Edie. 'Ask me again in a few hours' time when I go off shift and I'll be even better.'

Milan chuckled heartily. 'I will!' he answered, and twirled the empty silver tray he was carrying on his forefinger, one of his favourite party tricks. 'Keep smiling, Edie.'

Edie did, indeed, smile, at the same time as shaking her head in mock despair. There was simply no keeping Milan down; he was irrepressible. She wondered what it was that made her so relentlessly cynical, what trauma or trouble from her childhood had caused it. Perhaps always playing second fiddle to her twin

Laura was the root of the problem; the knowledge that Laura would always have the edge in looks, intelligence and charm. In response, Edie had resorted to affecting a generally world-weary and sceptical persona that meant that, whenever she failed – at a spelling test, a netball match or A-level history – and Laura succeeded, she could pretend that she hadn't tried and didn't care in the first place.

Nevertheless, despite their innate competitiveness, Edie thought the world of her sister and missed her like crazy. Not a day went by that she didn't think about her and wonder what she was doing. Today was no different to any other. Laura was always on her mind.

'Excuse me.' A customer calling for her attention broke her reverie. Edie deposited the seafood platter with its eager recipients and turned to address the enquiry.

'You didn't bring us any cutlery,' declaimed the bottle-blonde, her voice an exaggerated lament.

You didn't ask for any, Edie wanted to retort but restrained herself just in time. She was aware of the need to mind her step. You never knew when Vlad, the vulpine resort manager, was watching. Perfectly positioned at the centre of a horseshoe bay of golden sand, the location meant that the beach bar and restaurant was popular with tourists and locals alike. There was a constant stream of customers from opening time at 8 a.m. until they shut up shop at midnight or later. The resort itself was aimed at wealthy Russians and Europeans – French, English, German, Italian – hence Edie's job there, for Vlad felt that an English girl would understand the requirements of the cosmopolitan clientele better than a local. Edie had been somewhat economical with the truth about her ability to speak French (failed GCSE but he wasn't to know) and English was her mother tongue. That had been enough for Vlad to take her on, but he could equally get rid of her if her work wasn't up to standard.

'I'm so sorry,' Edie apologised to the customer, who gave a long-suffering sigh in response. 'I'll get you some right away.'

She turned back towards the bar and kitchen, trying hard not to drag her feet. She had cleaned cabanas all morning and then come straight here for the lunchtime shift and she'd now been taking food orders, pulling pints of pale yellow lager, preparing cocktails with coloured parasols and handing over bottles of fizzy pop with bendy straws for the kids for over two hours already. It was the first time in her life she'd had to work so hard, on her feet for hours at a time, her breaks never seeming long, frequent or restful enough.

Once she'd delivered the cutlery, she sought respite by going round behind the kitchen, ostensibly to fetch a crate of Coke but in reality to get five minutes' time out from the frenzy. Standing in front of the huge fridge door, Edie sensed a presence, someone near her, an uncanny sensation of being watched. She looked around. She couldn't see anyone but knew that she was being spied on. A curl of excitement slid through her, that feeling of playing hide-and-seek as a child and knowing that you are about to be found and starting to giggle even as delicious fear slides through your veins.

She stood quite motionless for a moment. It must be Vuk, playing games with her. Big, bad, incredibly sexy Vuk, deputy manager, Vlad's right-hand man – and Edie's latest and most covetable conquest. The slither of fear turned to a frisson of excitement that began in her belly and spread tantalisingly outwards.

Then came a stifled giggle, audible even above the music and voices and laughter filtering through from the restaurant. Not Vuk then; someone female by the sounds of it. Edie turned rapidly around, took two great strides forward that brought her to the corner of the building where she halted, almost falling over, momentarily blinded by the brightness of the light. Her eyes recovered, she looked up. And came face to face with herself.

Or rather, with her twin Laura, who was standing there with

a teasing, 'how long does it take to get noticed around here' look on her face, her perfect, pale pink rosebud lips drawn into a half-mocking, half-delighted smile, a tiny backpack dangling casually from one shoulder. Forgetting everything, her job, her customers, the Coca-Cola that was needed out front, Edie shot straight at her, hugging her vigorously and squealing incoherently in astonishment and excitement.

'How did you get here? Where have you come from? How long are you staying?' And then, 'Is that all the stuff you've got with you?' as she took in the minuscule size of Laura's minimal luggage. Her excited questions poured out of her, leaving little time for her sister to respond.

But Laura wasn't giving any answers anyway. She merely stood there, mute and smirking, letting Edie release her excitement unabated.

'I was thinking about you only a few moments ago, I must have sensed you were nearby although I never thought you'd just turn up, I can't even imagine how you found me, I didn't exactly give you precise directions ...' Her voice tailed off as she took in Laura's expression, the smirk having faded away and been replaced by a glassy-eyed stare.

'Are you OK, sis?' she asked, fear gripping her heart that Laura was really sick and had come to tell her so.

'I'm fine, Ed,' said Laura, wearily. 'Just fine. But now I'm finally here and I've found you, I've hit the wall. I've been on the road since forever and I'm too tired to talk. I'll explain everything later. But now ...' she held out her hand to Edie. 'Room. Key. Sleep.'

Edie pulled her key from her shorts pocket, gave it to Laura and pointed her in the direction of the staff cabins at the back of the resort, quickly telling her the number of hers. She could hear a voice calling her from the bar, telling her to hurry back. But she waited a moment, watching Laura drift up the path that wound between the cabanas and through the olive grove.

9

There was no one around, not a soul in sight, just the shimmer of a heat haze above the silver-leaved trees. Laura's slim, lissom body sported a perfect tan and even after hours of travelling, her wavy brunette hair swung buoyantly around her shoulders as she gradually disappeared from view. It was exactly as Edie was so well aware. Laura was, had always been, the top twin.

A lizard scurried out from behind the garbage bins and straight over Edie's toes, bare in her leather sandals. She squealed, just as the voice from the bar became louder and was suddenly right beside her.

'What you doing, Edeeee?' It was Stefan, the bar and restaurant manager, who always pronounced her name with a few extra 'e' sounds at the end. 'You been gone too long, you got three orders waiting.'

Edie shot a last glance after Laura, but she was no longer visible, swallowed up by the twists of the path and the sheltering tree branches.

'Sure,' she answered, flicking open the fridge, hauling out the Coca-Cola and pushing the door to with her foot. She wanted to go and hang out with her elusive sister, not get back to work. 'I just noticed we were short of this stuff. I was only trying to help.' She flashed a reproachful smile at Stefan, playing on the soft spot she knew he had for her.

'Here, let me,' said Stefan, pulling the crate from her hands. 'I take it.'

He was too much of a gentleman, too calm and kind and far too beguiled, to get truly angry, despite her many failings. His entrancement was nothing less than she expected; she and Laura had learnt early in their teenage years the power that youth and beauty could wield. This translated now into the fact that Edie could get away with murder on Stefan's watch. As Stefan lugged the crate of soft drinks back to the bar, she felt herself mellow, towards her job, the resort, everything. Her sister's electric presence brought the promise of excitement that overrode the mundanity of working. Despite the feelings of inferiority that Laura unintentionally engendered in her, when Laura was around Edie instantly became a better, nicer, happier person. And of course there was always the impact of 'double trouble' to enjoy; the two of them together somehow held more than twice the allure of one twin on her own. They would have some fun in the next few days and weeks, for sure.

As the hours wore on, however, Edie lost hope that Laura, whose capacity for sleeping during the day was infinite, would reappear anytime soon. It was a shame, as she could have got some free food for her and had her nearby as she plunked baskets of bread and bowls of tomato salad, cups of coffee and bottles of beer onto the rough-hewn wooden tables. The up-market atmosphere meant plastic was kept to a minimum; Vlad wanted to create a rustic, authentic feel, but it was hard to eradicate almost half a century of Communism with a few artisan accoutrements and some things just weren't quite right in Edie's eyes. The restaurant still sported those naff metal dispensers that contained paper napkins so small and flimsy as to be good for nothing and Vlad had stared at her in utter bemusement when she had suggested serving beer in jam jars, as the trendiest places in London and Sydney did.

He'd had to concede to plastic chairs, though, as diners in bikinis had not appreciated splintered bottoms, but had confined these to the area at the front on the sand, keeping the wooden ones for the fully covered section, where people were expected to turn up with the semblance of being dressed. Of course by the end of every long night the chairs had invariably been moved and mixed up and one of Edie's least favourite jobs was reorganising them all; she had about ten bruises on her legs from hefting around heavy, unwieldy lumps of pine. That was another legacy of Communism, Edie presumed; no concessions to ladies that they shouldn't put their backs into physical work. Doing it really, really slowly was the only way she'd found of mitigating the situation but Vlad had got her number and threatened to put her on toilet-cleaning duty so she'd had to speed up a bit.

Slave driver Vlad was an enigma. His height was average – about 5 foot 10 – and he was dark like most people here, clean-shaven and well-groomed. His brown eyes burned bright in his thin face and seemed to be always scrutinising, judging, appraising; when he smiled, it did not reach them. He was slightly built but wiry – Edie had heard that he'd been a long-distance runner in his youth but that he hadn't quite lived up to his promise and had only competed locally. Perhaps it was disappointment that lay behind his icy gaze.

Edie had never seen him with a woman and had found out, through not very discreet enquiries of other members of staff, that he was unmarried. What was puzzling – and unusual – was that he hadn't tried it on with her. It had crossed Edie's mind to wonder if he were gay. Now that Laura was here, this theory could be put properly to the test, as it was unheard of for any red-blooded male to refuse her sister. She was irresistible.

Although they were identical, with even their closest friends finding it difficult to tell them apart, there were differences between them that came from something intrinsic, primordial. Where Edie was pretty, Laura was beautiful. Edie was slim and attractive but Laura was something more, something harder to define, a heady mixture of sex appeal and mystery mixed with a pinch of dismissive contempt that kept every man she met drooling at her feet and coming back for more, however badly she treated them. Edie was generally considered a looker; her friends had nothing but envy for her appearance and figure and charm. But everything that Edie had, Laura had also, doubled. Laura was a stunner. At least, that's how Edie saw things.

Their parents had tried hard to make sure that they never showed any favouritism, constantly reassuring Edie that they

12

loved both girls just the same. Edie couldn't remember the birth of her brother James, who was three years younger, but she was pretty sure that during their growing-up, all three children had enjoyed nothing but fair, equal and unconditional love. They had lived a life of plenty; plenty of money, plenty of space in their five-bedroomed semi-detached house in a leafy Brighton suburb, plenty of support. Edie, Laura and James had never wanted for anything and for sure, Laura had made a career out of getting others – men, namely – to provide for her. Edie, on the other hand, having dallied with university and modelling and travelling, had tired of life and needed to get away from the superficiality of everything that surrounded her. She was fed up of being supported, protected and smothered by her parents, Laura, doctors – all of them making decisions about what was best for her or what she should or would do. She had had to escape. So she had come here and got a solid, honest job and now she was working her socks off on a daily basis and wondering what on earth had possessed her. And yet ... and yet she stayed. At three months and counting, it was getting to be the longest she'd ever stuck at anything.

The long afternoon dragged by. A group of lads, young and fit, provided the only entertainment, ordering beer after beer that kept Edie running backwards and forwards to the bar. She flirted with them a bit, out of habit as much as anything else, and also from a feeling she had that she was expected to provide the eye-candy at the beach bar that would keep the customers – the males, at any rate – coming back. She was glad when the group, half-cut and with glazed eyes, retreated to the beach to sleep off the alcohol, lying flat out on towels flung onto the soft sand under the pine trees, oblivious to the flies and the kids scuffling clumsily by and the volleyball game going on only metres away.

Even with the boys gone, there was no let-up from work; just customer after customer ordering meals and drinks and sandwiches. The resort itself wasn't that big – only two dozen cabanas amongst the olives, all with plunge pools and cleverly situated to have sea views. But it was at full occupancy at the height of the tourist season and, though the accommodation was self-catering, most residents didn't, and their custom was augmented by that of the constant ebb and flow of visitors, who came from far and wide to enjoy the beach's clean yellow sand and shallow, crystal clear water. All of these people couldn't be wrong and indeed it was an idyllic place. It could have been this that had made Edie act totally out of character and hang around so long, without ever intending to do so, and commit to the entire season working with Vlad. But in all honesty, her decision had more to do with Vuk; to being close to him by working with him. Or working on him. And now, working hard to keep Laura and Vuk apart, in all senses of the word.

Because Vuk, Edie realised, could be a problem now that Laura had arrived, the only blot on the rosy horizon of life with her sister. Vuk was devastatingly handsome and tall with it, well over 6 foot, strongly built with well-defined biceps and a six-pack to make a girl weep. His black hair was cut close to his scalp and a five o'clock shadow darkened his face even immediately after he'd shaved. The tan that enhanced his indisputable masculinity was deepening by the day now that the season was in full swing; Vuk was responsible, amongst other things, for running the sailing trips on the resort's luxurious yacht and so was almost permanently outside. He was the strong, silent type that Edie always fell for and mostly spoke in monosyllables, barked out in his deep, seductive voice. He rarely smiled and when he did it was sensually lopsided, as if only the right side of his mouth could be bothered to make the effort. He was utterly gorgeous and Edie was not only determined to snare him but also not to share him.

Little by little, perhaps not as swiftly as she had hoped, she was reeling bad boy Vuk in. They'd had sex a few times, each time better than the last; Vuk's hard, strong body the perfect complement to Edie's willowy, lithe limbs. Even to think about his white teeth on her breasts, his strong tongue probing between her thighs, his thick cock pumping into her, made Edie wet and set her clit throbbing in anticipation. He could circle her wrist with his thumb and forefinger and pull her towards him as if it were no effort whatsoever, could pick her up and throw her onto the bed as if she were nothing, could part her legs and pull them over his shoulders like she was a rag doll with no strength of her own. The power he had to dominate was dangerously attractive. But Edie still wasn't sure she really had him where she wanted him; namely committed to some kind of a relationship with her.

It would have been good if Vuk had been there to see how those boys had ogled her, to imagine how their dicks swelled in their swimming trunks, to feel the same himself. That would have been a minor triumph. In Edie's experience, there was nothing better than jealousy to make a man keen. But Vuk was nowhere to be seen, his comings and goings on the resort always erratic, his schedule impossible to pin down.

Edie just had to hope he hadn't bumped into Laura.

* * *

Finally, the sun shifted to the far side of the beach and the orders diminished. Edie threw her pad and apron into a heap in the kitchen and, shouting a hasty farewell to Stefan and Milan, set off as fast as she could bear in the still intense heat. As she walked, the sweat gathered on her back and chest and trickled down her spine and between her breasts. It was boiling.

In her room, she saw with relief that Laura was not only still there but still sleeping, face down, one slim, delicate arm flung out of the bed like the boom of an idling sailing ship. No sign she'd encountered Vuk or anyone at all. She looked as if she'd been asleep for ages. Edie sighed with relief. She dug around in the tiny fridge that nestled in one corner and pulled out the vodka she had stashed there. She'd bought cups of ice from the restaurant, and a water bottle filled with fresh lime juice. Mixing the drinks, adding sugar and stirring, she watched as the white crystals slowly dissolved. She slurped a mouthful; delicious. Putting the glasses side by side on the upturned crate that served as a bedside table, she sat down beside her twin. She shook her gently. No response. She tried again, more vigorously, and added in a little tug at her long tresses of brunette hair. Laura muttered something that sounded a bit like 'fuck off' but did not open her eyes. Exasperated, Edie stuck her fingers into one of the glasses, retrieved an ice cube and shoved it down the back of Laura's T-shirt.

'Christ!' Laura's cry was bloodcurdling. 'Shit! What the fuck ….'

Edie fell onto the floor, clutching her sides and gasping for breath as the laughter spewed out of her.

'Sleeping beauty, it's time to get up! There's fun to be had, drinks to be had, boys to be had. Every moment you're snoring is a wasted moment.'

Laura rubbed her eyes and wiggled her back, standing up to let what remained of the ice-cube slide out of her T-shirt. She shuddered.

'Oooh, that was actually quite nice. It's bloody bugger hot around here, I must say.'

'Yup. And you being here is just going to make everything even hotter. Drink up.' Edie handed Laura her vodka and lime. 'Ziveli.'

They lifted their glasses and drank. Laura exhaled loudly and shook her head. 'Wow. That's strong.'

'That's just for starters. Now you need to get yourself all tarted up cos we're going out.'

Edie threw Laura a faded beach towel. 'The showers are at the end of the block.' She looked around her, located a bottle of shampoo and chucked it in Laura's direction.

'By the way,' she added, as Laura turned to go. 'How on earth *did* you find your way here? I didn't give you the precise address. And where did you come from, where have you been the last few months?'

'My very own personal, inbuilt sat-nav, little sis.' Laura had been born first, by ten minutes or so, and never let Edie forget it. 'I could track you down anywhere.' She twirled the shampoo bottle round and round in her elegant hand. 'But – questions later. Right now, I need to wash. I can smell my own armpits and that's not even the worst of it.'

Laura glided out of the room and Edie drained her glass, still not quite believing that her twin had appeared as if from nowhere. She pulled a bundle of clothing out of the canvas shelving that was all she had for storage and dumped it onto the bed. By the looks of it, Laura would definitely be needing to borrow clothes – she didn't seem to have anything with her; her pack couldn't hold much more than a few pairs of knickers. Make-up, she always helped herself to anyway. Men – the same. Edie stopped short at this thought. Not Vuk. She was not giving up her claim on Vuk. This time, Edie would make sure she kept the big prize for herself.

TWO

Fatima

When the barrel bombs came to their neighbourhood, Fatima and the girls were not there. They had gone to visit friends in another suburb. They heard the explosions as they travelled home but explosions were nothing new so they tried to ignore them. You could never tell exactly where the bombs were falling anyway; sound ricochets and distorts, making distance incalculable. It was better to assume – to hope – that it hadn't hit your street, your home. Inuring yourself to the violence, the terror, the bloodshed, was the only way. So many times already it had been someone else's turn to take the brunt of this insane and insatiable war. Fatima gathered the twins protectively to her as the taxi proceeded through the deserted streets. For so long the fighting had taken place elsewhere and perhaps they had all assumed it would continue to be so even whilst knowing that there must surely be a limit to how often they could escape it.

As they neared home, it seemed that that limit had arrived. The taxi driver pulled over abruptly and told them it was finished; he would go no further. As if in a dream, Fatima got out of the car and pulled the children after her. She had had no phone call from Fayed, her husband, or his parents or brother with whom they lived, so she assumed things were all right at their place. But as the three of them stumbled onwards, picking their way through rubble, choking on dust, tripping in potholes, it was clear that their neighbourhood had been the target. And that it was bad. Really bad. She tried to remember what Fayed had said he was doing that afternoon, where, exactly, he would have been. Had he been planning to spend the hours that she and the girls were out at home? No, Fatima was sure he had mentioned popping into the office – his accountancy premises that were in the downtown business area about twenty minutes' drive away. He would have been far enough away to have avoided danger.

'Mummy, where are we going? What's happened?' asked Marwa, always the bolder of the twins. How to answer such questions? With the truth: 'I do not know', or with a platitude, blatantly untrue, 'Everything's fine, don't worry'? However much parents across the land tried to shield their children from the dreadful events that were occurring, it was impossible. They saw the images on the television, heard the news reports, gazed uncomprehendingly, but with full awareness of the horror of it all, at the pictures in the newspapers displayed on stands outside shops. Children, after all, were not stupid.

As Fatima searched for a response, Marwa's inquisition continued.

'Why did we come here? What are we doing? This is not where we live.'

And then, when greeted by Fatima's continued silence, more urgently, 'Mummy? Answer me.'

Children grow up fast in war. They have no other option. Today would mark a stage in that process for her twins, Fatima realised. There was no point in trying to hide what was plain to see.

'There's been a bomb.' Fatima took a deep breath. She looked around her, at the ruins that lay everywhere. 'Several bombs. Lots. We need to find out what has happened to our house.'

Maryam began to cry. Fatima gripped the girls' hands and held them tight as they walked on. Drawing closer to where they lived, she began to lose her bearings. Familiar landmarks were gone, buildings she had walked past a hundred, a thousand times, were no longer there. The main street, where she had drunk coffee with Fayed in happier times, shopped and chatted with friends, pushed the girls up and down in their pram when they were babies, had been badly hit. Some structures were still standing, upright but crooked teeth that only served to emphasise the gaps on either side. But most were wrecked and half-collapsed. The contents of shops and houses were strewn across the road; broken toys, smashed plates, ruined furniture. The carpet shop's façade was blown away, the handmade silk floor and wall-coverings still hanging forlornly inside, coated in dust that weighed them down and robbed them of texture, pattern and colour.

Both girls were sobbing now, wailing and screaming, not understanding, despite her explanation, why their mother was dragging them through this hinterland of horror. The sluggish surge of fear that had begun when the taxi stopped began to grow in Fatima's stomach, rising up through her diaphragm and into her throat. She coughed back the bile, shuddering at its bitter taste and caustic burn, trying to avoid the children seeing or sensing her fear. They were at the corner of a block, only five minutes from home. Their house was this way – just down the short side-street ahead, and then right where the fruit seller had his stall, into a wide, tree-lined boulevard that led towards the little park by the river where the children played in the sunshine. The winter her twins had been born it had snowed and she had wished the girls were old enough to build a snowman and join in the snowball fights. There had been no snow the next winter, nor the next. Looking around her now, it was as if the snowfall had come at last, out of season and discoloured, a thick, grey, flattening blanket that stank of staleness, dirt and desiccation and covered everything with the pall of devastation.

Should she walk down the side-street, take the right turn and amble past all the well-tended courtyard houses towards her own? What chance was there that it would still be standing? The trance-like sensation intensified and Fatima felt that she was walking on air, not really touching anything, distant from all that was unfolding around her, as if it were not real. The feeling was intensified by the absence of any other living being. Those who had survived must have fled already, fearful of repeated onslaughts. Or perhaps they were hiding in dark corners, too terrified and traumatised to emerge. Whatever the truth, no friend or neighbour could be seen; not even a cat prowling the pavement.

The dream-state propelled her onwards and, advancing cautiously along the rough stone sidewalk, at first things didn't seem as bad as all that. The concrete apartment buildings still stood firm and the only obvious signs of damage were broken windowpanes and shattered car windscreens. Even the fruit-seller's stall was intact, the cartwheels chocked with wooden blocks that were blackened with age rather than any more recent calamity. The carefully constructed piles of fruit, of apples and persimmons, mangoes and guavas, had collapsed into muddled rivers of greens, browns and yellows and the fruit seller himself was nowhere to be seen, but with a little bit of tidying up there'd be no sign that disaster had struck so close. Fatima had to stop herself from a compulsion to pause and right the fallen fruit, to rebuild the neat pyramids, as if somehow repairing this small piece of damage would mend the horror that surrounded her.

Instead, she turned the corner, tugging a twin on each arm,

and started down the boulevard. Each step was a step further into Hades. Bombs had fallen here; direct hits that had left craters in the road and taken rugged slices out of buildings as if a drunken giant had tramped down whatever lay in its path. Lazy flames licked around a battered, roofless estate car slung sideways across the road, the tyres on one side flattened so that it was crooked and lopsided like a small child's drawing. For a terrible, fleeting second Fatima thought it was their car; that Fayed had been coming home as death rained down.

But then she saw that it was the wrong make, and the wrong colour, beneath the grime. The relief was momentary; behind the pitiful vehicle, a building's steel rods, stripped of concrete and plaster, reached towards a sky leaden with dust and ash and full of the stench of obliteration. Fatima was staring all around her, struggling to make sense of the sights her eyes were relaying to her, when she heard the noise. Involuntarily, her gaze sought to find its source. With a sickening surge of terror she saw that there were people in the estate car, the fire-blackened corpses of a family who had tried to escape but been too late and too unlucky. And that one of them was moving, groaning, dying in excruciating agony and unimaginable fear.

Fatima froze to the spot, quite literally petrified. The feeling of being in a dream evaporated in an instant. This was reality and it was awful. Nothing in her life so far had prepared her for a moment such as this. She should help, do something, call an ambulance. She fumbled in her bag for her phone and drew it out, frenziedly trying to tap in the emergency number, forgetting that there was a shortcut button for this. She had never had reason or cause to use it before.

The children were whimpering in terror, but saying nothing, seeming to have lost the power of speech. She should get them away from this horror but still she hadn't managed to make the call and she couldn't leave that person to die like an animal. She stabbed furiously at the keypad again, missing the numbers, her hands trembling too severely to hit them accurately. It was a nightmare, one of those hideous ones where you are trying to run but your legs won't move and you keep replaying, over and over, your efforts – futile – towards flight.

A blast of intense heat, accompanied by a loud, fizzing hiss and the whoosh of fierce flames, brought her struggles with the phone to an abrupt halt. Nearly knocked off her feet, instinctively she grabbed the girls to her, hugging them close as if just her embrace could save them. The car's petrol tank had ignited and the vehicle was engulfed in a swirling ball of fire, blue, red and orange. A wretched, animalistic scream ripped out from its innards, rending the smoke-laden air apart. And then stopped. Even the roaring flames could not fill the silence that followed. The world whirled around her. Fatima was struggling to breathe, was drowning in fear. She turned towards the car as if she could help, realised immediately the stupidity of such an idea and tried instead to flee. Running, she tripped and fell, taking Maryam off guard and pulling her down with her. Dizzy and disorientated, all Fatima could think of was getting away from this apocalypse. She stumbled back to her feet, dragging Maryam up with her, not even checking to see if she were hurt.

She had to get home, to find Fayed.

THREE

Edie

'Ready to paint that town red?'

The sun had disappeared behind the mountains and much vodka had been imbibed by the time Edie pulled the scooter out from the shade of a handy oleander bush, clambered aboard and revved the engine.

Laura giggled, delightedly and drunkenly. She had had more vodka than Edie, and nothing to eat.

'Sis,' she announced, whirling her sunglasses in an exultant twirl, 'I'm so, so ready.' She jumped onto the scooter behind Edie. 'By the way, I hope you know how to drive this thing,' she added, resting her feet on the metal supports.

'Just call me Jensen Button,' shouted Edie, already speeding off down the steep track to the exit gate.

'He drives cars,' shrieked Laura as Edie increased velocity alarmingly quickly. 'Extremely fast cars!'

'Whatever.' Edie was having fun; she hadn't had anyone ride pillion since she'd taken possession of the scooter and she wanted to make the most of it before Laura insisted on being the driver. 'Hold on tight!'

'I am,' Laura hollered, 'believe me.' She gripped Edie's waist and attempted to blow a stray hair from her forehead.

At this time of year the heat lingered long after twilight and there was not the slightest breeze to bring respite. Being on the scooter, even at top speed, was like driving through treacle, as if the warm air had to be literally pushed aside to allow them to pass. The vodka, plus the unaccustomed weight on the back, meant that Edie wobbled on the sharpest bends, inducing shrieks of alarmed laughter from Laura. They were still laughing when they arrived at the marina, parked the scooter and used its mirrors to put right their dishevelled hair and make-up, bending low to get the fullest view possible.

The marina was the place to come for the smart set, home of super-yachts and their super-rich owners. Edie had notched up a few successful conquests here – before Vuk, of course. The quays were lined with boats flying flags from around the world, and the people strolling up and down and drinking at the numerous bars were dressed to impress; all designer labels and immaculate hair and smile-free pouts. Heads turned as Edie and Laura promenaded past; a perfectly matched pair in tiny shorts and crop tops. Spotting a table just being vacated at the bar with the best vantage point, Edie seized Laura's arm and dragged her towards it, ordering double vodkas for them both before they had even sat down.

'I'm a tad short of cash, Ed,' said Laura, pulling out the lining of her pockets in illustration. 'I had a bit of a mishap in Italy, got my rucksack stolen with a whole load of euros in it. I was just lucky my passport didn't go too.'

'You idiot!' Edie shook her head in disbelief. 'First rule of travelling: never keep all your money in one place.'

'Okay smart ass, rub it in.' Laura took a swig of her drink. 'It wasn't *all* my money anyway. Just a fair amount of it. I had enough to get the ferry across the Adriatic, find my elusive sister and beg her to rescue me.'

Edie snickered. 'Glad I'm useful every now and again.' She clinked her glass against Laura's. 'I've got enough for us to get by on. My enormous earnings from my marvellous job, for a start, plus I've still got some savings.'

They both drank and put their glasses down simultaneously onto the high glass table. Edie could see her reflection, distorted and watery, in the sheen of the polished surface. She thought for a moment before asking the question, cautiously.

'What about you? Have you spent all your modelling money?'

Laura was notoriously reticent about how she made her living and even more so about how she spent it. When they had finished university, they had both signed up with a minor modelling agency. At 5'9" (Laura) and 5'8" (Edie) neither was tall enough for catwalk work. Edie had got one job for a knitwear catalogue and then given up in disgust, finding it impossible to wear a pink fluffy tank top with a smile on her face.

Laura had done rather better, gaining work from various sources and going to America twice. Edie wasn't entirely convinced that her earnings were exclusively gained from putting clothes on. She suspected that the reverse activity might be involved somewhere. But Laura divulged nothing and suddenly, without warning or explanation, had given it up and told Edie that she was fed up with being a clothes horse and that they were going travelling.

They'd had a great few months in Eastern Europe – Krakow and Warsaw, Prague and Budapest – and then Laura had met a handsome Slovenian man, much older than her, and gone off to the mountains in search of inner peace and really hot sex.

Edie wasn't sure exactly what had transpired but had a feeling that the discovery that the man was married with children had had something to do with Laura's sudden disenchantment with her Slovene lover. The rest of the story, the gory details, the retribution that she was sure her sister would have wreaked on such a traitor, she had yet to hear but she was going to enjoy it when she did.

'I've got a bit of dosh left but it's in the bank at home – I've had to cancel all my cards because of the robbery, so I can't get hold of it at the moment.' Laura grimaced dolefully. 'Pants, isn't it, being skint.'

Edie reached across the table and squeezed her sister's hand. 'I can keep us in vodka, no worries. Although,' she made a sweeping gesture with her head across the crowded forecourt of the bar, 'the real skill is in not buying our own drinks.'

Laura giggled and nodded. 'Way to go, Ed.' Laura was the only person who called Edie 'Ed'. Edie liked it; it made her feel special and cemented the bond between her and her twin that no one could sever.

Edie continued scrutinising the clientele. She kicked Laura under the table. 'Those guys over there – you see them? Russian, probably. Let's see what we can squeeze out of them.'

Laura cast her eyes casually in the direction that Edie was indicating.

'I'll drink to that.' She gave a low wolf-whistle as she appraised the two men, both of whom were dressed in white shirts and chino shorts as if they had just stepped out of a casual wear advert. One sported an ostentatious watch on his left wrist, which even from this distance Edie could tell was a Bvlgari. The other had a pair of mirror sunglasses pushed up onto his head. Both were clean-shaven, blue-eyed and handsome, though one was slim and slight and the other much chunkier – not overweight but solid and sturdy.

It didn't take long to attract their attention.

***

The rest of the night had passed in a haze of flirting and alcohol and more flirting and more alcohol. Edie recalled going back to the men's apartment where they had put music on loud and played strip poker, which led quickly to nudity since they were all wearing so little. The watch, she clearly recalled, had stayed firmly on Mr Bvlgari's wrist although at some point Laura had grabbed the sunglasses and put them on, refusing to give them up for the rest of the evening.

Thinking back on it now, in the cold light of a new morning, tearing her memory apart to remember the details, Edie kept reaching a blank. Disjointed bits of dialogue, snapshots of her and Laura posing naked for pictures on the balcony, of the two of them in the bathroom taking turns to pee, collapsing into heaps of giggles whilst raiding the kitchen cupboards for food, dancing wildly to some Beyoncé number, kept appearing and disappearing in her mind, making no sense and giving no indication of timing or indeed veracity. One thing she knew for certain is that nothing – other than a bit of kissing and cuddling – had *happened*. It had all just been good, clean fun. Now that Edie had Vuk in her life, the casual flings and one-night stands that had peppered her existence previously no longer appealed. She craved a true partner, a companion, intimacy and *love*. She longed for Vuk to be the one and only. When – *if* – he ever reappeared from one of his damn sailing trips, trailing dreary tourists around hidden coves and picturesque harbours, she hoped she would find out for certain that he was of like mind.

In her room, feeling sick and confused, Edie stared around her once more. There really was no one else there. But *she* herself was there, had woken up in her own room in her own bed and she would never, ever have deserted Laura. That was the code, the rules of the game – one in, both in, never get separated, no one left behind. She slipped her feet into her flip-flops, went to the door and opened it tentatively. The sun hit her full in the face, making her pupils contract painfully and causing the throbbing behind her eyes to intensify. She stepped to the front of the narrow veranda that ran the length of the building and off which each of the staff bedrooms opened. At the far end, by an oleander bush, she could see her scooter, parked haphazardly, leaning heavily to one side.

A dim recollection of leaving it there in the early hours before the dawn surfaced, sending misty tendrils of memory through her sleep-deprived, hungover brain. Had Laura ridden home with her, holding on behind and screeching in alarm when she took a corner too fast or seemed to be coming off the road and heading for the clear water of the bay? She must have done. Edie could not remember unlocking her door, getting undressed and into bed. But she was wearing her pyjamas now so she must have done. It would have been a squash in the single bed with Laura but they had done it before. Had Laura slept beside her last night? *She must have done.*

It was completely clear that Laura *must have done* all these things. But beyond that certainty lay nothing. There was absolutely no sign of her.

FOUR

Fatima

There was no home.

Her house and those immediately around it had taken a direct hit. The tree-lined street, once green and peaceful, alive with birdsong and the gentle rustle of branches in the breeze, was now filled with noises of an utterly different nature. The sounds of carnage; of pain and despair. A man was running along the street carrying a child, a boy of about six. The boy was screaming with pain, his left leg bent at an impossible angle and his left arm dangling, limp and lifeless, by his side. Tears were pouring down the man's face so thickly that his vision must have been obscured and his frequent trips and stumbles testified to that. Fatima turned her head away, appalled by their suffering. There was nothing she could do to help.

She stared around her. Charred remains of tree trunks stabbed at the sky where the once majestic maples had provided shade. Colour had been obliterated and replaced by grey, interrupted only by spatters of blood, deep red blotches on the shattered concrete. And everywhere she looked she saw bodies strewn amongst piles of stone and plaster and roof tiles. Or not, in fact, bodies, only pieces of bodies, randomly distributed; an arm here, a blackened and filthy leg, ankle and foot there. A head lay face down in the arenaceous soil of what was once someone's carefully tended garden; its hijab soaked with so much blood it was hard to tell what its original shade had been.

Fatima walked forward a few steps, incapable of lucid thought. She would have screamed herself, like the young boy, but she had no voice, could not make her vocal chords produce any sound. A couple, ghostly in their dust-coated clothing, were standing on a pile of rubble, frantically but futilely sifting through it, lifting pathetically small pieces of wreckage and throwing them aside, their shredded hands raw and bleeding, making no impact on the huge mound beneath their feet. Fatima knew them; they were her neighbours, a young man and woman with a new-born baby. She put her hand to her head, covering her eyes as she realised what they must be looking for, and staggered on, away from them and their tragedy.

She continued her stumbling progress, the twins beside her. Somewhere here should have been their house with its court-yard and lemon tree, its almond orchard and its years of family history.

The house was gone.

In its place was a body. Its clothes were ripped to rags by the force of the bomb blast but it looked surprisingly intact, no injury visible. It was a body so familiar that Fatima knew instantly who it was.

Fayed.

Her husband; her children's father.

She sank to her knees and vomited, retching so violently it felt as if her stomach would burst apart. The girls were becoming hysterical, screaming and sobbing and Fatima didn't

31

stop them, couldn't stop them. Violently, she pushed them away to prevent them from seeing what she had seen. But, terrified as they were, they wouldn't go, instead clinging desperately onto her, burrowing into her back as she crouched down, hiding their faces in the folds of her scarf. Their weight took her by surprise and she lost her balance, falling forward and instinctively putting out her hands to save herself only to find herself pressing down on Fayed's stomach. The disgust of making contact with his dead flesh made her throw up again and again, her throat raw and burning, her mouth filled with the foul taste of bile.

Despite the warmth of the day and the heat from the fires that burnt amidst the remains, his body was already cold. Soon rigor mortis would set in and then, if the corpse were not buried, the flies would come, followed by the maggots. Fatima forced herself up and lurched away from what had once been her husband. The girls, clinging to her clothing, dragged behind her. They had seen the body, for certain, but Fatima didn't know if they had recognised their papa. Please God that they hadn't. They were screaming, and Fatima wanted to join them, wanted to howl at the dust-shrouded sky, wanted to make it all go away and not be true. But a mother's instinct to protect her young kicked in. She must get away. She wrenched the twins after her, speeding up to a hobbling, stumbling, wreckage-impeded attempt at a run. With no idea where she was going or how she would get there, she knew only that she must flee, must escape these killing fields and arrive somewhere that still had a pretence of normality. Run. All she had to do was run.

Running, barely feasible for an adult, was almost impossible for a child. Marwa's tiny legs could not navigate the treacherous terrain and she fell, banging her knee on the sharp protruding edge of a bent and contorted piece of metal that sliced into her flesh with the ease of a knife. There was a long pause before the first bellowing screech exploded out of her, far too loud for such small lungs, a yell laden with fear and pain and uncontainable panic. Fatima had no words with which to console her, nothing to say that would make it any better, no will in her body to tend to her daughter's injury, the seeping gash in her baby-soft skin. Marwa howled and sobbed without cease, on and on, whilst Maryam whimpered and Fatima's tears erupted from her eyes and poured unstoppably down her cheeks. She hauled herself and her children onwards.

A single gunshot rang out, close by, coming from behind one of the half-standing buildings of what had, until so very recently, been a peaceful and affluent middle-class street. Wiping snot from her nose with a filthy hand, Fatima's legs froze, paralysed by terror. Her gaze darted from side to side. The sniper fire had prompted forth shadowy figures from other nooks and crannies, creeping, scuttling creatures, the undead, fleeing like prey escaping an unseen enemy.

What have they done to us, Fatima's soul cried out. What have we become?

'Run,' a voice, dust-coarsened and gravelly, urged. 'Run, now.'

Swept up in his wake, driven by the urgency in his voice, Fatima grabbed up Marwa and placed her on her hip, took Maryam's hand in a vice-like grip and ran. She did not falter when the second shot came and her companion stopped in his tracks and languidly, as if in slow-motion, fell to the ground.

She just ran, on and on, through the dirt and destruction, between the mountainous heaps of boulders and rubble, iron and steel, traversing every obstacle, as if it were possible to ever truly get away.

Edie

Ripping off her pyjamas, Edie pulled on her bikini, then tied a sarong around her waist. She needed to think clearly, banish the fug that was clouding her mind. Grabbing a towel from the pile of stuff on the floor, she left the room, quelling the need to be sick; her temples pounding afresh from the sudden activity. She marched through the olive grove, where people were stirring, coming out of their cabanas in search of breakfast or, for those with children, heading for the beach even at this early hour. She should be at work already, collecting the cleaning equipment from the store and starting to scrub however many effing cabins Vlad had assigned to her. Sod that.

Veering off the path, she took a short cut that skirted through the trees and close to one of the plunge pools. A man stood there, casting a long shadow over the water, his net extended, capturing the silver-grey leaves that had fallen in the night. Zayn. Why couldn't it be Vuk? The trips he ran constantly denied them the time together that Edie yearned for. She waggled her fingers towards Zayn in a half-hearted wave. He made as if to say something but stopped as he noticed that her pace did not falter. His gaze followed her as she passed, fixated, Edie was sure, on her breasts that were only just contained by her tiny bikini top. She sighed to herself. Poor Zayn. She turned and gave him another, more enthusiastic wave. She didn't want to be cruel, but he simply couldn't hold a candle to Vuk.

Zayn had been the first person she'd got to know when she arrived on the site, basically because he'd hung around her like a moth around a flame. They'd had a fleeting dalliance but he'd got too keen and she'd had to cool the whole thing down, which was lucky as the next thing that had happened was that Vuk had shown up, back from a sailing trip and Edie had fallen for him, hook, line and sinker. He was more suitable in every way, apart from anything else because he was only a few years older than Edie, whereas Zayn was about thirty-five, Edie reckoned. Way too ancient to be taken seriously.

There was something intriguing about him, though. He was pale-skinned, paler than the local people, with heavy-lidded, dark eyes that were soft and forgiving. He wasn't from here, he came from somewhere else; he'd told Edie a bit about himself but she hadn't really been listening and now it slipped her mind, but she knew the place he was from he could never go back to for all sorts of complicated reasons from blood feuds to civil war. He had numerous ideological opinions that he liked to air, despite the fact that Edie had made it quite clear that she didn't do international politics; in fact didn't do politics at all. She left causes to Laura, who was always marching or fasting or writing letters for something.

Edie reached the tree-shaded concrete path that skirted the beach and headed for her favourite swimming spot. Come to think of it, she pondered as she meandered along, doing her best to avoid a pair of butterflies involved in an elaborate mating ritual, Zayn and Laura would probably get on like a house on fire and he could be a useful diversion, steering Laura well away from Vuk. She happily skipped a few paces off the back of this thought, threw off her sarong and, balancing on a protruding rock that just had room for her size 5 feet, dived into the cool, clear water. Laura might fancy Zayn, she always had a soft spot for the underdog, *and* she liked older men, viz the Slovenian guy – and if she did, that would kill two birds with one stone; provide a girlfriend for Zayn, who clearly really wanted one, and also ensure Laura would not be making eyes at Vuk. A marvellous solution, though Edie said it herself. Sorted – or it would be if Laura were here.

It was just so typical of Laura to disappear at precisely the moment that Edie had everything worked out and under control. She was, quite simply, the most unpredictable person on the planet. Once they'd left school and home and supposedly become independent adults, Laura had developed a habit of sauntering in and out of Edie's life – although Edie couldn't help but admit that it was a tad unusual that on this occasion, Laura had said absolutely nothing at all about her plans. She would probably materialise in a few hours and come over all affronted if Edie pulled her up on her unexplained desertion.

Coursing through the water, Edie concentrated on her breathing and then dived down, deeper and deeper. The underwater world was blue and green and grey, fish flitting between clumps of seaweed and submerged rocks, the occasional bright glint of some sunken litter the only discordant note. She relaxed her body, shut off her mind. She had spent some time with free-divers in Greece and tried to learn their techniques. Although she'd only managed to hold her breath for just over three and a half minutes so far, she was constantly working on it. Swimming was her passion – she'd been in a squad in her school days, won tournaments and medals. At one point it had been thought that she might compete nationally, perhaps even internationally. But then she'd become a teenager, discovered boys, got ill … and those ideas had faded away into the distance. She was still a better swimmer than Laura, though. That was one thing – the only thing – she'd always been best at, and what better place to show off her prowess than here at this idyllic seaside resort?

Now all she had to do was sodding *find* Laura.

FIVE

Fatima

Distant relatives in a nearby town that had so far avoided attack took them in. Fatima and the children, together with Ehsan, Fatima's dead husband's younger brother and his son Youssef, who had been at a football match when the bombs hit the house and so survived. Ehsan's wife Noor had died of breast cancer eighteen months ago, about the same time Fatima's own parents had been killed in a car accident, and he and Youssef had lived with Fatima and Fayed from then on, along with Fayed and Ehsan's parents. Death had seemed to surround them for a few awful months, but they had got through it, she and Fayed, because of the strength of their love. Missing her parents and Noor, who she had been close to, had diminished over time. Now death was back with a vengeance, claiming Fayed and so many others.

Fatima had not imagined that they would be subsumed by such loss again and had not contemplated having to pull through once more. At times, her grief was like being in an earthquake, nothing secure, nothing to hold on to; everything shaking and rocking out of control. She longed for her husband

and soulmate and knew the longing would never end. But she had two children to care for and had no choice but to do so. In this terrible war, which had seemed to come out of nowhere and to grow and grow until it engulfed them all, like being sucked inside the rapacious mouth of a giant monster, the only way to survive was to concentrate solely on the here and now, on how to get through each day and night and make it to the next sunrise.

Fatima knew she should be thankful that she was not entirely alone, that she still had her brother-in-law Ehsan. But she had always felt a little uneasy around him. He seemed to be constantly looking at her, observing and appraising her, following her with his eyes, noticing parts of her body that he should not. She'd never mentioned it to Fayed; he had a terrible temper that, when provoked, made him irrational and unpredictable and she didn't want to bring his wrath down on either herself or Ehsan, because she had no reason to cast aspersions against him. All she had were feelings and feelings were not enough to accuse anyone of anything.

Ehsan was a weak man, though, she knew that for sure. A few months ago Fayed had beaten Youssef for bringing a magazine into the house. It contained pictures of scantily-dressed women, as far as Fatima had gathered, although she hadn't seen it herself and couldn't imagine where a thirteen-year-old could have procured such a thing. Ehsan hadn't joined in the beating but he hadn't stopped it either. That just made him even more unappealing in Fatima's eyes – Youssef was his son and he should have taken the lead in disciplining him, not cowered in a corner whilst Fayed thrashed the boy.

Despite this, there was one undeniable fact to contend with. She was a widow now, a woman with neither father, husband, brother nor son to take care of her and protect her. That was not a good position to be in at the best of times, and these were the worst of times. Ehsan, whatever his failings, was a necessary evil. She would just have to put up with him, as with everything else that had befallen them. In thinking this, tears flooded her eyes and the grief clenched at her heart once more. Her anguish and misery were more than she could bear; she could not live without Fayed who had always led and guided and protected. She wanted to shout out at his ghost, release her fury that he had not, as he had suggested he would, gone to the office that afternoon but instead had stayed at home and been pulverised by the falling bombs. Why had he betrayed her like this?

But then the tears fell with renewed intensity, as if desperate for release, as she railed with herself for her disloyalty and evil thoughts. Fayed had not meant to die. He had not wanted to leave them. And now that he had, she must somehow and some way, find the inner resources to keep going.

A test of her resolve came from the rightful demands of Safa, the matriarch of the family with whom they had found shelter.

'We need food – bread and rice, and lots of other things that are nearly finished,' Safa declared bluntly to Fatima, a few days after they had arrived. She and Marwa were sitting in an armchair. Fatima was trying to read the little girl a story but she kept losing her place on the page, her thoughts drifting away, her voice falling silent. She swallowed hard and fiddled with Marwa's hair to cover her embarrassment. She should have thought of the need to contribute without having to be asked. Of course the family couldn't afford to keep them; everyone was struggling enough as it was.

The shock of losing everything had temporarily eclipsed all else from her mind and then the trauma of arranging a funeral for Fayed, once she had managed to get his body recovered, had also taken its toll. It had all been overwhelming and she hadn't been thinking straight but now that must change. Money must be procured to give to Safa, Fatima understood, immediately the demand had been made. She had not left Safa's house since they had arrived there so she had had no opportunity to get cash. She had told herself that she was not going out because there was no reason to and she was tired but she knew that really she was scared. Scared to leave the house and not know if it would still be there when she returned. So she and the girls had stayed at home, if you could call it that, but now she had to pull herself together and pull her weight.

'I'm sorry,' she apologised to Safa. 'I'll go to the bank and withdraw some money.' As she spoke, it occurred to her what Safa probably really wanted. 'And – I can do the shopping on my way back. Tell me what I should get.'

'Bread, rice, as I already mentioned,' replied Safa, disappearing into the kitchen to check the cupboards. 'Salt, meat, flour–,' she continued, reeling off a seemingly endless list of the household's requirements. Fatima wrote it all down on a scrap of paper.

Armed with the list and a veneer of bravado, Fatima left the girls drawing pictures in Safa's kitchen. The queue at the bank stretched all the way out of the door but Fatima only needed to use the cash machine so she didn't join it. Putting her card into the slot, she marvelled at how ordinary life continued amidst the mayhem, or at least the approximation of ordinary life. She could still shop. She could still go to the cinema or to a restaurant if she wished. Not that she could imagine doing either of those two things, but it was somehow unbelievable that such diversions still existed.

The machine bleeped and rejected her card. 'Transaction not possible' flashed up on the screen. Fatima frowned at the message. She reinserted her card and tried again. A line was forming behind her, of people anxiously shifting from one foot to the other, looking around them and up at the sky. Air strikes had become more frequent recently.

Once more, Fatima's card was spat back out at her, emphatically. Puzzled, and with a knot of anxiety forming in her belly, she joined the queue which was only fractionally shorter now than it had been when she arrived. She had never taken much notice of their financial position before; she hadn't had to. Fayed, older than her by ten years, already had a well-established business when they had met, fallen in love and got married. Fatima had been happy to take care of the children whilst he made the money. They were well off and she was able to continue studying English in her spare time, with the goal of going to university to do a degree in English literature when the girls got a bit older. She had plenty of time – she was only twenty-three.

Reaching the front of the queue, she handed her card to the cashier.

'I don't know why the machine wouldn't process my request,' she said, feeling the need to explain herself. The man tapped numbers into his screen and then looked at her incredulously. He had small, narrow eyes and a mean mouth.

'It's nothing to do with the machine,' he explained, speaking very slowly as if she were extremely stupid. 'It won't give you any money because you haven't got any.'

SIX

Edie

The mop handle clanged angrily and water sloshed onto her bare feet as Edie lugged the bucket into the cabin and began to clean, making wide, bad-tempered arcs across the tiles. Three cabins in two-and-a-half hours was too much, especially when so many of the guests were absolute slobs, leaving dirty dishes in the sink that she had to wash up and making sure that they'd messed up all the beds so that she still had to make them again even if they hadn't actually been slept in.

She snatched a clean sheet from the pile she had dumped on the sofa and snapped it out across the double bed in the main bedroom, tucking it in haphazardly. Really, if anyone thought they were paying for hospital corners, they had another think coming. Pillowcases next, then the same to the single beds in the twin room. She swept the floor, whisking the grains of sand swiftly across the tiles so that they flew and caught the light like mini crystals. Slowly, she backed towards the door, dragging the bucket with her and cleaning right to the threshold. She paused to flick the air-conditioning off and stepped outside into the broiling heat. Fumbling for the key in her pocket, she could feel sweat gathering on her forehead and trickling down her back and legs, running from the nape of her neck to her shoulder blades. The door slammed as she pulled it closed.

The next cabin on her list was number 15, which brought back a few fond memories. She'd spent an interesting night there with two Serbian lads whose willingness to muck in together and get themselves – and her – into some gravity-defying positions had been entertaining to say the least. Not so much fun in here now though, she mused wryly to herself, pulling pubes out of the shower trap and trying to rid the sink of a tide mark of grime. Eleven o'clock already and still one more cabin to go. It was simply too much.

It was after midday when she locked the door of her third cabin and emptied her bucket out, slinging the water towards the roots of one of the parched olive trees nearby. She turned around, pushing her hair behind her ears with the back of her free hand and jumped out of her skin. Standing motionless in front of her was a man. Edie shrieked and then, realising who it was, clapped her hand to her mouth to suppress it. Zayn. She glared at him.

'Not funny, Zayn, not funny at all. You nearly killed me.'

'Sorry, Eeedie.'

In contrast to Stefan the chef, Zayn stressed the first part of her name so that it rhymed with an elongated 'seedy'. *Seedy-Edie* – she was surprised the boys at school had never come up with that as a nickname, but they were mostly too preoccupied with Laura to bother their heads with her.

'It's OK,' she conceded, feeling a twang of guilt at how sad and perplexed he looked and sounded. 'Did you need me for something, because I'm in a bit of a hurry.'

'Why are you in such a rush? And looking so angry?'

Edie suppressed a quiver of irritation that slid through her; she could do without an interrogation right now. 'Sorry, Zayn.

It's not you – I'm just mystified about where Laura's gone, that's all.'

'Laura?' Zayn's bushy eyebrows knitted together in further puzzlement. 'I don't know any Laura. Who is she?' Edie sighed in exasperation; Zayn was evidently another one of those unobservant people who couldn't tell them apart, who thought identical twins were exactly the same in every respect, from appearance to number of fillings in their teeth and bra cup size. Whereas in fact Edie not only had no fillings to Laura's three but also was a D cup to Laura's C.

Zayn was staring at her expectantly, waiting for an answer. Slowly, it dawned on Edie that she was forgetting a crucial fact. Neither Zayn, nor anyone else, had actually met Laura nor even known of her existence. No one at all other than Edie had seen her when she arrived at the resort. Edie had been in no hurry to advertise her presence, partly because she had wanted to keep her to herself for a few hours at least, partly in case Vlad made a fuss about someone freeloading and partly, of course, to make sure Laura didn't get anywhere near Vuk before Edie herself had had a chance to consolidate her position.

'Laura's my sister. My twin sister,' she explained, a flicker of irritation causing her to frown. 'She came yesterday but now she's disappeared and I don't know where she is.'

Zayn said nothing for a moment. Then, gently, he asked, 'But can't you phone her and find out?'

For one fleeting second, Edie thought that Zayn had come up with the answer, the easiest and most obvious way to make contact with Laura. And then something Laura had said whilst they were drinking drifted back to her. She'd had her phone stolen along with everything else and had no money to replace it. That was one reason why she hadn't so much as sent a text to alert Edie to her imminent arrival. She had suggested that, if Edie didn't mind lending her the dosh, that's the first thing she would do in the morning. This morning, right now, Laura had intended to take the scooter into the town and buy a new phone. Edie would have told her where to go, drawn a map of the old town which was so confusing with its maze of cobbled alleyways and passages. She would have asked her to buy homegrown strawberries from one of the old women in the marketplace to bring back for them to feast on. But none of that was happening now and, as Edie thought about it, tears began to trickle down her cheeks. Honestly, it was too bad of Laura to leave her in the lurch like this.

'No, I can't,' she snapped back at Zayn. She folded her arms angrily over her chest. 'She doesn't have a phone right now.'

'That is not good,' answered Zayn, his brow furrowed in concern. 'But don't worry!' He released the frown and smiled at her encouragingly.

'We'll look for her, we'll find her.' He cast his gaze skywards, narrowing his eyes as he searched for the right words. 'How do you say in English? I'll put my thinking cap on and see what I can come up with.'

Edie shrugged. 'Yeah, thanks Zayn. That's great.'

He was trying to help, and she appreciated it, but in all honesty what would he be able to do? Being sweet and kind wasn't what was required right now. To work out Laura's whereabouts she needed someone with natural authority about them, someone who knew how to kick ass. A description which exactly fitted Vuk. She also needed someone who could console her for the brevity of the time she'd had with her adored sister. Surely he'd be back from whatever boat trip he was on soon? Suddenly she felt desperate for him, for the soulmate that she was sure he was beneath his taciturnity and undemonstrativeness. She yearned for arms around her, strong and capable arms. Vuk's arms.

Abruptly taking leave of Zayn, Edie sloped off to the bar for her shift. The afternoon dragged, each order an irritation, every customer an inconvenience. She kept looking around, anxious

46

for any sign of Vuk, simultaneously expecting – hoping – that at any moment Laura might also reappear, a taunting smile on her face, wondering what Edie was making such a fuss about, decrying that anyone might have so much as noticed her absence.

'Where on earth have you been?' Edie would ask.

'Here and there, shooting the breeze,' Laura would reply, and that would be that.

So much for the idea that twins are psychic. Edie had never been able to read Laura's mind. She banged down glasses and crashed piles of plates together for several long hours. 'Edeeee,' remonstrated Stefan. 'You need be careful. You break something.'

'Yeah, sorry.' Edie began shoving handfuls of clean cutlery into the grey plastic tray on the table behind the bar. 'I'd slow down but Vlad always tells me I'm letting the team down if I do that.' She smiled self-righteously at the long-suffering Stefan as she flung down the last handful of forks.

'You are a good worker, Edie,' countered Stefan, his voice eager and anxious at the same time. 'I've told Vlad that.'

'Thanks, Stefan,' said Edie, turning to survey the tables and assess what needed doing next. A tiny glow of pleasure seeped through her, despite herself. Stefan's praise was nice to hear; at least someone appreciated her.

And then she saw him.

Vuk was making his way across the dry, powdery sand that edged the beach. Tall and upright, attracting admiring gazes from every woman around, just the sight of him turned Edie's stomach upside down. Haphazardly depositing a pile of teaspoons on the counter, she raced towards him.

'Vuk!'

He looked in her direction. Flying across the loose, shifting sand, Edie could not focus on his expression. She arrived at his side, grabbing his arm and hanging onto it while she caught her breath.

'You are in a hurry today, Edie.' The few words he spoke were always in impeccable English, learned during a few years he'd spent as a student in Leicester. She looked up into his eyes and saw the outline of herself, perfectly reflected in his black pupils. He smiled his lop-sided smile and she melted.

'Oh, Vuk, I've been desperate to find you. I've missed you so much.' As soon as the words were out, she regretted them. She mustn't put Vuk off by being too available, too clingy; she'd made that mistake before. But he just riffled her hair with one of his dextrous hands and smiled, albeit somewhat distractedly.

'Let's go and get a drink,' she suggested hastily, to cover up her over-zealous greeting. 'I could do with one.'

She squeezed her fingers around Vuk's. His hands were so big, so strong and muscular. They were hands that could cope, that could fix things.

The bottles that Edie fetched from the bar bled with condensation and foamed pale and yellow as Vuk poured the beer into glasses. Edie stuck her finger into the middle of the spume and circled it, observing how the frothy bubbles attached to her skin and then quietly imploded and melted away. It reminded her of the tops of the breakers on the Atlantic beaches of home, where she and Laura would wave-jump, shrieking from the cold and even more so when they landed and felt the squirm of a disappearing crab underfoot. How James had longed to join them when he was small but their parents had said it was too rough. It must have been hard for him, Edie suddenly realised, to be always on the outside looking in, always chasing after them but never quite catching up. A bit like how she felt about Vuk right now. She seemed to be doing all the running.

'Edie, you should not play with your food and drink. It's not hygienic.'

Edie smirked in pseudo-embarrassment. 'Sorry, Vuk. I forgot

you were Mr Clean.' She put her finger in her mouth and sucked it, long and slow.

She expected a reaction to her provocative action but Vuk merely lit a cigarette and began to smoke.

'There's something I need your advice on,' she ventured tentatively, looking up at Vuk through her eyelashes and pushing out her chest in her skimpy T-shirt. Rather than dropping the flirting as a reaction to Vuk's seeming indifference, she intensified it.

Vuk raised his eyebrows infinitesimally in response. Edie nearly snapped with exasperation.

And then he reached out and ran his thumb and forefinger around her cheek and chin and along her lips.

Finally! Satisfied that he wanted her and that she had his attention, she was able to say what was burning her tongue.

'I don't know where Laura is.'

Vuk's eyes creased as they narrowed in perplexity. 'Edie, you are talking in riddles. I don't understand.'

Remembering again that Zayn was still the only other person who knew about Laura, she qualified her explanation. 'Laura's my twin sister, she came yesterday but now she's gone. I've been half-expecting her to turn up all day but there's still no sign of her.'

Edie put her fingertips to her forehead, covering her eyes. She shook her head, took a deep breath and slid her other hand down Vuk's forearm.

'So what do you think I should do?'

Vuk took a long draught of his beer.

'Nothing.'

'Uh?' Edie's surprise made her inarticulate. Surely Vuk could do better than that.

'She has gone travelling again,' he continued, laconically. 'That's all,' he shrugged.

'But I don't understand why she would have done that

without telling me,' protested Edie, flinging her arms in the air. 'Why would she? Why would she come one day and leave the next? It doesn't make any sense.'

'You are twins. Don't you know?' Vuk drained his glass and made as if to get up from the table.

'NO!' Edie slammed the palms of her hands on the table. 'That's all just bollocks. Of course we know each other inside out but we, like everyone else on earth, need a telephone or a computer to have a long-distance conversation. Cut the "twins are psychic" crap – everyone does it and it really annoys me.'

Her anger rolled off her like the hot breeze from the nearby fan. And then dissipated as Vuk pushed his chair back and picked up his sunglasses from the table.

'Wait, where are you going? Is that all the help you're going to give me?'

'I have an appointment. See you later maybe.' Vuk was already making his way towards the side path that led away from the beach and up into the resort. All he ever had was appointments, business to conduct. Where was the time for her?

'You need to stop fussing, Edie,' added Vuk as he retreated. 'Laura is okay. You just look after yourself.'

Edie slumped into her chair, her head in her hands. And then sat bolt upright, her eyes widening with horror. *No, no, no.* Surely the thing she'd dreaded hadn't happened? There had been something so strange about the way Vuk dismissed the whole story. He knew something, she was sure of it … could Laura possibly have got her hands on him so soon? But even if so, it still didn't explain why she had completely vanished, he would hardly be keeping her prisoner.

Edie hauled herself out of her chair and started to make her way up the sandy brown slope of the hill towards her room. She was tired after such a short night's sleep and, as well as her suspicions about Vuk and Laura, she couldn't get his words out of her head. '*Look after yourself.*' What had he meant by that? If anyone needed minding, it was Laura. Why on earth should she, Edie, need looking after – and if she did, why not by him?

SEVEN

Fatima

'I don't understand,' stammered Fatima, feeling her legs go weak. 'It can't be right. I – we – always have money, we – my husband was an accountant; he had many clients. Of course not the same as it used to be …,' her voice faltered.

'Maybe your husband was planning something,' the bank clerk shrugged, half-bored and half-enjoying her discomfort. 'I can see here that he withdrew all the money from this account and the associated savings account a week or so ago.'

Fatima leaned against the counter for support. She felt hot and sick and dizzy.

'You better ask him why,' continued the clerk by way of conclusion. 'Now if you don't mind, many people are waiting.'

Fatima inched herself along the counter just far enough for the next client to take her place. She rested her forehead against the cool glass of the empty booth in front of her. In that moment, she hated this war as she had never hated anything before and surely never would again. It had made Fayed do something which he would not have countenanced in any other circumstances – act in secret, without discussing his plans with her. Fatima knew his actions would have been driven by love and a desire to do the best for his family. But that was little comfort now that he was gone and all of their money with him.

All Fatima had was what she kept deposited in an account she had set up when the girls were born, that she herself managed and paid into. She took out every penny. The sum that had disappeared by the time she had bought the items on Safa's list was frightening; prices of the most basic goods were escalating by the day. That evening, Fatima sewed a secret pocket into the waistband of her trousers and stashed the remaining money inside it. There was only one explanation for Fayed's actions. He must have decided that they should leave; he probably hadn't wanted her to know to prevent her from worrying or perhaps because these days, it was often best to know nothing in case of summary arrest and interrogation. Aware of what Fayed had had in mind, and believing in her husband's ability to make the right decisions as he always had, she went to Ehsan to talk about their future.

It turned out that Ehsan had a fair amount of cash; between them, they might just be able to manage. Manage to get away, that was, not to stay. The widow Safa and the various members of her family who lived with her were kind but, like everyone, were struggling hard enough to keep themselves going in these terrible days. Often, there was not enough food, power supplies were intermittent and unreliable and the cramped conditions they were living in were bound to breed illness and disease. When the next winter came, everything would be a hundred times harder. By then, who knew what would be left of the country.

More and more bombs dropped by day and by night. Where they struck was random and indiscriminate. House raids could happen anytime; nobody knew when the door would be broken down and the men, such as were left, taken, imprisoned, tortured, killed. Towns in the north were besieged; starving residents reduced to eating grass and cats to stay alive. New threats arose all the time, bands of fighters more vicious than the last, their methods and ideologies ruthless and barbaric, devoid of mercy. Public beheadings were commonplace, mass slaughter just another everyday occurrence. The enemy was everywhere and everyone; most people no longer knew who was fighting who or why.

It was obvious to Fatima that they must make arrangements to leave. There was no time to apply for new passports to replace the ones that had been lost along with the house. That could take weeks or months in the current chaos, even supposing they were issued at all. Anyone could be accused of being on the other side, an enemy of the state, and then there would be no documents and probably no freedom. In any case, it was not a good idea to make yourself known to the authorities, to draw attention to yourself. They would have to take the chance of getting across the border illegally.

There had to be a better life for them all than this. There had to be a life.

***

In the idle days before they left, and the silent hours of the night when there were no air strikes, Fatima began to think about contacting Ali. For the first time since the war had begun, it seemed that perhaps now was the time to mend bridges and renew family ties. Ali was out there somewhere, in Europe Fatima assumed. He was in a safe place, and maybe if she could find him, he would be able to help, send money, get them a route out, support them into Europe also. But so much had been said; so many accusations been made against Ali by her father when he was still alive – accusations of betrayal because he had refused to have an arranged marriage, did not want to

54

take over the family business and did not follow all aspects of Islam – that it seemed unlikely the rift could ever be healed. Fatima had been instructed to join the rest of the family in disowning him, and she had done as she was told because she had been so young at the time, only twelve, although underneath she still loved her big brother like she always had.

She thought about contacting him now the chips were down and their lives might depend on it, but did not do it. He would most likely hate her for being party to the whole sorry affair of his banishment from the family home and subsequent exile, and for only getting touch when she needed something from him. To track him down and then have her requests fall on deaf ears would be worse than not hearing anything at all, because then she would know that she had lost her only brother for ever. She pushed thoughts of Ali from her mind. Imagining that out there somewhere lay a saviour, a guardian angel who could guide and help them to safety, was plain fantasy. She, Ehsan and the children would survive only on their wits, by the making of good decisions, and with a whole lot of luck.

Angels do not exist.

EIGHT

Edie

Abandoned anew by Vuk, Edie meandered through the resort, at a loss for what to do. She had thought about the whole Laura shenanigans almost without let-up and decided that in all likelihood, she had gone off with some bloke – perhaps one of the Russians they had met at the marina – and would amble back once his flight had departed for Moscow or St Petersburg or Vladivostok or wherever it was he was from. She had no idea where Vladivostok was but she liked the way the letters rolled off her tongue and it amused her to think what its inhabitants would be called. If people from St Petersburg were Peterburzhy, would it make them Vladivostokhy? Or Vladivostokites like Muscovites? Either one could double as the name for an unpleasant intimate infection or a particularly repellent insect.

She passed cabana 16, grumpily kicking at the sand as she walked. The cabana was quiet and still; the loungers piled on top of each other in the corner, the washing line free of swimming costumes and towels, the recycling crate by the front door empty of bottles – all indicating a property waiting for its next inhabitants.

Pausing only for a second to think about it, Edie slipped through the gate and disappeared behind the fence. Stripping off her clothes as she walked, she arrived at the edge of the pool in seconds. It was not deep enough for diving so she slid into the water and struck off from the side, reaching the opposite wall in just a few strokes. The cabana pools were small but kept at just the right temperature – cooler than the sea at this time of year, and in the middle of the afternoon, when the beach was at its busiest, Edie preferred to stay away. It was all right if you had nothing to do but lounge around and read trashy novels, but when it was only ever a brief respite from her life of drudgery, it made her too jealous of the holidaymakers.

Pushing her body down to the very bottom of the pool she practised her breath-holding, relaxing completely, slowing her heart-rate, counting to sixty as many times as she could. Three minutes twenty. No improvement, in fact a relapse; she needed to keep working at it. She surfaced and arched her body backwards, streaming effortlessly onto her back where she lay still, her arms and legs spread into a star. She floated with her eyes shut, bright red pricks of light pulsing behind the lids, the gentle swoosh of the water filling her ears.

'Mummy, mummy, this one, this one.'

'Let's go in, I want to go swimming.'

Voices filtered through to her, clearly audible but barely registering.

'There's someone in our pool!' A child's helium pitched squeal, suddenly much too close, seared into Edie's stupor.

Shit! The new occupants had arrived and were about to discover her, Goldilocks-like in their swimming pool, and not only that, but stark naked. Her body convulsed from back to front and into swimming position, and she opened her eyes to be greeted by two little faces bent low to the water. They were examining her as if she were an exotic bug of a type they had never seen before and were curious about.

'I'm so sorry, I just finished cleaning and I was so hot,' she lied, thinking off the top of her head as she climbed out of the water. As she did so, she noticed that the children were accompanied by two adults, one a woman, shortish and plump with a blonde bob that swung around her ears like a shaggy, past-its-best halo and the other a ginger-haired man, open-jawed in amazement.

Attempting to cover her breasts with one arm and her genitals with other, Edie executed a comedic, half-hopping, half-shuffling movement towards where her discarded clothes lay, distributed in random heaps on the poolside tiles.

'Who are you? Why are you here?' The woman's voice was well-educated, her words elaborately enunciated. 'Is this definitely our accommodation, Patrick? If so, I think we should complain,' she continued, turning to the man, presumably her husband, beside her.

It was a few moments before he regained his composure enough to reply. 'Oh no, Debs, that's not necessary.'

Edie had gathered up her clothes and was pulling on her shorts whilst performing a weird, fumbling run towards the gate. 'So sorry,' she called out behind her. 'Bye. Enjoy your stay.'

'We have disturbed Psyche at her bathing,' she heard the man say before she was through the gate. 'I can think of worse things …' and then Edie was out of earshot and never heard the end of the sentence or found out what the worse things were.

At least he didn't seem likely to complain to Vlad. The last thing she needed was to be chucked off the resort right now, when Laura might reappear at any moment.

On her way to the bar a bit later, she encountered Zayn hovering amidst the olive trees, almost as if he were waiting for her.

'Has your sister turned up yet?' he asked, his heavy eyes doleful as ever.

'Nope,' replied Edie, curtly. She couldn't hang around chatting as she was already late.

'And you have still heard nothing?' Zayn had secateurs in his hand and snapped off a stray olive branch as he spoke. It tumbled gently to the ground where its silver shimmer was quickly obliterated by the sandy soil.

'Nope,' repeated Edie, impatient to get on.

Zayn pursed his lips and nodded his head slowly up and down whilst making a low, tutting noise.

'What?' demanded Edie. 'What are you getting at?'

'Nothing.' Zayn forced a smile. 'Nothing at all. Just that I hope you find her. I know what it's like to lose a ....' he tailed off, without finishing his sentence. He looked as if he might cry.

'I wouldn't describe her as lost so much as temporarily mislaid,' countered Edie, horrified at Zayn's barely disguised emotion, and backtracking hurriedly on her previous assertions that Laura was, indeed, missing. Without pausing for Zayn's reaction she made her escape. 'Sorry, got to go,' she called out as she galloped off down the path, her sandalled feet sending sand flying.

But all evening, working behind the bar, she could not rid her mind of the seeds of worry that Zayn's words and troubled demeanour had, probably unintentionally, planted.

The fairy lights sparkled and the stars lit up the calm, flat water of the bay, and everything looked gorgeous but Edie found herself eyeing every male customer as a potential suspect in the Mysterious Case of the Disappearing Sister; presuming all were hiding knowledge of her twin's whereabouts. The only person she couldn't accuse of nefariousness in this respect was Patrick, the man whose pool she had invaded earlier, given that he'd only just arrived. When he came to the bar to ask for two Coca-Colas, a white wine and beer, she faced up to him, looking him squarely in the eye and serving him as if she had never seen him before. He responded in similar vein, although when Edie turned back from taking the glasses from the shelf, she was sure she caught the shadow of a smirk on his lips.

'Can I put it on my room?' he asked.

'Yeah, sure.' Edie took a notepad and a pen, which she tapped idly against her teeth as if deep in thought. 'That would be cabana 16, wouldn't it?'

Each flashed the other a complicit grin and Patrick walked away with the drinks.

A few moments later, Edie jumped when an arm encircled her waist and a pair of firm lips planted a kiss on the side of her neck.

Vuk.

Overcome with relief, she turned to face him and put her arms around him, her ally. 'Hello, stranger.' His hand grazed the back of her thigh and slid up towards her buttocks. She stiffened, her body tight with desire.

'Back already?' Edie couldn't hide her surprise. 'I didn't expect you so soon.'

Vuk shrugged, but didn't answer. His hands were inside her shorts now and he kissed her again, hard on the lips. And then brusquely detached himself and went to sit at a table with a group of locals where Edie kept a surreptitious eye on him until Stefan awarded her a break. Immediately, she joined Vuk, alone now, silently smoking and staring into nothing.

'Howdie,' she said, standing behind him and running her hands over his shoulders and down to his pecs. His muscles were hard, his body solid. She bent down and kissed the top of his head, smelling the sun in his warm, thick hair.

'Sit down, Edie. You look tired.'

Edie flopped into the chair next to him. 'I'm officially knackered,' she groaned, letting out a long sigh.

Vuk wordlessly pushed his glass of beer over towards her, indicating that she should drink.

'How was your trip?' asked Edie, wanting to break the silence.
'Fine.'

Vuk really took the prize for being economical with words. One-syllable answers were his speciality.

'Just a short one this time, then?' She desperately tried to elicit some more information.

Vuk merely flicked his head backwards in affirmation.

'I've made a decision,' she announced, only aware of this fact as she articulated it. 'I'm going to go to the police about Laura tomorrow. Just in case.'

Vuk said nothing, merely raised his eyebrows.

'Yes,' asserted Edie, as if convincing herself that the action she had just thought of was definitely the right one. Vuk's attitude was hardly encouraging and seemed to demand that she came up with some kind of justification. 'I'm sure Laura is fine but I'm thinking of our parents; they're away at the moment, trekking in the Andes, so they're out of contact. But I'm imagining what they would say if they knew Laura had vanished and I didn't do anything about it.'

Vuk drew on his cigarette, tipped his head back and blew smoke rings, small and perfectly formed, into the blackness of the night.

'It will be difficult to get the police to understand,' he replied, his voice deep and even as usual. But Edie thought she detected a flash of annoyance in his eyes.

'Look, I know I don't speak the language but there'll be someone there who speaks English, surely? Especially in a tourist place like this.'

She fell silent, expectant, waiting for him to say he would come with her. She was desperate for him to prove his devotion to her, could feel her need growing and swelling like blotting paper in a pool of water. She pressed her lips hard together and clenched her fists to stop herself from articulating that need. She had done this before, scared people off with her intensity. That could not be allowed to happen again.

She watched, all her muscles tensed to contain herself, as Vuk crushed his cigarette into the ashtray in front of him, pushing it down so forcefully that the stub bent and split at the side, spewing forth a few flakes of golden-brown tobacco that fell infinitesimally slowly onto the grey ash.

'I suggest that you do not go to the police, Edie,' he said. His countenance was calm, but his eyes had a steeliness that seemed to contain the inexplicable hint of a warning.

'I really do not recommend it.'

'Why not?' It seemed absurd. The police were where you went for help. Everyone knew that.

'There is a lot of corruption here. The old ways die hard and the truth can be a rare commodity. People say the police are in league with the drug gangs, that they don't try to prevent the wars that break out between them now and then. Foreigners should take care to stay away from authority, lest they get involved.' He sighed, as if he had the weight of the world and inefficient officials on his shoulders. 'The police will do nothing to help you, I can guarantee that.'

'What if you spoke to them, then?' retaliated Edie, even while Vuk's words played in her mind. She really didn't know what he was talking about, did not understand the pre-democratic era he seemed to be describing. 'Surely that would make a difference?'

Vuk emitted a short snort of incredulity. 'I don't trust anyone in uniform. If you had lived all your life in our world, you would not either.'

Edie gaped, open-mouthed. Vuk's cryptic words had floored her.

He reached toward her and stroked her cheek, gently and firmly. 'I only want the best for you, little one. Nothing but the best.' Bending forward, he kissed her on the lips, hard and purposefully.

Edie felt herself relax. Only the best. Of course that's what he wanted for her. And Laura, too, she was sure.

She kissed him back.

NINE

Fatima

The pudgy fingers of the man in the gold shop repulsed Fatima as he picked at her bracelets, her necklace, her wedding and engagement rings.

'They're not much, are they?' he stated disparagingly, his grubby glasses fallen to the end of his nose and dandruff from his greasy hair coating his shoulders.

You disgust me, Fatima wanted to say. *You are a horrible little man who feeds on the plight of others.*

She kept her mouth tightly closed. The odium she felt was not really for him; it was for the perpetrators of this conflict that allowed some to profit whilst most were reduced to utter ignominy. Watching the dealer distastefully poke her earrings she wondered how her happy, settled, ordered life had come to this. And then gave a contemptuous inner laugh at the idea that she had it worse than anyone else, at the audacity of even thinking that she didn't deserve what had been meted out to her. Millions of lives had been slashed to pieces, tens of thousands slain, a multitude left with scars that would never heal. And she was sad about selling her trinkets. She despised herself for the pettiness of her thoughts.

And yet her heart lurched in her chest when the dealer held a magnifying glass against the stones in the necklace that she always wore. The chain was pure gold and the pendant an interlocking figure of eight shape with two emeralds surrounded by tiny diamonds and seed pearls. Fayed had given it to her when the twins were born, an emerald for each of them to match their mother's green eyes, he had said. It had been in his family for years and Fatima had always admired it but never thought to own it herself, assuming that Noor, who possessed the status conferred by seniority, would get the pick of the most valuable pieces.

'This one – this is nice,' the man said, laying it carefully back onto the table.

Fatima gave an almost imperceptible nod of agreement. Remain implacable. Give nothing away. This had been her advice to herself as she set off for the shop.

'Take whatever you can get,' Ehsan had urged her, his brow growing taut and his eyes wide, obviously fearing that she would bungle it somehow and get ripped off, end up selling everything for a song.

Fatima had nodded whilst secretly concocting her own game plan. She was not going to panic and give the jewellery away. She was nobody's pushover. She'd been telling herself that since the day at the bank and she was beginning to believe it – or at least to make a good enough pretence. There had been bad decisions in the past, though. If only they'd sold the house and left at the beginning, when it all started, Fatima railed at herself now. Then she'd have cash in her pocket and could keep the jewellery for later, for the rainy day that would undoubtedly come all too soon. But no one had known, then, how bad it was going to get, how long it would all go on for. No one could possibly have predicted such a complete break-down of society, such carnage, such an exodus. Now Fatima had only her few pieces of jewellery to fall back on and thank goodness Fayed's accountancy business had been lucrative, once, and that he had been generous and rich enough to bestow gold and silver and precious stones upon her, and that she'd been wearing so many of them on the day the bombs fell. She was going to need every single pound she could glean from them today. There was nothing that mattered now except getting Marwa and Maryam out of here.

The gold dealer offered a price. It was derisory.

'I don't have time for this.' Fatima scooped up all the jewels, delicate chains dripping between her fingers, the stones of her engagement ring digging into the palm of her hand, and left. She said nothing more, just turned her back and walked away.

The man called her bluff, shrugging and busying himself with some paperwork. She almost lost her nerve and returned to the counter but just managed to hold on long enough for him to have to summon her.

'Wait,' he called out, 'let me take another look.'

She was at the door already and she paused, hovering on the threshold, making him wait for her to turn back.

His second offer was better, but still nowhere near enough. Fatima scowled scornfully and refused, but this time remained where she was standing. The dealer did some more poking and prodding and examining and scrutinising. Fatima put forward an amount that she would find acceptable. He laughed in her face. She almost capitulated, anything to get away from the humiliation he was joyously meting out to her.

Inside her head, a voice was crying out to her, *this is all you have! Nothing else, just this. Don't mess it up, you foolish woman.* She stood firm.

Pursing her lips tightly together, squaring her shoulders, Fatima steadfastly gave the dealer another sum, her absolute minimum. It was not much less than the previous number. Negotiations like these could take hours or minutes. It all depended on how much the seller wanted to sell and the buyer wanted to buy. However much she affected nonchalance, the dealer knew that a woman only sold her jewellery, her wedding ring, if she had to. She only had so much power to influence the outcome.

Eventually, they agreed on a price. It was far lower than the value of the items, but considerably higher than Fatima had expected to get.

'Thank you,' said Fatima, and actually meant it.

'No, thank you, madam,' said the gold dealer, suddenly jovial now the deal was done. 'It was a pleasure doing business with you.'

'Likewise,' nodded Fatima, and did not mean it.

She stashed the money in the waistband pocket, nodded a perfunctory farewell and left. It was small, but it was a victory. It was proof that she could cope, that she would continue to cope. She would do it for her children because not doing so was not an option, and for Fayed, for his memory. As she walked back to Safa's house, her thoughts strayed to how life used to be when they were all so happy together and had everything to look forward to. The twins were healthy and bright, they were comfortably off and, most importantly of all, she and Fayed were in love.

Fatima remembered how he had brought the emerald necklace to her one evening as she sat in the girls' nursery in the courtyard house, singing them to sleep with the songs she had learnt from her mother that had been passed down through the generations. He had hung it around her neck, gently fastening the clasp and then leading her to the mirror to show her how it complemented her dark skin and sparkling eyes. In that moment, Fatima's world had been complete. The rumbling protests and skirmishes in the big cities far away had been expected to pass over quickly; order would quickly be restored and life would go on as before.

How naive that complacency seemed now. Fayed was dead

and the country dying. Life itself could no longer be taken for granted. Fatima quickened her pace as the sky darkened. She had a feeling there would be a raid that night. She must get back to the twins before the bombs began to fall.

Edie

'So you will forget your idea about the police?' Vuk's voice was low, full of concern. 'Remember that you need to think about your status here. You do not have a work permit, for example.'

He squeezed her hand conspiratorially. 'It is not advisable to draw attention to yourself or the resort. Vlad would be most unhappy.'

Edie was speechless for a moment. No one had mentioned permits or any kind of legal nicety when she had pitched up and asked for a job. Typical of Vlad to use threats to keep people down. Suddenly, the tension that had been building exploded out of her.

'Fuck Vlad,' she shouted.

She got up, knocking her chair over in the process; it was one of the plastic ones, light and unstable. Exactly how she felt at that precise moment.

'And fuck this whole stupid place.' Without stopping to pick up the fallen chair, she marched off in the direction of her room. But her flouncing protest soon ran out of steam and she was already regretting her tantrum before she got even halfway through the olive grove and long before she reached her door. Once inside her room she flung herself onto her bed, clenching her fists tight and drumming them onto the pillow, tears of frustration pouring down her cheeks.

Edie needed Vuk right now, really needed him. She couldn't go to sleep after their argument. What had her mother always said to her? Never let the sun go down on a quarrel. Not that it had been so much a quarrel as a disagreement – her disagreeing with Vuk, him implacable as always. But still, Laura's presence, her support, could never be relied upon, whereas in Vuk Edie had seen the possibility of building the permanent, fulfilling, mutually beneficial relationship she so yearned for.

Slowly, she sat up and shuffled along her bed until she was facing the mirror she'd propped up on a shelf on the wall. She would have to go and see him, apologise, make up with him. Sniffing loudly, she rubbed her finger over the smudges of mascara on her cheeks whilst deciding what to do. Her make-up was strewn across the room and she gathered up the elements she needed – powder, mascara, some nude lip gloss that accentuated her pale rosebud mouth. She set to work on tidying herself up.

The heat still had not dissipated as she picked her way back though the olive trees, their silvery leaves shimmering in the moonlight. The paths were lit at ground level and by overhead lanterns, but she always deviated from them, preferring to take the most direct course possible, and she had already established an off-piste route to Vuk's cabin. As she drew near, she could see Vuk sitting on a lounger, his legs stretched out in front of him, his bare feet crossed one over the other. It was impossible to tell if he was asleep or awake, except for the twitch of his fingers as he tapped the ash off the end of his cigarette. Silently, Edie slid through the darkness and onto the terrace. She paused, sheltered by the huge fig tree that grew there. It was heavy with fruit, small and green, that clustered pugnaciously on every part of every branch like knuckles on a clenched fist. Hidden from view, she watched Vuk, his brown limbs at ease, his eyes shut, his breathing slow and relaxed.

'Edie.'

She jumped and her heart beat wildly. She had thought he couldn't see her, wouldn't know that she was there.

'Why don't you come over?' His deep voice set her pulse racing.

Stepping out of the shadows, she padded across the rough stone slabs, designed to prevent water from making them slippery. She had heard that in the winter the rain here was torrential, sheeting off the mountains and cascading downwards towards the sea, forming seasonal waterfalls that thundered during their brief revival and then fell silent when summer came again.

Arriving at his lounger, Edie stopped and took a deep breath.

'I'm sorry I shouted at you.' The blurted apology was hard to make, but necessary. 'It's just because I'm worried about Laura. I mean, I wasn't worried until Zayn put doubt into my mind and I probably don't need to be worried, but somehow I am.' She paused. 'Just a bit,' she added, lamely.

Vuk flicked his cigarette butt into the flowering oleander bushes that sprawled beside his cabin walls.

'You like a beer? Go inside and fetch one from the fridge.'

Edie took the invitation to be Vuk's way of saying 'It's OK, no problem, all forgotten.' She made her way silently inside and into the kitchen. The senior members of staff who lived on site, namely Vuk and Vlad and Ivana, the admin manager, had cabins of their own. Although not as luxurious as the guest cabanas, they were still comfortable and Edie saw how they could be made really nice with the right touch – some rugs to absorb the echoes, pops of colour to break-up the monotony of the white walls and floors. An enormous bowl containing nothing but fifty lemons or limes sitting on a counter-top, like in the interior magazines or the home sections of the Sunday supplements.

Vuk's cabin, though, had nothing homely about it. Containing only the bare minimum – bedclothes, a few mugs and a kettle in the kitchen, his toothbrush in the bathroom – the cabin could have belonged to anyone. It was utterly impersonal. She resisted the temptation to go into the bedroom and check it for signs of female visitors other than herself.

She came back with the beers, handed Vuk a bottle and kept one for herself.

'Sit.' Vuk indicated to his left hand side. As there was no chair there, Edie knelt down, resting on her upturned heels.

'Are you still cross with me?' Vuk was often so unreadable, so inscrutable that Edie could not tell what he was thinking.

'Of course not.'

Vuk drank and put the bottle on the ground. Reaching out his left hand, he caught hold of the back of Edie's head, his fingers tangling in her hair causing tiny stabs of pain in her scalp.

'I'll make some enquiries around and see if I can find anything out about your sister. You should stop fretting. Leave it to me.'

Adoration flooded through Edie. Vuk would not let her down.

His right hand was on his shorts zip, undoing it, opening the waistband wide. Whatever he wanted, she would give to him, in return for being her knight in shining armour. He wrenched her head roughly forward, grinding her face into his groin, and then releasing the pressure to allow her mouth to find his penis beneath the soft fabric of his underpants. Her lips felt him swell and harden, and she began to tease him, bringing him to full size. He pulled himself free and guided her mouth onto him. Controlling the rhythm, his fingers even more tightly wound in her hair, he made her take all of him in her mouth, arching his back to her until he came, emitting a groan that seemed to originate from somewhere deep within him, and then relaxing back into stillness.

Edie climbed onto the lounger and lay beside him, fitting her body into the spaces around his, nestling down between him and the arm of the chair. She shut her eyes and listened to the roar of the crickets and his steady breathing and the rustle of fallen leaves in the sandy soil as some night creature went about its business. She was so happy that she could please him, satisfy him. So happy he was finally here for her to do so. She didn't mind that the sex they had was so often about satisfying his needs and so rarely about hers. If she could give him what he wanted, she regarded that as a privilege.

'Shall we go to bed?' she asked eventually. She thought he had fallen asleep and didn't want to disturb him but it was getting uncomfortable wedged against the hard plastic and she had a sudden desire for sleep. She pushed herself upright and looked down at Vuk.

'I'll walk you back to your room,' he said, swinging his legs over the side of the chair and getting up.

She stared at him, wondering if she had heard correctly.

'What?'

'Come on.' Vuk had slipped on his shoes and was waiting for her expectantly.

Edie didn't know what to say and Vuk was clearly impatient to be off.

'Edie, please hurry. I have things to do.' He was walking towards the path already, striding purposefully forward, not even looking to see if she were following.

'What on earth do you need to do in the middle of the night?' demanded Edie, running to keep up.

Vuk didn't answer, just continued up the hill. When they reached the staff cabins he bent down and pecked her on the cheek.

'See you later,' he muttered, looking into the distance, his mind clearly on other things. And then he was gone.

In her room, Edie tried to think objectively. She was not Vuk's keeper. Her mother had tried so hard to instil in her how important it was not to overwhelm people with demands and impositions. It had taken her years to accept that it was OK for Laura to have other friends, to occasionally want to do her own thing instead of always being with Edie. That doctor-type woman she'd seen in her teens had impressed on her the need to let go, to live and let live. Now she must put this into practice with Vuk. To keep him, she had to set him free. And that meant not questioning him to the point where he would get annoyed with her, not keeping tabs on his movements. Free, easy and undemanding, coupled with sex whenever the bloke wanted it; that was the way to conduct a successful relationship, Edie was sure of it.

Remember those rules, she told herself sternly as she got into bed. It didn't stop her feeling lonely, though, and wishing Vuk were with her.

TEN

Fatima

Ehsan had been vacillating about leaving with Fatima, one minute certain, the next full of doubts again.

'How will we manage it with three children in tow?' he demanded, his voice gruff with anxiety. 'What if they get sick? What if we do?'

Fatima bit her lip. 'But if we stay we'll get sick for sure, next winter, if we haven't been blasted out of existence by then.'

Eventually, he made up his mind. He and Youssef would accompany her after all. Just like Fatima they, too, had nothing more to lose. It would work for both of them; she would do better with a male protector and Ehsan would benefit from the fact that she spoke much better English than him; an asset that would surely help them on their journey. And Fatima was happy to be with Youssef, who was a kind and loveably boy, and who deserved the same opportunities as her own twins.

They would all attempt to get to Europe where they could begin again. One thing was clear to both adults; neither had any intention of just crossing a border and staying put. They had heard about that life, from friends and acquaintances, from the internet. The appalling conditions, the abject poverty, the abuse and degradation suffered daily by the refugees, the lack of work, of opportunities, the reliance on charity handouts that diminished in line with thinning donations as compassion fatigue set in around the world.

Fatima knew also about the rape and domestic violence suffered by the women, the return of child marriage, families offering up their pre-pubescent girls for a fraction of the dowry they should have received in normal times, literally selling them into a life of early pregnancies and childbirth that would destroy them even if the bombs and shooting and soldiers didn't. The parents would tell themselves it was to keep their daughters safe. It was a safety Fatima would never accept for her children, however far off it might seem right now, when the twins were still so very young.

Above all, life in the camps was a life in limbo, waiting for a change for the better that would never come. That's why they had never even contemplated leaving before now. It had seemed preferable to stay put and pray for an end to the war and the violence and the suffering. Until now. Now, anything seemed better than remaining where they were. Fatima only had to recall in her mind's eye that vision of her once beautiful street crumpled and beaten, the lurking shadows of the injured and dispossessed scuttling like rats out of holes, the hideous sight of her beloved husband's body, lifeless and stiff, to know that she would never, could never go back.

The ancient cobbled lanes of the old town, suffused with scents of clove and cumin, the bright clothes in the shops, the bakery that smelt of warmth and cinnamon and everything good to eat, were all gone. The courtyard house, with its lemon trees and almond orchard and trickling fountain, was gone. The girls' nursery where she had soothed them to sleep, with its white-painted walls and matching beds covered with the counterpanes she had embroidered by hand in the months she waited for them to be born – gone now.

Her city, the only one she had ever known and where she had lived all her life, had been eradicated. Everything was in ruins. Nowhere to live, nowhere to work, nothing to eat. No Fayed.

The only choice left was to go and to keep going until they reached northern Europe. That there were so many hundreds of thousands of others doing the same she was well aware. But she couldn't think of them, couldn't let the fact that she would be just one woman in the midst of a nameless multitude put her off. Of the two routes available, both were fraught with danger. They could get to Egypt and try to cross the Mediterranean from there, or from Libya. Disadvantage: a long and extraordinarily perilous boat ride to Italy during which it was highly likely one or all of them would perish. Advantage: from Italy it was the EU all the way to Germany or Sweden. Alternatively, they could take the Turkish route. Disadvantage: the danger inherent in getting to and crossing the border, in getting to one of the islands and then traversing Macedonia and Serbia before reaching the European countries. Advantage: a much shorter boat ride – the possibility that they might all survive.

Fatima and Ehsan discussed the options until late into the night in the days following the destruction of their home and lives.

'Everyone says it's better through Turkey. Libya is full of warlords, cheats and traffickers without scruples of any kind.' Fatima knew that Ehsan wanted to be in charge and she worked hard to make him feel that he was, whilst at the same time trying to influence him to her point of view.

'That way it's such a long journey before we reach the EU,' countered Ehsan. He paused and rubbed his tired eyes with rough hands.

They bandied the possibilities back and forth until finally they reached an agreement that the Turkish route was the best one. Once the decision was made, Fatima spent hours online, on chat rooms and websites that updated people on the situation across the country, whose troops held what territory, where the worst of the fighting was, the best places to try to cross the border. Ehsan talked with the men in town, surreptitiously.

'It's getting harder every day,' he said to Fatima.

'I know,' she replied. 'We should go now, while it's still summer and we will have better weather for the sea crossing.'

There was nothing to pack, no reason to delay a moment longer.

They had just their phones, the jewellery money and a change of clothes for them all, two for the children (Safa had gathered together everything she and her friends and neighbours could spare) together with some food and water for the journey. No ID, no passports, no documents to show that they had once owned property, businesses, that they had had status. They had nothing to prove who they were or where they had come from. They simply had to take their chances with all the other homeless and dispossessed.

'They say of refugees that they leave *taking only what they can carry*,' Fatima commented ironically to Ehsan as they stuffed their few possessions into plastic bags and two small backpacks.

'If only we had a choice of what to take.'

ELEVEN

Edie

It was already scorching at eight-thirty the next morning when Edie surfaced from a fitful, troubled sleep. She stood on the veranda, a shaft of sunlight that filtered through the olive branches burning her cheeks, her eyes half-closed in protest. She needed a plan, she had realised in the hours during which she had tossed and turned in bed. A schedule to keep to, a process to follow. To systematically tick off the things that needed to be done and make sure they *were* done.

She would have put calling her parents at the top of the 'to do' list, but that was not possible due to their remote location right now. Should the need arise, it would take them time to get here even once they were back in touch. And anyway, Edie wanted to sort this for herself. She had always been the slightly hopeless one, the one who couldn't cope on her own or manage for herself. When her mother picked up the phone to find it was her, her voice would instantly develop a tone tinged with anxiety, the unasked question, What's happened now? hovering between them in the ether. This was Edie's chance to prove that she could confront a crisis head on and overcome it.

She went back inside, sat down on her bed and pulled a note-book out of her bag. 'PLAN TO FIND LAURA' she wrote in pencil. Her handwriting was large and shapeless, another thing she had never managed to accomplish the way Laura had, whose cursive script was impossibly lovely and perfectly formed, just like her.

1. Go to police.

Sod Vuk and his work permits and corruption rubbish blah, blah, blah … if she wanted to seek help from the forces of law and order she would, and let him try to stop her. And anyway, as he'd disappeared yet again for some so-called 'job' he was out of the picture right now which gave him no right to lord it over her and her actions. Wouldn't *he* try to find *his* identical twin if *he'd* gone AWOL? If, on his return, he objected, a blow-job would probably sort him out. Sex was always a reliable tool when there was a tricky bit of fixing to do.

2. Make 'missing' posters.

It had occurred to her that she should stick notices up around the resort and along the road into town, alerting everyone who saw them to the fact of a missing person. Someone might have seen Laura, and if they had they would definitely have noticed and almost certainly remembered her. She was hard to ignore.

3. Search the resort.

Surely somewhere there would be a clue as to where Laura was or where she had gone. Laura was impulsive and did crazy things; this wasn't the first time she had vanished into thin air. Once, at university, she had told Edie she was going out for a quick drink. The next time Edie had heard from her, she was in France. She'd met a bloke in the pub who suggested spending the weekend in Paris and off they'd gone, passing by Laura's student house to pick up her passport on the way. They'd ended up in a boutique hotel in the Marais where they had drunk champagne and shagged practically non-stop for forty-eight hours. Laura had dropped him once they got back to the UK because he had a hairy back and held his knife sideways between his thumb and forefinger, which was too vulgar for her to bear. Edie wasn't sure that either of these things were sin enough to dump someone, especially someone stinking rich and adoring, but Laura could pick and choose and so she did.

In the same way, when she'd met the Slovenian guy she had simply evaporated like a vapour trail and it had taken days for her to get round to emailing Edie with pictures of their sylvan love-nest and an – in Edie's opinion, unsatisfactory – explanation of her sudden disappearance. And there had been other times, of shorter and longer durations, a few hours to a few days, when Laura was simply off radar to everyone. In so many ways there was nothing unusual in her having melted away – and yet ... and yet Edie couldn't quite explain, even to herself, her increasing sense of unease. The Russian blokes were at the end of their holiday when they had met them and must surely have departed by now, which scuppered them as an explanation. And who else would Laura have had a chance to get to know and bed down with other than them?

For a while, Edie sat chewing the end of the pencil, the metallic taste of the paint contrasting with the dry earthiness of the wood. When she looked back at the list she realised that she'd run out of ideas after number three. Reluctantly, she pulled on shorts and a T-shirt. She had cabanas to clean and the sooner she got them done, the sooner she'd be on her way to town to see the police. There was no point in phoning, it would be even harder to explain what she was calling about. Better to do it in person and hope to find someone who spoke English.

Even racing through her cleaning schedule at top speed didn't see her finished, showered and dressed in something vaguely respectable until just before midday. She grabbed the scooter key from the nail she'd bashed into her bedroom wall and let her door bang shut behind her. As she was pulling back the scooter support, Zayn appeared at her side, his soft eyes with their cow lashes fixed on hers.

'Where are you going?' he asked.

'Into town.' Edie bit her lip and forced back tears that suddenly prickled at the back of her eyes. 'I'm going to speak to the police about Laura.' She swung her leg across the scooter and put the key in the ignition. *Despite what Vuk said,* she thought but didn't say.

Zayn made as if to reply, stopped and then blurted out, 'You want me to come with you?'

'No, you're all right, Zayn.' It was sweet of him to offer but getting him involved would only complicate matters. And she might have more chance of a sympathetic hearing if she cut a helpless damsel-in-distress figure. 'I'll go on my own.'

Edie turned the key, the engine sputtered into life and she pushed the scooter forward, the wheels spinning in the sandy ground for a moment before gaining purchase. Speeding away, she glanced over her shoulder to see Zayn staring after her, a forlorn figure with drooping shoulders. *Shit,* Edie thought to herself, filled with momentary regret. Poor lonely Zayn. Evil, cruel Edie, spurning his obvious devotion. She would *definitely* get him and Laura together when Laura reappeared.

In her impatience, she cursed every bend and turn in the narrow, single track road that led towards the town, the high rocky banks on each side sometimes falling away to reveal the cerulean sea below, flat, calm and limpid under the broiling sun. Wild hollyhocks in every shade of pink grew tall and proud all around. Ferns nestled beside ancient grey boulders that jutted forth here and there, and butterflies flitted between staging posts. Seen out of the corner of Edie's eye as she rode like the wind they seemed to be drifting streamers of colour, ephemeral and dreamy, never resting, always moving on.

***

At the police station, she was greeted in a perfunctory manner by the duty officer, who was almost certainly expecting a report of a lost camera or some car insurance document that needed a signature. Tourists were welcomed here and crime against them was rare; nobody wanted to scare them, and the cash that they brought, away. Edie asked if he spoke English. He shook his head dolefully. Why should he, thought Edie? How many foreigners pitching up at a police station in England would find that the local bobby was conversant in another tongue?

He disappeared into a back room and after some minutes, came back with a female police officer whose dyed blonde hair was tied into a tight ponytail.

'What do you need? I help if I can. My English is not so good.'

Edie shook her head graciously in denial. 'It seems excellent to me,' she replied and then, having got the niceties out of the way, she explained that she had a missing person to report and could they please go somewhere quiet to discuss it.

The woman, whose name was Lucia Šimovic, led her in the opposite direction from which she had come, down a long corridor and into a suspect interview room. It was a surprise to Edie to enter such a room, not just because she'd never done so before, but also because the room's very existence seemed incongruous in this place that was synonymous with sunshine and holidays. There must be a hidden underbelly of lawlessness that she had yet to encounter. She remembered what Vuk had said about drug wars. A sudden knot of fear formed in her stomach. Where there were drugs there were other underhand goings-on. Could that include abduction? Kidnapping? Edie forced such preposterous notions from her mind.

Lucia made notes in a spiral bound pad as Edie explained what had happened, hedging around the topic of what she herself was doing at the resort because of Vuk's warning that her position was not legal. She wasn't sure it was true and even less sure that anyone would care enough to do anything about it – but still, best not to take risks. It was disappointing to see how little Lucia wrote down, how sparse the information Edie had to offer her. Lucia asked a few questions and then, tapping her pen against her teeth, silently contemplated the white lined page of her notebook for a few moments.

'I will file report and,' she paused, resuming the teeth tapping again, 'to be very honest with you, Miss Edie,' she continued, speaking very slowly, as if Edie were a child or intellectually deficient, 'I do not think we can do very much. Your sister is adult and there is no evidence that points to anything suspicious. It seems most likely that she left of her own free will.'

Lucia smiled a smile that was clearly intended to be comforting. It was more genuine and effective than Edie had anticipated.

'OK,' she nodded, pursing her lips thoughtfully in the way she imagined very intelligent people did when mulling over a problem. 'I guess you're right. There's no need to do anything.'

Edie thought of her parents as she spoke. Would they buy this explanation? Or would it make them think she was even more incompetent than they did already?

Add 'losing sister' to the long list of all her other failings: screwing up GCSEs and having to retake, dropping out of university, being a crap model in ill-advised knitwear.

Lucia closed her notepad. 'If there is anything we should do, we do it.'

Edie shrugged. What could she do against such a shutdown? 'You'll let me know, though – if anything crops up?'

Lucia stood up. 'Of course. But in the meantime, try not to worry. There is no law against people coming and going, no law that says they have to tell anyone their plans or explain themselves. You know yourself that Laura has done this before, that she comes and goes as she pleases. In all my years as a police officer in this town, we have never ... a foreign girl like your sister has never been the victim of murder, abduction, rape or any such attack. There is absolutely no evidence of a crime.'

Edie laid her hands on the table, fingers splayed like starfish, her skin a strange reddish-brown under the fluorescent light. She had bitten her nails to the quick over the last few days, a terrible habit she seemed powerless to stop.

'Okay. I guess that's it then.' She got up and stood, waiting for Lucia to move.

'Do you have photo of your sister?' asked Lucia. 'To keep in file.'

Edie pulled her phone out of her bag and then stopped short. 'I don't think I do. I cleared them all ages ago and I didn't take any the night Laura arrived.' She bit her lip, trying to remember why not. 'I thought we had loads of time and so I didn't bother.'

'So if you find one bring it in to us, please.' Lucia walked towards the door, indicating to Edie to follow her.

'No, wait.' Edie remained motionless. 'Can't you use one of me? We are identical – most people can't tell us apart at all.'

Lucia's eyes widened as she halted and looked doubtfully back at Edie. 'I'm not sure if we can do that. It might be considered fraudulent or unethical in some way. I've never encountered this particular situation before.'

Edie folded her arms and stared at Lucia. 'It seems like a good idea to me.'

Lucia opened the door and ushered Edie through. 'Okay. I will take photo but we will replace if you find one of your sister.'

Edie skimmed through the photos on her phone to find something suitable to give to Lucia. She stopped at one, taken by Zayn soon after she had started work at the resort, and was taken aback by how different she looked then. She was pale from the winter and thin, her cheeks drawn and her eyes dull. As time had gone by, she had filled out a bit and her tan, together with her sun-lightened hair and newly alive eyes, made her appear thriving and vibrant. The modelling, with the dieting and indoor lifestyle it necessitated, had not been good for her, she could see that clearly now. And there was something about the air here, its purity as it rolled down from the mountains or in from the Adriatic, that seemed to impart health and vitality. If it hadn't been for Laura, and the situation now, she would be entirely happy with her decision to come here, and to stay.

Eventually she found a photo that she was happy with and gave it to Lucia to download and print out. She didn't bother to ask whether it would be distributed to other parts of the police network as it was clear that it wouldn't be, given the aforementioned lack of evidence of a crime.

Stepping out of the police station onto the sun-soaked cobbles she found the old town crowded with swarms of tourists just arrived off one of the cruise ships. Cameras ever ready, they followed their cardboard-lollipop wielding guides, their carefully chosen casual clothing in linen and cotton drooping in the sweltering heat. Weaving her way through the hordes and out of the main gate, Edie made her way back to where she'd left the scooter, shoved up under a bush in an attempt to ensure that the handlebars didn't get too hot to hold. The old ladies in the market tried to tempt her with their garden produce; heaps of sumptuous home-grown cherries and strawberries piled upon torn up cardboard boxes, enormous tomatoes with splits like crevasses built into pyramids alongside luscious bunches of fresh herbs.

Edie ignored them all. She wanted to get back to tick off number one on her plan, and to start on numbers two and three. She'd use the same photo she'd given Lucia to make the 'missing' poster but she needed to create it and then ask Vuk to write the wording in the utterly incomprehensible local language, made even more complicated than any language needed to be by virtue of the fact that there were two alphabets to choose from. Latin or Cyrillic, take your pick … what was that all about? Surely one set of letters was enough? Whatever, it would be an opportunity for Vuk to show how much he cared, which if he had any sense he'd grab with both hands. And at least she'd still be doing something, so she wouldn't look as if she didn't care about Laura or anything like that.

Gripping the handlebars tightly, Edie lent forward into the wind her speed created and hurtled back to the resort.

TWELVE

Fatima

Ehsan found a man with a car to take them to the border. They divided the cost between them, him and Fatima. Ehsan said that as the two girls were so small, they were equivalent to his one son, so they could just halve everything. Fatima counted out the notes and gave them to him before they even left Safa's house. The fewer people who knew where her money was kept and how much there was of it, the better. Ehsan pocketed it and left to make the arrangements with the driver. The first bit of our cash gone, thought Fatima. The first step of our journey paid for.

Before the first light of dawn they set off in the ancient car, its seats so sagged and worn it felt as if they were touching the ground beneath. It seemed as if every other vehicle on the road was heading the same way, but Fatima was sure they couldn't be. Not everyone was leaving. Nearly everyone, but not all.

'My leg hurts,' pronounced Marwa. And then when Fatima did not instantly react, said it again. 'It *really* hurts, Mummy. I need medicine to make it all right.'

It was what Fayed had always said if the girls had a pain or a cold or a fever. 'You need medicine. Then you'll be all right.'

The cold lurch of fear, combined with a vicious stab of grief at the memory of Fayed, stirred in Fatima's stomach. She couldn't think of him, could not put herself face to face with her loss. If she did, she would crumble and give up. She swallowed down her despair.

'Later, sweetheart,' she said, kissing Marwa's dark curls. 'I'll give you some medicine later.'

'Where is Daddy?' Perhaps her sister's words had reminded Maryam of their father because there was her tiny, high-pitched voice ringing out above the clanking rumble of the car engine, asking the worst question, the one most guaranteed to compound Fatima's torment. She rubbed her hands across her eyes and took a deep breath.

'Daddy is in heaven, watching over us, like I told you,' she stated, definitively. 'Remember?'

Unbelievably, both girls seemed to accept this apology for an explanation. Perhaps it was something in Fatima's tone of voice that precluded further enquiry. Marwa didn't ask about medicine again, either. This was fortunate because Fatima didn't have any. She had not even thought about trying to procure any, had been so preoccupied with making the momentous decision to go that she'd neglected the small details that were so important when travelling with children.

Perhaps they would be there, later. In that other country where there was no war and no bombs and no blood-chilling, heart-stopping, gut-wrenching terror. The most up-to-date information was that the border crossings were closed and being steadily fortified with hastily erected razor wire and fences. As the car bounced over potholes on its shot suspension, Fatima began to feel hot and nauseous, covering her mouth with the loose end of her headscarf as if that would stop her vomiting.

'We'll get across somehow,' Ehsan muttered, staring out of the window at the barren landscape of untended fields and desolate, bombed-out villages. Travelling anywhere these days was to run the gamut of sniper fire and air strikes, of gangs of armed bandits and religiously motivated militias. Black smoke was rising from a town in the far distance. 'There's always a way,' continued Ehsan before pausing; his confidence, such as it was, faltering. 'If only we had documents, it would be easier.'

If only, Fatima wanted to shout out. *If only!* But we don't.

Edie

The afternoon bar shift was tedium itself; nothing but families and screeching kids with their impatient demands for ketchup or a spare plate or whatever it was that she'd forgotten to take to their table. Edie got out of the restaurant as soon as she could, escaping before Stefan could corner her to refill the bar fridges or the beachside vending machines. Her beaten up old laptop was just up to the job of creating a template for the poster and once that was done she took it to the office to beg a favour from Ivana, to whose name Edie had added the prefix 'evil'.

When Edie had first arrived at the resort, Ivana had imme-diately made her feel small by telling her about her travel and tourism degree from some unpronounceable university in the back end of nowhere and had been disparaging to say the least about Edie's lack of language – or any other – skills. Ivana was, of course, fluent in English, German and Russian as well as her mother tongue. Today, however, Ivana surprised Edie by being friendly and helpful; she printed off a copy of the poster in between dealing with a flurry of guest enquiries and wished her a nice day when she left. Grudgingly, Edie had to concede that she wasn't all that bad, even if she did dress as if she were twenty-seven going on seventy.

It was too hot to continue with the plan so Edie went down to the beach and sat for a while on the damp, golden sand right at the water's edge. Being there, especially in her current bad mood, reminded her of why she usually avoided it in the daytime. Tiny brown babies splashed in the warm, clear water of the shallows, whilst further out, older children threw balls and dived down under the surface like tousle-headed seals. Mums and dads lazed on the shore, reading, snoozing, listening to music. Far out by the rope barrier were plastic sun loungers where those unafraid of burning, mostly young people and teenagers, offered up their bodies to the fiercest rays.

A few yachts dipped and swayed beyond the rope and Edie could make out figures upon them, talking, eating, drinking and occasionally diving overboard into the deep water, tiny heads bobbing up and down like a string of baubles cast afloat. Everyone seemed to be playing happy families or happy friends or happy lovers. It wasn't really the crowds Edie didn't like, but the togetherness of those crowds. Only she was alone.

Shedding her shorts and T-shirt, Edie waded through the shallows to where the water became deep enough to swim. The sand yielded beneath her and she wriggled her toes as she walked, enjoying the feeling of the abrasive grains against her feet. Sinking gradually under the surface she concentrated on the blissful relief from the heat that the water imbued to her skin. A leisurely breaststroke soon got her to the rope barrier. Pausing momentarily to look back at the beach, she ducked under the rope and struck out in a strong front crawl. She swam past the moored yachts, with their swaying orange dinghies and flags that drooped in the windless air, and further on out until she had cleared the rocky, pine-topped cliffs and had reached the peak of the headland. Turning over onto her back she lay still as a star and let the rhythm of the sea's steadily beating heart lull and soothe her. Conquering the water somehow gave her the hope and self-belief she lacked on dry land.

When she had completely relaxed, she rolled over onto her front. Without a snorkel it was harder to take the deep, slow breaths that went before a free-dive, but she did it as best she could. Then, in a single smooth movement, she bent at the waist and raised one leg. Letting one arm glide alongside her body, she used the other to clear her ears and made a perfectly vertical descent. She had no fin so could not cover much distance but it was practice she needed, as much of it as possible, refining and honing the techniques the free-divers in Greece had taught her, constantly striving for longer times underwater.

Resurfacing, the calm that free-diving brought her suffused her body and her mind. She made her way back to shore thinking only one thing. There must be a reason Laura had left, whatever everyone else said and if she could solve that mystery, she would not only have her sister back but also know she had achieved something that would make people – namely her family, her parents – proud of her.

Fatima

Many hours later they arrived at the border, enabled by good luck or fate or the will of God to get there in one piece. Small worn out groups of dusty-looking people were gathered under the trees near the barbed-wire fence and the four-metre trench that marked where one country ended and another one began. Staring across at where freedom – of a sort – lay, Fatima marvelled at how the parched brown grass of late summer was exactly the same on both sides. It felt as if her country should be black and shrouded in perpetual darkness whilst across that thin divide they would be able to see sunshine and rainbows and brightly-coloured butterflies.

'What are they all waiting for?' Youssef asked.

Fatima's sorrow rose up inside. How to explain to a child the pitiful lengths his country's people had been reduced to? To expect a child to understand that the people have to wait there until they get the signal from the smuggler on the other side that the border guards have passed by and they should attempt to cross. 'Attempt' being the key word; the barbed wire, the ever-widening trench and the increasingly trigger-happy soldiers all playing their part in preventing the desperate from making it. But they were doing all right so far; they'd got here unscathed, in a journey that had been made tense by boredom and the fear of what might happen rather than by anything that actually had happened.

'Maybe they're waiting to meet someone,' she replied. 'For a friend or relation to arrive.' She paused and fumbled in the plastic bag that carried her few possessions. She passed each child a sweet from her rapidly diminishing horde. The distraction allowed her a brief word with Ehsan.

'He said we had to phone when we got here.' Fatima had the paper with the smuggler's number on it inside her secret pocket, along with her money. He had been found through the refugee grapevine, contacted initially through encrypted messaging services. He came highly recommended but verifying anything was almost impossible. You had to go on trust, combined with a large dose of hope.

'But I'm not sure if this is the right place,' she continued. 'How would we know?' She looked around at the little groups of young men, of women and children sheltering from the scorching sun under the scrubby trees.

Who to ask, who to have faith in or believe?

They had sent the smuggler a money transfer with the payment for the crossing. Included in the price, he had told them on the phone, in a tone of voice that left no doubt as to his magnanimity, was transportation to the nearest big town from where they could get to the coast. *So generous*, thought Fatima, unable to quell the sarcasm. A bargain. It cost $500 for her and the children and the same for Ehsan and Youssef. And so the money, so carefully collected and preserved, had begun to slip through their fingers, with no hope of replacing or replenishing it.

Ehsan made the phone call. Fatima had to stand close – too close for comfort – to hear what might be said. The phone rang and rang until the call was dropped. Fatima and Ehsan looked at each other. Both knew what the other was thinking. They had been duped; there was no smuggler. They stood in silence for a while. Waves of fatigue swept over Fatima; she felt light-headed and giddy, unable to think straight. The stress and anxiety of the days since the bombs fell threatened to engulf her. She looked down the long, dusty ribbon of road that swept back in the direction from which they had come, and imagined she could see the deadly fires of destruction creeping up behind them. There was no going back. She straightened her shoulders and along with them, her resolve.

She turned to Ehsan. 'I think we should keep trying the number. Who knows what these people do all day, it might just be that he can't answer the phone right now.'

Ehsan nodded. He didn't seem to have a clue what to do.

'Why don't you have a chat with some of those guys over there?' Fatima gesticulated with her head towards a cluster of four or five dishevelled men who were standing smoking in the full glare of the sun. 'Ask them for a light or something and get into conversation. Find out what they know, how they are planning to cross.'

Ehsan looked doubtful. 'I don't smoke,' he said, hesitantly.

Fatima had to work hard to quell the irritation that rose up inside her. 'Well, start,' she hissed. 'We've got to do something. I can't talk to them, can I? They're not going to give their secrets away to a woman.'

She busied herself with the provisions she had in the plastic bag, setting a small cloth on the ground and laying some bread and olives on it. Calling the children over, she let them all have a small drink of water and encouraged them to eat something. Nobody was very hungry.

I should be pleased they're not eating, thought Fatima, as she packed the food back up, wrapping the bread carefully to keep it away from the dust and dirt that was all around them. *It'll make our supplies last longer.* She sat back on her heels and shut her eyes for a moment, gritting her teeth as she concentrated on holding back the tears. A mother's first instinct is to feed her children and now even the ability to do that adequately was gone, joining everything else in the graveyard of what was once a proper and civilised life.

Ehsan had finally plucked up the courage, or whatever it was that had been necessary, to approach the men and talk with them. Grim expressions were exchanged and there was much shaking of heads and making of vociferous gestures. Fatima thought about joining some of the other women and children and seeing if she could glean any information from them. But she didn't want to draw too much attention to their little group. It was selfish of her, but she knew that if she got involved in anyone else's story, in their drama, she would start worrying about it and their problems would become hers and she would feel obliged to help in any way she could. And she didn't want to help anyone else right now. She just wanted to get across that border. After that could come a time for compassion and selflessness.

The twins soon became bored and fretful.

'Maryam wants to go home,' announced Marwa, coming to stand by Fatima where she crouched on the ground, her back resting against a tree trunk. The little girl loomed above her, blocking out the sun.

'Not now.' Fatima couldn't think of anything else to say. As she stared at her daughter's solid little frame poised against the backdrop of the brown soil and the blue sky, she noticed that her leg was red around the knee where she had cut it open when she fell on the day the bombs hit. The gash had not healed and now looked angry and raw. She reached out her hand and gently rubbed it with her thumb. It was hot and Fatima could almost feel it throbbing. Marwa let out a cry of pain and stumbled backwards, out of her mother's reach.

'Mummy, that really hurt! Don't touch me,' she shouted in outrage.

Fatima bit her lip so hard it began to bleed and her heart missed a beat. The cut must be infected. That was why Marwa had been complaining that her leg hurt earlier. Fatima didn't know what she could do about it. There would be a doctor on the other side. A pharmacy, at the very least. She would deal with it then. What else could she do? She quelled tears. It wouldn't help Marwa to see her cry. But she had always looked after the girls so perfectly, tending to their every need both physical and emotional. She had nurtured them tirelessly. And now she could only sit by and watch Marwa suffer.

Perhaps it was good that she had had almost exclusive care of the girls, leaving Fayed free to work long hours to provide for them all, as it meant that they were used to their father's absence and, apart from every now and again such as on the journey here, they rarely asked for him. But whether they missed him or not, their daddy was gone and she, their devoted mother, didn't seem up to the job of caring for them alone. She shut her eyes and prayed, even though she was sure God wasn't listening.

The waiting was interminable. Time crawled. There was nothing to do but listlessly wave away the flies. Youssef stood with drooping shoulders, tracing patterns in the dry, dusty soil with his toe. He found some stones and began to throw them against the stub of an iron pole, remnant of some sign or post long destroyed. He aimed the stones carefully, giving himself a point for every time he hit the post, collecting them up and doing it again and again. He hardly spoke.

He misses his mum, the mother that he barely remembers, thought Fatima. His home, his school, his friends. Security and routine and lots and lots of love is all that children need. The first two are gone and he doesn't get much of the last from his father. It hadn't occurred to her before, when she was so busy with the girls and Youssef so busy with his football and schoolmates. But now, stripped down to just the five of them in this hostile landscape at the beginning of their epic journey, it was so obvious that the boy lacked affection that Fatima couldn't believe she'd been so unfeeling. She just wasn't sure that she had the capacity to make the difference anymore.

She pondered all of this whilst the twins curled up beside her and dozed off as the sun began to set. The flies circled and landed and took off again, all the while buzzing dementedly, and Fatima waved them away from the sleeping children whilst trying to not let them drive her crazy. At least Marwa was able to rest, despite her leg. Perhaps it wasn't so bad, after all.

Eventually Ehsan returned from his protracted discussions.

'What did they say?' asked Fatima.

Ehsan shrugged. 'It's the same for everyone. Sometimes the smugglers answer the phone and sometimes they don't. You just have to keep trying.'

'And they always come good?' demanded Fatima, unable to stop the impatience showing in her voice. 'How long do you wait before you give up?'

Ehsan seemed to have taken Fatima's exhortation to take up smoking seriously. He stubbed out his cigarette on the trunk of the tree they were standing by and then ground it beneath his foot. 'Two days. Three days. If we can't make contact, we'll just have to tag along with someone else. Make a run for it when they do.'

Fatima's eyes fell to the ground. An ant crawled busily amongst the crumbs of bread that had fallen from the earlier attempt at a meal. It looked as if it were trying to choose which morsel appeared most tasty. Fatima wanted to kill it, to squash it and destroy it, just because she could, because it was smaller than her and defenceless and it would feel like a bit of power amidst the general impotence and humiliation. But she didn't. It was wrong to take a life, even of an ant. Pity the government and the rebels and all the rest of the warring parties didn't know that.

'Right,' she said, flatly. She cast her eyes towards the sky and the horizon. 'It'll be dark soon. Do we stay here for the night?'

Shaking his head, Ehsan pointed back down the road they had come by. 'There's a town off to the left, about five kilometres away. We should go there tonight.'

Day one had ended in failure. How many more such days would have to be endured in the weeks that lay ahead?

THIRTEEN

Edie

When the sun disappeared over the sea that evening, Edie was ready to get started on number three of her plan. She had bargained with Stefan to have the evening off, pointing out that she hadn't had a break in weeks. She had worn her skimpiest T-shirt to talk to him about this, together with her shortest, tightest shorts and had quickly gained his agreement.

Phone in hand ready to use as a torch, Edie locked the door of her room and looked surreptitiously around her. Establishing that the coast was clear, she set off into the olive groves. Creeping around the resort in the gathering dusk suddenly struck her as insane; she was like some bizarre parody of Inspector Clouseau, himself a bizarre parody. All she needed was a false moustache and a magnifying glass to complete the picture. And then she remembered the serious nature of her task and the smile faded from her face. Noises emanating from cabana 18 that indicated a couple having a good time made her cover her ears and hurriedly divert her path; the last thing she wanted was to come across anyone having better sex than her. Vuk's failure to reciprocate the pleasure she had given him the night before was rankling. She wanted more from him and did not want to face the possibility that what she wanted was more than he could give.

Edie continued through the olive grove, picking her way across the sandy soil, frequently having to pause to impatiently kick out the stones that kept finding their way into her sandals. She knew that there was a derelict old building somewhere around here – Zayn had shown it to her during her early days on the resort. The ruins of a shepherd's hut from a bygone age, he had said, but she couldn't remember exactly where it was. Remnants from the modern day were also still in evidence; there had been a Soviet-era high rise hotel on the site that had been razed to the ground and although the rubble had long since gone, there was still a bizarre row of huts that resembled changing rooms for a municipal pool that she had seen when exploring one day, right at the beginning of her stay. Why she had got it into her head to look for Laura here, she had no idea. She must have read too many rubbishy thrillers and filled her head with far-fetched tales of woebegone women gagged and bound in darkened rooms, awaiting their fate in a pitiful yet alluring way.

Poking around in the semi-darkness – the sun had fully set now and only the moon and the stars lit her way – she found her way to the concrete huts. They stood, forlorn and empty, the doors of those that still had them swinging open, graffitied and ugly. There was no sign of life, or any indication that anyone ever came near them. A lizard darted out from under a pile of leaves making Edie start, stifling a scream. She forced herself to go right up to the huts and peer inside each and every one of them. All were empty. And then she arrived at the last one and saw that on the door was a padlock and chain holding it tight shut. Nervously, Edie shrank into the shadows. She paused, listening to the sound of her own breathing, waiting until the thumping of her heart had stilled. Eventually, summoning all her courage, she stepped towards the locked door.

What the fuck are you so scared of, wuss, she demanded silently of herself. It's a padlock, not a werewolf or a mad axe murderer. But it was the fact that the lock, together with its accompanying chain, was so shiny and new that disturbed her. She tiptoed closer, trying to make no noise at all. She reached the door and shone light upon it. The lock was pristine, not a rust mark to be seen, the door solid; no gaps, no cracks. She crept around the side of the hut, hoping to find a window through which she would be able to see inside. There were none, but at the back, right up at the top beneath the flat, corrugated iron roof, was a horizontal ventilation hole about the size and shape of a household brick.

Edie stood looking up at it, defeated. There was no way she could reach it, not even to get a handhold on it and haul herself upwards – and she knew without a shadow of a doubt that she lacked the upper body strength to do that anyway. It seemed that she had reached a dead end with this part of the search and the quiet was so absolute and intense that she did not imagine that there could possibly be anyone inside the hut. If they were, they were locked in from the outside … And then an icy cold trickle of fear ran through her body, from her stomach to her legs, making her feel weak and unstable. What if Laura was in there? What if some mad man had snatched her and hidden her away, before or after doing terrible things to her? Just because Lucia the policewoman had gone on about it never having happened before didn't mean it never would. You heard these stories of girls who get taken as teenagers and locked up and kept as sex slaves by evil perverts who make them have their babies with no medical care – Edie had seen the film *Room* – and, and …

Calm down! Edie spoke severely to herself in her head. You're getting hysterical. This is totally ridiculous, there's no one here and it's just some private storeroom – it's probably got someone's fishing gear in it, nice and near to the beach, save taking it home all the time. She was being absurd, skulking around a dark olive grove in what was by now practically the dead of night on some half-arsed mission to find someone who everyone else believed had left of her own accord. Who in all likelihood was absolutely fine. And yet … that feeling that there was something amiss wormed its way back into her attempts to rationalise once more. Emboldened anew, Edie took a deep breath.

'Is there anyone in there?' she shouted at the top of her voice.

'There – there – there?'

Her words echoed around the silent hillside and faded away into the blackness. She began pounding at the metal door with her fists and booting it ineffectively with her foot, her open-toed sandals a distinct impediment to the job. And then the noise she was making became terrifying and she suddenly stopped, not wanting to draw any extra attention to herself, to bring anyone up here wondering what was going on and finding her beating up an old concrete hut having apparently lost her marbles. She sank down onto her haunches in the dusty soil and put her head in her hands. This was hopeless. She had no idea what to do.

And then she heard it. A snap of twigs underfoot and a rustle of fabric brushing against itself, as a man's thick shorts do. She held her breath. One more crack of dry wood breaking and then silence, complete and utter, apart from the deafening roar of the cicadas.

Edie got up, shaking her head angrily. You just imagined it, she told herself sternly. Overactive imagination, isn't that what Mum always used to accuse you of? Well then, she was right and you need to stop, right now.

Stepping forward deliberately boldly she began to sing a

Miley Cyrus song that she and Laura both loved, the words of which she knew by heart. She was not scared and let no one prowling in the bushes think that she was. She struck on up the hill to where she believed was the ruined hut, determined not to fall prey to stupid presuppositions that might hinder her progress. By serendipity, she soon reached the glade where the ramshackle building lay. Here, the atmosphere seemed completely different to that at the concrete huts. By the light of the moon, the stone construction now seemed to be more of a cottage than a hovel, romantically rustic and unspoilt.

Edie went up to the paneless window and looked inside. It was empty. But as she shone her phone-torch around, she noticed that the dirt floor was scuffed as if many footsteps had trampled it and there was a clearly discernible print of the sole of a shoe that appeared to have been made recently. Peering more closely at the ground, she saw cigarette butts littered everywhere, and a discarded packet nestling between two stones at about hand height where someone had presumably stashed it to protect it from the sand and dust. There were a few pieces of dilapidated furniture; chairs, a table and an iron bedstead complete with soiled mattress. Probably where the local kids come to hang out and smoke weed, she pondered. She herself didn't do drugs anymore; one too many nasty experiences had put her off and anyway it was a stupid way to waste money when she didn't have much to spare.

Having satisfied herself that there was nothing more to be seen here, she turned away and began walking back down towards the resort. She had gone a few metres when she tripped on a half-buried olive branch that splintered apart, dry and brittle. Falling forwards, she only just stopped herself from ending up flat on her face. It was as she was righting herself that she saw it. Trailing from the spikes of some unidentified bush, caught up in a tangled bunch at one end with the other hanging free, was a scarf. Edie couldn't make out its exact colour in the moonlight, but it was made of a thin, gauze-like material and had a pattern of stitches in the shape of 'x's upon it. Biting her lip and staring at it intently as if it might escape if she took her eyes off it, she crept forward. She reached out her hand and fingered the flimsy fabric. It was soft and yielding. Carefully she disentangled it from the bushes and held it up close before her. It seemed to be a shade of grey, the crosses white. Edie buried her face in it. It smelt of the sun and the earth and the sand – and something else, familiar, evocative.

It smelt of Laura.

FOURTEEN

Fatima

'Town' was an ambitious word for the shambolic collection of dwellings they arrived in, where a few families scratched out a living selling food and shelter to those trying to get out. Fatima couldn't imagine what induced them to stay. She and Ehsan found a room, negotiating a price that seemed exorbitant, and bought a meal. Fatima insisted on ringing the smuggler every fifteen minutes. At least they were able to keep the phones charged whilst here. Ehsan had also brought with them a back-up mobile, with spare batteries. He said that it would enable them to 'keep in contact', though there was no one they needed to communicate with except the smuggler. At the twelfth attempt, when they had been about to give up for the night and try to get some sleep, the call was answered.

'You try tomorrow,' ordered the smuggler. 'There was no chance today, border guards everywhere. Tomorrow. Early.'

They left at 4.30am. They had decided to walk, to save money, but Marwa's knee was getting worse and Ehsan had to give her a piggy-back. That was difficult because holding onto her right leg to keep her stable was impossible, it hurt so much now. Fatima knew that she needed antibiotics but there was no pharmacy in the place they'd spent the night and Ehsan didn't want to waste a morning going further afield to look for a shop when this might mean missing the opportunity to get across the border.

The sun was rising and the darkness slowly vanishing behind the distant hills when they got back to where they had been so few hours ago. Time was beginning to lose all meaning. Dozens of their compatriots were already gathered to wait under the trees near the barbed wire fence, praying for the opportunity to reach safety. Perhaps word had got round that today might be the day thought Fatima, gazing at everyone. There were many more people than the day before, youngsters, families with children, the elderly, some carrying laundry bags of food and clothing and anything they had managed to salvage or find space for, others equipped only with a carrier bag and a phone. Apart from the children, everyone's eyes were scanning the border, waiting for the sign to run, hoping that if they did so they might get lucky and evade being apprehended and turned back.

Fatima fell into conversation with a couple who arrived to stand next to her. She didn't ask their names and they didn't offer them; anonymity seemed to be the order of the day here. Both husband and wife were clutching a small child, a one-year-old and a two-year-old. They wore their fatigue and exhaustion on their white, taut faces.

'It's the sixth day we've come,' the man said to Fatima. 'We've tried but we haven't made it yet. It takes time and if the border guards are being vigilant in their patrols, you can't do it.'

Fatima nodded, wordlessly. She was sorry for this family just as she was sorry for her whole country. But she must focus on herself, the twins, Youssef and Ehsan. No one and nothing else.

In the distance an armoured truck, windscreen glinting in

the rays of the rising sun, sped past. The flag and official markings showed it for what it was. The border patrols were regular and efficient. She hadn't seen them yesterday because she hadn't been looking, hadn't known that was what they were waiting for.

'They check the guard positions all the time. Except sometimes, they disappear for a few hours and then you have your chance,' the unnamed man explained. 'The smugglers are watching them and they give you the signal.'

Fatima didn't want to give the impression that she was completely naive, that she didn't know the score. 'Yes,' she nodded, nonchalantly. 'And your smuggler,' she asked, working hard to keep her tone casual. 'He's reliable?'

'If it wasn't for him telling us we'll get through soon, we would turn back, go home.'

Fatima digested this information slowly. Back home. She supposed that such a decision made sense, but only if you had a home. If you didn't, the limbo of living in no-man's land could go on indefinitely. She stared at the road beyond the wire and the trench. They would make it. They had to.

For the first hour or so, Ehsan walked out of earshot of the crowd to make the calls to the smuggler but as the number of people increased it got harder to push his way back through and so they gave up on privacy. The smuggler hadn't answered yet anyway. Fatima could feel the sweat in her armpits and trickling down her neck and back and she knew she smelt. Everyone did. They were like a herd of cattle, reduced to their base elements, stinking and wretched. If she had had any energy Fatima would have felt disgust but she didn't so she just stood amongst the fetid multitude and did what everyone else was doing. She waited.

Worsening the ordeal was having to hold Marwa, burning with fever and listless, in her arms. Fatima's self-assurances of the day before that it wasn't as bad as it seemed had clearly been false. The little girl now stirred only to scream if anyone so much as brushed against her. The infection had taken hold and spread rapidly. Her entire calf was hot and swollen now, the crimson skin stretched taut. When she opened her eyes, they were glassy and unfocused. Fatima held her tight although every muscle ached. There was no help available, no medicine, no disinfectant. Maryam clung silently, desperately, to Fatima's legs. She had shrunk into herself, her usual babbling chatter extinguished, her expression one of constant wariness, her melting eyes dulled by fear as Marwa's were by pain. Fatima had always noted how they seemed to feel each other's suffering, to experience their own pain and each other's, and now she knew it for certain, getting the proof in the worst of circumstances.

Suddenly everyone started running. The only way to stay upright was to run with them. Ehsan swept up Maryam, Youssef picked up Fatima's bag and his own and they joined the stampede. The front runners were all young, unaccompanied men, unencumbered with hangers-on or baggage; a few were already at the top of the fence. Most of the time all Fatima could see were people's backs, dark clothing, rucksacks hoisted onto shoulders. But every now and again her field of vision cleared for a second or two and then she saw the men ascending, dropping, sliding, climbing, over the fence and across the trench and then, on reaching the other side, running. Running for their lives, because the armoured vehicle was back, all glinting metal and flashing lights. Fatima heard shots echoing out into the morning air, along with cries of 'Git!'

Just as suddenly as it had begun, the surge halted in its tracks like a flood of water stemmed by the turning of a tap.

The people at the back of the crowd stopped too late and bashed into those in front of them, setting off a domino effect of lurching, stumbling bodies. Marwa woke up, screaming with pain as her leg was continually knocked and jostled in the crush. Fatima, concentrating on keeping hold of her, tripped and fell. For an instant she saw herself being trampled like a fallen animal and began frantically groping for the floor with her hand, trying to stabilise herself so that she could push herself upright. She started to breathe quickly, too quickly, to hyperventilate, as panic took over. Her heart was racing, fleeting moments of blackness shuttering across her vision. Rivers of sweat coursed down her forehead and into her eyes, blinding her. Marwa's leg was pressing on the floor and the child was uttering high-pitched, uncanny yelps that brought to Fatima's mind memories of a dog that had once been run over on her street and had dragged itself to the roadside to die.

For a moment, everything stopped, darkness surrounded her and Fatima blacked out. And then immediately came to, screaming in agony, for someone was standing on her hand, crushing her outstretched fingers, pinning her to the ground. The pain roused her from unconsciousness and then subsided as the foot moved and a strong grasp clutched her elbow and pulled her to her feet. The swarm parted and she could see again, but the temporary relief at being upright and alive was soon replaced by the heavy weight of dread settling in her stomach. There was no sign of Ehsan, Maryam and Youssef. Fatima stood stock still, searching, willing God to catch a glimpse of them, praying that they had not been the recipients of the bullets she had heard fired.

Marwa was not moving at all but Fatima could not take her eyes off the people milling around her for so much as a second lest she miss a sighting of the others. She was hot, so thirsty she thought she might die and she could do nothing about it, dare not risk getting out water and drinking until she knew where they were, where Maryam was.

At last, she saw a face she recognised, walking towards her, arms opened wide, smiling. It was Fayed. Marwa whimpered as Fatima let out a cry of relief and began to stumble towards him, clutching the child's dead weight close to her. But as she approached he disappeared, melting into the backdrop of the chaotic mass of humanity all around. Fatima remembered that Fayed was dead. She was hallucinating; it had been a mirage, her husband's familiar, longed-for face taking the place of the oasis in the desert. Nausea rose in her throat and she was sick, the vomit splattering against the hard, dusty soil and onto her ankles.

Close to collapse, Fatima began to drag herself back to the dismal trees. She found a space there and wearily crouched down. Marwa had lapsed back into a deep sleep and she laid the child on the ground next to her. She regarded her daughter, so sick, so similar to her other daughter, now missing. She was about to lose everything and she was too numb to care.

The thump of Maryam's little body against hers destabilised Fatima, causing her to lurch to the side and almost crash down on top of Marwa. It was half an hour at least since the surge to the border and she had been sure Ehsan, Youssef and her daughter were gone for good. She had begun to convince herself that it was good news, that their absence meant that they had got across and that three of them, at least, had succeeded. Now, incredibly, here they were and suddenly the time without them seemed like nothing because everything was back to exactly how it was before. Fatima couldn't work out if that were good or bad.

Ehsan, catching her eyes, shook his head. 'We didn't make it,' he said, unnecessarily. 'Not a chance.'

There was nothing to do but stay in the shelter of the trees and continue to wait.

The smuggler answered the phone at some point in the afternoon.

'You should have come before, when it was easier,' he railed at them. 'Now it's very hard, since the last four, five months. Very hard. You keep trying but I don't know if you make it. It's very dangerous.'

'We got it wrong,' said Fatima, her eyes burning as she tried not to cry. 'We've left it too late.'

The tears began to flow despite her efforts to quell them, dropping onto Marwa's blue shorts where they left a dark stain. Her leg was even more swollen now. Fatima had hoped letting the air get to it might help, in the absence of disinfectant, drugs, bandages. But it was getting ever worse, and had begun to ooze thick, yellow pus that stank of fetid decay.

'There's no point in weeping,' said Ehsan, roughly, his inability to solve the problem seeming to turn into anger towards everyone and everything. He glared hopelessly in the direction of the border. 'All we can do is wait.'

Marwa's silence was worse than the noise of her earlier screaming had been. She had passed into semi-consciousness, a slick of sweat covering her body, her skin, where it wasn't scarlet, an unnatural shade of grey. Every now and again a swell of air from the movement of the crowd or the breeze brought the stench of rot wafting to Fatima's nostrils. Marwa's infection was destroying her flesh and would soon destroy her.

Fatima could no longer hold back the full force of her despair. 'If we wait any longer,' she sobbed. 'Marwa will be dead.'

FIFTEEN

Edie

It was a relief to arrive back amongst the lights and activity of the resort. Although it always seemed quiet around the cabanas in the olive grove, Edie realised now that there was a comforting amount of coming and going; imperceptible when you weren't thinking about it but like Piccadilly Circus in contrast to where she had come from.

She set off to look for Vuk; she needed to ask his opinion about the scarf. Perhaps now she had a piece of the much vaunted 'evidence', people – namely Vuk – would start taking her seriously. As well as that, there was the poster to complete. There was no sign of him down by the bar or restaurant and he was unlikely to be in the office this late, so having made a detour to her room to collect her poster prototype, Edie set off for his cabin, clutching the scarf tightly in her hand.

If Vuk was around, he was usually sitting outside smoking as he had been the night before but tonight the chair was empty. She tried ringing his phone. No answer. She tried the door handle of the cabin. It was locked. She wandered around, peering in the windows to see if he were asleep and had not heard her.

He wasn't there.

Pondering what to do, she decided to leave him a note and then remembered that she had neither paper, other than the poster, nor a pen. She was bound to find both such items inside if only she could get in. The bathroom window was open; it was quite low and just big enough for someone her size. She reached her hand up to the clasp on the inner edge, released it and pulled open the window. Placing both hands on the ledge she launched herself into one great effortful push upwards. Puffing and panting with the exertion, and really hoping that Vuk didn't show up right now to see her engaged in such an inelegant activity, she hauled herself into a sitting position. From there it was a simple matter to kick shut the lid of the toilet, which was positioned directly below the window, and lower her feet down onto it.

Padding from the bathroom into the open plan kitchen/ sitting room, she saw the spare key hanging from a hook on the wall. It occurred to her that it was somewhat annoying that Vuk had never offered it to her. But at the same time, he'd never told her that she couldn't have it. The phrase that she and Laura had always parroted forth, in sing-song voices, when appropriating something of James's that he'd left lying around – his sweets, the 20p pieces he begged from every passing friend and relative, the key-rings he collected – came to her now. Finders keepers. Putting Laura's scarf down on one of the dining chairs, she added Vuk's key to her lanyard that held those to the kitchen storeroom and the cleaning cupboard.

Flicking on the lights she looked around for the things she needed to write Vuk a note. As usual, the cabin was utterly bare, impossible to imagine that anyone actually lived there. She poked her head around the door of the bedroom, just in case that yielded anything. No pen and no paper, but she did see something that made her frown in puzzlement. A woman's skimpy white camisole top hung from one of the wardrobe door handles. Edie went up to it. She put her hands on each side of it, widening it out to wearing size, studied it and then dropped it to the floor.

It wasn't hers.

Was it Laura's? She stared at it long and hard, wanting and simultaneously not wanting to know whose it was and what Vuk was playing at. As she considered it, a profound silence fell on the room and the white noise of nothing became deafening. Edie was suddenly paralysed with an inexplicable fear, an innate sense of impending doom. There was someone watching her. She shook herself. This was ridiculous; she had worked herself up into a state of paranoia with her covert actions of earlier.

A bird squawked outside. Edie's heart thumped so hard that she thought her chest would explode. She did not dare turn around. She was not imagining it; there was someone there, creeping up on her. A shadow slid across the wall and her heart stopped.

A pair of strong hands flattened over her eyes, blinding her. She screamed, long and shrill.

'No one will hear you with the doors shut,' a voice whispered in her ear.

For a second, she felt as if her legs would give way. Laura had been abducted and now her attackers had got her, Edie, too.

Then her brain registered the voice and relief suffused her.

Vuk. It was just Vuk.

The hands fell from her eyes, releasing her.

Edie looked up at him to see that he was appraising her with a half-smile curling across his face. He was handsome, familiar, her lover. She smiled back. This Laura stuff was making her loopy; she was in Vuk's room, the safest place she could possibly be. Wasn't it? That's how she had thought of it up till now.

'What are you doing?' he asked. 'Was I expecting you?'

Edie sat up and pouted crossly. 'No, but that doesn't mean you have to creep up on me like a mad axe murderer.'

'You are in my room, Edie.' Vuk clearly had no intention of apologising. 'Don't polite English girls know they should wait to be invited?'

Edie looked up at Vuk through her eyelashes, sensing the changing mood. 'Don't mean, lean, bad, Balkan men know that not all English girls are ladies?'

Keep true to type, she heard Laura instructing her. Entice him by being flirty and frivolous. Men liked that.

Vuk regarded her silently for a moment. And then laughed; a short but robust guffaw.

Relief coursed through Edie. He wasn't cross. She could ask him to help with the Laura poster and he would see what a good plan it was and think how clever it was of little her to have hatched it. She waited for him to ask what she was there for.

Instead, Vuk stepped forward and around her, picking up the discarded camisole. Carefully and deliberately, he hung the flimsy garment on a hanger and put it in the wardrobe, then quietly shut the door.

'You know I don't like mess, Edie.' He clearly wasn't going to explain its presence in his room. Jealousy burned through Edie, only dampened by the thought of her mission, the reason she had come.

He turned to her. 'So what can I do for you, little one? You are here for a reason?'

Vuk's words were followed by a deep silence. The air-conditioning was off and there was just the white noise of emptiness.

'I was looking for you.' Edie pulled her face into an expression which she hoped said innocent-but-knowing. 'It's becoming my full time occupation, looking for people. You, Laura ...'

Her voice tailed off as Vuk strode towards her.

'Perhaps I should add the owner of that top to the list,' she added defiantly, momentarily unable to resist the childish envy that suffused her.

In response, Vuk threw her unceremoniously onto the bed, slid her shorts off and pulled her knickers to one side. He bent his face close to hers, his lips nuzzling her ear.

'If you're thinking that the top belongs to Laura,' he whispered, his breath hotter even than the air that sweltered around them. 'It doesn't. I've never set eyes on your sister, let alone undressed her and fucked her.'

Sitting herself up, Edie grabbed Vuk's arms, wanting him to face her and tell her the truth. Why was he mentioning Laura with regard to the top, what gave him the idea that she might suspect it belonged to Laura? His biceps were rock hard. Her fingers made no impression upon them at all. Vuk moved towards her as if to kiss her, then pushed her backwards to lie on the bed where he held her, unable to move.

'It is not a girlfriend's, either. It is my cousin's. She was staying here recently.'

Edie gazed up at him, overcome by bewilderment, fury and disbelief in equal measure. *Cousin, my arse.* How come she hadn't seen or heard of this elusive relative? But there was no chance to interrogate further as Vuk was on top of her, his weight pinning her down, biting her nipples, his hand between her legs. The questions, the doubts, the idea that if he could lie so easily about this he could lie about anything, fought with her devotion to him. Vuk entered her, pushing himself deep inside her, his mouth narrowed in concentration, his gaze focused on something far, far away as he pumped into her time and time again. She loved him, she knew she did. And, to make love to her like this, he must feel the same about her, mustn't he?

As soon as he had finished, Vuk got up and went to the bathroom. She heard the whoosh of the water and the thud of the shower door closing. Edie lay on the bed, close to tears.

Now it was over, she realised that she hadn't come to have sex, unusual though that might be. Vuk hadn't asked her either, hadn't considered at all how she might be feeling. Confusion suffused her. At moments like this, she realised how inept she was and probably always would be. She was sure that, by having sex with her, Vuk was trying to make her feel good and to show her how much he cared. Perhaps to take her mind off her sister. She was sure he was trying to do what was best for her.

It just didn't feel much like that right now.

***

When they had both showered and Vuk had poured two glasses of home-brewed rakija, Edie pulled forth the poster from her bag. She had fought against and resisted the urge to leave, to cut and run in the face of her bewilderment. The plan was, must be, her priority.

'I need your help, Vuk. There's a couple of things.' She looked down at the poster, from which her own smile – or was it Laura's? – shone up at her.

'Firstly, can you write the script for this poster? In both alphabets? I've done the English version here; you just need to translate it into your language.'

Vuk said nothing. Edie wasn't sure whether to go on, whether to take his silence as inviting her to continue or the opposite. She ploughed on regardless.

'And the other thing is – that I found something ...' she blurted the words out as she retrieved the scarf from the chair where she'd dumped it. She held it up for Vuk's inspection.

'This scarf. I think it belongs to Laura.'

She stopped, eyeing Vuk expectantly. The scarf was a silvery grey she could see now, under proper lighting. The crosses, which had seemed pure white in the moonlight, were actually ivory. The overall effect was pretty and delicate; just like Laura. Vuk took it from her and examined it closely as if precise identification that it was Laura's might reveal itself upon rigorous scrutiny. Finally, he put it down onto the table and turned back to look at Edie once more.

His face was utterly expressionless but Edie was sure that something lingered behind the façade. Anger, perhaps, or disdain.

'You shouldn't go poking around the old buildings, Edie.' His demeanour was still completely neutral, as was his voice. He could have been asking the time. 'They're not safe, they might collapse at any time. And sometimes there are – undesirables, shall we say – hanging around there.'

Edie let her gaze drop away from Vuk to the scarf, and then the poster. He was just concerned about her safety, that was all; that was why she sensed fury bubbling beneath his blank visage. He cared about her; how sweet was that?

She pushed the poster around the scarf and towards him. 'So will you write it?'

Vuk went to a drawer in the kitchen and returned with a pen. 'Of course.'

He read the English out loud:

Missing
Have you seen this girl?
If you know where she is or have any information, please call: 07977710939

Considering it carefully, he wrote down the translations.

'Can you make my handwriting out?' he asked Edie when he had finished, passing the paper back to her.

She went over it with him, word by word, to be sure.

'Thank you,' she said when it was finished, leaning forward as if to kiss him and then suddenly pausing, retracting, standing up straight again. 'I really appreciate it.' This at least was still one-hundred per cent true. She faltered and frowned before continuing. 'But back to the scarf ... how do you think it got there?'

Something was troubling her, something didn't sit right, but she couldn't quite get her head around what it was.

Vuk twisted the pen around in his fingers. 'You said Laura had all afternoon on her own, while you were working.' He shrugged and placed the pen deliberately onto the table. 'She went for a walk, went exploring. Dropped the scarf and it's been there ever since.'

Edie grimaced doubtfully.

'You English girls, with your insatiable appetite for exploration. Your search for new experiences,' Vuk interrupted, a sardonic smile spreading over his face. 'She's just the same as you.'

They sat in silence for a while, Edie contemplating the mystery, wondering if she were being as insanely melodramatic about it as Vuk seemed to be implying.

Feeling Vuk's gaze intent upon her, she lifted her eyes to his.

'What are you staring at?'

'You. You look so beautiful. And much, much more interesting than a scarf.'

He got up, took Edie's hand and led her to the other end of the table. Undoing the towel wrapped around his waist he let it fall onto the tiles and then removed hers. He turned her around and bent her forward over the wooden surface. 'Laura is your identical twin, after all,' he whispered in her ear, his breath soft against her skin. 'No wonder she's as nosey as you.'

And then he was fucking her again, so hard she felt the breath knocked out of her. It lasted a long time and when he had finished, he went to sit outside and lit a cigarette.

Edie joined him, standing on the edge of the pool and staring at the still water. She suddenly understood what, precisely, was odd about Vuk's comments about where she'd come across the scarf.

'Just one more thing,' she said, dipping her toe in and swirling it backwards and forwards, watching the smooth lines she created form and dissolve in the water.

'How did you know I found the scarf by the old buildings?'

SIXTEEN

Fatima

A kind young man saved them. He was a doctor, fleeing like everyone else but perhaps better prepared, certainly better equipped. He could have stayed, could have continued to patch up the fighters and their victims and he might have been OK, if he'd managed to keep on the right side of whoever was currently dominant in the incomprehensible confusion of it all. But his hospital had been hit by an airstrike one night when he had been operating and he had decided enough was enough. Having arrived at the border, despite his education, his qualifications and skills, his fluency in three languages, he had to take his chances along with everyone else. It was luck that led him to end up sheltering from the sun under the same tree as Fatima. He saw Marwa, noticed immediately the horrible sight that was her leg and put out his arms to take the child.

'I'm a doctor,' he said, in a tone of voice so concerned, so solicitous, and at the same time so matter-of-fact and author-itative, that Fatima could no longer stave off the tears.

'Oh dear,' the doctor said as he inspected the area more closely. 'That doesn't look too clever.'

He wasn't paying attention to Fatima any more, all his training and expertise directed at Marwa. Fatima couldn't speak. Her head was pounding, the deep thirst that desiccated her throat making her want to reach out her tongue and lap up her own tears, however salty.

'Have you anything clean you can put down?' he asked, indicating towards the ground beneath their feet. He ignored Fatima's crying. She supposed he was used to it. Sobbing relatives were an occupational hazard.

She laid out the scarf she had been using as tablecloth and bread wrapper. It wasn't exactly clean but it was better than the bare earth.

'My name's Ahmed,' the doctor told her as he laid Marwa on it. 'I have some antibiotics I can give her, if we can get her to swallow them. She should have liquid ones but here— ' He looked around as if to emphasise his point.

Ahmed had antiseptic wipes which he used to clean the area, his touch tender and light. He murmured words of comfort to Marwa as she squealed in agony, her body bucking involuntarily with every excruciating contact with the wound and surrounding area. Fatima clenched her fists and bit her lip, her heart thumping against her chest as she bore Marwa's distress.

When Ahmed was ready, Fatima held Marwa's nose whilst Ahmed put the pill on her tongue. As he filled her mouth with water from a plastic dosing syringe, Fatima blew strongly onto Marwa's face and even in her half-conscious state, the little girl swallowed instinctively, gulping down the water and the pill. It was Fatima's own proved method of getting the children to take medication.

Ahmed was impressed. 'Well done.'

He took the antibiotics box and showed it to Fatima, explaining the dose to give her and how often. 'By the time you've finished them all,' he said, 'you should be on the other side and you'll be able to take her to a hospital. It should be properly stitched. They have excellent doctors, there.'

Fatima wasn't sure exactly what he meant by 'there'.

'Thank you,' she stuttered, still not quite believing what good fortune had struck. 'Thank you so much. But I must pay you for the drugs.'

Ahmed shook his head. People all around were shouting and there was a rush of footsteps passing by their little huddle.

'I must go.' He thrust the box and the plastic syringe into her hand.

'Good luck,' he called over his shoulder, already running with the crowd. 'You'll make it. Just keep trying.'

Fatima gathered Maryam into her arms as she watched Ahmed go. Youssef and Ehsan were standing watching, seeming as shocked and overcome as she was. It was clear they were not going to run with him, not this time, not with Marwa lying supine on the ground.

As she stared after Ahmed's receding figure, Fatima had only one thought in her head.

Maybe angels do exist, after all.

**

Ahmed must have made it because they didn't see him again. Their wait continued. Youssef did his best to cheer the twins up, performing funny walks, pulling faces and pretending to magic sweets out of their ears. But even he fell silent by the end of day three. Fatima tried to make it all seem like a fabulous game of hide and seek.

'We're all going to play. We have to see if we can run from here to …,' she gesticulated wildly into the distance, '– to over there, and then we hide!'

The twins were gazing at her with wide, uncomprehending eyes. Youssef just looked puzzled and slightly disgusted. He could see straight through the pretence and he was not impressed.

'What fun!' she concluded, so lamely that no one, not even three-year-olds, could possibly be taken in.

It wasn't anything like hide and seek. It was an interminable torture of waiting in the hot sun with not enough food and barely any water, unwashed, unrested and increasingly losing their last reservoirs of resolve. They snatched sleep on make-shift beds of cloths and pieces of cardboard they'd gathered up, with rolled up clothes for pillows, not wanting a second to pass when they were not poised ready to leave, always anxious that the signal could come at any time. As the hours and the days went by it was clear, despite all Fatima's talk of running, that Maryam was too exhausted to do more than walk and Marwa, though vastly improved, was still not able to run. She and Ehsan agreed that they would carry one twin each and Youssef would take his own backpack plus two of the plastic bags. Fatima was grateful for Ehsan's support. There were women here on their own with one, two, six children. But she was preoccupied with the idea that he harboured resentment about the burden she and the girls were.

He's wishing he came on his own with Youssef, she couldn't help muttering to herself as she opened one can of fish for five of them to share. *Of course he is, it would have been so much easier for him, for the two of them.*

She wondered how Ali had got out; where he was now. Europe or the States, most likely. Canada, maybe. He had probably just gone to the airport and got on a plane. Fatima gave a snort of anger and resignation. That was the old days. Everything was different now. But wherever he was he might be able to get them all there, too? Angrily, she pushed the thought away. She didn't have the effrontery to approach the brother she had not tried to get in touch with all the years before – before thinking he might be useful to her. He would think she was the worst kind of gold-digger, looking for favours where none were owed.

The others ate but she couldn't face anything. The smell

revolted her. This was what made it all so much worse, made her even more of a dead weight. Because soon Ehsan would be bound to notice the other problem they had.

She had.

Having missed four periods, there was only one possible conclusion to come to. She was pregnant. She had tried to put the first, and the second, down to stress and fear due to the ever-worsening crisis engulfing the country. She hadn't said anything to Fayed. But it wasn't just not bleeding that made her sure, it was the metallic taste in her mouth, the physical exhaustion that was more intense, more overpowering than any ordinary fatigue, the craving for oranges and the nausea, which had continued throughout the time she was expecting the twins and seemed to be doing so again. The signs were all there and as much as she tried to ignore them, she knew what they meant.

She told no one.

They waited some more.

***

And then suddenly, in the early evening of the fifth day, word went around, confirmed by a hasty call from the smuggler, that now was good. A hiatus further up the border had redeployed the guards for the time being and provided an opportunity. Young men, the bravest and fittest, scrabbled to the front of the waiting hordes and launched themselves bodily against the fence; some scaled it with ease but others had to use the concrete posts to support themselves as they hauled themselves up, metre by metre. Once they had reached the top a few, the kindest perhaps, stationed themselves astride the wire to help others. Ehsan followed suit, managing somehow, even though he was overweight and unfit, to clamber clumsily to the summit where he balanced, half-standing, half-crouching, one leg on either side.

126

The fence was flimsy, built in haste to hold back the human tide, and it rocked perilously to and fro with the conflicting weights of those climbing up on one side and down on the other. Fatima watched as Ehsan swung around high above her, his lack of balance only too apparent. She muttered a brief prayer but had not had time to finish it before Youssef was in front of her, gesturing to her to give him a leg up, to help him follow on where the men had led. More and more these days, he was showing that he had left childhood behind. And yet, at only thirteen, he was far too young for adulthood – especially the brutal travesty of true manhood that their circumstances engendered.

Somehow, between Fatima hoisting and Ehsan pulling, Youssef conquered the fence and dropped down the other side. For one brief moment, they caught each other's eye, and Fatima saw in his expression the hunted, panic-stricken look of the animal that has broken out of its cage and into freedom and feels not elation but utter terror, having no idea what to do with the hard-won liberty now it was achieved.

There were people behind her, hundreds and hundreds of them, bearing down on her, pushing her forward. Word got around quickly and refugees were arriving, by foot or taxi or car or by whatever means possible, from all over the place, desperate for the chance the brief absence of patrols offered. The sheer weight of bodies pressing towards her meant that Fatima would have to get up and over that fence quickly or she and the girls would be crushed by the mob. But the jostling and elbowing, the screeches and shouts of instructions, exhortations and warnings that filled the air threatened to overwhelm her. She wanted to put her hands over her ears and scream to drown out all the noise and the panic and the hysteria.

A woman flopped down off the fence next to her. She had got about half way up and then fallen, hampered as she was by a full abya and two enormous carrier bags of food and clothing. Undaunted, she pushed her hijab back from where it covered her eyes and began again. Her determination brought Fatima to her senses. She seized hold of Marwa and lifted her as high as she could. Ehsan grabbed her arm and for a split-second she dangled there, hanging above the scorched earth and crowds of clamouring men, women and children. And then Ehsan pulled her up enough to get a hold of her body and swung her over the summit of the fence and down to Youssef's waiting arms. Maryam was soon also over and then it was Fatima's turn. Her paranoid fear of heights, her hatred of climbing anything, evaporated in a heartbeat. It had to. There was no other choice.

As she turned to make her ascent, she noticed a little boy, about six, who was standing next to her, seemingly alone. Incongruously fastened around his neck was a pair of sunglasses on a thick, elasticated band and under his arm he clasped a hastily bundled up piece of plastic sheeting which presumably served as his bed. His clothes were tattered and torn, little more than rags, but the expression on his face was new and unfaded. It was utter, profound, raw fear.

Fatima faltered, staring wildly around her. She could not leave this child here, abandoned. Where was his family, his mother? Just as she was working out what she would say to Ehsan about the fact that their party had added another to its number, the little boy was seized by the arm and swung up and over the fence. Fatima followed, hating herself for the relief she felt that she hadn't, in the end, been called to act, hadn't had to choose between a moral action and a selfish one.

Looking upwards as she began her ascent, Fatima saw that next to Ehsan was a youth of about twenty, curly haired, filthy clothes darkened by sweat stains down his back and in his armpits. They were both waiting expectantly for her to reach them. Between the two of them they managed to manhandle Fatima over the top of the fence and down the other side, where she fell heavily and painfully to the ground. The jolt sent a flash of pain searing through her stomach and for a fleeting second she wondered if it would harm the baby, cause a miscarriage, and if so, whether that would be a good or a bad thing. Frantically, disgusted with herself, she chased the thoughts away; it was sinful to wish a death of anyone or anything. She would never have let such a notion enter her mind before. Never.

The youth who had helped landed beside her and Fatima started to thank him but he was gone already, almost rolling down the trench in his hurry to get away, to get on with his journey. The fence was still rocking back and forth and the wire was now adorned with scraps of fabric torn from fluttering veils or abyas too voluminous to keep out of the barbs' way. It resembled some sort of macabre bunting.

Most people had little with them, but just beyond where she stood Fatima saw a couple manhandling two enormous suitcases over the fence. One of them still bore the remnants of airport security tape, reminiscent of happier, normal times when one took a plane to a holiday and always packed too much.

Ehsan was trying to get down from the fence but had got involved in bundling across an elderly woman in traditional dress, her clothing completely incapacitating her, her skirts ridden up around her waist, her helplessness turning her into a pathetic overgrown baby, all dignity gone. Finally, she was over and deposited unceremoniously on the dusty, stony ground, looking dazed and confused, unable to comprehend how she had got there and what to do now. Through the wire diamonds of the fence Fatima beheld, approaching in a seething torrent, more and more people, all intent on one thing. They rippled up and over and down the fence, leaving more tattered remnants of skirts and scarves to join those already there, a ceaseless human tsunami.

Bags of provisions were dropped and spilled, ripe red

tomatoes left to roll down the crumbling sides of the deep trench like so many tumbling balls. Anything extraneous was left by the wayside; nothing let go of could be gone back for. Somebody lost hold of a bag of rice that split open as it fell, showering everything with an incongruous confetti cloud of white grains. It was mayhem, a scene of Biblical intensity and dread.

Ehsan's feet hit the ground beside Fatima with a thud. Urgency sent adrenalin shooting through her veins. She and Ehsan grabbed a twin each, checked Youssef was there too and descended into the trench. The sides were flaky and unstable, hard to get down and even harder to climb out of. Some were being hauled up with makeshift ropes fashioned out of hijabs. Fatima's head spun with the exertion of clawing her way up the steep bank with Marwa in her arms. But she managed. She and Ehsan paused at the summit to pull Youssef out and as they did so, Fatima saw it again, the tide of humanity that kept on coming, surging across the fence, down into and up out of the trench, more and more and more people.

Joining the flow of the human flood as it built up speed again, Fatima, Ehsan and the children crossed the patrol road and fled, into the scrappy, untidy undergrowth of another country. If the border guards caught them now, they would send them back. So they kept on running.

SEVENTEEN

Edie

Edie's question hung in the air like one of Vuk's smoke rings.

'I guessed.' Vuk's tone was as laconic as always. 'I was behind you when you arrived at my cabin and I saw the direction you came from; there's only one place that path leads to.'

'You were spying on me?' Edie's voice was far louder and higher than she intended.

Vuk took a long draw at his cigarette.

'Edie, you are the one who entered my room without permission.'

He blew another smoke ring that shimmered in the moonlight like the ethereal outline of a planet before dispersing. 'If we are talking about prying ...'

He let the end of the sentence hang and Edie said nothing. She took her foot out of the pool, droplets of water darkening the tiles.

'So,' she paused, running the evening's earlier events through her head. 'You know how I got in?'

Vuk grinned. 'You looked very funny, dragging your sizeable arse through such a small opening. I thought you were going to get stuck.' He stubbed out the cigarette in a flower pot. 'But you made it – just.'

Edie flushed deep pink. She had always been sensitive about the size of her bum. Vuk had picked the right subject to make her self-conscious. She said no more.

'Bed time, Edie,' concluded Vuk, once it was obvious she wasn't going to respond to his joke. He gestured towards the bedroom.

Edie almost got up to obediently go where he indicated. And then changed her course and headed for the door instead. She was tired and she didn't want to have sex again; it wasn't as if he'd asked her permission the last two times.

'I've got to go back to my room and send some emails,' she lied. 'And – well, yeah, just that really.'

Scuffling along the sandy path she could hardly fathom her own behaviour. Turning down eight hours in Vuk's bed, held by his arms? Not wanting sex?

This Laura stuff must be getting to her even more than she thought.

***

Evil Ivana surprised Edie again the next day when she readily agreed to copy her poster fifty times. Vuk had told her not to put it up in the resort as it would unnerve the guests but bollocks to that. Edie intended to pin them up anywhere and everywhere. It was the local custom to announce a death by putting a picture of the deceased on display, usually on a conveniently situated olive tree. Edie had bought some of the tape and pins she'd seen used for this purpose and, armed with this and the sheaf of posters hot off the photo-copier, she set off to find suitable places to advertise her missing sister.

She was struggling to break off the first piece of tape whilst holding the posters wedged under her arm when Zayn appeared, pool-clearing pole and net in hand.

'What are you doing, Edie?' he asked in his characteristically downcast way.

Edie barely spared him a glance. 'Trying to find my sister,' she replied. Mounting anxiety was making her short-tempered.

Zayn said nothing but continued to stand there, watching her battle with the roll of tape.

'Grrrr! This stuff is useless.' Edie flung it to the ground in frustration.

Zayn bent down to pick it up. 'Let me help,' he said.

'Go on then, if you really want to make yourself useful you can hold these for me.' Edie thrust the sheaf of paper at him. He looked down, studying the top one carefully. She managed to peel back a section of tape, bite it off with her teeth and, grabbing one of the posters from the pile he held, stick it onto the tree.

'She's pretty,' Zayn said, contemplatively, as if he had made a great discovery.

'Well, yeah, doofus.' Edie regarded him with raised eyebrows. Zayn gave no impression of having noticed.

'And just so you know,' she continued. 'It's actually me, not Laura – I didn't have any pictures of her on my phone.'

Zayn nodded, still scrutinising the poster.

'I think you have a problem, Edie.' His words were slow, deliberate.

'Zayn, I've got a lot of problems, most importantly of all right now being that I don't know where the hell she is,' retorted Edie, rolling her eyes dramatically. 'I thought you were here to help, not find fault.' She tried to be nice to Zayn but really he was testing her patience today.

Zayn's expression was pained. 'I want to help.' He paused, then seemed to summon the courage to continue. 'The thing is – if someone rings up and says they've seen this person ...'

He indicated towards the poster with an incline of his head. 'How will you know it's Laura they've seen and not you?'

Edie closed her eyes and sighed heavily.

'You'll get hundreds of phone calls and they'll just be distractions because they won't be Laura.'

Having said his piece, Zayn fell silent, looking as if he wished the ground would swallow him up.

Edie was about to snap back at him to stop being so negative and obstructive, had opened her mouth to do so, when she shut it again. He was absolutely right. Totally and completely right. The poster plan was a disaster and would more than likely lead to calls and 'sightings' that were a distraction from the search rather than assisting it in any way.

She sank down onto a hummock of rough grass. It scratched her bare legs and she knew she'd be bitten by something, some bloody ant or mosquito or another type of creepy-crawly; this god-awful place was full of them. But she didn't move, feeling suddenly deflated, exhausted.

'Sorry.' Zayn squatted down next to her, resting easily on his haunches. 'I didn't mean to distress you.'

Edie let her head fall onto her knees and blinked back tears. When she was sure she had suppressed them, she turned towards Zayn. 'It's okay. I hadn't thought it through. How could I be so stupid?'

Zayn tentatively stretched out his hand and patted her on the shoulder. 'We'll think of something else.'

There was silence for a moment, filled by the incessant humming of the cicadas. Edie's phone beeped to signify a text message and out of habit she pulled it out of her pocket and looked at it. Maybe it would be Vuk with some news, or just a kind greeting that would dispel the uneasiness that lingered from the night before. Perhaps he wanted to find out how she was. She read the message. Then read it again, hardly able to believe what she saw.

Hi Edie, sorry to disappear like that, I decided to move on already. I still dont have a phone I just asked someone a favour to send this so dont bother replying but I'll call you soon. Dont worry about me, Im fine.
Laura xxx

She held the screen towards Zayn as if there would be confirmation that it were real if he saw it too.

'It's from Laura,' she stuttered. 'A text to say that she's OK.'

Zayn read it, an expression of intense concentration on his face. Gradually, a beaming smile spread across his normally careworn features.

'So it's fine, Edie. Your sister – she's good, just like I said, like everyone said.' Zayn stood and pulled her up to stand beside him. He made a gesture towards her that looked as if he intended to hug her but she stepped quickly sideways.

'Thanks, Zayn, thanks a lot. It's great news. Really good.' Edie slid the phone into her pocket and looked uncertainly down at the bunch of paper still in Zayn's hands.

'I'll put them in the bin,' he suggested.

'Yeah.' Edie bit her lip as the tears threatened again. Why was she crying when Laura was alive and kicking?

'I need to get to work,' she blurted out, turning on her heel and hurrying towards the cleaning store and away from Zayn. 'I'll see you around.'

Alone with the mops and buckets and bottles of detergent she sat on a box of washing powder, took the phone back out of her pocket and studied it again. It was unusual of Laura to call her Edie rather than Ed, and the phrasing didn't sound like Laura's. But if she'd borrowed a phone from a stranger, and was trying to send the message really quickly, that was perhaps hardly surprising. Edie thought about answering the message but there didn't seem to be much point. By the sounds of it, Laura and the phone this had come from had nothing more than a passing connection – this, along with the fact that she'd expressly told her not to reply was reason enough not to respond. She would just have to wait for Laura to call as she promised to do.

Edie picked up a bucket, a mop, some cleaning cloths and the local version of Cif. She hauled herself out of the storeroom and towards Vlad's office where she stood waiting while he finished a phone call.

'Where am I today?' she asked as soon as he hung up.

Vlad handed her a list of cabanas to be cleaned and any additional information, such as extra bed or cot requirements and whether a welcome grocery pack was to be included. Edie scowled as she took it from his hand and turned to go.

'Edie.' Vlad's tone was harsh.

Edie made a deliberate show of stopping and looking round at him excessively slowly.

'Yes?'

'Please put a smile on your face. The guests are on holiday. You need to show them cheerful, happy.'

His thin face showed not a hint of the jocularity he was urging on her.

'Right you are.'

Fuck this stupid camp and stupid Vlad and stupid bloody everything. Edie was struggling to distinguish between the right reasons she had for being here: independence, showing that she could hold down a job, a healthy lifestyle, opportunities to free-dive. And the wrong ones: putting off getting the qualifications she'd so far failed to achieve, avoiding facing up to her lack of a 'career'. She'd been given so much help over the years by so many people – her parents, professionals, doctors, even James, who'd always stood by her – and how had she repaid it? By running away to somewhere most people had never heard of and investing so much in pretending to be happy that most of the time she actually kidded herself that she was. She dragged her feet along the path to her first cabana. She should be over the moon that Laura was all right and there was nothing to be afraid of anymore and no more searching to do. She should be seeing it as an achievement, although strictly speaking she hadn't had anything to do with it. But she wasn't. Laura hadn't even begun to explain why she had 'decided to move on' so soon after arriving; why she had deserted Edie anew.

Banging and crashing around, she cleaned her cabanas in the skimpiest of manners that day. In her room after taking a shower she stood in front of the mirror she'd nailed to the wall. She examined her face, which was hers but could also be Laura's; their likeness binding them together superficially as all their other similarities did beneath the surface.

She had read in one of the many twin studies she followed that psychologists believed you could tell the future relationship that a set of twins would have by observing how they reacted towards each other in the womb. There were playful twins, competitive twins, affectionate twins; twins with pre-natal habits and ways of behaving that would last after their birth and into childhood, adulthood and old age. She wondered what kind of relationship she and Laura would have been deemed to have, so close together for nine months in their watery world. Although it hadn't been nine months as they had been born six weeks early, as her mother had frequently told her. Maybe that's why I'm so hopeless at everything, Edie sometimes thought about herself. Born too early; brain not ready or something.

She looked back at the mirror and imagined that the person standing facing her was Laura. When they were little girls they had barely spent a moment apart. Every child longs for a best friend – unless you're a twin, because in that case you already have one. She and Laura had shared everything, done everything together. They had had a secret language and although they had grown out of it years ago, Edie could still remember some of the words. Sweets were 'goggles' and the park was 'balala'. She gave a brief snort of laughter at the memory. They must have driven their parents mad, sometimes refusing to talk English for days at a time, relishing their secret world that excluded all others. Edie felt bad for James, remembering how they had petted and patted him, making him part of their games whether he wanted to be or not, but never inviting him to join them in their made-up universe. Just as she wasn't including him in Laura's disappearance. He couldn't know that she had lost her own twin, his beloved sister. He would never forgive her.

A knock on the door startled her thoughts away from James.

'Who is it?' she called out, not bothering to fumble around for clothes. She couldn't imagine it would be anyone she wanted to talk to right now.

In the mirror's reflection she saw the door opening.

'Wait! I'm naked,' she shouted out involuntarily, casting her eyes frantically around the room for something that might cover her.

'That's what I was hoping.'

It was Vuk.

'Quick, get in and shut the door! I don't need the whole world to see me in the buff!'

What on earth was Vuk doing here? He never came to the staff cabins.

Vuk was dressed in a business suit. She always found it incongruous to see people wearing formal work wear, in a holiday resort, in the heat and dust of high summer.

'I wanted to see you.'

'I thought you'd be off sailing. You usually are,' replied Edie, pointedly. Her feelings on seeing him were not what they usually were. The usual delight was tainted by something else now, something she couldn't put a name to and didn't properly understand.

138

'Not yet.' He went over to her and rested his hands on her hips. 'Don't you want to see me?'

'I just wasn't expecting you.'

Vuk clicked his tongue regretfully and stepped backwards, holding her at arms' length.

'I wanted to say sorry; maybe you think I have not been sympathetic enough about Laura.'

Edie's eyes widened in disbelief. Vuk apologising? This had to be a first.

'You mean so much to me, Edie,' he went on, his eyes still fixed on hers. 'I am guilty of taking you for granted, not showing you how much I care for you. I'm sorry that my work takes me away from –' he paused, as if his next words required a lot of effort '– from us. But when I am around – like now – I hope you'll let me make it up to you.'

Edie was flabbergasted, and at the same time subsumed by a warm feeling that spread slowly through her veins to the tips of her fingers and the ends of her toes. She had been about to add 'Vuk' to her list of wrong reasons for being here, but now he could go firmly back to the top of the column of right ones. All her qualms faded away; she had let her crazy notions get the better of her for a moment when she had refused to stay the night, when she had wondered if he knew more about Laura than he was saying, but at least she hadn't done any lasting damage.

She tilted her head back to look up at him. He was so tall, so handsome and masterful. Her hands strayed over his body, his buttocks taut inside the suit trousers. 'Of course I will.'

She must have been losing her mind to have doubted him. No one could speak and act so lovingly if they didn't mean it.

He bent down and kissed her, tightening his grip on her as he did so.

Edie turned her head away so she could talk. 'I had some good news today.'

Vuk pulled her face back round to him so that he could continue to nibble at her lips. 'What good news would that be?'

'Laura's OK. She sent a text. She left because she wanted to carry on travelling.'

Vuk spent a long time developing and then finishing the kiss, his tongue probing into her mouth, insistent and exploratory.

'So it's exactly as I told you, then,' he said, finally relinquishing her lips and drawing away from her.

'I guess so.'

'You can abandon the search and concentrate on more pleasurable things.' Vuk's hands were clasped around her waist now. He moved them down and pressed his fingertips into the fleshy tops of her buttocks. It felt as if his nails were piercing her skin. 'Can't you?' He pressed harder and the pain intensified. She squirmed out of his grasp.

'You're hurting me,' she protested.

Vuk smiled the slow, lop-sided smile. 'You don't usually complain.'

Edie had no time to reply before he had picked her up and carried her over to the bed.

His love-making was rough and uncompromising. Edie knew she'd have bruises where he had gripped her forearms like a vice. She should have felt replete, safe in the knowledge that Laura was alive and kicking and that Vuk ... Vuk what?

That Vuk loved her, of course. She smiled to herself, her face buried in his shoulder. He really did seem to love her. Mission accomplished.

She couldn't explain the vacuum inside herself.

Vuk shifted his weight off her and, running his hand through his hair, sat up.

'Are you going?' asked Edie. She suddenly, desperately, didn't want him to leave. If Laura was OK but just finding better things to do elsewhere she needed Vuk even more than ever. He was all she had.

'I've got things to do.' He pulled his trousers up, fastened the zip and buckled his belt. 'I'm not going to be around much for a day or so. Another trip, I'm afraid.'

Edie grimaced.

'You're so in demand.' She tried to seem light-hearted, but her voice cracked mid-sentence.

Vuk smiled. 'I'm sorry, little one.' He kissed her tenderly on the forehead.

'When I return, I would like you to come with me on a trip to the canyon. It will be good for you to work with the tourists more directly.'

Edie contemplated this idea silently.

'Edie?'

She looked up at him. His eyes questioned gently but there was a steeliness in his tone of voice.

'You do want to come, don't you Edie? It's a great opportunity for you.'

In what way it was an opportunity Edie wasn't quite sure. It wasn't as if her job on the resort was a career choice.

'And just think – three days and two nights for us to spend together.'

The opportunity became clear. It would seal the deal, cement their relationship. Some quality time in each other's company, no boat trips to keep tearing them apart, no cleaning and waitressing to steal the hours of her day.

'It sounds great.' Edie smiled, and didn't have to try to make herself sound convincing. Laura was fine, no longer a concern. She had nothing to worry about except enjoying herself with her lover, Vuk. What could be more perfect?

Three whole days with Vuk, two nights camping out under the stars, snuggled up in a tent, sleeping bags zipped together for warmth, holding each other tight as the wolves howled and the brown bears stalked the ancient black pine forests. Of course, the wolves and the bears were unlikely to show up but the very fact that they existed was enough to increase the impossible romanticism of it all. And then the canyon, which she hadn't seen yet, which was the second deepest in the world after the Grand Canyon.

'I can't wait,' Edie added, sensing Vuk needed something more from her.

He landed a gentle peck on her forehead, got up and walked to the door. He put his hand on the handle, paused and turned to face her.

'So that will be the end of looking for Laura, yes?'

'Yes, of course. She's – well, she's all right.' Edie frowned. 'I'd still like to know exactly where she is, though,' she added.

As she spoke, she could see the corner of the grey scarf peeking out from under a pile of clothing on the floor. An inexplicable clutch of fear made her stomach contract. Irritated, she dismissed it. What was wrong with her? Did she want Laura to be missing?

'But I guess I'll just have to wait to hear from her,' she concluded.

'That's right, Edie.' Vuk nodded. 'Good girl.'

He opened the door and disappeared, closing it gently and precisely behind him. Edie listened as his footsteps receded along the wooden veranda.

EIGHTEEN

Fatima

It was a moonless, starless night. The pitch dark worked in their favour, making it harder for the border guards to spot them as they waited in the undergrowth for the smuggler's van. Every now and again Maryam let out a whimper of fear; she had always been terrified of the dark. Fatima hastily stifled her cries as best she could, holding her tight and showering her with silent kisses of reassurance but not daring to utter any words of comfort. Disaster could still strike if they were found; the thought of being taken back across that border after so much effort was too terrible to contemplate.

They waited and waited. Every now and again, headlights roved into vision and they would throw themselves down into the long grass and hide until the patrol jeep had sped past. Each time, they wondered if it were the smuggler and each time it wasn't and they were left with nothing but the sound of the crickets whirring all around them. Using their phones to track them, the smuggler knew exactly where they had been and where they would be crossing. But it had all taken so long that their phones were dead, even Ehsan's emergency one, so they had no way to make another call to confirm their arrival. The smuggler had their money – lots of it – and he had told them to trust him so they had. But as the minutes turned to hours it became apparent that their trust had been misplaced.

Eventually, Fatima crawled close to Ehsan and whispered in his ear.

'The smuggler's not coming. We will have to walk.'

She could tell that Ehsan was angry, and so was she. But anger was not going to get them to safety.

She looked around her and saw no sign of light, not the smallest glimmer that could signal an approaching vehicle. Standing up, she picked up her plastic bag of possessions and took Maryam by the hand. Youssef followed her lead and, once he had shouldered his load, he took hold of Marwa.

'Ehsan, you lead the way with the compass,' instructed Fatima, not caring any more whether he liked it or not that she should be giving the orders. Somebody had to make the decisions around here. 'We have spent enough time looking at the map, we know the direction. So let's go.'

Ehsan mutely did as she directed. He, like them all, was too tired to argue or debate. One foot in front of the other was the most any of them could manage.

It took two hours blundering and stumbling along half-made paths in the darkness to reach the dusty town they were headed for. Even there, they were still not safe but at least they were on their way again. In the still of the night in which the whirr of the crickets held dominance, newly arrived refugees were being herded into minibuses. It was like some kind of surreal school trip, thought Fatima as they joined the queue; apprehensive and potentially disorderly students guided by bored and cynical teachers; no one quite knowing what the day would bring.

'You pay $50 each person,' growled the man in charge.

Fatima saw Ehsan bristle at the demand. There was no point

in getting riled; this guy didn't care that they had been ripped off. The only way they would get on that bus was if they shelled out the money he asked for. She whispered in Ehsan's ear to give him the cash. Ehsan reluctantly did so.

It took an hour to get to the bigger town and all the way there the danger was ever present. The security forces had stepped up patrols of the mountain roads and were looking specifically for vehicles loaded with those who had entered the country illegally. Interception would mean a night in jail and back 'home' in the morning. Everyone on the minibus was tense, the atmosphere taut and strained. Nobody spoke. Everybody's story was as bad as or worse than everybody else's and everybody had the same aim in mind. There was nothing to discuss.

***

The large town they eventually arrived at was a bustling conurbation of houses, shops, factories and schools. Here they could blend in with the crowd and Fatima knew that she should be relieved but instead she just felt sick and exhausted beyond all imagining. There was a café near where the minibus stopped. The smuggler-driver, who told them his name was Muhammed, advised them that they could get something to eat and he'd be back in an hour. If they were heading to the nearby refugee camp they could make their own way there. If they were intending to get to the coast he would take them to where they could get a long distance bus.

'How much will it cost?' asked Fatima.

The smuggler named a price.

Ehsan caught her eye. Fatima gave an almost imperceptible shrug. If he wanted to argue about it, let him. She was past caring.

A long discussion ensued which Fatima only half listened

to. She noticed, as she had done several times over the last few days without really taking it in, that Maryam kept scratching her head. She pulled the child towards her and sat her in her lap. On the pretext of stroking and soothing her, she ran her fingertips through Maryam's thick dark curls. It was exactly as she had suspected; her hair was full of head lice.

For some ridiculous reason this seemed to Fatima to be a catastrophe, worse than all the misfortune they had so far encountered. After everything, Fayed's death and Marwa's near-fatal infected wound, the destruction of their house, the perilous crossing of the border, incomprehensibly this felt like the worst of all. It represented an utter dereliction of her duty as a mother; parasites were feeding on her child's blood and she could do nothing about it. She had neither metal comb nor shampoo nor a hot bath at her disposal. Maryam, and Marwa too, for if one had nits the other would surely also have them, would have to remain infested until such time as Fatima could deal with them.

And this was the reason it struck so hard. Because in such a small detail was the utter destitution of their life laid bare.

Fatima wondered if she would ever be a 'proper' mother again, with a safe house for her children to live in, a comfy bed for them to sleep on, good food for them to eat. Clean water. The most basic things that she had always taken for granted seemed utterly out of reach, and not just for now but for the foreseeable future. And soon, in just a few months, she would have a baby to care for – or rather, to fail to care for. She had nothing to welcome this baby with, not even a cloth to dress him or her in. Fatima rubbed her belly with her hands. *Stay in there,* she whispered under her breath to her unborn child. *You're better off safe inside than out in this terrible world.*

Ehsan's conversation with Muhammed had become increasingly belligerent and now the altercation reached its apex. It culminated with Muhammed uttering swear words that Fatima hoped the children didn't hear and storming away into the bustle of the crowds.

Fatima looked at Ehsan enquiringly.

'He wanted too much money,' Ehsan snapped sharply at her. 'And he wanted it upfront, now. How do we know he would come back? What guarantee would we have? We have experienced this once already and that is once too much.'

Fatima nodded. She would have given him the money for the chance of a swift beginning to the onward journey but it was too late now. They finished their juice, pastries and eggs and Fatima went with the girls to the bathroom. She cleaned their faces, and her own, with cold water from the tap and wiped them dry with toilet paper. Desperately she wished she could bathe properly; she could smell the ripe, unwashed smell of herself and it disgusted her, made her feel repellent. But there were no showers here and they needed to press on and put distance between themselves and any chance of repatriation.

They found the bus station after a long trudge through the baking streets and bought tickets for a city on the coast. From there they could get to one of the small towns where the sea crossings took place. They stocked up with water, bread, fruit, cheese and olives. Fatima didn't want to take any meat, even cured or smoked, as they could not keep it cold and she was sure it would make them sick. The heat was intense and unrelenting. They were wandering in a foreign country with no documents, stateless, homeless and rootless. The relentless stress and worry, combined with the secret pregnancy, nauseated her constantly; the slightest whiff of bad food would surely finish her off.

The first bus they could get onto didn't leave until late that evening. More waiting, during which time Fatima and Ehsan decided it was best if they pretended they were married. That was the safest way, because then, if one 'parent' got to Europe and the other didn't, they would have the right, or at least the possibility, of being reunified. Without papers, no one could prove or disprove the fact of their matrimony.

'Call Ehsan daddy, not uncle,' Fatima instructed. She uttered a silent apology to Fayed, begging him to understand, to appreciate that the desperate situation they were in called for desperate measures. The girls stared, their eyes ringed purple with exhaustion, their faces white.

'It's another game,' she explained, 'like when we climbed that funny fence! We're going to pretend that Uncle Ehsan is your dad, and Youssef is your brother.'

No one laughed. Marwa and Maryam nodded and Youssef emitted a strangled grunt. Fatima had no idea what that meant and no inclination to find out. The girls were so young, far too young to have any real comprehension of what was going on. Their total trust in their mother, in Fatima, was pitiful when she was so inadequate for the job. She wanted to take Marwa to a hospital to have her leg checked. It was so much better now, the swelling completely gone, but the gash itself was large and obvious. She would be badly scarred, that was for sure. Ehsan refused to countenance either the visit to a clinic or the time by which it would delay them.

'The scar is there now, it's too late to fix it, plus it will be expensive,' he insisted, as if he had some medical know-how that Fatima didn't. 'We must press on.'

Fatima knew that Fayed would have insisted that she get proper care for Marwa. She was letting him down again. As if reading her mind, Ehsan grabbed her by the wrist.

'You know that a good wife obeys her husband.' His expression, up close as it was now, was terrifying, a leer that Fatima struggled to interpret.

'And does what he says,' added Ehsan.

Disgust caused Fatima's stomach to churn as she recognised the look. It was one of barely-disguised lust. If it hadn't been so horrific, it would be laughable that in her disgusting state she could arouse such an emotion in anyone. She dismissed it. Thank God Ehsan was not really her husband and never would be.

***

It was a long journey and despite the uncomfortable seats and constant snorting and spitting of phlegm by the man behind her, Fatima fell almost immediately into the drugged, profound sleep of utter fatigue. They had saved money by saying the twins were two and therefore didn't need a ticket with the consequence that they didn't get a seat. But even the dead weight of a child on her lap could not keep Fatima awake for any amount of time. Occasionally the girls asked for water or the toilet and she managed somehow to force herself to see to their needs before immediately falling back to sleep again.

Late the next day, the bus drew into the outskirts of a city. At the bus station, a small cluster of men split apart and drifted towards the vehicle as it came to a halt. They descended on Fatima and Ehsan as they clambered down the steps and into the sultry heat of a summer night. At first, Fatima wasn't sure what they were saying and thought they were representatives of local hotels or guesthouses, drumming up trade by greeting new arrivals. But then it became clear that they were smugglers, too. Everyone was a smuggler now.

Despite the hours and hours of slumber, Fatima still felt weary beyond belief. One of the men had a sweet smile and less insistent tone than the others and she singled him out to tell them what he could do for them. This turned out to be transporting them to one of the small resorts further down the coast and arranging their passage across the sea to the nearest island.

Once he had outlined his offer, there was a pause.

'There's a camp about an hour's walk away,' he went on to say, with a dismissive shrug. 'You must stay there if not come with me. On the streets – the police will pick up you.'

His English was broken and his tone of voice had become accusatory. Perhaps the sweet smile had been an illusion.

'Unless you have money for a hotel,' he added, derisively.

They obviously no longer looked like that kind of refugee.

And it was true, they didn't have money for a hotel. Each and every dollar had to be saved for what was absolutely essential and, in the height of summer, shelter did not fall into this category. After a quick discussion, Fatima and Ehsan agreed to pay the smuggler $50. He disappeared into the night, to get his van and fill up with petrol.

'I'll be back one hour,' he told them.

Two hours later he had not shown up.

Youssef went crazy, kicking the plastic signs that advertised the different bus services, his fists clenched and his face taut with anger. All his pent-up fury, all the petty humiliations and deep betrayals were vented as Fatima and Ehsan looked helplessly on. They had nothing to offer in mitigation, no reassurances to bestow upon him.

By midnight, it was obvious the smuggler wasn't coming back.

'Let's find somewhere to sleep,' said Fatima, her voice barely audible from fatigue and despair.

'What about the police? He said they'd pick us up from the streets.' Youssef was frightened as well as incandescent.

'He was full of bullshit.' Ehsan spat the words out as if he were spitting in the smuggler's face.

They set off, their little group rag-taggle and bowed, its spirit gone, heading in the vague direction of the refugee camp the smuggler had mentioned but with the intention of sleeping in the first suitable place they came across.

We are nothing more than a bunch of hobos, thought Fatima.

It was impossible to imagine that they could ever escape this situation, rise phoenix-like from the ashes of their impoverishment. But they must, she and Ehsan at least, because if they both rose they could all rise together but if one fell, so surely would they all follow.

They didn't get anywhere near the camp because they came upon a small area of flyblown grass, in the far corner of which was a child's swing and rocking horse. Ehsan indicated towards a patch of ground underneath a sad looking, dusty leaved tree.

'Here will do.'

They had bought a piece of tarpaulin and a few blankets at one of the stops en route to the coast and Ehsan unrolled these whilst Fatima took the girls to pee under some scrubby bushes. They were so tired that they fell asleep immediately after she had settled them under their thin covers. Youssef was still raging and had argued with Ehsan; he walked angrily to the swing and sat on it, staring at the worn brown earth beneath whilst he scuffed the toe of his shoe repeatedly back and forth.

'Aren't you going to go and talk to him?' asked Fatima. She didn't like them to be any distance apart from each other. It seemed as if the only safety there was, or would ever be, came from the five of them together, whatever their personal antipathies.

Ehsan sneered unattractively. 'He'll come back. He's not brave enough to go it alone.'

Fatima despised Ehsan then for his disloyalty towards his son. Youssef was only thirteen, just his size made him look much older. But he was still a child, and he was scared. It was not wise to cross Ehsan, though, and challenge his treatment of his son; it would only enrage him and lead to more discord. Fatima could do nothing but stand by and watch and hope that the situation would right itself once tempers had calmed. She made herself a space next to the girls and drifted into a fitful sleep.

The discomfort of being pressed against the ground, of an elbow pinching the skin of her arm, combined with a strange sound close to her ear, woke her. As she fuzzily came to, she felt something ripping at her clothes, at the secret pocket where she kept her money. Realising that she was being robbed, or worse, murdered, she struggled and opened her mouth to scream.

A hand slammed onto her face, crushing her skull against the hard earth beneath her, stifling her cries, its force threatening to break her neck. The back of her head ground against the stony soil and her ribs ached from the weight on top of her. Her belly, with the baby inside, was being squashed, the pressure making her gasp in pain. Fatima writhed and twisted and freed one arm with which she tried to fend off the attacker, thumping and punching wildly at him. But it was no use; he was far stronger than her and all her efforts to release his hold on her, to get him off her, were futile.

She was going to die, leaving the twins abandoned and defenceless, and there was nothing she could do about it.

NINETEEN

Edie

Edie put her phone back in her pocket and tried to listen to the customer's order. She had been reading Laura's text again, as if she hadn't already read and re-read it a hundred, a thousand times. She was tormented by all the unanswered questions that it raised. Why? Where? What? Why had Laura gone, where was she now, what had happened for her to change her plans to stay awhile? In the end, she had sent a text in reply to Laura's, on the assumption that the phone's owner must surely know something about her sister if he or she had let her use it. But her message received no reply. She had called the number but it rang out, ending in an incomprehensible message in a language she couldn't understand.

As Edie went through the motions of her job the puzzlement ate away at her like a plague of voracious locusts.

The evening bar shift was monotonous as usual. To make it even worse, Vlad was there, poking his nose into everything, critically observing how Edie addressed the customers and served the drinks. It was one in the morning before the bar emptied out and the last drinkers padded away into the olive grove. Cloud had come over and Stefan predicted a storm; one of the electric storms that came when the heat was too intense and sent shocks of lightning radiating over the mountains. It would rain up high, he said, but the rain rarely came to the bay and the coast in summer time. The temperature had soared so high that day that a downfall to soak the parched ground and dampen the heat would be welcome.

Edie remembered summer days at home in Brighton, when she and Laura would wake early and go outside to tiptoe through the dew, delighting in the sensation of the moisture squidging up between their toes whilst the grass tickled their feet. They would play on their swings, pretending that they were on a flying carpet upon which, if only they could get high enough, they would be able to travel the world. Soaring up and up, they would shriek with laughter as the swing supports thumped in and out of the ground, constantly threatening to teeter over and bring them crashing to the floor. So that he would not be left out, their father had hung a seat in the shape of a horse from a nearby tree branch for James. It took him years to learn how to swing himself and so he would patiently watch the twins, waiting for one of them to relent and get off to push him. It was nearly always Edie who did so. She loved her baby brother almost as much as her twin sister.

In her room, Edie lay on her bed and stared at the pine-clad ceiling. She picked up her phone and read Laura's text once again. She turned onto her stomach and let the pillow absorb the tears that ran from her eyes. She was tired and she didn't know what to do and there was no one to ask and no one to help. Even Vuk, who had been falling in and out of grace, was gone again. At that moment, another plan that she'd had in mind for a while but done nothing about became of sudden and paramount importance.

After completing her cleaning rota the next morning, and making sure her phone was securely pushed deep into her pocket, she put on her helmet. She dragged the scooter out of the oleander bush and put the key in the ignition. Nothing. After trying several more times with increasing impatience, Edie dismounted, angrily kicked the front tyre and tore the helmet back off again.

Fuck! Fuck, fuck, fuck. She stormed off down to the office. Perhaps Ivana could be persuaded to conjure forth a little of the milk of human kindness and shout Edie a taxi. But that turned out not to be necessary for as she passed the road towards the exit gate, a cloud of dust heralded Zayn in the pick-up truck. Waving her arms frantically in the air she stepped dangerously into the road and flagged him down. He slammed on the brakes, causing them to let out an agonising whine.

'I need a lift to town,' Edie announced as she climbed into the cab. She decided to overlook how he had left it until the last minute to stop for her. Everyone seemed stressed right now; everyone except Vuk, anyway.

As if to confirm this, Zayn's normally lachrymose face bore an even more woebegone expression than usual today, his eyelids drooped over weary, bloodshot eyes, his smile when he greeted her strained.

'I'm going to the phone shop to try to trace the text,' said Edie. '—You know, the one that arrived when you were with me – to see if they can tell me who owns the number. I need to speak to her for myself, put my mind at rest. And then I'm going back to the police. Somebody must know something and they should be made to talk!'

A flash of fear that was visceral crossed Zayn's face. He crashed the gears and narrowly avoided colliding with a mother pushing a baby in a stroller. Edie stared at him, watching a cloud of anxiety settle upon his shoulders as he revved the engine and forced the pick-up to its top speed. His eyes were fixed on the road ahead, to the steep hill they were currently ascending.

'Zayn, do you know where Laura is?' Edie asked, doggedly. 'Are you protecting someone who's involved?' She added this last because poor Zayn couldn't possibly be the instigator of any nefarious plan; he simply didn't have it in him.

There was a long pause before Zayn replied. 'I know nothing about Laura. Nothing at all. I will help you any way that I can to find your sister. There is nothing more important than family, than a sister.'

His words carried a weight of history about them, as if there was more, much more, to say on the subject. But he didn't elaborate and Edie didn't ask. She believed him when he said he had no idea what had happened to Laura.

'I'm just not sure that the police have any interest in assisting you,' cautioned Zayn. 'And their involvement could cause trouble for everybody.'

Now he was being melodramatic. Edie decided to ignore him. If she listened to other people's opinions nothing would get done.

The rest of the journey passed in silence.

The visit to the phone shop did nothing to allay or explain Edie's fears. The guy there was as helpful as he could be. He confirmed that the number was a Greek one and the message when the calls rang out was from Greek Telecom. But more than that he could not say. It was perfectly possible for Laura to have got to Greece in the time between last seeing Edie and sending the text; the country was hardly far away. And if Edie went to Greece to try to find her – well, the idea was nonsensical. She had no clue as to where to start looking; Laura could have headed for the mainland, for Athens or Halkidiki, but she also could be on one of the islands and there were scores of them. Forget needle in a haystack, this would be pinhead in an entire threshing mill.

A wave of exhaustion flooded over Edie as she sat in the air-conditioned shop. She was tired of worrying about Laura, wished it was not her responsibility. She tried to tell herself what others had told her – that Laura was a grown-up now and could take care of herself. She tried to tell herself what any well-wisher might say, that it wasn't fair of Laura to be putting this weight of anxiety onto Edie; that she needed to prioritise herself.

But nobody knew all the reasons that Edie had come here on her own, probably not even Edie herself, or at least she would have found it hard to articulate them. It was something about the fact that, for all she couldn't bear to be parted from her sister she had also needed to get away from her, to be independent of the twin who, naturally and undisputedly, dominated. And now she felt that those feelings had somehow brought bad karma; Laura's disappearance was a direct consequence of, and punishment for, Edie's subconscious desire to have her sister but not have her. Whatever. The deep foreboding that sat deep in her gut was not to be shifted, however much she analysed and over-analysed.

Her visit to the police station was as perfunctory as she had thought it would be. They took details of the message and the phone number to put in the file they assured Edie they were keeping of Laura – though she wasn't convinced such a file actually existed – and informed her that they had no reason to ask for the phone records to be made available to them so that they could check ownership of the Greek number. Edie's suggestion that they check immigration records to see if Laura's passport was recorded, to check an exit date for her leaving the country, also met with short shrift. They needed evidence of a crime to do that kind of thing, and there was none.

Bloody evidence of a bloody crime. Those two words, 'evidence' and 'crime', had become the ones Edie hated most in the world.

Zayn had numerous errands to do in town and Edie would be late back for work if she waited for him to do them. Disentangling herself from the cruise ship crowds, she headed for the roundabout where the road led out of town and back towards the resort on its isolated peninsula. Hitch-hiking was alive and well here which Edie thought was both quaint and a bit sad. Her mother had told her about the custom that, in her youth, had been widespread in England too, but was now almost unheard of. Stranger danger, a wealthier society and the proliferation of private cars had put paid to that. But in this country, where most people could not afford to own a vehicle, hitching a ride was taken for granted and those who had space in their cars stopped for them. The only problem was that, at this time of year, the majority of those on the road were tourists who tended to totally ignore the hitchers.

Standing by the side of the road with her thumb out wouldn't have been so bad if it weren't for the searing strength of the sun. Edie wished she had water, a hat, anything that someone with any sense would have brought with them. A car stopped but was heading in the wrong direction; she would have had to get out as soon as they were through the tunnel under the mountain. A steady stream of hire cars packed with vacationers in brightly coloured clothing passed her by. Nobody seemed to have any room for her. Edie was on the verge of giving up and going back into town to mooch about until Zayn was done (and accept the wrath of Vlad when she missed the beginning of her shift) when a car indicated, slowed and pulled in. She sauntered along to it, refusing to succumb to an undignified run. Bending down to look through the window she hesitated, knowing she had seen the driver before but unable to place him. He was wearing a dark blue baseball cap with an extra-long peak and mirror sunglasses, resulting in not much of his face being visible.

'Get in,' he said, leaning over to release the passenger door handle for her. 'I assume you're heading back to the resort?'

Edie played it cool, pretending that she knew exactly who this over-friendly man was. Nonchalantly, she nodded and slid into the seat, using the time taken to shut the door and do her seatbelt up to search her mind for his identity.

'Had a good morning?' he was asking, and then it came to her. He was the man – she knew his name but couldn't for the life of her remember it – whose pool she had been caught skinny-dipping in and who she had seen around the resort with his family a fair amount. Unable to suppress a grin at the memory of his captivated gaze upon her naked body in that pool, she turned her face away to the window.

'Not bad,' she lied, referring to his question. She wasn't in the mood for a conversation, had too much churning around inside her head.

'Have you been working here long?' he tried again, his attempts to engage her in conversation aggravating and somehow cute at the same time.

'A few months,' she answered, noncommittally.

'This is our first time,' he continued, seeming oblivious to her monosyllabic replies. 'We absolutely love it. It's a great little country, isn't it? I can see why they call it Europe's undiscovered paradise, the pearl of the Adriatic and so on.'

'It's nice, I suppose, if you like that sort of thing.'

'I guess it might seem a bit slow for a young person like you,' suggested the man, hesitantly, as if responding to her reticence. 'Away from that place down the coast where all the action is. But it's just right for us old has-beens and our kids.'

Edie demurred politely.

'My name's Patrick, by the way.' Of course; she recalled now how his wife had enunciated his name when expressing her disgust at finding someone in her pool, her posh accent with its clipped syllables.

Having introduced himself, Patrick took his eyes off the road to glance at Edie expectantly.

'Edie,' she acquiesced.

'My wife is Debs and the kids are Lucy and Tom.'

'That's nice.' She tried to sound interested in his dullsville family.

'I'm a journalist. I don't do travel writing but I might give it a go now I've been here; there's so much to write about.'

Edie nodded.

'We're going on the trip to the canyon tomorrow – you know, the rafting and camping one. The children are over the moon, they can't wait.'

Edie suddenly took notice. This was the trip Vuk had asked her to go on. Her enthusiasm for it waxed and waned as did her feelings towards Vuk. Encouraged by the shadow of a response, Patrick continued. 'Have you been? It sounds fantastic.'

'I haven't yet but I'm going on the same trip as you.' Edie twisted the end of her hair around her finger. 'I'm told it's amazing. Although apparently the rapids are fairly tame at this time of year, when there's been so little rain for so long.'

'Better for us, Edie.' They were on the homestretch now; not too much longer to make small talk. 'I'd love to get the adrenaline going but the kids are only ten and eight; they're too young for high-octane danger.'

Edie contemplated a life of domesticity and restriction; unable to do exactly what you wanted when you wanted. She was sure she would never have children. She felt sorry for the man. But then, it was his choice.

'I might give the zip wire a go, though.'

Edie regarded him, a smile curling around her lips. He was actually quite endearing but he didn't look like the adventurous type, with his barrel of a belly, sunburned nose and thatch-like Boris Johnson hair-do. The idea of him attached to a wire rope hurtling across the canyon at thirty miles an hour like a superpowered pocket-rocket fur ball was simply too ridiculous.

Patrick gave a short snort of laughter. 'Well, maybe not,' he continued in an ironic tone of voice, as if he could suddenly see the same mental picture as Edie. He slowed down as they approached the corner just before the gatehouse that gave entrance to both the resort and the public car park for the beach.

'Debs would have a heart attack if I suggested— ' His sentence petered out as he took in the scene before him, three police cars blocking the road, sirens flashing.

'What on earth's going on?'

A hot flush of fear suffused Edie's body and she began to sweat despite the air-conditioning that was pelting out at full blast.

'Laura,' she gasped. 'Maybe they've found Laura.'

TWENTY

Fatima

The hand lifted from her face and she managed to utter a small, pleading cry for help, more a whisper than a shout.

'Where are you, Ehsan?'

Her stomach was churning with terror and she felt sick and faint, but she had Ehsan. It was precisely for protection that travelling with him had always been preferable to going it alone. Now she was glad of that choice.

'Ehsan, please, I need you.' She hated the begging note in her voice but could not eradicate it.

A snorting moan filled her right ear, vibrating deep inside it.

'Oh, yes, Fatima, yes.'

Her assailant knew her name, knew who she was. The voice was familiar, unmistakeable. 'I need you, too.'

The fear that heaved in Fatima's bowels turned to disgust and horror. It was Ehsan. Her attacker was Ehsan.

Her blood ran icy cold. She was being assaulted not by some deranged stranger but her own brother-in-law.

All the events of the past, his eyes that had so often lingered too long upon her in the courtyard house, his lecherous look of the day before and countless other times that Fatima now understood she had ignored and pushed aside for fear of confronting them; his decision that they should say they were married – all flooded through her mind in a few short seconds.

Ehsan was still grunting and muttering in her ear, saying 'I need you, too, and I want you.'

Fatima lay motionless, stunned. A hot, wet sensation, first on and in her ear and then on her face and cheeks and lips, brought bile rising in her throat.

'It's about time, isn't it?' Ehsan's voice was gravelly, rumbling against her skin and making it crawl, and tinged with frantic urgency. 'Married for days now. Oh yes, it's time.'

He was pawing at the waistband of her trousers again, wrenching it down and she couldn't stop him. He had her arms pinioned underneath her. She was whimpering in fear, but whether he noticed in his frenzied state or took it for encouragement, she couldn't say. His hand was between her legs, forcing her thighs apart.

The horrendous realisation dawned on Fatima that she had brought this upon herself by agreeing to the husband and wife plan he had initiated.

Fatima's breathing slowed at that thought, and as what Ehsan was doing registered in her frozen mind. Her lungs refused to work as horror seized hold of her and gripped her tight. All she could think of was the girls and how much she hoped they would not wake and witness what was happening. They had seen so much already, in their three-and-a-half short years. To watch their mother's rape would signify the end of any innocence they may, despite everything, have retained. And then her horror gave her strength and with all her might she sat up, gulping in air as she did so, shoving Ehsan off her, suppressing the urge to howl because of the proximity of the children.

'Ehsan, what are you doing?' Her voice was a hiss, released under pressure, desperate. 'Have you lost your mind? Get off me.'

For a moment Ehsan relaxed his grip, taken off guard by her sudden action. But then something changed and Fatima felt the atmosphere cloud and darken to match the starless, moonless night. Ehsan took her upper arms in a vice-like grip and pushed her back down onto the ground.

'You're my wife now; a wife gives a husband what he wants.' He wasn't wearing any trousers, proof that he'd prepared for his assault. Fatima had seen in the brief moment when she'd sat up that Youssef was not with the group; he'd obviously decided to keep his distance. It was his absence that had given Ehsan his opportunity.

Fatima renewed her defence, squirming and fighting, wriggling and bucking beneath him. But it only seemed to fire him up and renew his strength and vigour, and his lust.

'You're not going hungry, are you?' he leered at her, a drop of spittle landing on her eyebrow. He pinched her waist, thickened already even though she was not five months gone yet. She seemed to be putting on weight more quickly this time, despite the lack of food. Or maybe it was just that the difference between her swelling belly and her sunken torso and skinny arms became more marked as her calorie intake diminished. Ehsan seemed completely oblivious to what was really going on and in that moment Fatima realised she could not tell him. For a fleeting second she had been about to cry out to him that he was raping a pregnant woman, believing that this truth might bring him to his senses. But now she understood that knowing she was expecting would put him in an even more powerful position over her. He would know how much more vulnerable it made her and would be able to take advantage of that fact. The secret would have to remain with her.

He had her trousers down now, and her underwear and he

entered her clumsily and began to thrust into her, his hands all over her breasts and stomach. She gave up and lay still, resigning herself to surrender, trying to pretend it wasn't happening. Passive acceptance seemed to be the only way.

Ehsan groaned and grunted, flopping flat on top of her and then rolling to one side. Within moments he was snoring. Fatima lay still and inert, silently weeping, the tears rolling down each side of her face and soaking her black hair, released from its scarf during the battle. She could not imagine where the tears were coming from, what part of her body had the energy to produce them. But now they were here, she did not possess the strength to stop them.

Edie

'Who's Laura?' Patrick asked as he applied the brakes. The way ahead was blocked by the police cars and the resort's security barrier was firmly down.

Edie's throat was tight and restricted, her heart racing. She could think of no other reason why the police should come to a peaceful holiday resort in the middle of an August day but to investigate a missing person. Or the discovery of a missing person … personal effects … a body … Could Laura have died between sending the text message and now? Edie had to stop her thoughts right there to prevent herself from becoming hysterical.

Taking no notice of Patrick's question, she flung herself out of the still-moving vehicle and ran at full tilt towards the security hut where the guard stood looking officiously serious.

'Tomas,' she cried, 'what the fuck is going on?' She threw herself against his solid bulk and asked again, before he had time to give any response, 'What's happening?'

Tomas shrugged. 'I don't know anything, Edie.'

He did not meet her eye and shifted awkwardly from one foot to the other as he spoke.

166

'I don't believe you,' she shouted, pounding her fists against his broad chest. 'Tell me what's going on. Is it Laura? Is it? You have to tell me the truth!'

The tears were cascading down her cheeks and she could almost feel them evaporating in the unrelenting heat of the sun at full strength. She was about to pummel Tomas again when she felt someone take her gently by the wrist and lead her away.

'Calm down,' said Patrick, in a soothing voice that should have been patronising but in fact was strangely comforting. 'Wipe your face and tell me what on earth this is all about.'

He handed her a tissue and waited patiently for her sobs to ease. Quickly and amidst intermittent bouts of further crying, Edie explained about Laura to the quietly listening Patrick.

'OK,' he nodded, when she had reached the end of the story. 'Why don't you go back to the car and get a drink of water – you can bring a bottle for me, too. They're on the back seat. And I'll see what I can find out.'

Not entirely sure why, Edie followed his instructions. She found that the water was exactly what she needed and drank an entire bottle before returning with one for Patrick. By this time, he had had a chance to talk to Tomas and, with Tomas translating, with one of the lingering policemen. The conversations involved much nodding and casting of serious glances in the direction of the resort, the office, and then the cabanas, the restaurant and the beach.

'I don't think it's got anything to do with Laura,' he reassured her. 'They'd want you involved if it were. The police aren't saying anything and this guy,' he gestured towards Tomas, the gate man, 'doesn't know much, just that they've been here for an hour or so already and they've got sniffer dogs in there.'

'Dogs?' Edie felt faint, her legs weak and her head swimming in the heat. Surely dogs indicated something really bad, something terrible.

'It's probably drugs, Edie. These aren't the local police either, they're from the capital. To be honest, I think that indicates a greater crime than a missing foreign girl when there's absolutely no evidence at all of foul play.'

Edie reeled and almost fell over. So much for the sympathy and understanding; now Patrick was showing himself to be just the same as all the rest, dismissing her concerns, belittling the idea that Laura might be in trouble. And using the dreaded 'e' and 'c' words.

'There have been a recent spate of drug wars in Kotor, shoot-outs in the streets between rival gangs, things like that,' Patrick continued, seemingly oblivious to Edie's trauma. 'I think the government is very keen to stamp such occurrences out; it does the tourism industry, on which the country is so dependent, no good at all.' Patrick started to walk towards the gate, then paused to wait for Edie. 'We can go in, anyway. We just have to leave the car here for now.'

Automatically, she followed him, unable to think of anything else to do. Vuk had mentioned the problems with drugs. Maybe Patrick was right and that was the reason the police were there.

They made their way in silence along the eerily quiet road where the tarmac reached as far as the office before reverting to a sandy track that took them into the centre of the resort. They arrived at the restaurant and bar, where people were eating and drinking as normal, seemingly unperturbed by the police presence. Perhaps they didn't even know about it; there was no sign of anything out of the ordinary here. No one seemed to be looking for Edie so maybe Patrick was right and the drama with the police didn't have any connection to Laura.

A woman was waving and Edie recognised Debs, Patrick's wife. She was sitting with the two children at one of the tables, plates piled high with food in front of them. Debs was wearing a floral bikini that, in Edie's opinion, did her no favours, the sides of the pants pinching into her ample spare tyre. Poor woman, thought Edie. It must be awful to be fat.

'Bye, Edie.' She had forgotten Patrick was still by her side. 'It looks like my lunch is waiting.'

The children were shouting: 'Daddy, daddy, did you get the lilo for me? Did you buy me a blow-up whale?' Edie's eyes followed the voices and distractedly flicked to Debs, now tucking into her meal.

'No need,' she uttered under her breath. She felt a frisson of enjoyment at her unkindness; it was a sop to her own distress.

'Come and see me if you're worried about anything. I'll help you if I can,' Patrick called over his shoulder, his attention on his family now. 'You know where I am.'

Edie felt momentarily guilty for her mean thoughts. Patrick was a kind man and Debs might have been better-looking, slimmer, in her youth. It wasn't her fault she hadn't aged well. Some people didn't. Of course it went without saying that Edie would not be amongst that number, she would make damn sure of that, however much Botox and filler it took when the time came.

Patrick reached the table and embraced his wife, hugging her tight and kissing her forehead, then bending down to the children and bestowing kisses on them, too. He sat down next to Debs, his hand on her knee, his focus on her, thanking her for ordering the lunch, apologising for the length of his absence.

A strange sensation of deflation overcame Edie. He seemed to really love them all, despite his wife being old and plain. He didn't seem to find his kids demanding or annoying. The togetherness and intimacy that Patrick seemed to have with his family was exactly what she so desperately craved for herself. She had had it with Laura when they were children but as adults – well, of course a sister, even a twin, isn't enough anymore. Everyone wants a mate, a partner, a significant other, to use a phrase Edie hated. Vuk was the person she had set her sights on for that – and what an attractive couple they were, how good they looked together. But what if that wasn't enough, either? What if Vuk wasn't the person she had hoped he was, had decided he was when, in all truth, she barely knew him. What would she do then?

TWENTY-ONE

Fatima

It was late by the time they got to the beach of the small town on Turkey's Aegean coast. The lilos and deckchairs that colonised it during the day had been replaced by empty expanses of sand, darkly glowing in the moonlight. The sea lay flat and still, almost motionless. Black. Fatima gazed at it, longing to wade into it, to wash away the layers of dirt of the last week that had now been intensified by the scourge of the rape so that filth seemed to cover every inch of her. But she knew that even all the liquid in that great body of water before her could never make her clean. She was sullied forever. The shame, the embarrassment, the disgust, would live with her for all time.

Even though the tourists had gone safely back to their hotels, B&Bs and apartments there were still plenty of people about. Migrants were gathered in groups all along the road that curved around the bay, shadowy figures lurking in the atramentous night, waiting for the smugglers. In just the same way, having reached the small resort town by local bus, Fatima and Ehsan had once again shelled out a large sum of their remaining money to a man called Khalid, a broker for the smugglers, in the hope that at some point in the night they would be afloat and on their way to Europe. The more you paid, in theory, the less overcrowded the boat and so, again in theory, the less likely it was to capsize. If it had been a choice they had to make it would have been a bleak one, but there was no choice. They could only afford the cheapest – $650 per person – option. Khalid told them there would be 'just' forty-five people on board. He also told them where the departure point would be; they were to hide in the dunes that backed the beach until the smuggler arrived with the boat. During the hours they waited, Fatima went over and over what Khalid had told them, in answer to her insistent questions, about the danger of the crossing.

'God decides who survives and who does not,' he had said to her with a complacent shrug and disinterested tone. 'If you don't make it – it's not my fault. It's fate.'

There was no way to argue with such an opinion, nothing to say in response or retaliation. Fatima pulled the twins close to her and nuzzled their hair and necks and cheeks like a mother bear tending to her cubs. She could still turn back. She didn't have to go through with this. Youssef and Ehsan could go on ahead and get established and then she and the girls could follow.

Lying in the soft, yielding sand dune in the pale moonlight, a tiny, fractious breeze blowing the salt air towards her, Fatima angrily bit her lip so hard she drew blood. What ridiculous way of thinking was this? Of course she was not going to give up now and let him forge the way, the idea that she would be indebted to, that she would have to count on, the despicable Ehsan was intolerable. She was the one who had set in motion the idea that they should leave, it had been her who had done the bulk of the research into the most preferable route. Somehow, from a lifetime of relying on another to make plans and decisions – her father, her husband – she had somehow mined and drawn up reserves of strength deep within her and shown that she was stronger than Ehsan, even though he was the man.

Now, after what he had done to her, without apology, explanation or any sign of remorse, there was no way she was going to slip back into the pattern of letting him think he was in control, of letting him think she owed him anything. The very thought repelled her. And besides all else, deep inside herself she knew she didn't trust him enough to be sure that, if they did part ways, he wouldn't just forget all about her and concentrate on feathering his own nest.

Fatima shuddered, feeling cold despite the balmy Mediterranean night. She itched all over, and particularly the parts of her that Ehsan had touched, that had had flesh to flesh contact with him. She scratched and scratched but it brought no relief, just left her skin red and raw with ugly white weals where her stubby, ragged nails tore at herself. Just being close to him made her feel nauseous, the sickness rising up within her in bilious waves that made her gag.

She wanted to be a million miles away from him, to never have to set eyes on him again. Instead, he lay only a metre away from her, just the three children and some stubby seagrass between them. Fatima reached out and held Marwa's tiny hand in hers, rubbing her thumb over her palm that was still silky-soft despite all the hardship they had endured. Everything she was doing now was for her girls, and her unborn child. They were the only thing that mattered, her only motivation to keep going. She must do what was best for them.

Right now, and for the immediate future, the best for the children was that they all stayed together.

Nobody slept, not even the twins, despite their obvious exhaustion. They were grumpy and grizzly but seemed to have lost the capacity to cry, their huge eyes staring out blankly from pale, drawn faces. Fatima couldn't decide whether it was worse that they didn't fully understand what was going on and what was in store for them than if they had. Is it better to know you might die in the next twenty-four hours or to be blissfully unaware until it happens?

The night stretched onwards, seeming never-ending.

By the time that dawn was breaking behind the high rise hotels and apartment blocks of the town, it was obvious that Khalid's smuggler was not coming tonight. According to Khalid, he himself held on to the refugees' money until they had boarded a boat. Only then did he hand it over to the smugglers, minus his cut of course. Apparently, by the way he explained the system, Fatima and Ehsan were supposed to take comfort from that and to be reassured that their money was in safe hands. There was not much comfort now as the small groups of people who had been lying in wait all night began to trickle out of their lairs and drift away, towards the pine woods or into the town. Some still had plentiful resources and they might find accommodation in a hotel or guesthouse. Fatima longed for a bed and a shower, clean clothes, a glass of fresh water with ice and lemon and hot coffee served in a proper set like the one she had had at home. And then hated herself for such trivial desires. Who was so superficial as to want to drink out of a china cup when they were about to stare death in the face, and when they wore clothes that still bore the stains and smells of the ultimate humiliation?

Anyway, there was no chance of any of those things, now or any time soon. Just another day of interminable boredom under-scored at all times by ceaseless, debilitating anxiety.

Fatima picked up the life jackets they had bought earlier that day and gathered together the rest of their meagre possessions. Perhaps they would have more luck the next night.

***

Sheltering from the midday sun in the pinewoods, Fatima got talking to a young man named Yasin who was also waiting, with three others, for a chance to get to one of the islands. He was not from her country and did not speak her language but they could communicate in English. Yasin and his mates' first attempt had ended in disaster – their boat had hit rocks and been ripped to shreds, shipping water in seconds and sinking in less than five minutes. They had been fortunate not to be too far out and all fifty-odd passengers had made it back to the shore, including a woman who had held her newborn baby clasped to her chest throughout the ordeal. Yasin didn't know where she was now.

'We wait for the smuggler to bring a new boat,' he explained, seemingly unperturbed by the experience. 'We will keep trying until we get there.'

He was the loquacious type and the conversation was one-sided. Fatima didn't have the strength to join in, but Yasin seemed personable and she had nothing else to do but listen.

'When we get there – to Europe, to the EU, to Germany or UK,' he continued volubly, 'We will pretend to be from the same country as you because that way, we will receive papers that allow us to stay.'

Despite his preoccupation with himself, he seemed to notice Fatima's expression of doubt tinged with disapproval because he stopped short. His hesitation didn't last long though, as he clearly felt the need to defend himself against her accusatory glare.

'Everyone's doing it – all the peoples from all the countries. If we say we are the same nationality as you but we have no papers, we can get in. Nobody can prove it's not true. It's our best chance.'

Fatima couldn't think of anything to say. It seemed unfair, exploitative even, to pretend to be from a country ravaged by war and destruction just to get a better chance for yourself – but on the other hand, who could blame Yasin, and all the others like him? The problem was that Fatima wasn't sure there was room in the EU for everybody and if Yasin and his travelling companions got in when they didn't really need to, they might take the space that Marwa and Maryam needed, and Youssef, not to mention her and Ehsan. Fatima had a vision of the European continent slowly sinking under the weight of the desperate, the dispossessed and the homeless, each one clinging on for dear life whilst the native populations tried to throw them out, one by one, to save themselves.

Fatima's thoughts drifted, as they did more and more frequently these days, towards Ali, the long-lost brother, the sibling who had fled from a different kind of conflict. He had left a war of words, of arguments and disagreements that became intolerable. He had been told that he should go and take the disgrace he was bringing on the family away with him. It must have been terrible. Not as bad as this, not as horrendous as what they were going through – but everything is relative, isn't it? He had no doubt experienced despair, even if it had been whilst enjoying the comfort and safety of an aeroplane. So he would understand.

Fatima reasoned and reasoned with herself but still could not make the decision about whether to try and find him. He might berate them for leaving when it was so dangerous, or for not leaving sooner, when it was easier. She wanted neither pity nor criticism; she just wanted help and couldn't face not knowing whether she would get it or not.

Ehsan returned from the town, from Khalid's 'office', an untidy, broiling room in the underbelly of a concrete block where most of the doors had been shuttered and bolted when they had visited for the first time.

'He says it'll definitely be tonight,' he blurted out, before noticing Yasin still standing by, uncharacteristically quietly. He threw the young man a hostile glare and took Fatima by the arm, forcing her to follow him further into the trees.

'Who's that guy?' His yellow, uneven teeth, bared in the dull light beneath the canopy, were like a wolf's as it tears into its prey.

'I don't know,' answered Fatima, honestly. 'I mean, he told me his name – Yasin – and that he's on the way to Europe too. But other than that,' she faltered, suddenly afraid of the menace contained in Ehsan's silent consideration of her. 'Other than that – I don't know.'

Ehsan's face came close to hers, and she could smell his breath, sour from lack of tooth-brushing.

'Don't you ever ...' Ehsan paused, pulling her further round towards him, forcing her to meet his gaze, his eyes, bloodshot from lack of sleep, heavy with hatred. 'Don't you ever make up to another man again. What kind of a woman are you?' He thrust her violently away from him. 'A shameless one.'

He'd been drinking, Fatima realised, and found that the only reason she minded was because it meant that he'd spent money and they had so very, very little left. He wasn't coping with the situation at all, with the frustration, despondency and continual disappointment that they were facing. Rationalising it, she knew that the rape was but one symptom of his internal rage. As long as he didn't take it out on Youssef and force the boy away. The relationship between father and son had become increasingly distant and bitter since the night of their argument – the night Ehsan had attacked her – and Fatima was terrified that Youssef would just disappear one day, decide to make his own way into his future. There were many children, mainly boys, travelling alone and it was known on the migrant trail that they often fell victim to sexual predation and exploitation. She could not let that happen to Youssef.

Khalid had given Ehsan instructions for how to find the bay they would leave from that night. Plans had been changed because of an increase in police patrols on the original beach. Once again, Fatima, Ehsan and the children picked up all their worldly goods and began to walk. Even if they had money, they would not be able to take a taxi or bus; all such modes of transport had been banned by the local government in a bid to stop the refugees. But it was clear, as they trudged along the ragged coastline, that the ban was having no effect. Groups of itinerants were everywhere; families of two, three or even four generations, more bands of young men like Yasin, women alone with small children, young men singly or in groups.

All human life is here, thought Fatima as she forced herself to put one foot in front of the other. *Not that there's much life left in any of us.*

TWENTY-TWO

Edie

'Where have you been?' Vlad's voice was thin and accusatory and, when Edie turned to face him, his eyes were thunderous. 'You're supposed to be on shift.'

'I had something I needed to do in town.' Edie put her hands on her hips defiantly. 'I'm only a few minutes late.'

'Clear this.' Vlad threw his arm towards a cluster of tables where plates and cups and cutlery lay heaped in untidy and unstable piles and bunched up napkins rustled in the breeze from the ceiling fans.

'Yes, sir!' Edie raised her arm in a mock salute but Vlad wasn't looking, her sarcasm lost on him.

'What's going on with all these police here?' she demanded. 'Where's Vuk?'

'Vuk's doing what you should be doing.' Vlad's voice was low and harsh, the words spitting furiously out of him. '*Working.*'

Stefan was hovering, wanting to speak to Edie but not daring to whilst Vlad was still around.

'And as for the police – it's nothing to do with you.' Vlad's body was tense with controlled fury, his shoulders hunched, a muscle in his cheek twitching involuntarily. Vuk must have told him that Laura had come and gone again in a matter of hours and that Edie was worried about her.

'And they're not here because of anything to do with your sister, so you can get that thought out of your stupid head, too.'

Edie opened her mouth to protest, realised it was futile and shut it again. She worked hard for the rest of the afternoon, conscious despite her posturing that pissing Vlad off too much ultimately put her job at risk. And the last thing she wanted right now was to have to leave.

She had nowhere else to go.

***

It was late afternoon before she went to her room. On approaching the row of staff cabins, at first she thought it was someone else's door swinging open as she knew she had locked hers when she had gone out in the morning. But almost as soon as she had this thought, she had dismissed it and realised the truth. It was her room, and it had been ransacked. Edie felt in her pocket for her key and found it there. She was sure she remembered locking up but then the scooter had broken down – had she put the helmet back into the room and forgotten to close the door behind her?

Everything was turned upside down, clothes strewn even more wildly around than she could manage on her own, her make-up bag emptied out onto the bed, her rucksack taken apart, every single compartment unzipped, not a single item left inside. It was clear there'd been a burglary; panic surged inside her as she thought about her passport, unprotected when she should have taken it to the office and put it in Ivana's safe, together with her cash, the last of her savings which she had intended to use when the season here ended and the work dried up.

What had she said, so mightily, to Laura? First rule of travelling – never keep all your money in one place. She had failed on that score.

But on examination she found that both passport and money were exactly where she had left them, in an envelope under the crate that was her bedside table. She picked up knickers and bras, dresses and T-shirts and dropped them back down onto the floor. Nothing appeared to be missing. But whoever had been in here had come for something. She stood, leaning against the door lintel, thinking, racking her brain for what it was that was niggling at her.

And then it came to her. The scarf. Laura's scarf. It was the one thing that wasn't there anymore. Someone had got into her room and taken it.

Slamming the door and locking it despite the fact that this action now seemed pointless, she set off in the direction of Vuk's cabin. He was the only person who knew she'd found Laura's scarf. Maybe he would know why it had attracted the attention of the police. Vlad had been so adamant that their visit was nothing to do with Laura. Really? Edie could hardly be expected to believe that in the light of this new discovery, could she? She called Vuk's number as she ran, not at all sure of what she would say to him but almost as a reflex action because she always called Vuk when she needed help ... But as usual there was no answer. He never answered his phone – at least, not to her.

She was running so fast and so blindly that she almost cannoned straight into someone. She stopped short. Her breath was coming thick and fast and she was sweating, her armpits damp, her shirt clinging to her back.

'Where are you going?' The voice was low, controlled and calm. 'Vlad?' It came out as a question even though she knew it was him. Looking at him properly, she saw that the inscrutability he commonly displayed had replaced his obvious anger

181

of earlier. The silence that followed her interrogatory saying of his name seemed to last for hours and Edie found herself filling it although she could not have explained why.

'I'm going to see Vuk.'

'I think I told you earlier that he is working.'

Edie's breathing had steadied now and she forced her voice to steadiness also. 'My room's been broken into. I don't feel safe there anymore.'

'The police went into your room, Edie. The dogs took them there.'

Edie could feel that Vlad was furious, incandescent, despite the lack of expression on his face. The only hints at anger were his tightened lips and the even greater than normal intensity of this gaze.

'But ... but why?'

'You are very lucky that they found no drugs, Edie. You would face a long prison sentence if you were caught.'

'I don't do drugs – I never have and I never will.' Edie shouted, incensed that her reputation should be so tarnished. The 'never have' bit wasn't entirely true but it might as well be and it was accurate enough for Vlad. 'If you really thought I was taking or dealing drugs, you'd throw me out in an instant. So why are you lying to me?'

Vlad stood motionless, staring into the distance.

'Stop screaming, Edie. The whole resort does not need to hear this.'

'Because you know I'm right. You know it! And I'm the one who should be complaining. Who took the scarf?' She was screeching uncontrollably, shaking with rage and hysteria. 'Who took Laura's scarf?'

Vlad reached out his arm and took Edie by the hand. She was too surprised to resist. He led her onto the path to her room and she went with him, silent now, her confusion and exhaustion precluding further protest.

'You don't need to work at the bar tonight, Edie. Go to bed. Do not mention Laura, the scarf or the police again.'

He wasn't tall but his slight frame seemed to loom over her, blocking out the moonlight.

'Do I make myself clear?'

Edie nodded, defeated. She turned and scuffled through the sandy soil back to her room, her feet dragging dejectedly. Once inside, she made a half-hearted attempt to clear up the mess. She wanted it all to go away, to go to sleep and hopefully wake up with all the problems solved and the doubts and uncertainties swept away by a fresh day. That was all she wanted, just then.

She kicked a stray pair of sandals underneath the bed, and then leant forward to pick up an empty water bottle. The door of her room was behind her. It swung slowly open. Prickles on the back of her neck told her there was someone there. She stayed stock still, bent down, her hand halfway to the bottle. She waited, tensed for the pounce, for the steel grip of hands around her throat. Her heart was pounding, her veins pulsating as her blood ran cold. A sound, like a footstep. Yelling out her fear, eyes closed, she turned around, thrusting her fist forward, bracing herself for the counterblow. She encountered only air. Nothing else. She summoned the courage to open her eyes. The door swayed lazily to and fro.

There was no one there.

Outside, darkness shrouded the still olive trees and cloud cover partially obscured the moon. The cicadas thrummed their endless tune. There was no intruder, just her imagination. She fell forward onto the bed, her head drooping between her shoulders. She reached to the fridge and yanked out the vodka bottle, pulled off the top and took a long slug. It was freezing and foul-tasting, much too strong. It burnt her oesophagus. She shuddered and swigged another mouthful. Getting up, she lurched to the door, staggering slightly already from the effect of the alcohol; it had gone straight to her head. Locking the door firmly and putting the key under her pillow, she lay down on her bed. She was becoming delusional. Vlad was right; she needed to sleep.

Fatima

When she saw the knife Fatima knew that they had made a terrible mistake. And that they had been lied to. There were not going to be forty-five people on the boat. At least seventy were gathered together on the beach, jostling and pushing in the shallow water that lapped softly against their feet in a way that would be enticing in any other circumstance.

'We're not getting on,' she shouted, raising her voice to be heard above the muttering of the crowd.

The knife was against Ehsan's waist, prodding him on board. At that moment, seeing him under threat, Fatima realised exactly the extent of her hatred for Ehsan. But also that she didn't want him to die, not like this, not at the hands of an unscrupulous, parasitic people smuggler.

Ehsan climbed aboard, ignoring Fatima and obeying the knife. Youssef followed, mutely. Maryam was clinging to Fatima's legs and screaming, whilst Marwa stood, tight-lipped and grey with fear.

'I want to go home,' sobbed Maryam. 'Go home, Mummy. Go home.'

And then Marwa, always the stronger and feistier of the two, seemed to cave in on herself and she too began screaming.

'Daddy! I want my daddy!'

It was the first time either girl had mentioned their father since they had set out on their journey. And now she had started, it seemed that Marwa couldn't stop. She howled and wailed and pleaded for Fayed and Fatima could not calm her. The smuggler was still herding people aboard, pushing the boat a little further into the water as each body added weight that lowered the rubber floor onto the sandy bottom.

Another child, a boy of about eight, was crying out, 'I don't want to die, I don't want to die …' Endlessly, over and over again, his cries rang out.

The smuggler was getting impatient, wanting his vessel filled and on its way. Some of those on board had just arrived at the coast, having spent three hours packed like cattle in a windowless van to get there; a woman had told Fatima that story but Fatima couldn't see her now. The boat was so crowded it was impossible to make out individuals in the feeble half-light of the moon.

Now the knife was at Fatima's waist. She thought about the island they were heading for, how close it had seemed when seen by daylight, the sea so calm and welcoming. Behind her lay only misery; even death at sea was preferable to going back. She passed the girls into the boat. And if it wasn't okay, as long as they all died together, it would not be so bad. She clambered aboard and the boat slipped a little further into the water.

TWENTY-THREE

Edie

The mood of excitement and anticipation amongst the assembled guests the next morning, eager for the rafting excursion to begin, was not one in which Edie was able to share. She had slept badly and felt tense and unrested.

'Have you brought some warm clothes, Edie?' Ivana asked, concern pervading her tone.

'Oh yes,' Edie replied, airily.

'It can get cold in the evening,' Ivana continued, as if Edie hadn't understood.

All the more reason to snuggle up close to Vuk. This is what Edie would have thought only a few days ago. But now – his absences, his failure to be there when she needed him, his inability to find Laura for her, his feeble excuse when confronted about the place Edie had found the scarf – well, now it all seemed a little different. Was she starting to think that Vuk wasn't being completely straight with her? Edie struggled with such a thought, wanted to dismiss it outright. But just the fact that there was a 'but' was desperately worrying. Everything she had thought certain, all she had believed in, had been turned upside-down in a matter of a day or so. And Edie felt entirely lost because of it.

'And,' Ivana hesitated, still taking an unprecedented and frankly irritating interest in Edie's attire, 'do you have a more substantial T-shirt?' She eyed Edie's skimpy top disparagingly up and down. 'It's important for resort employees to look professional at all times.'

'I'll get one,' replied Edie, with no intention of doing so but wanting Ivana to leave her alone.

Ivana gave up, turning on her heel and heading back to the office, saving Edie the necessity of responding. Instead, she stuck her tongue out at Ivana's receding figure. Giggles from behind her made her jump and look around. The journalist's children – what were they called? – were standing behind her, grubby fists clenched around chocolate croissants.

'Why don't you like her?' asked the boy.

For a moment Edie was going to tell him but then she thought better of it; remember the resort's effing reputation ...

'It was just a joke,' she explained, feebly. She could tell they were about to engage her in conversation so she walked away, looking ostentatiously around her as she did so as if she had urgent business to attend to.

Zayn turned up, as lugubrious as he always was these days.

'Morning, Zayn.' Edie tried out a bright, cheerful voice. 'Are you coming too?'

Zayn did not respond in kind. 'I'm driving the bus,' he replied, kicking at one of the tyres. Edie was silenced by the misery that emanated from him. A fleeting pang of sympathy seared through her. He had seemed so desperate for love when she had indulged in her brief flirtation with him. She was sorry she'd had to let him down.

A sudden, hideous burst of self-realisation made her wonder if she had come across the same way. Had the salvation she sought in Vuk been as piteous?

'That doesn't sound bad enough to account for how miserable you look,' she countered, unsympathetically. Of course she could never seem as pathetic as Zayn. How ridiculous.

A half-laugh, half-snort of derision erupted from deep in Zayn's throat. 'The bus, this trip, the resort – all are nothing compared to the real worries of the world.'

Edie opened her mouth to question him further, but he was already climbing into the driver's seat, making it clear that the conversation was over. His words rang in her ears *The real worries of the world.*

What was he talking about? Laura's disappearance? Did he know something he wasn't saying?

Edie watched him as he fiddled with the side mirrors, and then took his phone out of his pocket and studied it, seeming to read something intently before putting the phone away. Then taking it out again.

It was clear that he was deeply troubled but *she* was the one who had lost a sister; a twin. What could have happened to him that was worse than that?

Fatima

They obviously had not done their research thoroughly enough. Neither Fatima nor Ehsan had realised that the smugglers do not generally drive the boats themselves. Each rubber dinghy is an expense on the profit and loss account that is only ever expected to make one journey; a refugee is given the job of skipper. That way, if the boat is intercepted by the coastguard, there is no one to arrest, no trafficker to hold to account. Just hopeless, desperate people who have a right to claim, if not to receive, asylum.

In this case, on this voyage, Ehsan had been given the job of getting the vessel and its human cargo to the island. Fatima knew for a fact that he had never been in a boat in his life. But then again, neither probably had most of the rest of them. And Ehsan, of all people, had the spirit of survival, an instinct for looking out for number one, that would ensure he gave it his best shot. So perhaps he was a good choice, even though one made completely at random and certainly without any concern on the smuggler's part that he had the ability to do it. To him, it was merely a duty discharged and a pocketful of dollars.

Fatima found herself next to an elderly man who cradled his youngest granddaughter on his lap like a piece of priceless treasure. At first, as they ploughed gently out of the bay, the sea was calm and smooth. The man told her that his family business, a bakery, had been razed to the ground in the bombing a year or so ago, and his house also destroyed.

'All my family, me and my wife, my son and daughter-in-law and their five children, we had to ask relatives to take us in.' The old man wiped his hand across his mouth as if to take the badness and foul taste of his words away. 'Imagine the embarrassment. We had been the rich ones, the ones who others asked for help. Now we were the beggars.'

Fatima nodded in the darkness. She knew that scenario only too well.

'But then their village came under fire and we all had to flee again. They decided to stay in a camp just over the border but we –' he gestured around him, to the family he had come here with but could no longer see, spread out as they were on the overcrowded boat – 'we knew we had to get as far away as possible, away from all the fear and bloodshed. And so here we are.'

He clasped the slumbering child so tightly Fatima thought he might suffocate her. 'Here we are.'

A single tear fell from his eye but he did not brush it away.

In the time it had taken for the grandfather to recount his miserable tale, the boat had reached the open sea. It began to buck and fall on the waves like a defenceless cork. Fatima did not manage to ask his name due to the nausea that overcame her; she was soon vomiting unstoppably, and though she tried to aim into the water the strong wind blew it back into the boat, onto her face and that of the twins and those sitting nearby. With every roll of the sea, the passengers rolled too, clinging onto each other, unable to stay in position, constantly destabilising the boat.

Soon everyone was vomiting and the stench and the cries of the children and the roar of the sea became a nightmarish vision of hell. The stars that twinkled so brightly and cruelly above were utterly indifferent to their plight. A cloud blew across the moon and Fatima felt an invisible rush of water fall into her lap and soak her.

And then the engine cut out. The sudden silence was deafening, thundering in Fatima's ears so that she wanted to clasp her hands to them to shut out the sound.

The sound of the end.

Edie

Thoughts of Laura, of where she was and what she was doing, and of Zayn, locked in some private torment, were still eating away at Edie's thoughts like an infestation of unpleasant insects when she felt a hand on her shoulder, steady and calming. She turned, knowing who she would see. She could tell Vuk's touch from anyone's. He looked more handsome than ever, his skin burnt a deep brown and his hair bleached even lighter at the ends than it had been the last time she had seen him. He bent forward to kiss her briefly and then, as she was trying to bury her face in the comforting bulk of him, wanting this to be the moment when all the doubts that pestered her were dispelled for good and all, he pushed her away.

'I'm at work now, Edie,' he whispered, his eyes not on her but on the rest of the small crowd of people, smiling at all the gawking tourists rather than devoting himself to her. He held out his hand to Patrick who, unseen by Edie, had joined the group with his loud children and plain wife.

'Morning sir!' Vuk shook Patrick's hand vigorously. In the past, his vociferousness in this had always made Edie laugh, as if Vuk believed that the object of the exercise was to take the person's arm off. Now she scowled. She wanted to go back to normal, to the time when she had unquestioningly adored Vuk, set her heart on claiming him for her own. Now she didn't know what normal was, or if she wanted it anyway.

'Morning lady!' Vuk shook Debs's hand too, hardly any less forcefully, and then moved through the rest of the raggle-taggle bunch, being so friendly it was almost as if he genuinely liked them and was truthfully glad to be there.

Edie threw her rucksack into the luggage compartment and climbed into the van. She sat there for a few minutes, a sudden, unpleasant thought fomenting in her tired mind. Should she actually be leaving the resort right now, when so much was at stake, when she knew so little about Laura's whereabouts? Shifting uneasily, she gazed out of the window, thinking hard. The minibus was packed with stuff; bags, suitcases, travel pillows and handbags crammed into nooks and crannies and underneath seats as well as in the luggage area at the back. Edie's eyes flitted wildly from side to side. She shouldn't be here, she should go, now. She was half out of her seat when Vuk was suddenly next to her, sitting down beside her, taking her hand and kissing it, and then placing it on his leg, his thigh, not only blocking her way but also ordering Zayn to drive on, urging him to get a move on as they were already running late.

'What's the matter, little one?' Vuk's voice, deep and sultry, was full of tenderness. 'You seem agitated. You should relax; you have been working hard and worrying too much. Now is your time to do nothing, sit back, enjoy the view.'

He put an arm around her shoulders. It was heavy, anchoring her to her seat. She tried to cleanse her mind of all the noise and clutter, the buzzing doubts and worries. Vuk was right, there was nothing she could do right now. It wasn't Laura the police had come about and it was probably true that no news was good news. She should make the most of this opportunity to see some more of this beautiful country and to put her relationship with Vuk back on track. He was so sweet, so caring. She was going mad, thinking there was anything suspect about any of his actions. He worked hard, he had a lot of responsibility, it was natural that sometimes he was distracted, preoccupied. She had not been paying enough attention to his needs, she'd been so obsessed by her own. Now was the time to put that right.

She settled back into the upholstery, leaning her head against Vuk's muscular biceps. Zayn drove skilfully and the minibus ate up the miles. It was a perfect day, the sky cloudless, the light so bright that it bounced off every surface and made harsh outlines of the cars and buildings that they passed as they sped towards the north.

However many pictures she had seen of the river canyon, they had nothing on the reality. When the great gash in the ancient limestone appeared before them, cut through by the turquoise and white river, it was so deep as to literally take her breath away. Here and there, the gorge sides were studded with black pines, some of which grew at impossible angles, stretched out at right angles to the rock and clinging on with giant twisted roots. A restaurant perched on the cliff edge provided a bird's eye view of the tumbling water far, far, far below; here Zayn pulled up the minibus and they all got out.

Edie, who had never been good at heights, had to suppress the feeling of sickness and vertigo that rose up inside her. She noticed Debs corralling the two children as if they might disappear and plummet over the edge and for the first time she actually felt sympathetic towards the woman. The depth was terrifying.

Her phone buzzed and she pulled it out of her pocket to look at it. For a few seconds, her eyes could not focus, were not able to decipher and decode what she was seeing. When she had managed to read the message through and understand it, the words made her feel even sicker and giddier than the precipice below.

Fatima

They had run out of fuel. The smuggler must have known that there wasn't enough to reach the island. What did he care? They'd be in European waters by the time it happened so it would be someone else's problem. Or they'd capsize and die; nothing to do with him anymore. Seventy plus people, the old, the young, the unborn, were floating in the middle of a heavy sea, utterly helpless. There were no oars. Nothing. Ehsan repeatedly tried to restart the engine, pulling on the cord with a force that eventually ripped it off.

But it didn't matter because it was obvious it was not going to work. Some of the passengers started to get angry, shouting and moving around on the boat in a way that pushed its already dubious seaworthiness to the limit. It shipped in water every time there was too much of a commotion, its sides so low anyway that even the slightest increase in weight on one side or the other put it under the water level. People were bailing out the brine, with their hands or cups or water bottles, but it was seeping in quicker than they could get it out, spilling insidiously over the grey rubber like an ominous lava flow.

Fatima was soaked and freezing; a strong wind was blowing and the air was cold and harsh. She was trembling uncontrollably, from the chill and the convulsive vomiting and the heart-stopping fear that they were floating there only for the brief period of respite before they drowned. She tried to comfort the sobbing children but couldn't. The pretence that she had started out with – that they were going on a midnight picnic – seemed not only ridiculous but now also cruel. In the unlikely event that they survived, they'd never want to have a picnic again. Arguments were breaking out, people shouting and fighting about what they should do, but it was all pointless because one moment's thought was all it took to know that there was nothing whatsoever they could do.

The grandfather was weeping quietly into his granddaughter's curly hair.

'What kind of a man am I that I can't save my family?' she heard him mutter. It was a question, wrested from the soul of someone so desperate and invested with so much pain that there was no possible answer.

The infant, miraculously, remained fast asleep, oblivious.

Time passed; it was impossible to know how much. She tried to soothe her twins, stroking their filthy, matted hair, nestling them against her body as best she could, what with the bulk of her life-jacket and the incipient bump of her baby. She didn't know what else to do.

Time goes slowly when you are waiting to die, Fatima discovered.

And then a light was spotted, to the west, and not too far off. Seized by excitement, everyone moved towards it.

'Sit tight!' Ehsan's voice was authoritative and sure. Fatima almost felt proud of him and then immediately threw up, or would have done if she had anything left inside her. Proud of her rapist? What madness – but then nothing made any sense in this utterly surreal, completely terrifying environment.

198

'For God's sake, sit down, don't move!' Ehsan had taken off his shirt – it had once been white but was now a dirty shade of grey, but it still appeared pale and luminous in the feeble light of the moon. He began to wave it in slow, regular circles around his head. Fatima couldn't believe that the approaching boat could really see it, but miraculously, unbelievably, it continued to make its way towards them. Soon they could discern its markings; those of the Greek coastguard. A cheer rang out and people leapt to their feet, ignoring Ehsan's previous instruction, behaving with the lack of foresight that is the penance of the desperate.

They lurched towards what they saw as their salvation, leaning towards the approaching vessel, wobbling precariously in the flimsy dinghy, every movement bringing them closer to their doom. Water flooded in, cascading over the rubber sides in an unstoppable torrent, filling up the boat with a dead weight. Panic ensued, a frantic scrabbling for a position in a part of the boat that was still above water. The end came quickly. Within seconds, the boat had sunk, the grey rubber that had been their only protection from the sea gone.

We have our life-jackets, was all Fatima could think as she wrapped the twins' arms around her neck and struggled to keep afloat. The boat was there, almost upon them. Surely we can't die now, surely they'll get to us in time? The placid acceptance of whatever fate should have in store for them which had been the only way she had got on board now disappeared. Like the little boy who didn't want to die, she knew, with a desperate, searing lightning flash of realisation, that she didn't, either.

'Hold on tight. Don't let go,' she urged the girls. The wash of the coastguard boat drawing near sent a rush of water over their heads and they emerged, sputtering and spluttering but still breathing.

'You can do it. Not long now.'

She went under again, and felt the girls go down with her. She pushed her arms upwards, kicking her legs frantically, desperately trying to keep Marwa and Maryam above the surface. But the more she tried to do this, the more she herself sank down. She couldn't understand how the life-jackets, far from supporting them and giving them buoyancy, seemed to be dragging them under. They should have been enough. But they weren't because she was sinking down and down, the girls going with her, the sea closing in above them, her frenzied fight for breath at an end. She reached out her arms, stretching them as far as she could, holding the twins above the water, but it was impossible. Her strength deserted her. As she blacked out all she could think was, save the children first.

Save them before me.

TWENTY-FOUR

Edie

Edie sat in the restaurant playing with her food. She should feel justified in her decision to go on the trip, not to pull out at the last moment as had crossed her mind. She should feel that everything was OK, because the text on her phone was from Laura.

Hey Edie! I am having a great time. Hope you are too. Love Laura.

The message was followed by a row of smileys, a cocktail, a palm tree and a balloon.

Edie had read it over and over again. The country code was the same as before – Greece – but the number was a different one. Edie ran the details back and forth in her mind as Vuk and the other guests ate slow roast lamb and made small talk. Patrick and his family were chattering away, seemingly oblivious to Vuk's habitual taciturnity and Edie's troubled silence. As people finished eating and began to drift off, to the toilets and the smoking area or outside into the fresh air, Edie could remain silent no longer. Suspicion was crowding her mind, doubts and questions pervading her thoughts. She showed her phone to Vuk.

Slowly, chewing his last mouthful of lamb, he read what she held in front of him. 'Great news. If she were … if anything had happened to her, she wouldn't be texting, would she?' He swallowed and lifted his eyes to meet hers. 'So now you really know for absolute certain that Laura is safe and well.'

Edie shut the phone off and put it back into her pocket.

'No, I don't. In fact, I know precisely the opposite.'

Vuk raised his eyebrows and tapped a cigarette out of a battered packet and onto the table.

'I know nothing about Laura,' reiterated Edie. 'Because that message is not from her.'

The waiter came and cleared away the plates.

'So the message says it's from Laura but you know that it isn't.'

The way Vuk said it belittled Edie, made her seem stupid. But she knew she was right.

'It's not from Laura. Firstly, she never calls me Edie, only Ed. That was odd about the first message. Secondly, she never, ever, ever, not in a million years, would use emoticons. She despises them.'

Vuk shrugged and flipped the cigarette from end to end in his hand.

'She's changed. People do.'

'Not Laura. She's the most stubborn, unbending, uncompromising person I've ever met.' Edie was resolute. 'After me, that is.'

Vuk did not respond.

'What's going on, Vuk?' she demanded, to break his silence as much as anything else. 'Someone is sending me messages pretending to be Laura and I don't know why they're doing that other than to make me think she's OK when she's not and it's doing my head in.'

Vuk stood up and turned to leave the restaurant, motioning to Edie to follow him. Angrily she did so, wanting to shout after him that she needed answers but not wanting to create a commotion and embarrass Vuk in front of the guests. She still had her wretched job to think of. He led her to an outside seating area with a view of the canyon and lit his cigarette. He offered one to her even though she had told him a hundred times that she didn't smoke. She shuffled a little closer to him on the bench they were sitting on, desperately wanting some comfort, some reassurance.

'There are weird things happening, Vuk,' she pleaded, despairingly. 'The hut on the hill, Laura's scarf, the messages. None of it makes any sense.'

Vuk drew on his cigarette, long and hard.

'It is all perfectly straightforward, Edie.'

She listened, desperate for a rational explanation that she could believe.

'This is small and poor country,' he explained, speaking quietly and unequivocally. 'Some people are homeless. Plus there are Roma here.'

He paused, wrinkling his nose in disgust as if something smelt bad. 'You've seen them, getting their children to beg in the old town. They are not good people. They have been using the hut. They probably stole the scarf from Laura and then dropped it up there.'

Slowly and deliberately, Vuk let his cigarette butt fall onto the stones where he ground it down with his right foot.

'You don't think ...,' Edie ventured hesitantly, frantically twiddling her hair between her fingers. 'I mean, I thought – could these people have abducted Laura or killed her or something ...? If they're bad people like you say, it's possible, isn't it?' Her voice had risen and was tinged with hysteria. 'And they're sending the texts to keep me off the trail until it's gone cold?'

The cigarette butt had split apart and disintegrated under the pressure Vuk had applied. He was smoking another one already, still staring at the ground, seemingly fascinated by the tiny stones that lay there, rubbing the toe of his shoe into them and watching the white dust rise.

'When we get back from this trip – I'm going to the police again. I'll chain myself to the furniture there until they do something.' She had spoken far too loudly, a high-pitched whine that she hated in herself but couldn't stop, filling the silence left by Vuk's failure to answer.

Very, very slowly, Vuk turned towards her. The look he gave her warned of things she could not fathom.

'Edie, you are exaggerating as always. You will not go to the police because they do not care. And as for the messages – whatever your addled mind is telling you, they are from Laura. Who else would have your number?'

Edie bit the inside of her cheek as she considered this fact. It was true and stupid of her not to realise it. The knot of anxiety in her stomach tightened. Vuk was cross. She had really blown it now. Totally ruined everything. Vuk cast his second cigarette aside and, reaching out for Edie's hand, gripped it firmly. She stood up and their feet tangled together and she almost tripped; he was standing on the lace of her Converse and as she pulled forward, the lace untied itself, letting a long cord of dirty white trail behind her. She ignored it, wanting to keep up with Vuk's rapid march. He paused, planted a kiss on her head and smiled, his sexy, lop-sided smile.

'It's cute, the way you care so much about your sister.'

Edie didn't reply. She couldn't imagine that anyone *wouldn't* care about their own sibling, identical twin or not. But then, there were always people who questioned the bond and disparaged it, perhaps even more than they would do about an ordinary brother or sister, perhaps because twins scared them with their togetherness and its associated exclusivity. Whatever. Vuk wasn't angry after all and that was good because she needed him on side, needed his help. Or was it so she could keep track of him, of what he was doing? Right now, she wasn't sure.

She watched as he strode towards the little clusters of guests and began to round them up. He led the group to the view of the bridge across the canyon, where angles for photos were discussed as well as awe at the feat of engineering required to build it. There was a narrow path that led away from the viewpoint to a lower rocky outcrop where an even more expansive vista could be seen. A few of the more intrepid guests, including Patrick, were heading down there, and Vuk followed, indicating to Edie to come along.

'Get your camera ready, Edie,' he instructed her. 'These will be the pictures for the folks back home.'

Reluctantly, swallowing her fear, she stepped tentatively off the platform, attempting to walk exactly in his footsteps as if this would somehow offer protection from the chasm below.

Zayn appeared behind them, but Edie's stifled terror was too great for her to care.

'You should do your shoelace up, Edie,' he advised her.

Inadvertently, she looked down and in so doing, caught a full on glimpse of the dizzying depths of the gorge. *The fucking deepest in the world after the Grand Canyon.* Edie could not imagine what had possessed her to come so close to the edge. She hated heights, was terrified of them. She felt dizzy and sick and nauseous with fear. But she could not go back now; there was a trail of people behind and no possibility for one to pass another. She had to keep going. The lace could wait, she couldn't possibly bend down and retie it here, she might lose her balance and – and what might happen after that was too terrifying to contemplate.

She was right behind Vuk, not leaving his side, sheltering in his bulk and relying on it to keep her from falling. The path ended and the person at the front, who happened to be Patrick, stopped short. An almost comical effect of each one behind jarring to a halt ensued. Edie could hear Debs calling from above, presumably admonitions to Patrick to come back, not to be so stupid as to take a chance on this crumbling path. Whatever she was saying or doing was pointless as her words were lost in the air that filled the giant space beneath.

They all stood, speechless. Vuk reached out to Edie and pulled her gently towards him. She wondered fleetingly what had brought on such a public display of affection but assumed that the potency of the location was responsible. Being up here was enough to make anyone feel light-headed and cause them to act out of character.

Time seemed to stop and there was nothing but the bridge and the grey-white cliffs and the tumbling water, so far below as to be utterly silent. Edie managed, with trembling hands, to take a photo. As long as she didn't look directly down, she could cope. Cameras snapped and videos whirred and Edie was suddenly aware of the birdsong all around. She breathed deeply two or three times, trying to put into practice her free-diving relaxation techniques. It was actually all right, hovering above this precipice, if she concentrated exclusively on being all right. Sort of all right, anyway.

She shifted her position. There didn't seem to be room for her feet, even though they were so much smaller than Vuk's giant ones, and she thought about the shoelace and wished she had followed Zayn's advice and retied it. Vuk was pointing at something, some kind of bird – an eagle? – on the other side of the canyon and she turned her head to look, and caught another inadvertent glimpse of the vast distance below her that was so overwhelming that panic overcame her and she began to laugh hysterically. And then she stumbled.

Stumbled, and fell, the air parting for her, letting the gorge swallow her up, the laughter halted by the terror that caused saliva to rise bitter in her throat, her arms flailing, windmilling, her hair covering her face and getting into her mouth as she screamed, a scream wrenched from the depths of her being.

And the only thought in her head, as the gaping chasm claimed her, was of Laura and how she'd never find out what had happened to her now.

TWENTY-FIVE

Fatima

Fatima regained consciousness to find herself wrapped in a survival blanket and propped up against the cabin of the boat, a plastic mug of hot tea beside her. The twins were there, next to her. She couldn't understand how the three of them had survived; maybe it was up to God as Khalid had pontificated and He had been kind to them.

A man in uniform passed her. He paused when he saw her eyes upon him.

'Are you all right?' He spoke in thickly accented English, hard to decipher.

'Fine, thank you,' she answered politely.

'I want to kill those bastards who sold you those life jackets,' the man went on.

Fatima stared at him uncomprehendingly. Of all the people she felt hatred for, the person she'd bought the life jackets from had not, so far, featured.

'Filled with newspaper, worse than useless,' the man sneered. 'Those fucking bastards, selling them; making them in the first place.'

He wandered on along the deck, muttering to himself, 'fucking bastards'. It was scarcely believable. Life-jackets that were actually death-jackets. She recalled how she had seemed to sink as they spent time in the sea, how the jacket she wore had felt ever-heavier around her shoulders. She had thought it was the weight of the twins hanging on, but the weight had grown and grown just as it would if three bundles of newspaper were absorbing water by the litre. They would only have lasted another few seconds, if the coastguard hadn't got there.

The boat was already coming in to dock and on the quayside, in the gathering dawn, Fatima could see a flurry of activity. Another coastguard vessel was lined up ahead of them, a steady stream of people disembarking from it. Looking around her, on their boat, there seemed to Fatima to be only women and young children. Where were all the men? Surely not left in the sea? Someone helped her up and onto the tarmac, passing the girls to her. She saw the prow of the boat crowded with standing figures, the men, old and young, and the boys who were of an age and size to be grouped with the adults. With a sick feeling of relief, she spotted Youssef amongst them. There was no opportunity to wait for him though, as they were being directed onwards. Handsome, efficient looking Europeans wearing fluorescent tabards with the name of an organisation Fatima had never heard of were handing out bottles of water and casting their eyes expertly up and down everyone who passed them.

'Do you need a doctor?' the one at the end of the line was saying as the shambling group of the saved passed by. She thought about saying, *Yes, I'm pregnant, I don't feel at all well. Can you help me, please?* but didn't. She just kept moving, along with everyone else. A couple of the tabarded men – for they were all men as far as she could see – were on their knees beside a child of about five. They were performing CPR but even Fatima could tell that it was useless. As she drew level with them, they stopped, sitting back helplessly onto their heels and staring at the little figure. Next to it was another, already covered from head to toe with a black cloth.

'An hour in the water,' one of the men was saying. 'Poor little mite didn't stand a chance.'

She could hear tears in his voice and her heart felt heavy and slow. It could so easily have been one of her girls – or both of them – but it wasn't. Somehow, for some unfathomable reason, they were amongst the lucky ones and had survived. They must take heart from that and be strong for whatever other trials and tribulations were going to come their way.

It was in that instance that Fatima decided that she would try to contact Ali after all. No one in the world could be unaware of what was happening in this sea and on these islands. They had looked death in the face and somehow survived and now she felt braver than she had ever thought possible. And surely, if Ali knew of his own sister's and nieces' predicament, he would help.

Anyone would, wouldn't they?

Edie

The jarring pain that seared through her spine as she landed on a sharp, protruding piece of rock made Edie's teeth rattle and set stars jumping before her eyes. She pulled her knees protectively towards her, an instinctive reaction to the agony, as someone pushed her head between her legs. Vomit spewed out of her, covering the rock and the dusty soil. She was sick again and again and then, when it had finally stopped, found herself taking great sloughing gasps of air, desperate for oxygen.

Her whole body was shaking, her teeth jolting furiously together. She could hear voices all around her but not what they said. Then two strong hands lifted her under the armpits and she was being transported along the path and over the viewpoint platform and out to the other side of the restaurant, far from the gorge and the danger which she had thought was going to end her life.

'What happened, Edie?' It was Zayn and Vuk who had borne her to safety. Zayn was questioning her, gently, confusion and bewilderment suffusing his voice.

She couldn't answer, had lost the power of speech.

'She tripped on her shoelace.' Vuk did the talking for her. 'She should have tied it up.'

Zayn said nothing.

'Get everyone into the bus,' Vuk ordered him.

Zayn walked slowly away, motioning to the group to follow him.

Edie staggered to her feet. She couldn't speak, was stunned by what had occurred – by the fact that she had just looked death in the face. Her eyes fell on Zayn, retreating towards the carpark, the guests trooping behind him, and then her gaze moved to Vuk who was lighting another cigarette and standing, his back to her, staring at the gorge.

Back in the minibus, driving to the first campsite on the banks of the river, Vuk reassured her.

'You were never in any danger, Edie. You weren't going over the edge.'

Zayn, listening silently from the driver's seat, wrenched the gears, clumsily and noisily, missing second and almost stalling as their descent grew steeper.

Edie shut her eyes and pressed her fingers into them as if the pain would give her clarity. It didn't.

She no longer knew who was lying and who was telling the truth.

Fatima

All along the dockside, all along the dusty road into the city, there were tents and flattened cardboard boxes and rolled up sleeping bags. On every bit of waste ground, in every doorway and alleyway, there were people sitting slumped in exhaustion or staring despairingly into nowhere or holding their heads in idle hands. Fatima had not imagined anything like it. In the time since they had left their country, during which period she had hardly heard or read the news, thousands upon thousands of her compatriots, their number augmented by those from any number of other failed or poverty-stricken states, must have been coming, daily, nightly, never-endingly.

Marwa and Maryam were exhausted and Fatima had to drag them along, sweating with the exertion as the heat of the day built. When they arrived at the so-called camp, it was to find a place of utter squalor and total disorganisation. In her dreams, Fatima had imagined order, had thought after so long that all the necessary procedures would be in place and that registering for documents and refugee status or asylum or whatever it would be called would be straightforward.

213

She had been utterly wrong. There was no one in charge, no one to ask what they should do or where they should go. Hanging in the air was the choking smell of urine, and flies buzzed around piles of rubbish, soiled nappies and faeces. It was disgusting.

Everybody they saw wore on their face their desperation, hopelessness and hunger. Where would all these people *go*, thought Fatima, gazing at them all, of whose helpless number she was now one. Where will any of us get houses, jobs, schools, healthcare? It was impossible to imagine that those things really existed anywhere, for any of them. We're all just pretending, realised Fatima. Duping ourselves into thinking that there's a future for us somewhere.

Looking at the destitution all around, Fatima tried to make the hazy, half-remembered picture of Ali that she held in her head more solid, more real, more recognisable. Most of the photographs of him had disappeared when he had. There had just been one that she had kept in her bedroom, of him pushing her on a swing, that she had taken with her when she married. Of course it had been destroyed along with the house and anyway had been old and faded. Despite the vagueness of her memories, Fatima was sure she would still recognise her brother – she just doubted whether he would recognise her. But that was no reason not to try and track him down, and whatever the consequence, it could hardly make things any worse than they were already.

The idea formed and reformed and finally cemented in her mind. She would find the right moment to put it to Ehsan and then pray that it would all work out.

Ehsan found a space, recently vacated by the look of the sparse clumps of dead grass, where they could put down their tarpaulin. There was a tiny bit of shade from a miserable looking, half-dead shrub and Fatima tried to settle the girls down to sleep. They were hungry and thirsty but they had no food or water. Youssef said he'd go to find a tap to fill up water bottles. He was gone for ages, during which time the twins grizzled and whined. Fatima wanted them to be quiet, felt momentarily impatient with their complaints and fussing and then hated herself for being so cruel. They were so tiny and helpless, just three years old. They had done nothing to deserve any of this and the least they should be able to count on should be her constant and unwavering love and patience.

She patted their backs and soothed them with a gentle lullaby she had sung to them in the white nursery of their beautiful old courtyard house. She tried to take no notice when they scratched their heads. As soon as she could, she would go into town and buy a comb and conditioner and get rid of the damn head lice, one by one. Youssef returned with the water.

'There's a tap over there.' He pointed at some random location deep amidst the forest of tents and tarpaulins. 'But there's only one and the water comes very slowly so it took a long time.'

He watched Marwa drink, gulping the water down so fast that Fatima had to stop her for fear of choking.

'Sorry,' he added, his voice dull and toneless.

Fatima snapped a glance towards him. He was suffering badly from their daily degradations and humiliations; teenagers are proud and uncompromising anyway, and Youssef was even more so than most. Fatima doubted he would ever get over his experiences on this journey, let alone whatever horrors were still to come. Gazing around at the swarms of other children wandering aimlessly around the camp, their movements listless and their heads bowed, she realised what a cataclysmic problem was being stored up for the future. The young people, battling their despair and hopelessness, lacking even the semblance of an education, were a simmering pot waiting to boil over.

The girls went to sleep despite the broiling heat and Fatima left them in Youssef's charge whilst she took a look around. There were a couple of portaloos along the edge of the camp where it was bordered by a wire fence. She opened the door of one and was almost flattened by the stench that hit her, knocking the wind out of her. Just about managing to shut the door, she fled in the opposite direction. Putting her hand to her waist – and immediately feeling sick again with the reminder of her pregnancy – she felt the little secret pocket that held her money. There was hardly any left. They had no food, no shelter and no idea how long they would be here. The word doing the rounds was that it took days to get registered and receive the papers necessary to move on, to take the ferry to Athens to begin the long walk to northern Europe. She had no choice but to spend some of the precious funds that still remained on the search for Ali.

That evening, she broached the subject to Ehsan. The area of land adjacent to the camp, where the wire fence divided the rootless and homeless from the locals and tourists, was an open-air cinema. They could clearly hear the soundtrack – sirens, momentous music, urgent dialogue – carried to them on the still, hot air, between the wails of hungry, bored and spiritless children and the raised voices of adults arguing; there were frequent fracas between different groups of refugees. The irony of the movie world next to the real word was inescapable.

'What will your good-for-nothing brother do to help us?' Ehsan was scornful, his face twisted into an ugly scowl.

Fatima was taken aback by the strength of his antipathy. She wasn't aware that Ehsan had such strong feelings about Ali. Against him. Whichever. She couldn't allow his aversion to her brother, their last – their only – salvation, to foil her plan.

'I think he'll understand our predicament, if I can reach him and explain,' she replied patiently, determined not to let Ehsan rile her. 'I'm sure he's doing well, wherever he is; he was always such a hard worker. If he could get us out of here ...'

Her voice tapered off as she looked around at the wretchedness of their surroundings. Glancing back towards Ehsan, she saw that the idea that Ali might have money, and contacts, that he might be able to expedite their way out of the dirt and filth, had taken hold. His eyes held that same look of greed that she had seen when he had been lying on top of her. She suppressed a shudder at the memory and seized the moment.

'You know what everyone is saying, getting registered is a nightmare. There's only one place to get the papers, it has two officials working there, the queues are enormous, people wait for days and don't get anywhere near the door … I'm sure Ali is a better option, our best hope. An option we should at least try. If you agree, I'll go to the internet café tomorrow, first thing. You can find anyone online, absolutely anyone.'

She pursed her lips and took a deep breath. 'If we don't find him – if I don't get into contact with him within a couple of days – we'll forget all about it and join everyone else who's waiting in line.'

It was a gamble, but Ehsan was the kind of person who needed to know that he had a get out.

'All right,' he replied, dismissively, making it plain that he thought her over-optimistic but was prepared to indulge her. 'Two, three days, maximum. And then we'll give up.'

***

The next day Fatima began the search for her brother. She walked into the town and found an internet café. It was in a basement where a few dilapidated fans stirred the soupy air, providing no relief from the summer heat. Facebook was her starting point, then Twitter, followed by every other social media site she could think of. But Ali is a common name and their surname, too, was one shared by many millions of others the world over. She found nobody and nothing that seemed to lead her any closer to her brother. The walls sweated and throbbed as the sun rose high in the sky outside and the heat built. Fatima spread the search wider, to friends of Ali's, those she had heard the names of over the years, many of whom had also left their homeland for a better life elsewhere. There weren't that many that she knew of, due to being so young when Ali had disappeared, but she racked her brain for any small snippet that might help.

She worked quickly, concentrating so hard she began to feel sick and lightheaded. A tinge of desperation underlay each click on the mouse; every minute, every hour online cost money, every cent she spent on the computer meant less for food, less for the onward journey that they had almost run out of funds for anyway. They were already eating only twice a day, bread and olives mostly.

Finally, just as she was going to give up for the day, perhaps give up on the whole idea, she struck gold. She found the website of a man who had been a student with Ali; Fardeen Muhammed. She remembered him for some reason, had a recollection of an ebullient person who would tease her and embarrass her, commenting on her beauty and asking Ali to let him know when she had passed eighteen.

'Perhaps he'll remember that now,' she thought wryly as she tapped out an email. Fardeen was living in a town called London. At first, Fatima thought London, England, and her heart leapt. Perhaps Ali had gone to England, too, and would live nearby and be instantly and easily contacted, and not too far away for them to get to him. And then her heart sank again when she saw that it was London, Canada. But still, even so, if he knew where Ali was it didn't matter where either of them actually lived. Easy communication made the world a small place.

She finished her message. She wrote in English, thinking that might make her seem more genuine, but ended with a traditional greeting in their own language. As an afterthought, she attached a photo of herself. It might bring back memories for him. After all, purported relatives and friends and hangers-on were probably coming out of the woodwork in these terrible times. Composing the English sentences, choosing the English words, sent pangs of wistfulness running through her. Her dream of going to university to study English literature was well and truly dead now, along with so many others.

***

Once she had sent the email, Fatima decided to give up for the day. Her current paid-for time was almost up and she was feeling weak with hunger and dehydrated from sweating profusely for so long. As she walked back to the camp, a green-grocer was packing up his shop for the siesta. He gave her a box of peaches that were on the turn, pressing them upon her and refusing to take any money for them. Fresh fruit didn't last long here in summer, out of a chiller. Perhaps the shopkeeper discerned how her eyes feasted on them, how ravenous she looked. Carrying the box stiffly in front of her, the saliva gathered in her mouth and her stomach growled. But she waited until she got back to their slovenly abode to eat any, wanting to share each and every one with the others rather than greedily help herself. Ehsan and Youssef ate two each but she and the girls couldn't hold back and gorged themselves on the delicious orange flesh, dribbles of juice running down their chins and onto the parched brown grass beneath them.

That night the three of them suffered the consequences of their gluttony. They had terrible stomach cramps and the resulting diarrhoea was crippling. The toilets could not possibly be braved and it was the utmost humiliation to have to use a corner of the camp, up against the fence that separated them from the open-air stadium, as a toilet. Fatima had nothing to properly clean the girls with, let alone herself. She was repelled by herself, by her foul odour, by the dirt that was engrained under her fingernails and into her skin. Wretchedly, she longed for a shower and clean clothes – clothes that fitted properly and did not dig into her ever expanding waist – and a bed.

That night, lying on the stony ground, Fatima gave up. It was all useless, pointless. They would never get to Northern Europe and even if they did, for what? For life as outsiders, hated, persecuted.

Prostrate on the hard ground, weak from dehydration, stomach still cramping, she knew she would never get up again. She could feel the baby moving, its feather touch like the brush of a butterfly's wings against her belly. She could not understand how it was still alive and kicking when she was dead, finished.

TWENTY-SIX

Fatima

The long night passed. By the morning, Marwa and Maryam were listless and fatigued, staring dull-eyed at the sunrise as it spread over the trees and rooftops.

'Aren't you going?' demanded Ehsan, when Fatima had made no move to get up and start the walk back into town.

Wordlessly, she hauled herself to her knees and stood up. The world spun and she stumbled and nearly collapsed. The girls looked at her, appalled. Children fall over all the time. Mummies do not. Fatima broke a smile.

'I'll be back soon.' She blew them both a kiss; anything to reassure them. She had no energy for anything else. It seemed too much to hope that the Canadian friend would have replied, and yet without hope what else was there? There was the despair of the night before and she couldn't give way to that again.

On the way to the town, she passed a primary school, closed for the long summer holidays. The day before, the gates had been padlocked shut and the building's windows darkly shuttered. But today, the gate was open and there was a big sign, multilingual, advertising clothes and baby equipment, available to all refugees on the island, donated by the local people. Fatima could hardly believe it, that those whose beautiful island had been so overrun, could still find it in themselves to be so generous and warm-hearted. A woman with dyed blonde hair and a cigarette dripping from her lips gestured to her as she stood, unsure, at the threshold.

'Come in,' she said in English. 'We have many things here.'

Fatima stepped inside. Trestle tables were loaded with garments that had been roughly sorted according to size or age. She found a pair of cotton trousers with an adjustable elastic waist that would be perfect for her, plus a long skirt and two long-sleeved tops. There was a shirt that would fit Ehsan, hardly worn. The irony of choosing clothes for her rapist did not escape her but in order to carry on, she'd had to push that night's experience into the depths of her subconscious. Now, though, holding up the shirt and estimating its size relative to Ehsan's form, the memory of his body, the stench of his sweat, the roughness of his sweatshirt, that had become hard and stiff with lack of washing, rubbing up and down against her flesh, suffused her so that she gagged and stumbled and had to hold onto the table to support herself so that she did not fall to the ground again.

When she eventually recovered, she looked around her. No one had noticed. Everyone was preoccupied with other things, busily arranging and rearranging the piles of garments, bustling around, kind and friendly but not seeking out problems that they knew they would not be able to solve.

Burying her hands amongst the heaps of soft fabrics and her memories along with them, Fatima forced herself back to the task in hand. She found a couple of T-shirts for Youssef to replace the ones he had that were torn and ragged from their travels, and some track pants that seemed to have been hardly worn. Next, her delving unearthed two cute T-shirts with beads and ribbons that the twins would adore, together with two tiny pairs of jeans, faded and thin, but better than what they had.

Gathering everything together, she held her haul up to the blonde woman, who she had located organising the unloading and distribution of more items.

'I think this is too much,' she said, apologetically. 'Tell me which I can have, please. And how much.'

Secretly she was hoping that the cost would be minimal or she would have to put some back anyway. But there was no harm in at least asking; it might be cheap enough for her to afford.

The blonde woman removed the cigarette from her mouth and laughed, a hearty, friendly, tired laugh. 'You can take them all, my love. As much as you like and you can carry.'

Fatima frowned doubtfully. 'But what is the cost? I'm sorry, but I don't have too much money.'

'It's free. Gratis. You pay nothing.'

Fatima looked down at the clothes in her hands as if she expected them to disappear or turn to stone.

'Really? Free?'

'Yes, really.' The blonde woman turned away, her attention on an argument that seemed to have broken out in the far corner of the playground. 'Now take your things and get on your way. Safe journey to you.'

Fatima wandered out of the tarmac yard and on down the street to the internet café, her little bundle clutched tightly to her. She had never imagined a time in her life when she would be overjoyed to be in possession of hand-me-down clothes, but now was that time.

At the computer screen in the sweating underground room, another miracle unfolded before her. The Canadian friend had replied. Amidst his trite enquiries of 'how's it going', his news of himself, his house and, rather far down the list of priorities it seemed to Fatima, his wife and children, was the news she had been craving. He knew where Ali was.

Ali's email address was there, in front of Fatima, waiting to be used. The message she wrote took a long time to compose. What to say to the brother you idolised but who left you so many years ago? How to ask for help without coming across as whingy, melodramatic, needy? She wanted to sound strong, independent, in control. The fact that she was none of those things right now was immaterial.

Finally, after an hour of contemplation, she was happy with what she had written. As soon as she pressed send, he would have her email address and Ehsan's phone number; they had agreed ages ago to keep only one phone charged and topped up with credit to save money, and despite everything that had happened, she had not had the energy to challenge the decision.

Lumbering exhaustedly back to the camp, down the same long, dusty road, clutching the second-hand clothes to her bosom, she considered the bounty that fate had visited on her – on them all – today. The girls, recovered now from their upset stomachs, set upon her and showered her with love and kisses. She took them to the tap which gave, at its most enthusiastic, a thin dribble of water, washed them as best she could and dressed them in their new clothes. How lucky I am, she thought, with my girls and my unborn baby. Even here, even in this hideous place, I have something – three things – to live for. I must remember that. Please God help me remember that, whatever happens.

And then, that evening, the third miracle.

Ali called.

When the phone rang, Fatima could hardly believe it. And yet at the same time had expected it; had been sure that this was the moment when their luck would turn. Even Ehsan had to crack a smile of relief and happiness and to admit, afterwards, that she had been right and that it had been worth spending the money in the internet café. More than worth it. Because, once the greetings and exclamations were over, it turned out that Ali could help.

He had connections, people he worked with who could arrange their transportation to Europe and all the documents they would need. Fatima had many questions, but Ali reassured her on all of them; it would all be fine, nothing to worry about. No, no, not illegal at all, just a circumventing of the law and other obstacles that stood in the way of deliverance. He demanded to hear the twins' voices, to see pictures of them, the nieces he did not even know he had. Fatima longed to tell him about the new baby but couldn't whilst Ehsan was in earshot.

'I'm sorry,' Ali ended the call by saying. 'I'm so sorry for all you've been through and that I wasn't there to help you from the start. I think all day, every day, of my family and my country. Of what is happening to our people. I'm so sorry.'

Fatima smiled, though he couldn't see her, and shrugged. 'It's okay,' she replied. 'You're here now.' Her instincts that he would help had been correct.

Ali promised to keep in touch daily, to send them money and to let them know when they would be able to leave the island.

'But we haven't registered yet, Ali,' Fatima reminded him urgently. 'It's chaos here, it can take two weeks waiting in line – and then you have to wait again for a ferry.'

'You won't register,' he instructed her. 'Whatever you do, don't do that. Don't give fingerprints, nothing.' His voice had become hard and stern, a tone Fatima had no memory of from before. 'Wait for my instructions.'

'All right.' She held the phone out so the girls could shout goodbye.

'Thank you, Ali,' she said softly, as she ended the call. And then, clutching the phone to her chest, muttered 'thank you' again as the tears rolled down her cheeks. Now, maybe it would all be okay, exactly as Ali insisted.

Edie

The rest of the canyon trip passed in a blur. Edie couldn't stop thinking about her brush with death and going over and over in her mind how it had happened, how she, who was not normally a clumsy person, could have had such a near-fatal slip. This, together with the ever-present anxiety about Laura, caused Edie to be unsettled and on edge. Everything with Vuk was falling apart, too. She felt that Vuk had lost faith in her and knew that she had in him. But even if she had felt inclined to talk to him about it, which she didn't because she didn't know what she would say or accuse him of, he was always busy, arranging activities or meals for the guests or disappearing with Zayn for muttered conversations by the van or under the black pine trees.

In her more paranoid moments, Edie had them plotting something, conspiring against her, getting ready to consign her to a loony bin, thinking her delusional, neurotic, crazy because of her belief that the messages weren't from Laura and her increasing suspicions that they knew something they weren't telling her. Nearly falling into a fucking canyon would only make her look even more unpredictable and unstable. So she said nothing and kept her own counsel.

The group was divided into three for the rafting. Zayn had already driven off to the next campsite so there was no way out of the gorge but by river. Edie had no choice but to join in. She was placed by the guide into a boat with Patrick and his family. Vuk went in the lead boat. As the day wore on, Edie relaxed slightly. It was actually quite fun watching the children's delight in the experience, seeing how they screamed at every bump of the boat's bottom against the rocks and how hard they paddled in accordance with the guide's instructions every time the water became remotely turbid. For much of the journey, though, the river was calm, its turquoise colour a reflection of the clear sky above. The massive sides of the canyon rising up on either side ceased to seem sinister but instead were rather comforting, hugging them tight as the current bore them serenely onwards.

They passed waterfalls and shingle beaches that looked untouched by human hand, and indeed the only access to them was by boat so there were no casual visitors or day-trippers. A simple sandwich lunch was taken on one such beach, a thundering waterfall providing a dramatic backdrop.

'How are you feeling today, Edie?' Patrick asked, joining her as she idly paddled in the crystal clear, glacial water.

She looked sharply up at him. 'Fine, thanks.' No need for him to know her doubts and worries. She didn't need another person thinking she was ready to be dispatched to the funny farm.

Patrick nodded. He picked up a flat pebble and skimmed it across the river. Edie counted sixteen hops before it sunk beneath the surface.

'Wow.'

'Years of practice. Long holidays on the west coast of Ireland.' Patrick pulled a face. 'Beautiful, but nothing to do while my parents bickered except throw stones into the sea.'

'Oh.' Edie grimaced in sympathy. Her family holidays had always been of the adventurous and philanthropic sort, volunteering in marine conservation projects in Mozambique or teaching English in Malawian mud hut schools. She thought of her parents now, in some remote and generally inaccessible part of the high Andes, researching the travel guide they had long planned to write about mountain hikes around the world. Who they thought would want to embark on such a trip and call it a 'holiday' Edie couldn't imagine but this was the kind of crazy undertaking her parents had always got involved in. At least she was old enough now not to be dragged along with them. Her brother James was really into all that stuff, though, and he was spending his uni holidays building a health centre in Sierra Leone or Liberia or somewhere like that, when any normal, sensible person went to Ibiza or Inter-railing.

Her heart ached and suddenly Edie recognised the feeling. She was missing them. Debs called Patrick over to admire some achievement of one of the children. It was like a punch to the diaphragm. Everyone else had someone special except her. Neither Laura nor Vuk had shown themselves to be up to the job.

'Be careful, Edie,' Patrick said, as he waved to his wife to indicate he had heard and was coming. Edie looked around, wondering what she was doing that carried any risk.

'I mean in general,' he elaborated, looking her straight in the eyes. 'Just watch your step.'

'Yeah, right.' Edie felt foolish; her stumble on the cliff had made her a laughing stock, clearly. She turned away and walked towards the waterfall, the spray cooling her burning cheeks even from a few metres distance.

She was desperate for this horrid trip to be over. It had been a disaster.

TWENTY-SEVEN

Fatima

True to his word, Ali sent funds. Fatima picked it up from a small international money transfer office near the internet café, using a special password because of her lack of official documents. She couldn't believe how easy it was. They could afford to book into a guest house for a night, now, and there were plenty of rooms available. But she was still reluctant to spend too much, feeling that they should preserve all the cash they could. And anyway, it felt wrong to be living it up on Ali's generosity; she was sure he must work incredibly hard for what he earned and the last thing she wanted him to think was that she was a spendthrift and taking his assistance for granted.

So instead of booking a room, she just paid for them all to use a bathroom for a few hours, so that they could wash. Combing and combing the twins' hair she felt a maternal satisfaction she had not experienced for a long time. It was lunacy to enjoy delousing her children but that was precisely what the sensation felt like. It was something normal, which served to make it precious. It was doing what a mother should do; caring for her children, making sure they were clean, healthy, happy.

Every parasite she removed was one less left to feed on her precious offspring. If only she could find and destroy all the smugglers and traffickers and border guards who had tainted their journey, and the journeys of so many others, so easily and efficiently.

She herself had not worn her new clothes yet and the sensation of pulling on garments that smelt of sunshine and laundry powder instead of dried sweat and fear was almost as good as the feeling of stepping off that coastguard boat and onto dry land had been. Plus the trousers with the elastic waist were so much more comfortable than her old ones; she could almost see her belly spring out now it was no longer constrained by a too-tight band, blooming and blossoming. She could feel the baby inside her moving and kicking as if stretching out its limbs in delight at its new freedom.

She had to tell Ehsan. Waiting until the girls were occupied playing on the dismal broken metal roundabout that listed on its side in a doleful corner of the camp, she confronted him with it. Truly, she could not believe that he hadn't noticed but it seemed not. His reaction was one of indifference. He had not tried to have sex with her since that terrible night when they arrived at the coast. The constant proximity of the children, combined with the ever-present fear and anxiety, seemed to have dulled his craving for her. For now. Fatima hoped that this new information would keep it suppressed. But he just grimaced off-handedly and carried on smoking. Fatima thought ironically of how she had urged him to take up cigarettes as an excuse to get in on the man chat, the local know-how, before they crossed the border.

Now he never stopped and his breath, when he came near enough for her to notice, smelt sour and stale and somehow always moist, like an ashtray left out in the rain.

The next few days, without the draw of the internet café and the quest to find Ali, were even more interminably boring than they had been before. Hopelessness, hunger and depression invaded all corners of the sordid, decaying camp. Fatima felt guilty about the cash in her pocket and the promise in her heart, when so few of those around her possessed such things. But even these precious, cherished attributes were hard to hold on to, to believe in, during the never-ending monotony of the long days and nights.

A girl, about twelve or thirteen, a similar age to Youssef, took to hanging around with Fatima and the twins; she taught them clapping games and had somewhere found a piece of chalk which she used to mark out a hopscotch grid on the bumpy, crumbling tarmac of one of the camp's dilapidated paths. Marwa and Maryam were entranced by her, and by the entertainment she provided.

Just like how Youssef used to play with them, at the beginning, thought Fatima sadly. Now Youssef had no fun left in him and she marvelled that this girl, whose name was Sondes, had retained any of hers. Sondes was bright as a button as well as playful; she spoke some French and even better English. Fatima mourned on her behalf for her lost education. A whole generation of children deprived of the right to knowledge and learning, for when would she next see the inside of a school?

Fatima had bought a cheap notepad during one of her visits to the internet café, and a pencil – the two items had cost less than two euros and she wanted the twins to practise forming their letters, which she had begun to teach them back home. Some said the girls were too young but Fatima didn't agree and they had both mastered the writing of their names.

'I can help you with English,' she told the little girl. She offered the paper to her. 'Show me what you know.'

Sondes looked around her, at the sprawling dump that was home for the moment, at the haphazardly placed tents and flattened cardboard boxes that marked each groups' territory. A stray dog was nosing around a pile of discarded meat bones, sending a cloud of black flies whirling into the tepid air above.

She started to write. When she had finished, Sondes sat looking at the piece of paper with wide, tearless eyes.

'Show me,' said Fatima, gently. She took the paper out of Sondes's hands and read what the child had written.

I like park.

I don't like dog.

I love my country.

A child's poor, pathetic life in eleven words.

And then, underneath the writing, a picture of a blown-up building, a fire and the small figure of a child with a roughly drawn speech bubble coming out of her mouth: HELP!

Fatima thrust the notepad and pen into Sondes's lap.

'You keep it.' She had to speak quickly, before she lost control. 'Keep writing, Sondes.'

And then she got up and ran along the jagged path, until she was out of sight behind some bushes by the barrier fence. Holding onto the wire, the view of what lay beyond segmented into diamond shaped sections, she rested her head forward. She and her girls were getting out; Sondes, in all likelihood, was not, at least not any time soon. And when she did, she would face a long and punishing walk where she and her family, such as it was, would encounter obstacles at every turn, would discover their way barred time and time again, would inevitably spend time in other, equally horrendous, camps.

The worst thing of all was that Fatima knew she was going to walk away from Sondes and all her sorrow, was going to put herself and her children above all others. There was simply no other way.

TWENTY-EIGHT

Edie

Edie just wanted the trip over now. The foaming white water, swirling in furious eddies all around the boat, mirrored her muddled mind. The only alleviation from her introspection was provided by one of Patrick's children – the boy – falling out of the boat, causing much consternation (from Debs) and mockery (from Patrick). Edie kept stumm but she knew he'd done it on purpose. What eight-year-old boy wouldn't? Surely going over-board was half the fun?

In the afternoon was one further stop to have cold drinks and snacks. Zayn was waiting when the boats pulled up, cool-bags by his feet. He said nothing, seeming morose and disinterested in anything other than his phone, which he kept checking, appearing to be scrolling through messages, his eyes flicking up and down as he scanned the screen at the same time as he handed out his wares.

'What's wrong?' asked Edie, taking an ice-cold Coca-Cola from his outstretched hand. 'Bad news?' She indicated towards the phone. By rights, he should be checking up that she was all right after the canyon debacle. But she'd given up thinking

234

anyone cared about her now. And Zayn's ever-increasing shift-iness, combined with Vuk's ever-darkening mood, served only to increase her ever-growing feeling that she was on her own in this – whatever 'this' was.

Zayn looked nervously over his shoulder then back at Edie, hurriedly shoving the phone into his pocket. 'Nothing,' he said. 'Nothing's wrong.'

'Why so cagey, then?' She opened the can, waiting for the hiss to subside before taking a long drink. Zayn shrugged. 'Forget it, Edie,' he muttered, and scuttled away to the minivan.

'Be like that then,' muttered Edie under her breath. She drank the coke. The bubbles fizzed against her tongue like the simmering anger and apprehension she felt inside her. She put her head in her hands in despair. She didn't know what was happening or what to do about it.

***

Edie had hoped that she might have been forgotten about in terms of the work schedule for the evening after the trip, but unfortunately not. The minibus was met by Ivana in full-on officious mode, and Vlad. As soon as Vuk was out of the door, Vlad was muttering in his ear and they rapidly disappeared together, Zayn trailing behind, heading in the direction of the small marina where the resort's boats, jet-skis and its beautiful yacht were moored.

Ivana sent Edie straight to the restaurant. Even walking as slowly as she possibly could, she was still there in under ten minutes. Stefan was delighted to see her, sending her to a table of Russians who had some problem with the menu that he couldn't fathom. The main complainant, who had a distinct look of a younger Putin about him, initially eyed Edie belliger-ently but once he'd run his eyes up and down her body a few times, he calmed down considerably. For the first time in her life, Edie did not congratulate herself on this. It was utterly inconsequential. The sheer vapidity of what had hitherto delighted her induced a feeling of self-loathing that she did not know how to deal with.

The sun was dipping in the sky and she was hard at work when her phone beeped and vibrated in her pocket. Startled, she nearly dropped the tray of crockery she was carrying. She always viewed her phone with trepidation these days, aware that it could be Laura. Or whoever was pretending to be Laura.

It wasn't Laura. It was Vuk, thanking her for her help with the guests over the past few days. A message that, only a few days before, would have sent her into paroxysms of joy now just made her feel sick. He never thanked her for anything. Why now?

To avoid thinking about it all, she buried herself in her work, stunning Stefan with her new conscientiousness. Previously, he had told Vlad she was a good worker just to be nice, Edie couldn't help inwardly noting. Now she really *was* one, and for all the wrong reasons.

Bending down to stash a pile of ashtrays away on a low shelf, she saw Zayn pass by the restaurant entrance. He had a couple of suitcases in his hands that he must be taking to the cabana of some new arrivals. He was striding up the path and as he walked Edie could see his jeans pocket was stuffed uncomfortably full of something. She crept forward a couple of inches, not wanting him to notice her. When she got closer her suspicions were confirmed. Half-protruding from Zayn's pocket was a silver-grey piece of material. Upon it was a pattern of ivory crosses.

Laura's scarf.

As she watched, Zayn arrived at the big garbage wheelie-bin beside the restaurant wall. Pausing to put down one of the bags, he pulled the scarf from his pocket and shoved it into the bin, pushing it deep inside. Glancing hastily around him, he shut the lid, reclaimed the bag and went on his way.

Edie remained crouching by the ashtrays until Milan almost fell over her and she had to move.

Fatima

Sailing out of the port, Fatima's gaze was drawn towards a mountain that blazed in the sun like an inside-out volcano. It was comprised entirely of life-jackets, just one of many such man-made peaks that had grown up around these islands as a testimony to the unrelenting stream of human traffic that was arriving – still – on a daily basis. Their fierce orange was like the fires back home that had raged in the ruins of buildings after the bombs fell. The nausea that held Fatima in its grasp only increased at the sight. She knew she would never shake the memory of the jackets she had bought and worn herself and put on the twins in such good faith.

She was not sorry to say goodbye to the island, but waved a farewell nevertheless. She was sure that she would never be coming back. It was as if their journey were being continually rubbed out behind them, no traces left behind. In a symbolic gesture, she took the key to her house that she had been carrying since the day it was blown up and flung it into the water. She had no use for it ever again. Their past had been erased by the conflict, all that made them what they were dissolved away.

They were now defined by what they didn't have rather than what they did, as refugees, migrants, asylum seekers, all words that symbolised desperation and need, a reliance on others that rankled in every pore of Fatima's being. All they had was the possibility of a future, the future that Ali had promised to provide, if only they could get there in one piece. He'd sent them a complicated schedule to follow, involving this ferry followed by a series of smaller vessels that would, eventually, bring them to him – and to safety.

Standing and gripping the ferry's handrail, the metal burning into her skin, Fatima felt a twinge cross her belly. Sea-sickness again, like on the rubber boat that had borne them here. She had thought a bigger boat would not be as bad.

Youssef came with the twins. 'Can we buy Coca-cola?'

Fatima smiled weakly. She would never have let the girls have fizzy drinks at home. But now, if a sweet, cold can with a bendy straw brought them pleasure, why not? After all they had been through, it seemed a small reward.

'Of course.' She fumbled in her pocket for some money. Ali had been so generous, they could afford the odd treat.

As the boat ploughed on, it grew windy. Gusts buffeted Fatima's face, taking her breath away. The rocking motion grew stronger and stronger and Fatima began to vomit. The sickness was dreadful but it didn't matter because they were on a proper ferry, piloted by a proper captain, equipped with all proper safety features. However sick she was, she would be safe.

Ehsan, thank God, stayed well away from her. Fatima could see him, far along the deck, leaning on the barriers like her and chain-smoking. She retched again.

A crew-member passing by faltered in his step, then stopped and turned to her.

'Are you OK?'

Fatima took a deep breath. 'Oh yes, thank you.' She didn't dare attempt anything else in case she threw up in the middle of speaking.

'It's the Meltemi. It's always bad – everyone on board will be puking by the time we dock.'

Fatima grimaced. Flashes of memory of the vomiting hoards on the rubber boat flitted before her eyes.

'We might be held up there a few days,' continued the sailor, narrowing his eyes and sagely regarding the horizon. 'Are you going far? Or disembarking next stop?'

'Next stop,' gasped Fatima. She wanted the man to go away. The twinges in her belly had suddenly become deep, wrenching aches like period pain.

'You're doing the right thing, staying out in the fresh air.' He turned to go, calling over his shoulder 'You take care now' before disappearing through a door to the interior.

Fatima sank to her knees, doubled over in pain. The realisation of what was happening was beginning to dawn on her. But it wasn't how it had started before, when she had had the twins. They had come early, as twins often do, and of course the birth was a C-section. At that time, the health service still functioned, there were doctors and nurses and operating theatres and electricity and you could go into a hospital without fearing that it might be bombed in the night. Despite the operation being booked well ahead of the due date, the labour had started anyway – Fatima had been alerted by her waters breaking in the middle of the afternoon, when she had been cooking for the evening meal – and, after a mad drive with Fayed slaloming through the commuter traffic, the twins had been born in a rush in the twilight of a late November day. They were tiny but gorgeous, beautiful little parcels of white-swaddled, black-haired perfection.

Fatima struggled to tell them apart; a tiny birthmark behind Marwa's left ear was their only point of difference. Now, of course, they had developed their own characteristics and although strangers never knew one from the other, Fatima could always pick out Marwa, with her perpetually defiant eyes, and Maryam, with her sweet, wistful smile.

Because of the C-section, Fatima had not experienced labour so had no idea what to expect. Now she understood everything any helpful friend or acquaintance had ever told her about the horror of childbirth. Another gut-wrenching, scream-inducing, vice-like pain overtook Fatima's whole body as the land mass of the island on which they had spent such a dreadful few weeks disappeared completely from view. Struggling to her feet, she stumbled into the cafe compartment. Youssef and the twins were still there, savouring every drop of their precious drinks.

Fatima pulled some more cash out of her pocket and almost threw it onto the table. 'Get the girls something to eat,' she instructed. 'Chips, ketchup, anything you like. And afterwards – afterwards you can take them to the entertainment centre, see if you can win them a teddy bear from one of those grab machines …' She was starting to feel faint, desperately trying to hide how bad she felt from the children. Youssef's guarded eyes told her nothing. The girls were so delighted with the unaccustomed freedom that they giggled happily, high on sugar and adventure. Fatima was continually amazed at how they seemed to arise anew every day, without bitterness, always hopeful.

Back outside, she found a quiet space behind a lifeboat where she clung anew to the ferry's metal railings, vomited copiously into the sea again, and then half-crouched, half-lay as the contractions took over.

The ferry was headed for one of the much bigger islands to the west and there they would be met by Ali's friend and taken on smaller boats further into Europe, to the hallowed territory of the EU. It had all sounded, at the end of such a tortuous journey, so simple.

As Fatima faced up to the fact that she was strongly in labour, weeks, months, too early, all ideas of simplicity blew away like thistledown in the throes of the Meltemi wind.

***

The labour, that was in reality a miscarriage at only halfway through her pregnancy, seemed to go on forever. Far from blowing out, the Meltemi intensified, rocking the ferry from side to side, gusting so forcefully that it stirred up the sea and washed waves over the empty decks. Fatima was soaked, shivering and retching repeatedly when finally they reached land – one of the many islands on the ferry's itinerary – and disembarked. By this time, she could only just walk, had to stop every few paces for another contraction. Ehsan took barely any notice; he seemed incapable of comprehending what was happening, and it was Youssef who put his arm around her waist, hers around his shoulder and bore her weight as they stumbled down the gangway.

Unbelievably, there was a man waiting for them, pretending to be a taxi driver with whom they had to have a protracted pretend negotiation over price and destination to obfuscate the harbour police and allay any suspicion of what was going on.

The man drove them to a deserted beach with a tiny pier, all the while casting anxious glances over his shoulder to where Fatima lay, half-prone on the backseat, the twins and Youssef somehow squashed in beside her. He cottoned on pretty quickly to what was happening and clearly wished he could dump them all by the roadside but didn't, presumably because that would bring some terrible consequence from his paymasters, not least of which would be lack of his fee.

Somehow, Fatima, Ehsan and the children got aboard the motor boat that powered into the bay as soon as they arrived there. Fatima knew that it wasn't just that she was losing the baby; something else was going badly wrong for it to take so long, to make her feel so ill. But there was no one to help, no medical assistance available. She began to drift in and out of consciousness, unaware of where she was or how long they had been travelling for. Day merged with night and turned to day again and she couldn't grasp hold of any of it.

In her few cogent moments, she found herself thinking of Fayed, longing for him, missing him more than she had had time to, or had allowed herself to, in all the preceding weeks since their odyssey had begun. When she had first realised she was pregnant, she had hoped it would be a boy; she had always wanted a son. Caring about the baby's gender hadn't lasted long, though, in all the horror that surrounded them. And now she could only remember how Fayed hadn't been bothered about ever having a boy, was content with his two daughters who he doted on and adored. They had decided to wait a while, anyway, before adding to their family. Double-trouble was enough to be going on with, Fayed used to joke as he threw the girls in the air or dandled them on his knee. He had died without knowing about the baby, but even though it hadn't been planned Fatima knew he would have been overjoyed. He loved children.

***

They changed from the motorboat to a yacht. The sea broiled and bubbled between them.

'What the hell's wrong with her?' Fatima heard a harsh male voice rasp. She wanted to cry, to sob, to tell this person what was happening, to ask him for help. But the tone of the voice told her that the question was asked in anger, not concern.

She flopped down onto the deck. Dimly, fighting the urge to close her eyes and sleep, she watched through half-closed lids as the twins were brought aboard, and then Youssef. Waves were washing over the sides of the boat and they soaked her clothes, making her shudder and shiver. She put her hands to the deck and the liquid surrounding her felt slimy and thick; not like water usually felt. The moon was bright and full. Fatima raised her hands to her face and saw that they were red, covered in thick, viscous blood. Her blood.

Someone grabbed her, pulled her sodden trousers off her

and wrapped her in a sheet, rolling her over so that it encased her as if she were mummified.

'Clean this!'

On hearing the order, Fatima thought it was addressed at her. She was drifting in and out of awareness, the light of the moon merging into the light that formed behind her closed eyes. She felt that she was above herself, looking down, seeing her prone body, feeling pity for the poor human who was in such a state.

Someone lifted her bodily, throwing her over their shoulder and marching across the wobbling deck and then dumping her on a raised seat of some kind. Behind, she heard the sound of water sluicing onto boards. The cleaning. A little water clears us of this deed. The words, so familiar from the time when she had studied English literature in the hope of taking a degree in the subject, floated around in her head.

'What the fuck do I do with this?'

The voice was a different one, a deeper, lower one. What were they talking about, Fatima wondered. The answer, being barked out as she lay incapable of movement, was lost in the sound of the wind and the waves. She was lifted once more, and taken inside; she heard the catch of a door and the sudden absence of the breeze rushing in her ears. And then she must have slept, because she remembered no more.

***

Coming to when they finally got to land, someone told her that she'd given birth to a son, a tiny little boy far too undeveloped yet to have survived. The voice of the person who told her this was familiar from some deep recesses of memory but it wasn't until much later that she realised it had also been speaking her language, not English. She vaguely registered her surroundings as a stone building on a hot, dry hillside. She could not imagine where they were. The nameless man told her that the baby had been buried at sea.

Fatima heard herself scream, an inhuman, visceral lament that wrenched her heart from her body and tossed a piece of it into the roiling water with her son.

Her last thought before she lost consciousness again was that she had neither seen nor held him.

TWENTY-NINE

Edie

Edie headed up to the back of the resort, towards the staff cabins and her room. She was tired but the sight of Zayn secretively disposing of the scarf had energised her, an energy born of disbelief and growing fear. She now had the actual evidence that even feeble, forlorn Zayn was in on whatever egregious villainy was going on. Oh yes, she had the 'evidence' that the police had so loved to emphasise the necessity of; she just had no idea of what crime it pointed to.

Bypassing her door, she found that her feet were taking her of their own accord deep into the olive grove where the trees grew thicker together and the discernible path petered out. At first she disregarded the noise she made, the breaking twigs and the dragging of the fruit-heavy branches of the wild pomegranate trees against her arms. But as she got further away from the restaurant and the cabins and clambered higher up the hill, she walked more slowly and carefully, even though all reason told her that there was no one to hear her but the lizards in their lairs in the tree roots and the owls hunting in the night sky above.

And then she saw it.

At first she thought she had imagined it. But then there it was again. A tiny pinprick of light wandering haphazardly, stopping and starting, appearing and disappearing. She stopped dead, waiting, finding herself holding her breath. There was nothing. And then, as soon as she crept forwards, it shimmered into view again, the same golden beam making erratic progress ahead of her. Her breath catching in her throat, she paused once more. The light was nearer now, much too near, and she shrank back into the bushes, wincing at the noise of branches bending and yielding against her back.

The footsteps came closer, crunching through the dry undergrowth. It was definitely more than one person although it was impossible to tell how many more. The blood stilled in her veins. A branch snapped beneath her feet with a retort as loud as a firework. A barked command rang out and the footsteps came to an abrupt halt.

'Who's there?' It was a man's voice, speaking the local language, and its tone was icily threatening. Vlad's voice? Edie wasn't sure. She waited, frozen in terror.

The silence and the waiting seemed to last forever. Eventually, just as Edie thought she was going to faint with holding her breath, the footsteps brushing through the undergrowth resumed.

Emboldened by having evaded discovery, Edie crept a few steps closer, slinking along the line of oleander bushes, bent down low. The hut, as she thought, was ahead of her and moving towards it were vague figures in the blackness, bowed and hunched. Two were small, child-sized and somehow pitiful-looking. They had already cleared a trio of olive trees that stood to the left of the hut and were approaching the ruined threshold, following the gradually receding shadow of a man of a similar size and height to Vuk and tailed by a slighter person behind, whose movements were light and fleet. And then a man carrying someone over his shoulder, firefighter style, emerged from behind the olive trees. This man, though not tall, appeared strong and was bearing the weight with ease. Something about him reminded Edie of Zayn.

In just a few seconds the little group had disappeared inside the stone walls of the hut. The cicadas' constant roar was deafening in the now complete silence. And then a faint sound of voices floated across the clearing in front of the hut, and became louder and louder until the air was torn apart by a howling, heart-rending scream. A white-hot flash of terror subsumed Edie's body and stilled her blood in her veins. The noise was animalistic, raw, hideous. It had seemed to be wrenched from the heart of whatever poor woman – Edie was sure it was a woman – was making it. And then Edie heard the slap of flesh against flesh, a growling bark and a dragging, scuffling noise that seemed to indicate someone being pulled across the sand and dirt floor.

Edie's head was reeling, her eyes aching from straining in the darkness. So there *were* people using the hut and they didn't seem to be there entirely willingly. Should she go up there and try to help them, to rescue them? But how could she; where would she take them, what succour could she offer? Could Laura have been taken here, too? It was possible but that didn't explain why or what had happened to her after. And had that really been Vuk at the front and Zayn at the back of the group? If so, what were they doing? Where was Vlad, whose voice she was sure she had recognised. There were too many unknowns tumbling around her mind and not a single certainty anywhere.

Edie's veins were pulsating with heat. It had got a lot hotter whilst they had been in the mountains, or perhaps she had already got out of the habit of the kind of heat that sapped your energy and prevented you from thinking straight. Because that was how she felt right now. Her mind was full of suspicions that ran through her bones and her blood and chilled her despite the forty-degree heat.

It was the feeling of terror.

***

Having fled back to her room, Edie stared sleeplessly at the ceiling. Laura was missing, and someone pretending to be her was sending Edie messages. There were strange people hiding out at the hut on the hills and despite Vuk's assertion that they were tramps or gypsies, Edie wasn't so sure. Every hideous story she had ever heard or read or seen in a film, of kidnap or murder or slavery or trafficking, flitted across her mind. She wanted to help but at the same time was scared of getting involved. And what could a foreign girl who couldn't speak the language and had no friends, other than the ones who now didn't seem so friendly after all, possibly accomplish? Even going to the police, which might be thought to be the sensible, not to mention obvious, course of action looked dubious; what had they done so far? Were they, as Vuk asserted, corrupt? Maybe they were in on what was going on, too – that would explain their laconic lack of interest. You just never knew in places like this.

With so much going around and around her head, Edie was not aware of falling asleep. But she must have done, because at some time towards dawn, she jerked violently awake.

Someone was turning the door handle, trying to get into her room. Hardly daring to move, she rolled her eyes towards the source of the sound. The handle was still. The door remained closed. She listened intently. It was light outside, but too early for the other staff members to already be up and going about their business. She remained stock still for minutes that felt like hours and then, when she didn't hear anything else, forced her shoulders to relax, pushing her body down onto the bed. Every muscle was stiff with tension.

249

She turned over and felt a twinge of pain in her right arm, presumably from when Vuk had grabbed her back from the abyss at the canyon. Although he had been standing on her left, she realised now. This was puzzling and Edie couldn't work out how it could have been that he had got hold of her right arm.

Another noise from outside, from the back this time, by the window, sent fear surging through her again. She huddled into the bedclothes, wrapping herself up in the sheet as if in swaddling clothes, trying to make herself invisible to any intruder like a little child who's afraid of ghosts and thinks that if she can't see them, they can't see her. Her mind, however, could not be so easily stilled. Vuk had let her go down that precarious path with its precipitous drop with a dangling shoelace. The shoelace that he had trodden on and caused to come undone. Zayn had urged her to do it up.

Once in position and admiring the view, Vuk had been standing on her left, Zayn on her right. It was her right arm that was bruised from being hung onto with enough strength to prevent her from descending to her certain death. The thought slowly emerged from the fog of truth and untruth, fact and fiction, that clouded her mind - the thought that Vuk had tripped her up and Zayn had saved her – But no, that could not conceivably be true. Whatever love was, or was not, lost between her and Vuk he was hardly a murderer. Was he?

She lay, every fibre of her being straining for further sounds of someone trying to enter her room. There was nothing but silence, and the cicadas' relentless strumming. Stupid, stupid girl, she snapped at herself. Of course there was no one there; this was as much nonsense as the figures by the hut resembling Zayn and Vuk; just a figment of her overactive and increasingly paranoid imagination.

What wasn't nonsense was that she had absolutely no idea what in hell was really going on. And, in addition to the fear and the uncertainty, was the sneaking realisation that there was no one who seemed to be above reproach and beyond suspicion.

There was no one she could trust.

***

The next morning, Edie cleaned on autopilot. In the sleepless hours until daybreak, she had decided that she must not draw any attention to herself, must not do anything out of the ordinary and most certainly must not risk angering Vlad to the point that he might suspect that she knew something. So she had to complete her chores, do what she was asked and quietly, under the radar, take steps to solve the ever-increasing number of mysteries that surrounded her.

The time she was working could anyway be thinking time, given that everything she was required to do was utterly mindless. Cabana 19, then 8, then 3 ... She counted cutlery, replenished loo roll, stripped and changed bed linen, all the while churning over in her mind a plan of action. In cabana number 5, she cursed guests who had left it in such a mess it took her much longer than normal to sort out. She could never understand how people could leave the sink piled high with dirty dishes, or dump their wet towels on the bed so the mattress got damp. Did they think some elf came along to magic everything right? She was sure that if they associated the cleaning with a real person, they would take more care. They bloody well should do, anyway.

These guests had clearly had a few picnics and there were several teaspoons and forks missing, plus a sharp knife. There was also an extra item – one of the corkscrews Edie and the other staff used at the bar. The guests must have borrowed it, or more likely swiped it when someone inadvertently left it on the counter rather than putting it away. Edie tucked it into her pocket to take back later.

Despite her disaffection, for the first time ever she was disappointed when she'd finished cleaning for the day. Disappointment that was born out of the fact that she now had to confront her worries and do something about them. During the night, she had dismissed the police as useless – or worse. But now it was day time and the sun was shining so brightly, she considered it once more. The problem was that she still had little more than conjecture and suspicion to convince them with, plus her own sixth sense that all was not well. None of that would win over an officer of the law.

On the other hand, they were precisely that – officers of the law – and should get involved if there were potential infringements of said law going on. Unless they were in on the wrong-doing, taking backhanders or whatever ... Edie wanted to scream out loud. It was all just going round and round with no end and no beginning and certainly no resolution.

Locking the door on her final cabana, Edie stepped out into the glare. The brightness of the day, the fresh breeze that was blowing, the cheery shouts of children that came drifting up from plunge pools and the beach, somehow coloured her fears as unfounded and overblown. It seemed impossible that there could be darkness amidst such an abundance of sunshine. Suddenly, she knew what to do. The truth was most likely there, right in front of her – she just had to ask for it.

From her room, she collected a bottle of vodka and a net of oranges. As far as she knew, Vuk was on the resort so she'd go to his cabin on the pretext of a lovely afternoon drink and, once he was nice and relaxed and in a good mood, she'd bring up the subject of the hut on the hill. Just discuss it, all casual-like, giving no hint of any untoward notions about what was happening there, merely innocently stating the facts so that he could no longer fob her off with stories about Roma. She'd give him the chance to come up with some reasonable, believable explanation and see what transpired. Then, once that was done she could take the final decision about whether to go back to the police or not.

She used the key she'd taken on her last visit to get into Vuk's cabin. He'd left the air conditioning on, something the resort asked guests not to do, and the temperature was beautiful. Edie waved the front of her T-shirt up and down a few times to aid the cooling effect. The heat outside was punishing. Vuk's cabin was as bare and bland as ever. It lacked colour, and soft things, was all hard edges and white surfaces. In the past, Edie had sometimes amused herself by imagining what feminine touches she could bring to it to make it more homely. Now she laughed at herself for her naivety. Vuk couldn't care less about his living quarters – or her – and so why should she? His recent, rather transparent, pretences at showing affection for her were proof of his dissemblance.

Edie roved the kitchen, pulling out drawers and opening cupboards until she found a juicer and a knife to cut the oranges. She squeezed them and poured generous slugs of vodka into two glasses. Searching for ice, she found the top two drawers of the freezer empty but the bottom one contained two bags of cubes. Edie plunged her hand into the nearest bag, grappling around trying to secure a handful. As she did so, the bag slipped to the side, revealing a plastic container buried beneath it. Inside the container was a pile of small, dark red notebooks and some things that looked like credit cards or driving licences.

Edie's heart missed a beat. She dropped the ice, her hand already numb with cold. She knew she shouldn't pry, just as one knows not to open someone else's mail or read their diary but she couldn't stop herself. She picked up the plastic container, held it firm against her body and took off the lid. Inside, individually wrapped in thin plastic bags, were the credit cards. But they were, in fact, ID cards. Vuk seemed to have an awful lot of them. Or rather, an awful lot of someone else's. The woman who stared sightlessly out of the picture of the top one was young and beautiful, and wearing a headscarf. The notebooks were in fact passports. The first was German. Edie opened it. The photo inside was of a man. He bore no resemblance to Vuk.

Edie could almost hear her brain whirring into action, slowly and creakily, trying to comprehend what she was seeing and make some kind of sense out of it. She leafed through the other four passports and ID cards. None of them were Vuk's. An utter silence descended on the small kitchen in the bare cabin. Time seemed to stand still.

A high-pitched, screeching sound rent the air and reverberated around the cabin walls. Edie's heart leapt and juddered, beating wildly, incoherently, and she broke into a cold sweat.

The beat of flapping wings brought her to her sense. It was just a bird, squawking on the terrace outside. But still she stood, motionless, listening.

Vuk could arrive at any time. A lightning flash of terror slithered through her bowels. She slipped the first card she had picked up into her shorts pocket, fastened the lid back onto the container and busied herself gathering up a fresh handful of ice, humming light-heartedly all the while, as if nothing untoward had gone on at all. She slammed the freezer drawer closed, then kicked shut the door whilst already leaning towards the jug on the side into which she threw the ice. The glugging of the juice as she poured it helped to slow her thumping heart.

And then something made her stop pouring; put the jug back down. The saliva gathered at the back of her throat and icicles of fear, as cold as the cubes in the jug, crept through her veins. She turned to the front door. It was tight shut. There was no one there. She breathed hard and fast, struggling to quell the inexplicable thud of foreboding that was engulfing her. Goosebumps prickled her flesh. Dread enveloped her like a shroud.

She could not see anyone. But she was definitely not alone.

Very, very slowly, her heart in her mouth, her legs weak and shaky, she turned towards the French windows which had been firmly shut on her arrival. They were wide open.

THIRTY

Edie

'Edie.'

She screamed and jumped out of her skin, her hand clapped to her mouth, sweat breaking out on her neck and back and under her breasts despite the air con. Vuk emerged from where he had been partially hidden by the edge of the curtain. He crossed the threshold, a strange half-smile on his face. As Edie recovered from the shock and the turbulence of her mind began to settle, she was able to inwardly name Vuk's expression. It was mocking.

'Hi, Vuk.' She just about managed to make the sounds come out in a way that approximated normal. She had no idea how long he had been there. Whether he had seen her examining the contents of the freezer.

'Are you okay?' His steady gaze was unnerving. He couldn't have been watching her, surely she'd have heard him open the French windows?

'Why are you staring at me like that?' She laughed to make light of it, turn it into a joke. 'Have I got dirt on my face or something?'

Vuk shut the French windows, turned the key in the lock and put it in his pocket. He took a few paces towards her across the sparsely furnished room, his footsteps echoing against the tiles. 'You look very pretty, as always,' he said, stopping a metre or so away from her. And then added, abruptly, 'I wasn't expecting you. You really should let me know when you are coming to visit. I thought I made that clear last time.'

Edie skipped to the tall cupboard where the few glasses that Vuk possessed were kept. 'It was such a hot day and I thought, I know what Vuk would like right now. He'd like a nice, long vodka and orange.' She gurned at him like a geeky sixteen-year-old.

'So – I came to give you one. And the drink.' She giggled. Out of the corner of her eye she could see that Vuk did not crack so much as a hint of a smile.

She took the glasses to the table and put them down.

'Sit,' she gestured.

Vuk didn't move. Edie paused, her resolve momentarily deserting her. He was going to challenge her about what she'd found and she didn't know whether to 'fess up or deny it. She picked up one of the glasses and drank heftily. Dutch courage; it couldn't make things any worse.

'You know I don't drink during working hours.' Vuk's tone was even, displaying no emotion.

'Well, maybe you should start.' Edie smirked playfully. 'It's fun!' She took another slug of her drink, then licked her lips seductively. Distraction was the only strategy she could think of. She went over to him and ran her hands over his torso. If she behaved exactly as she normally would, perhaps he wouldn't suspect anything.

Vuk pushed her away. 'Edie, I don't have time for this now. What did you come here for?'

Edie could feel the ID card in her pocket, flat and stiff behind the corkscrew that she'd forgotten to take back to the bar. 'I came for you, as I already told you. But if you're not up for it …' she wandered airily towards the window and looked outside. '… I'm sure I can find something else to do. Or perhaps I should say "someone".'

He needed to believe she was as vapid and lustful as she made herself out to be.

Vuk shrugged. He went over to the counter where the coffee maker sat and turned it on, opened the cupboard to retrieve the coffee, took a spoon out of a drawer. Then stopped, poised to pour the grounds into the filter paper. 'How did you get in?'

'I took a key last time I was here. Don't you remember?'

Edie shoved her hands into her pockets. Her right hand closed around the card and corkscrew. She had to get out without him seeing what she had with her. She didn't even know why she'd taken the card now but she couldn't confess to the theft.

'Anyway, I know where I'm not wanted. I'll see you later, perhaps.'

Vuk didn't seem to be listening. The coffee machine gurgled and spluttered into life.

'Bye then.' Edie glided nonchalantly through the sterile room to the French windows. She was glad she hadn't had any more of the vodka. The idea that she might get the truth out of Vuk evaporated in all its absurdity in the same way the ridiculous notions she had once had of improving his living quarters with interior decoration had done. She tried the door. Remembered that she had watched Vuk lock it.

'Wait.'

She turned and stopped, not going towards him.

'Come back.' His voice was low, not raised at all, but what he had said was still an order not a request.

She could refuse to obey, walk on, walk away, try to get to the front door instead. But that would look suspicious; she never walked away from Vuk. If she went back to him, though

– what would she say if he challenged her? Searched her pockets? Demanded to know how long she had been in the cabin without him, and what she had been doing?

Slowly, she returned to him, her flip-flops slapping lazily against her heels. She moved as provocatively as she could, all swaying hips and thrusting tits. Best if he believed her mind was empty of anything but her fixation on him. She sat down and watched as he drank the vodka, seeming to have forgotten both about the percolating coffee and the fact that he didn't do daytime drinking. Draining his glass, he handed the other to her.

'Aren't you joining me? You made it, after all.'

She took a sip, filling her mouth with the not quite melted ice cubes to make it look as if she had drunk more than she had. She needed to keep a clear head.

'Get undressed.'

Vuk's face was impassive as he stared at her.

The card in her pocket felt huge and conspicuous. If she dropped her shorts to the floor it might fall out. And anyway the thought of having sex with him left her feeling cold in a way she could never have imagined it would.

'I just need the loo. Back in a mo.'

Fleeing to the bathroom, she locked herself in. Her eyes fell on the window. She could climb out and run away, use it for escape the same way she had used it for ingress only a few days ago. She reached up to open it, but no matter how hard she wrenched on the handle, it did not budge. Vuk had locked it and removed the key.

Edie sat on the toilet and peed, playing for time, her mind racing.

A sharp knock on the door made her start, her heart skipping a beat.

'Edie, what are you doing?'

She flushed the toilet. She waited until the cistern had

emptied and she had heard the last gurgling sounds of it refilling itself. Fuck. This was not a good idea. Keeping Vuk waiting like this would only wind him up, make him angry and more likely to question her about what she had been doing.

Slowly, she opened the door. Her way was completely blocked by Vuk's huge frame, filling the threshold. Edie suppressed a shriek of shock and surprise. Before she had time to think or move, his hands were on her shorts waistband, undoing the button, unzipping the zip. They dropped to the ground, as Edie tried to stick her toes high in the air to break their fall and protect her phone in the back pocket.

Edie felt as if she were watching from a distance as Vuk undressed her. Trancelike, she observed him removing her knickers, her bra and her top. The stirrings of physical desire that she had always felt towards him fought with the revulsion she was beginning to feel against someone she was sure was lying to her and had been for some time. She thought of Laura. The best chance she had of getting to the bottom of the secrets that were mounting up around her disappearance was to keep Vuk on side, give nothing away.

Vuk led her into the bedroom, pushed her onto the bed and immediately entered her, thrusting into her so violently that she gave a small, involuntary moan. She had not even had time to protest, to say she wasn't in the mood.

'Is something the matter, pretty one?' Vuk's voice rasped in her ear, his breath hot and damp. 'You said you only came for me. So that's what you're getting.'

His hands clasped her head, fingers twisting uncomfortably through her hair. Her scalp burnt. She tried to look into his eyes, as if by doing that she might be able to read his mind. But he kept them closed.

He had had a haircut and his thick, dark hair was bordered by a line of freshly exposed, paler skin. It made him look younger, less intimidating; a look that belied what Edie was increasingly beginning to believe.

He came, grunted something incomprehensible and jumped up, his huge bare feet landing on the tiled floor with a loud slap. He disappeared into the bathroom. Trepidation gnawed at Edie's stomach. Her clothes were in there, her phone. The corkscrew in her pocket, and the fake ID card. Please don't find it, she pleaded internally.

A sudden buzzing noise and vibration amongst the tumbled bed covers indicated a call to Vuk's phone. Edie leant over and picked it up. The message showed a number but no name and was written in Greek. She could make neither head nor tail of it. She tossed the phone back on the bed covers. Immediately, it buzzed once more. Another message had come through. Edie picked it back up again, but this time she continued to stare, transfixed, at the screen. She could not decipher the words but she recognised the number, she was sure. She read it out to herself in her head, over and again. Slowly, it dawned on her. She needed her phone to check her theory.

She tried the bathroom door. Locked.

'Sorry,' she called out, gaily. 'Just need the loo when you're done.' Vuk would wonder what was wrong with her bladder, going to the toilet so often, but who cared. What did matter was whether he was looking through her stuff.

She bent down to peek through the keyhole. The bathroom was hazy with steam through which she could see nothing at all.

The smack on her head sent her flying backwards onto the bed. Pain brought tears to her eyes and set stars dancing before them. For a moment she wasn't sure exactly what had happened and then, as the emergent Vuk stood before her, his rippling torso sprinkled with water droplets that shone like crystal in the light that shafted through the window, she realised that she had been in the way when he had opened the bathroom door, her forehead smashed by the door knob.

Fighting the searing agony, she darted between Vuk and the door jamb and sped into the bathroom, pulling the door hurriedly shut behind her. She studied the paltry pile of garments huddled on the tiled floor. Was they all as she had left them? She couldn't recall.

She picked up her bra. Her phone was underneath; silent, darkened screen reflecting the single ceiling light. It had been in her pocket, she was sure, unless it had fallen out. She put on her underwear and T-shirt. Nausea rose in her stomach and into her throat as she reached for her shorts. They felt light and insubstantial. She pushed her hand into the pocket. The corkscrew was there. A piece of scrap paper and a hair band, wedged right in the corner. But no ID card.

Edie sank onto the toilet seat and put her head in her hands. He'd found it and taken it. He had known it was there. Somehow, he had got the French windows open without her hearing and stood there watching her, had seen her rummaging in the freezer, opening the container, examining the contents. Removing the forgery – for that was surely what it was – and secreting it in her pocket.

Fuck! *Fuck, fuck, fuck.*

She remembered the text message she'd just seen and the number. Hurriedly, she entered her pass code into her phone. She scrolled down the messages to the ones sent by Laura. The number of the second one she did not recognise. But the first one – as she had thought, it was the number that had just appeared on Vuk's phone. There was only one conclusion to come to. Vuk had some connection with the person who had sent one of the texts that purported to be from Laura. She stared at the screen, lost in thought.

The door creaked slowly open. She'd forgotten to lock it. Vuk's two huge feet appeared before her. Her stomach turned over again as she raised her eyes to his. He smiled. There was a long pause. Edie had lost the power of speech, physically couldn't make her mouth work.

'It must be something interesting.' He indicated towards the mobile in her hand. 'Another boyfriend, maybe.'

Soundlessly, Edie shook her head. She gulped.

'No,' she blurted out, too fast and too loud. 'No. Ha, ha.' She forced herself to regulate her voice, to make it sound light and breezy as a spring day.

'You know you're the only one for me, honey.' She stood up. He was right in front of her, blocking her way. All she could see was the hair on his chest and tanned skin beneath.

She began to whistle, as if that would somehow lighten the atmosphere. She had always been proud of the fact that she could whistle and Laura couldn't. Hours and hours of practice as a child had perfected her technique. Greensleeves was her best number, once she'd even recorded it and used it as the ring tone on her phone. Such trivialities seemed light years away now.

Vuk's phone rang, loud and insistent.

'Better get that,' Edie cried out, making as if to move forward even though there was absolutely nowhere she could go with the bulk of Vuk between her and the door. There was a heart-stopping moment of silence in between rings. And then Vuk reeled around and into the bedroom, scooping up his phone and barking into it.

Edie seized her chance and fled.

THIRTY-ONE

Edie

Edie's feet were sore by the time she reached her room; she'd left her flip-flops behind in her rush to get away. The ground was hot, and although it looked smooth it was in fact covered in a myriad of tiny stones, sticks and twigs that were sharp as thorns. She delved under the bed to find her trainers, untouched since she had got there, put them on, snatched up the scooter key and was outside again in moments. She was sure she was being followed, constantly felt the ominous presence of someone behind, just beyond her shoulder. She couldn't stop to look. If someone was after her, wanted to murder her for what she now knew, they'd have to catch her first.

Now, at last, she had 'evidence' of a 'crime'; enough for the police to have to take notice of her, to take her seriously, whether it had anything to do with Laura or not. Surely this they couldn't overlook? And really – corruption? Edie suddenly doubted it. Vuk had just been trying to put her off the scent, to stop her doing what he dreaded. But getting the sodding evidence of the sodding crime had taken too long and she might not make it to the police station before it closed for the day.

The heat was deadening, a blanket that enveloped and stifled, making it hard to see, to think. The olive trees were still as stone, not the slightest hint of a breeze ruffling their silver-grey leaves. Edie wanted to shake off the suffocating pressure that weighed down on her, the unfathomable secrets that surrounded and enmeshed her. There seemed little option now but to think Vuk, amidst all the dodgy goings-on, was involved with the disappearance of Laura, that he was neither Edie's saviour nor her protector but her enemy, along with everyone else.

He'd tripped her at the gorge, she was sure now, but of course set it up so no one could think it anything other than an accident, making sure that Zayn had seen, and commented on, her trailing Converse shoelace. She was sure Zayn was in on it all as well as the two of them had sandwiched her between them – but Zayn must have been the one to grab her arm and pull her back, so that didn't make sense. *Shit!* She couldn't make head or tail of it. Perhaps Zayn just hadn't had the nerve to see Vuk's plan through?

The scooter was red hot. Its cheap plastic seat burned her thighs when she climbed onto it. Ivana had had the fault fixed for her; she hadn't bothered to find out what had been the problem, but it was back up and running now. She backed out of her improvised parking place and started the engine. It was almost out of fuel. She must fill up somewhere but she'd do that after the police station. The rush of wind as she sped down the track that joined the tarmac road out of the resort sent her hair flying around her face, sticking to her clammy cheeks and forehead. She'd forgotten her helmet but she wasn't going to go back for it.

She arrived, sweating and flustered, at the police station in town at ten past six. The doors were firmly locked. *Fuck!* At night time, responsibility for law and order was transferred to a much bigger station in the large town about half an hour down the coast. Should she go there? Perhaps, but first she needed fuel.

She'd take the long route, stopping at a garage on the way, and think it through whilst riding. Some head space in the serene beauty of the bay might help her see straight, calm her down a bit. Remounting the scooter and checking the gauge, she reckoned she'd have just enough petrol for this plan to work.

It didn't matter how many times she traversed the narrow road that hugged the seashore bend for bend, inlet for inlet, she always saw things she'd never noticed before, and this evening was just the same, despite her frazzled state of mind. Another ruin, ripe for renovation, ivy and vines clinging to the crumbling walls and covering the windows, inside which some fairytale princess might languish. A tiny chapel nestled between houses, where sea-faring families would have prayed and sung for their captain's safe return. It was all enchanting, and made so much more so in contrast to the evil that Edie felt was lurking on the resort.

This evening, the old stone houses basked in the last rays of the sun and the road was quiet, most people still seeking refuge from the heat inside. Soon the sun would disappear behind the mountains, giving welcome relief and bringing everyone forth. Whole families would jump into the water and stay there, bobbing up and down, chatting and joking just as if they were sitting around a table, sometimes for hours at a time.

How Edie wished she were one of those people now, enjoying the summer, worries and cares set aside. She wasn't cut out to be an adventurer, still less a hero. She didn't want to uncover crime or detect misdeeds. All she had ever wanted was to find Laura.

She took the corner where the hidden driveway led up to some Russian oligarch's lair, and then sped up where the road straightened out for a few metres. There was a car behind her that had been there since she'd left town, waiting for a chance to overtake in a patient manner that was uncharacteristic in these parts. Must be an unusually timid tourist. Edie pulled as far over to the right as she dared, given that there was no wall separating sea from road, and decelerated. The car did not pass. Her mirrors, small and smudged with a zillion sweaty fingerprints, did not allow her much of a view. All she could see was a small, dark coloured vehicle, headlights on as was the law here at any time of day or night. The car dropped back a bit. Definitely an exceedingly cautious vacationer. There were those who were too intimidated by the narrow winding road that was flanked on one side by the water and the other by houses and a deep, narrow drainage canal to ever overtake anything, even a tiny 500CC scooter. She sped up again. The car increased its speed, also.

Without indicating, Edie veered suddenly to the right, into a small parking spot between a *konoba* restaurant and a rusty vintage camper van. In one almost seamless motion she cut the engine, got off the scooter and walked to the edge of the concrete pier. Standing facing the water, she angled her body so that she could still see the road. She waited for the black car to sweep by. It didn't.

Slowly, she turned her body in a full circle. The car, engine idling, had pulled up behind the scooter. Edie couldn't see if there was anyone inside but the headlamps were off, indicating it was intending to stay awhile.

Just going slowly because they were looking for somewhere for dinner, Edie reassured herself. It didn't work. Her brain froze. So much for thinking things through. Fear had blinded her ability to think anything. She couldn't get back on the scooter because the car was blocking it. If she tried to walk anywhere, she could be followed. Looking out over the mirror-flat water, it seemed to represent the only option. Slipping out of her clothes and shoes, she piled them in a heap by the iron steps and then descended gracefully into the bay. Diving beneath the surface, she swam far out from the shore and surfaced to see, at a distance, the waiter putting a match to the candles on the tables of the rapidly busying restaurant. The normality of the action made her want to cry.

Further down the bay were two huge cruise ships which, with all their lights ablaze, resembled giant glowing water beetles. Behind them, the illuminated walls of the old town were like a daisy chain that had been casually dropped onto the precipitous hillside. And on the waterside, she could no longer make out the squat shape of the black car. Thank God for that. It had probably just been tourists stopping to admire the view, after all. She was going crazy with all the stress. Anyway, the car was gone, thank goodness, and it was safe to get out of the water.

Back on land and dripping wet, Edie helped herself to a handful of paper napkins from a dispenser on the table nearest to her and mopped herself down a bit. She put her shorts and T-shirt back on over her sodden bikini. Hunger made her stomach growl but she ignored it. The scooter fuel dial didn't seem to have changed much since she left the resort but Edie knew it was unreliable and often inaccurate. It would probably just about get her to the garage. She hoped so, anyway. She manoeuvred it backwards, carefully avoiding the tree trunk, waste bin, signpost and camper van. She started the engine, flicked on the lights and set off.

Focusing on navigating the increasingly busy road, filling up with evening shoppers and diners, Edie did not notice exactly when the black car appeared behind her again. Several vehicles sped past, and even the bus, driver honking the horn at full volume, skilfully negotiating the narrow road whilst also talking on his mobile phone. But the black car stayed right behind.

Edie slowed down. There were no turn-offs or cut-throughs to go for – any road leading to the left went back at most four or five blocks and then reached a dead end, further progress impeded by the small hurdle of a massive mountain. She could take such a turn, and see if the black car followed her – but if it did, what then? She'd be blocked in front and behind and have no option but to face a confrontation with whoever was inside. The number plate was local; it could be a resident's car or a hire car, there was no way of knowing. A steely chill of fear slithered through Edie's stomach and into her bowels.

She slammed on the brakes. Lost in her thoughts, she had almost missed seeing the Audi in front slowing to a standstill, hugging the bay side to allow room for an enormous German tour coach coming from the other direction to get by.

The force of her sudden stop sent the little scooter shuddering and Edie almost went over the handlebars. Once recovered, she attempted to use the mirrors, protruding like antennae from the handlebars, to examine the reflection of the black car. But all she could see was the blinding light of its headlamps.

A subtle noise, just discernible above the engine of the tour bus as it eased its way between the row of houses and the queuing vehicles, sent a spike of adrenalin racing through Edie's veins. Without her helmet, small sounds that would otherwise have been obscured were audible. It was the soft sound of an engine cutting out. Straight after, Edie heard the solid clunk of a car door opening and then shutting; it came from behind her on her left, and was immediately followed by an identical sound coming from her right.

Edie was off the scooter and across the road in the slipstream of the coach in seconds. She heard the dull thud of the scooter falling to the ground and heavy footsteps skidding in the sandy gravel that fringed the tarmac by the water's edge. And then the pace of the footsteps quickened.

She ran.

***

There was a small, roughly paved track straight ahead of her that led steeply uphill; Edie followed it. At first, it was fairly wide but it quickly narrowed to nothing more than a footpath, thickly overgrown with brambles and dark from the scrubby trees that closed in overhead. Beneath her feet, a dense carpet of dead brown leaves crunched as she ran. It was impossible to go quietly. She had no idea what it was that she was running from but was driven on by the dead weight of cold fear in her belly. Pushing her way through the ever-thickening undergrowth, branches whipping in her face, thorns tearing the skin on her bare arms, she did not dare pause for even a second to find out if she could hear the sound of footsteps behind her.

A dog barked right next to her and she jumped out of her skin. It was the other side of a fence, in the garden she was passing, but it made her exact position even more obvious to any pursuer, the way it was following her and barking its stupid head off. The path reached a turning, where she could either go on up or take a left. She went left. It was only just wide enough now to put one foot in front of the other and Edie had no way of knowing if it would lead anywhere. The hillsides that rose so precipitously from the bay were full of ancient rights of way that ran behind houses and through gardens. But some of them had been blocked off, and some led only to boundary walls and rainwater gullies that were too small for a person to get through. There was no guarantee that she would reach another access road.

She was breathing so heavily, her heart beating so fast, that she could no longer hear anything but the blood pounding in her head. At last she left the idiotic hound behind, thwarted in its attempts to track her by the limits of its enclosure. The footpath was overgrown, the grasses taller than her thighs and she couldn't see where she was putting her feet. Someone had told her there were poisonous snakes in the hills but that was the least of her worries. Pausing to disentangle herself from a branch that had got caught in the belt holder of her shorts, she listened hard, straining her ears for any sound that might reveal how close her pursuers were. All her senses were heightened. The wild mint that grew in abundance had a pungency to its scent that she had never noticed before and seemed to fill the air all around her, and the tugs on her skin from the spikes and thorns were as sharp as pinpricks. From a terrace lower down the hillside the chatter of voices floated up, reminding her that all around her lay normality. She was trying to calm herself with that thought when she heard it.

The sharp, unmistakeable sound of a stick snapping followed by a muffled curse.

Edie's breath caught in her throat as panic almost made her cry out. She fled on, stumbling and tripping on the undergrowth but heedless of the danger of a broken ankle or a branch in the eye. The path opened out again; thank heaven, it had led to another access road, a wider one this time that led up to the houses that were third, fourth and fifth row back from the sea. The road was paved and smooth, radiating the heat from the day. Edie looked frantically around her, not sure whether to go on up the hill and hide or to run down towards the sea and hope she would reach the main drag before her pursuers reached her. Down there would be people and cars and the ordinary hustle and bustle of a summer evening that would make all of this horror go away.

She heard heavy breathing behind her. Running down the road would put her in plain sight; she could not do that. Seeing a tiny lean-to shed that probably once housed chickens, she ducked behind it and under the makeshift corrugated iron roof, crouching in the dust and shrivelled chicken droppings within, desperately trying to calm her breathing so that it would not be audible.

She waited. Nothing. She sank down further onto her haunches, resting her back against the brick wall and letting her head fall forwards as she forced herself to breathe long, deep and slow. She was pouring with sweat and raging thirst burned in her throat. She became conscious of pain biting at her arms and legs and looked down. It was dark now, but the moon was full, and there was enough light filtering through the gaps between the sheets of iron that made up the roof to see bloody marks where the brambles had torn at her flesh.

A noise sent a thrill of fear rippling down her spine. But it was just a car, rumbling past her hideaway on its way down to the road. After that, nothing.

Edie wasn't sure how long she stayed scrunched up in the chicken shed. Eventually, she realised that she would either have to stay there forever or at some point venture out. Cautiously, she crawled to the hole in the wall that served as a doorway. She stopped there, listening intently. She could hear nothing. Her strategy was simple; burst out, get to the paved road and hare downhill as fast as her legs could carry her. This would give her the advantage of surprise; whoever was waiting for her, if they were still there, would have to try to follow at the same pace.

Her plan went well. At last, she bolted out of the chicken coop so quickly that a couple of small boys cycling past almost came off their bikes, so severely did they swerve and sway at the sight of her. There was no one else around. No one lying in wait. Edie could feel her T-shirt sticking to her back and her feet sliding around inside her sweat soaked trainers. Her hair was plastered to her cheeks and neck and her denim shorts rubbed against her thighs as she raced on. She burst out of the access road right into the stream of traffic coming from town. Brakes screeched and lights flashed as she stopped, not sure where she was or what was going on. Her head spun and she thought she would be sick.

A car door opened.

Shit, she thought, *they've got me. I've walked straight into their hands. Whoever 'they' are.* Staring wildly and futilely around her, she could not make her legs move.

A voice shouted her name.

'Edie!'

She was done for.

THIRTY-TWO

Edie

Edie's first instinct was to run, again, run to the sea and jump in and swim out into the bay where the currents would carry her to the open water and she would be away from all of this nonsense and all of the things that were happening that she didn't understand.

But she didn't run. She stood stock still, a rabbit in the headlamps, not knowing where to look but seeing nothing anyway, blinded by terror.

'Edie.' The voice again, that she was sure she recognised but couldn't place right now.

'What on earth are you doing? What's happened?'

It was Patrick.

Relief, confusion and embarrassment coursed through her veins. She couldn't think of anything to say, just stood there, aware of her own bedraggled state, mute.

'You're covered in scratches, blood and bits of someone's garden.'

Edie shook her head and tried again to reply. 'I don't know. Someone's – people – chasing me ...' she stuttered, knowing she was not making any sense but not sure what sense there was to make.

'Jump in.' Patrick gently took Edie's arm and led her to the car. 'We're holding up all the traffic.'

'Oh n-no,' she stammered, suddenly immobilised beside the passenger door, subsumed by mistrust and misgivings. Patrick didn't seem as if he could be mixed up in what was going on – he appeared to be a genuine holiday-maker – but on the other hand, he'd given her a veiled warning on the canyon trip that indicated he knew more than he was letting on. She had to be careful, take no risks with who to trust. 'No – I need to … to find the scooter. I can't just leave it here!'

Patrick pursed his lips and frowned. 'I don't think you should be in control of a moving vehicle, the state you're in. I'll arrange its collection.'

Edie still didn't move. Patrick waved on the cars that had accumulated behind his. He patted her back as if she were one of his children. The gesture seemed so normal, and genuine, that she felt some of the tension that had built up inside her during the chase dissipate.

'Get in the car, Edie. You're OK now. You're safe.'

She wasn't, and she knew it. But it seemed more likely than not that Patrick's car was a sanctuary, if only temporary. She bent down and climbed into the passenger seat. It was about ten minutes before she had relaxed enough to engage in a conversation.

'So what, or who, are you running away from, Edie? What's going on?'

Edie bit her lip and half-closed her eyes.

'I don't know. I thought someone was following me.'

Patrick tutted loudly, but kept his eyes firmly on the road ahead. Edie found it was easier to talk when someone wasn't looking at you.

'A car – it tailed me from the town, stopped when I stopped. When I ran, someone chased me.'

'A bloke? Some kind of sexual harassment?'

Edie almost laughed. But it wasn't funny.

'No. No, nothing like that.'

'Then what? You seem absolutely terrified, not to mention looking as if you've been dragged through a hedge backwards.'

Edie stared blankly out of the window. They had rounded the end of the bay now and were on the fast road that led to the marina where she and Laura had met the Russian boys. Such halcyon, carefree days seemed a lifetime away.

'Edie.' Patrick's voice cut through her thoughts as they sped past the entrance to the dockside. Edie breathed a sigh of relief; she didn't want to go there now or possibly ever again. 'I'm going to stop at that place in the village – you know, the one next to the fire station.'

Edie nodded. The fire station was like something out of Camberwick Green – two or three antiquated fire engines, not a firefighter to be seen.

'And you're going to tell me all about it.'

Edie did her best to explain the events of the evening to Patrick over a restorative Coca-cola and spinach pastry. She did trust him, she realised after all. He seemed firm and solid, a gentleman, and completely honest in a way that Vuk and Vlad certainly didn't. As for Zayn – Edie still couldn't believe he was up to no good but all the evidence pointed to the contrary. Even if she hadn't been a good judge of character in the past, she was sure she was getting better and she thought Patrick was all right. What he thought of her was another matter.

'You think I'm crazy, don't you?'

Patrick, who had listened patiently throughout, shook his head. 'No. I think you're overwrought and overtired.' He led her back to the car.

As they entered the resort gates, Edie suddenly thought of something. 'What were you out and about for, all on your own? Where are the family?'

Patrick flashed her a wry smile. 'I was on a mission to get takeaway pizzas from the place in town. But it was closed. So I decided to try the one at the marina.'

He glanced at Edie as he negotiated the turning up to his cabana.

'I sent Debs a text once I found you to say I wasn't going to come up with the goods.'

'I'm really sorry.' Edie wanted to cry. The thought of the children deprived of their dinner because of her felt like the last straw. 'What will they eat now?'

Patrick laughed gently. 'Suppertime was ages ago. Debs will have cooked them some pasta.'

'Will she be cross with you?'

Patrick drew into his parking space, pulled on the handbrake and cut the engine. 'Favours withdrawn for a week or so, probably.'

Now Edie did cry, big fat soft tears coursing down her cheeks. Their saltiness stung her scratches and grazes.

Patrick reached out a hand and squeezed hers, clenched together as they were on her lap.

'I was only kidding, Edie. And the children will survive without pizza. Debs probably let them have fizzy drinks or something to make up for it.'

He seemed worried, but not about his offspring or their sugar intake.

'Don't cry, Edie.' He patted her awkwardly, his plump fingers incongruous on her slim, lithe forearm. 'You're under ... you seem very stressed and ... I'm wondering if you should ...'

'I should what?' The thunderous noise of her own voice took Edie by surprise. 'Everyone likes to tell me what I should do, think, feel, say ... and it's all bullshit!'

She leapt out of the car. Patrick followed her. He had rounded the bonnet and was facing her before she had a chance to move. She stood there, trembling.

'Whatever the matter is, whatever's going on – you can trust me, Edie.'

The tears were now a flood, so thick and free-flowing Edie was almost blinded.

Patrick came up close and put his arms around her. He pulled her towards him in a deep hug.

By the time he released her, she'd stopped crying.

'I think you should get some sleep. Why don't you come back to our cabana; you could crash on the sofabed? A good night's rest will give you some perspective on all of this.'

Edie smiled but shook her head. 'No. Thank you – but no. I want to be on my own for bit.'

Patrick's look of concern deepened but he didn't insist. 'OK. So meet me at the restaurant for breakfast at 7am. I'm always the first one there; the kids are early risers. We can talk it all through then.'

Edie sniffed, loudly.

'Is that a yes?'

She gave a reluctant smile. 'All right.'

'Would you like me to walk you to your room?'

Edie shook her head, violently. 'Oh no. I'll be fine.' She turned on her heel and made off into the olive grove. 'See you tomorrow.'

She would go back to her room, but she wasn't going to bed. That was impossible; she doubted she'd ever get a wink of sleep on the resort ever again. In her tired and fuddled brain, a plan was forming and she needed to be on her own to put it into action.

Sitting on the bed in her room, the door firmly locked, Edie pulled her legs up in front of her and rested her back against the wall. She could feel the bits of grass and seed heads and twigs that she had encountered on her evening escapade scratching her skin but couldn't be bothered to do anything about it. Her thoughts revolved around the hut on the hillside, the boat and Vuk's frequent sailing trips, which so often seemed to last longer and occur more frequently and at different times than the tourist excursions he purported to be on. None of it made sense.

A burning feeling in her stomach reminded Edie that she was starving despite the snack she'd had with Patrick. She dug around the shelf by her bed and found a half-empty packet of crackers. Absentmindedly, she finished them off, chewing slowly at first and gradually speeding up until she got to the last one, which she crammed into her mouth in one go. She gulped down water from a bottle that was rolling around under the bed and then got up and stood looking at herself in the mirror, steeling herself for what she knew she must do.

Locking the door behind her, she hid the key under a loose board on the veranda. It would be safer there than where she was going.

***

It was quiet at the resort's tiny marina. The motorboats were lined up, ready for the next day's business. The jet skis pulled gently against their moorings, and the dinghies that were used for the sailing lessons bobbed serenely up and down, naked masts reaching into the star-studded night. Further out, where the water was deeper, lay the yacht *Radomira*, her name painted in blue on her elegant white flanks. She gleamed in the starlight, but Edie couldn't make out any light coming from on board. She seemed deserted.

Edie slipped along the pontoon that reached furthest into the water. She looked down at herself, at her shorts and sleeveless T-shirt, under which she was still wearing a bikini. She decided not to jettison her clothes; even if sodden, they seemed necessary to deal with whatever it was that might confront her. She left just her shoes behind, secreted behind the rough planking at the edge of the walkway.

Once in the water, it was no distance at all to reach the *Radomira*. The yacht hardly moved as Edie gripped hold of the ladder, pulled her slight body onto the bottom rung and cautiously climbed upwards. On deck, everything was quiet and still. There was no sign of anyone. The decks were clean, the lounging cushions stored away to keep them from the dew, the sun awnings folded back so that every piece of polished metal reflected the glimmering stars.

Edie crept forwards, towards the door that led into the cabin. She had only been on the yacht once before, not long after she had arrived, when Zayn was still trying to impress her and had taken her out on it for a sunset sail. Vlad must have been in a very good mood to allow it, Edie thought now. She had been so green then, so naive that, not knowing anything about all these new people, she had been quite taken in by how swish it all was. Before long, the place had seduced her. And so had Vuk.

A tiny breeze rippled across the water. Edie shivered as she tried the cabin door. It was locked. Of course it was. Why had she imagined that she would just be able to walk straight in? It wasn't going to be that easy.

Instinctively, she ran her hand along the ledge at the top of the door. But there was nothing there, no secret hiding place for a spare key. Edie was pretty sure that there was no other way into the living quarters of the yacht, but still she climbed up to the walkway that ran between the cabin and the safety rails to give access to the front deck. The boat's design meant that here the cabin roof extended only a couple of feet proud of the walkway. There were skylights in the roof but Edie was sure they would be fixed closed and further investigation, kneeling on the slippery fibreglass, proved her supposition right. Crouching down and peering through into the cabin, she ran her fingers around the edge of the square of glass above the kitchen area. There was absolutely no seam, no

279

possible place to prise it open. This was a serious yacht, ocean-going, designed for all sea and weather conditions.

Edie sat back on her heels and sank into deep contemplation. Thinking about it like this, it was obvious. This yacht was far too luxurious, specialised, above all *expensive*, for the resort's means. However successful, however popular, the rental of a few holiday cabanas or the sale of bottles of beer and tomato salads could not fund such a purchase and any old boat would have done for the trips Vlad advertised to hidden coves, caves and grottoes.

There had to be another reason for the *Radomira*.

THIRTY-THREE

Edie

The sudden motion of the yacht on a heightened swell shocked Edie to her senses. She realised how acutely visible she was, here on the roof, and scuttled crab-like down to the walkway on the seaward side. She stayed in a crouching position until her heart had stopped racing and her breathing slowed to something approaching normal. Then she raised her head and peered towards the shore. Making steady progress across the water towards her – or rather, towards the *Radomira* – was a small rubber dinghy. No motor was in use, but rather the craft was being propelled forward by the powerful thrusts of the oarsman. Edie could not at first make out who was on board but in just a few seconds the dinghy got near enough to see more clearly. Her heart skipped a beat.

It was Vuk.

In just a few seconds he would have reached the yacht, would get on board and find her there. *Think*, Edie screeched at herself, soundlessly. Gazing wildly around her, her eyes settled on the seating area behind the cabin. The bench-type seat tops lifted up to provide storage, she remembered from her trip with Zayn. The yacht had turned slightly in the wash from the dinghy and she was hidden, at that moment, from the fast-approaching Vuk. She lifted up the nearest seat. No good; it was stuffed to the brim with cushions. Frantically, she moved to the opposite side. This one was emptier; she was slim, it would have to do. She climbed in and let the seat close silently on top of her.

It was pitch dark. Edie hated the dark; had always relied on Laura to be the brave one, the one who didn't need a night light and would comfort Edie if they were staying in a strange place where the lamps were switched off at bedtime. But Edie was on her own now and she had to be courageous and strong, for Laura, because maybe, just maybe, this madcap venture would lead to finding her sister and then it would all be worth it.

The *Radomira* rocked with the unmistakeable movement of someone boarding. In the blackness her eyes were redundant but every sound became amplified, every tiny shift in the yacht's position felt as if it were tossing and turning on a violent sea. Edie lay, her body uncomfortably following the contour of the uneven mound of cushions beneath her, her fist stuffed in her mouth to prevent herself from whimpering with fear.

Another, more intense rocking, the sloshing sound of water against the boat's smooth flanks and the vibration that signalled the mechanised pulling up of the anchor. The motor started up, a discreet purring that was far from the noisy cacophony that an inferior outboard makes, and Edie felt them glide into motion. She imagined how beautiful the *Radomira* would look, slipping elegantly between the few sparse moorings in the tiny harbour and out to the open sea, exuding the confidence of affluence and superb design from each and every one of her glowing lights. She realised how absolutely stupid and ridiculously melodramatic she was being, stowed away in a cramped storage box like some kind of fugitive or (pathetically incompetent) amateur sleuth.

She could jump out of the box, present herself to Vuk as the sexual plaything he seemed to treat her as and, when he was in her thrall, get him to confess what he knew about Laura and about the hut on the hill; beguile him into telling her whose ID cards he had in his freezer, and why. Or, if that was a no go, at least sail her back to dry land so that she could ... So that she could what? Not run away, not leave. No, she had to toughen up, step up to the plate, be brave enough to see this through and sort it out.

She sank back down into the cushions.

'Hello.'

The voice barked out beside her, causing her heart to jump into her mouth and her breathing to momentarily cease. The game was up. She'd been found.

And then the talking continued and she realised it was Vuk on the phone to someone, his English, with its hint of a northern accent, so familiar to her. After his initial greeting, he seemed to lower his volume and Edie struggled to hear through her prison walls. Only odd words were discernible: 'quick', 'twenty minutes' and, at the end of the short conversation, a cold 'goodbye'. There was something about the words, the tone of voice, the purposeful nature of it all, that made Edie's blood chill in her veins. Definitely not a good idea to show herself now. She would just stay put, and pray.

***

It was impossible to tell how much time passed before Edie felt the slight tremor of the anchor's release and descent to the sea floor. She was stiff and aching, and getting tired of constantly flexing her ankles and wrists to try to keep her circulation going. Something hard and awkwardly shaped was pressing against her leg and she shifted slightly to release the pressure. She remembered the corkscrew, still in her pocket from earlier that day, from a time when there had been nothing

283

wrong with her life except that she didn't know where Laura was. She couldn't imagine why she still had the bloody thing with her but she couldn't do anything about it now, couldn't even reach her pocket to get it out.

The deck beneath her trembled as Vuk moved along it in the direction of the cabin. She pictured him unlocking the door, opening it, going inside. It was hellish, and frightening, and at the same time absurd not to know what was going on, where she was or why. Edie felt tears prick beneath her eyelids and the heat of imminent weepiness suffuse her.

The sound of the cabin door slamming shut snapped her back to her senses and she felt the yacht rock once more as Vuk descended the ladder – into the dinghy? – and then a few more gentle undulations from the wash he created as he power-rowed away before all was still.

Edie waited. She counted to one hundred once, ONE-hippopotamus, TWO-hippopotamus, THREE-hippopotamus, as she remembered learning in childhood in order to be sure of each count taking one second exactly and as she did when free-diving. When she had reached one hundred, she started again. At two hundred, she stopped. Slowly, cautiously, her heart pounding and her blood coursing through her veins, she reached her hand up to the seat-lid. She rested her fingers against the cool, silky flatness of it. Pausing, she summoned all her courage. She could still pretend it was a surprise for Vuk, a game, a light-hearted casual thing, something that had occurred to her he might be amused by. She could rely on her innocence, her perceived empty-headedness; Vuk would dismiss her as a silly little girl rather than a cunning investigator of crime. She could still do that. But where up to now she had managed to convince herself that Vuk would not harm her, that he was not that bad, she no longer believed it. Vuk had no more loyalty to her than to the resort cat.

She was on her own, with only her wits to rely on.

Flinging the lid open, she leapt out, amazed that her limbs still did her bidding after such bunched-up confinement. Once out and having encountered no one, she instinctively ducked down between the two facing benches. All of her senses were on high alert as she listened and stared, hunting for signs that she was not alone in the darkness. Unlike the picture in her imagination, there were no lights lit anywhere on the *Radomira*. But the moon was almost full and the stars gleamed and shone. She waited a few seconds, searching with eyes and ears. There was nothing. She slunk along the deck until she reached the cabin door. The handle seemed still to be warm from Vuk's so recent touch. She pressed down on it and the door swung open.

There were no lights on inside the cabin, either, but there was enough illumination to see by coming through the skylights in the roof. Edie crept through the kitchen and dining area and towards the prow of the boat where the sleeping cabins were. In the furthest one – the master bedroom she was sure the yacht-designers would promote it as – there was a comfortable looking double bed and small shower room. It was all in pristine condition, clean and new. What would a boat like this cost? Second-hand, 200 or 300K US? New, at least half a million, probably more.

Edie ran her hand along the white sheets on the made-up bed. It was peculiar and she didn't understand it but there was something very wrong going on aboard this yacht and whether it had to do with Laura or it didn't, she was going to find out what it was. At that thought, she almost snorted with derision at herself. She had left herself no choice.

The boat swung on its anchor and the subtle change in its lilting motion signified the arrival of someone. Right in front of her was the wardrobe door. Edie snatched it open, flung herself inside and pulled the door closed. It was tiny, smaller in dimensions than the seat she'd just got out of, but at least she was upright. The other advantage was the view offered by the small gap above one of the door hinges; although minuscule, Edie could see a small slice of the bedroom through it. It was through this gap that, in utter disbelief, she watched the scene that unfolded before her eyes.

***

The first person to enter was a boy, a teenager. He was dressed like teenagers everywhere; blue jeans and a T-shirt. But his clothes were old and worn, the T-shirt so faded that its original colour was impossible to tell. In the brief glimpse she caught of his face, Edie saw his mouth set in a sullen frown and sensed the air of barely suppressed anger that hung about him. Behind him came a man, slight and wiry, whose eyes within his pinched face darted all around him like a frightened bird. Edie heard a small child's voice call out something in a language she did not recognise. She thought it was a girl but it was hard to tell and whoever it was did not appear in her field of vision. And then the doorway was filled by the next person and it was Vuk, and he was half-supporting, half-carrying a figure wrapped in what looked like a blanket despite the heat. The bundled figure turned its face towards the wardrobe and Edie as they passed and Edie saw that it was a woman. That briefest of glances was enough to see the sweat shining on her skin and the fever burning in her eyes. She looked barely alive.

A smell had accompanied the people into the room, of body odour and unwashed clothes, of rot and decay. Edie could feel a sneeze building inside her and frantically wrinkled her nose, expanding and contracting her nostrils to prevent it from bursting forth. Attention back on the group now gathered within the room, it suddenly occurred to Edie what was familiar about them. With a jolt of her stomach, she recognised them as the string of people she'd seen silhouetted against the night sky at the hut on the hill.

Vuk got the sick woman to the bed and heaped her upon

it. She emitted a groan as she sank down. A child – the one who had spoken as she entered? – began to cry. Edie heard the sharp slap of flesh against flesh and imagined the hand that had landed on the child so violently. Was it Vuk's? She hoped not, and then realised immediately that it didn't matter anymore anyway. Whatever Vuk was doing, it was not pretty and it almost certainly was not legal and so her association with him was over.

She heard herself think this and had to struggle to stop herself from laughing out loud. It suddenly occurred to her that she was in the gravest danger, that what had begun as a simple quest to find a missing sister had led to her being witness to a crime, and the people committing that crime – Vuk, Vlad, maybe others as well – were not the kind to understand or appreciate that her involvement was well-meaning and not in any way meant to be a threat. If they found her, she could not even imagine what they might do to her.

'Stay here.'

The words, barked out in a ferocious whisper, made Edie jump and almost give the game away. It was Vuk speaking, just inches away from her. Squinting through the gap, all Edie could see was the black expanse of his torso right in front of the wardrobe.

'You stay here,' he repeated. As he spoke, Edie could feel the boat turning. So Vuk definitely wasn't alone; someone else was driving the *Radomira*, and from the sensation in her stomach, they were picking up speed fast.

'Make no noise. The children must be quiet.'

Vuk was speaking in a truncated version of English, the way you speak it when either you don't have a good command of the language or the person you are addressing doesn't. So these pitiful people did not speak the local language, nor English – or at least, not much English.

'How long?' The voice was soft and low, but fear was audible in every syllable. Was it the man or the boy speaking? Edie couldn't tell.

'Not long.' Vuk snapped back his answer as he turned to leave, the dark shadow that blocked Edie's view moving away.

Now she could see the bed, with the sick woman lying upon it, and gathered in a little huddle on the corner nearest to Edie's hideaway, the man, the teenager and two tiny girls, their faces piteously white and drawn, dark circles of exhaustion around their eyes. One of children began to whimper, a fretful, desperate sound that seemed to encapsulate the terror and despair that suffused the atmosphere of the room. Neither the boy nor the man tried to silence the girl, or to comfort her. Vuk had shut the door of the bedroom behind him and Edie hoped that her sobs would not be audible outside.

The movement of the *Radomira* indicated that they had reached open water again. Edie thanked her lucky stars that she had good sea legs. But the heat inside her tiny enclosure was becoming unbearable and she was desperately thirsty. Despite the advantages of being upright, the air inside the wardrobe was so thick and hot that breathing was difficult. Perspiration was trickling down her brow and off the end of her nose but she didn't dare try to move her hands or arms to wipe it away. Instead she tried to ignore the sweat beads' tickling motion, to take deep long breaths to combat the incipient claustrophobia.

And still the heat suppurated around her. The wardrobe walls were pulsating, condensation building and running downwards, the air thick as treacle. Her clothes were drenched. She felt light-headed and dizzy; was it possible to go on sweating even when you were dehydrated? She squeezed her eyes tight shut and then opened them again. The brown pattern on the wood of the wardrobe door swirled and turned before finally settling to stillness. Edie was not sure how much more of this she could bear. Vuk had said not long.

She forced herself to stay calm, clenching and unclenching

her fists, licking the sweat off her upper lip only for it to gather again in seconds. She imagined diving off the boat and into the cool water through which they streamed, pictured the clear depths beneath her, the darting fish and waving fronds of seaweed. Concentrate on your breathing, she told herself again and again. That's all that matters. A breath in. A breath out.

The bedroom door banged violently and Vuk entered. Edie was struggling to stay conscious, awake and focused. Her head was spinning, her legs trembling, threatening to give her away. She heard Vuk speaking but the words were fuzzy and unclear and coming from far, far away. Then there was an echoing emptiness all around her that filled her ears and reverberated around her brain. The boat lurched on a high wave causing Edie's head to fly backwards and hit the wall behind her with a dull thud. She lost her balance and lurched forward, crashing against the wardrobe door with all of her body weight. The door flew open. Edie shot out and collapsed onto the bed in a sprawling heap, barely aware of what had happened she had been so close to fainting.

She opened her eyes to be greeted by Vuk's face looming above her, his mouth twisted into a hideous grimace of rage.

THIRTY-FOUR

Edie

'What the fuck are you doing here, you stupid bitch?'

Edie flinched at the language; not in front of the children, Vuk, she was thinking as another part of her brain was trying to tell her something, to make her aware of something.

She sat bolt upright, her forehead smashing against Vuk's nose.

'Shit!'

His hand shot up to his face in a protective reflex action at the same time as he aimed a slap at her that hit her cheek with a stinging bite. It served the purpose of bringing Edie's fuddled mind to its senses. She had to get out of there. She leapt off the bed, evading Vuk's outstretched arm, dodging around the teenager and the man who now stood, dumbstruck in bewilderment, in one corner of the room. The two little girls, she observed, were curled up against the woman who was presumably their mother. They, too, were watching what was going on with fear-widened eyes. The woman appeared dead to the world, face pressed into the bedcovers.

Speeding along the short corridor that led out to the deck,

Edie desperately tried to formulate a plan. But there was none. She was on a boat, out at sea, alone and vulnerable. The idea that Vuk would not harm her seemed laughable now. It was clear that he would stop at nothing.

She pushed the cabin door open and stepped out onto the deck. Her muscles were tense, her heart pounding and now a different kind of sweat, the cold sweat of terror and dread, was running down her back and thighs. The ship's wheel was right in front of her, positioned to give a clear sightline over the cabin roof and into the distance. Standing behind it, appearing perfectly calm and relaxed, was Vlad. On seeing Edie, the merest hint of surprise flickered in his eyes.

'Edie,' he said. 'How unexpected. To what do we owe the pleasure?'

Vlad's laugh, falsetto, not in the least masculine, and tainted with undisguised hostility, rang out at the same time as she heard Vuk approach from behind. She spun round, not sure who she was most in danger from, and then back again to face Vlad, squaring up to him, determined that he should not see her cower.

'Howdie, Vl—' Edie had not managed to get the words out before her arms were grabbed from behind and a knee against the backs of hers caused her to crumple. Vuk propelled her body towards the ship's wheel and held her, as if some kind of sacrificial offering, in front of Vlad.

They began to speak in their language. A few words, here and there, Edie caught, words that she had picked up during her time on the resort. 'Night', 'police', 'no good' and 'soon'.

Vlad reached out his hand and clasped it around her neck. He looked into her eyes. She stared back, defiantly. She was up for the fight now, he wasn't going to intimidate her, ugly little man that he was. His hand tightened. Edie gulped, involuntarily. Vlad snickered and Edie almost laughed; he was like the worst kind of cartoon villain. But she could not have imagined

291

that such a small, weedy man should have such an iron grip. She was struggling to breathe in his stranglehold.

'Stupid, stupid, stupid little girl.' The cruelty in Vlad's voice made Edie shiver. He dropped his hand from her neck.

'I know what you are.' Edie's tone was rebellious. 'People smugglers.' There was a sense of triumph in her voice; at least she'd worked it out. Maybe she wasn't so dumb as her school reports indicated after all.

'That's what you do, isn't it?' she continued, fired up now, not caring that neither Vlad nor Vuk looked the least bit impressed, on the contrary, seemed unconcerned about the fact that she had uncovered their secret profession. 'I suppose we're headed for somewhere in the EU, to Italy perhaps, where you'll dump those guys and leave them to fend for themselves, when you can see that that poor woman is *dying*. Or maybe you won't even bother to get them that far, just get rid of them anywhere that suits you.'

The unearthly screech of her voice startled her and she fell immediately silent. Vlad turned and spat into the sea, and then looked back to meet her gaze, his poise stiff with menace, his eyes dark with fury. He resumed his grip of her throat, so tight that she choked. He laughed. Edie shut her eyes and then opened them again, looking in the opposite direction to where Vlad's spittle had been directed. She could make out lights across the water; they were not as far from the shore as she had thought. But no one would take the blindest bit of notice of an expensive yacht on a night voyage; people did it all the time, it was normal. That was the whole point of the *Radomira*; she was the best cover there was. Wealthy people spending their summer cruising the Croatian islands – what could be more delightful?

The boat lurched on a wave. Vuk was taken off guard and momentarily lost his balance, letting go of her arms as he did so. Vlad's attention was on one-handedly steering the boat and he, too, slightly relaxed his hold on her. It was not much, but it was enough.

Quick as lightning, she pulled the corkscrew from her pocket and stabbed at Vlad's arm, smashing the sharp point into him with a blind fury. The surprise attack made him fully relinquish his grip on her, and Edie was off, across the deck towards the stern of the yacht. Vuk had recovered and grabbed hold of a long strand of her hair as she passed; the pain in her scalp was intense and blinding. Wildly, she stabbed into the air with the corkscrew and met flesh, stabbed again and again. She wrenched her hair free from his grasp, leaving a great clump of it in his hands, staggered to the end of the boat. Jumped.

In the panic of it all, she did not take a big enough breath and, despite her terror and the desperate knowledge that she must stay hidden, she could not stay underwater. The waves slapped hard against her face as she surfaced to breathe and to assess where she was, where the boat was.

It was just a couple of metres away. Vuk had the boathook in his hand and was aiming it at her, trying to catch it onto her T-shirt. Vlad was barking instructions; Edie was glad she could not understand what they were. She was sure they would not be comforting to hear. She swam away, but it was as if she were in one of those terrible dreams where you are trying to run but cannot make your legs move, or you're desperate to get somewhere and never make it.

'Edie, I'm trying to help you,' Vuk called out to her plaintively. The innocence, the pleading in his voice was almost enough to convince her. But it was a lie, and she knew it.

She felt the hook catch onto her top and almost immediately lose its hold, and then manage to latch on again so that she could not free herself and was being dragged through the water at speed, surging over the waves like some kind of supersonic mermaid. She was at the steps and Vuk was reaching out for her arm, at the same time as holding tight to the boat hook that was entangled in her T-shirt. Edie suppressed every instinct within her that was telling her to fight and let her body go completely limp, allowing Vuk to bear all her weight on the end of his boat hook. His grip was tight around her wrist but he could not get enough of a purchase on her to bring her out of the water. She made her breathing deep, slow, calm. She was a rag doll, inanimate. Vuk struggled to raise her from the sea, hauling on the boat hook and her arm, battling to lift the fifty-three kilos of dead weight hanging on the end of it.

Edie took her final breath. With one swift, smooth, skilful movement she jerked her wrist out of Vuk's hand, stretched her arms straight above her head and, using the fact that Vuk was pulling so hard on the boathook and therefore offering resistance, pushed herself backwards and let her body slip out of her T-shirt. Free once more, she continued her dive, down and down into the deep black water. She could stay under for around three and a half minutes. Would that be enough for them to give up on her, to sail on and away, to leave her for dead? Neither Vlad nor Vuk knew how well she could swim or anything of her dabblings in free diving; they would presume she had drowned if she disappeared for long enough.

Edie focused everything on her mission, knowing that her life depended on it. She had seen the rope beside Vuk when he was reeling her in; far from rescuing her, his intention had been to make her drowning a certainty rather than a probability. In order to stay under for the maximum time, complete calm, a total absence of panic was a necessity. Edie forced herself to be so. She let the water bear her, and felt her heart rate slowing as she began to count. At three minutes thirty she knew she was near to her limit. She began to ascend, not wanting to but knowing she had to. Surely she was far enough away now? Her head broke the surface.

And then it was over, because Vuk had caught her, a huge net had trapped her arms and was tangling itself around her head, her hair was all over her face and she couldn't work out if it was the net or her hair that was throttling her. She was struggling frantically, using all her energy, wasting the oxygen that was still in her lungs and veins and blood and powering her heart. In her panic, she breathed in, and her mouth and nose and lungs filled with water. As she choked she began to sink.

The liquid sea closed over her head as firmly as the solid lid of a steel box, impossible to escape from. The life was ebbing out of her but still she could not give in; she was too stubborn and bloody-minded for that. She gave one last huge kick, using every ounce of strength and life she had left even though she knew it was too late. The net closed in around her again. It pulled her down to her watery grave. Everything was over.

THIRTY-FIVE

Edie

It wasn't over. Suddenly Edie was free, her head above water heedless of whatever enemy might be waiting for her. She was gulping down great heaving breaths of air and throwing up bitter, saline vomit as water streamed from her nose and ears. The net was drifting around her waist and she pulled at it, lifting it out of the sea and in front of her eyes so that she could see it only to find it was not a net at all but a bunch of dark green, thick-fronded seaweed. She shut her eyes and lay back in the water, floating in the black sea whilst her heart rate steadied, her pulse returned to normal and her breathing became light and easy once more.

Opening her eyes, she saw the vastness of the sky above her, and the glittering multitudes of stars within it. Not one of them was going to help her. She would help herself or die.

There was no sound at all, just the echo of the washing water in her ears. Righting herself, she looked around. Other than the far off galaxies there was nothing to see, either – no reflection of a yacht's pale flanks in moonlight. And then, far in the distance, she spied an almost imperceptible glow that could be a white boat moving swiftly to the north-west. She turned herself slowly in a circle, her hands pushing aside the water's resistance. Straining her eyes she made out, far away, a few sparse spots of light dotted randomly along what must be the coastline.

Edie pushed her hair away from her face, instructed herself that she could do this and began to swim.

**

Edie swam and swam and swam. She swam until her arms ached and felt heavy as iron. Her legs kicked at half-pace, then quarter and then she could hardly move them at all. But still she swam. There was no other option. As she propelled herself onwards, increasingly slowly, the sky clouded over in readiness for one of late summer's occasional rainstorms and it became harder to see where she was heading. She carried on.

If she died out here, at least she would have died trying. And then, just as she felt she could continue no longer, that she would rather drift away on a current and let the kind old sea take her where it would, something hard grazed against the toes of her drooping left leg. She stretched her foot out and it made contact with solidity. She lurched herself forwards and reached down again. Nothing. And then another great lurch and both feet were on firm ground and she could faintly make out the dark line of the shore ahead.

She half-swam, half-waded further in, reaching rocks that rose out of the water and were backed by scrubby bushes and trees. There was no beach here, no welcoming resort with a bar and café and campsite where she could rouse someone and get help. Not help for herself; she'd be fine now, but for the people on the boat and that woman who was so very sick and didn't look like she was going to make it to wherever Vlad and Vuk were taking them. The stench of flesh and decay that had filled the room still clung to Edie's nostrils and festered in her mind, despite the ocean of salt water that should have washed it away. The woman was a mother and her children were there with her, watching her fade away, and Edie couldn't bear the thought of it.

She clung to some rocks, scrabbling for a handhold, her legs waving in the cavity underneath, trying to find something to push against to help her body upwards. Her foot hit rock, hard. A searing pain tore through her and she screamed, liberated by the thought that it no longer mattered who heard her, the more people the better, but also secretly knowing that there was no one remotely close enough to notice. Hauling herself onto the rock as the water swirled and eddied around her, Edie was oblivious to the scratches and grazes that she sustained. All she could think about was the throbbing agony of her foot.

When finally out of the sea and sprawled on the clammy surface of the stone, she pulled her ankle towards her, not daring to touch the foot itself. It was too dark to see anything. She ran her fingers as gently as she could over the ball of her foot where it hurt the most but there was nothing to feel but pain. The only thing she could think of was that she had slammed against a sea urchin and that, despite how much the spines embedded in her skin hurt, it would not kill her.

She had no energy to stand up, knowing that she would most likely slip and fall, but crawled to where the rocks gave way to sandy scrubland. Only there did she attempt to walk, gritting her teeth against the torturous throbbing of her foot whenever she put the smallest amount of weight on it. Limping onwards, she tried to focus on the positive. She was on land. She'd survived the swim. She must surely be able to survive a short walk, however long it would take to hit a road or a village or maybe a farmhouse.

This country could hardly be described as over-populated but neither was it deserted and eventually, she would arrive somewhere. She had to. She hadn't done all of this to fail now. She had been determined from the outset, but then it had been for Laura. Now it was also for the dark-haired woman on the boat, and for her children, for the man and the boy, for those people who needed help right now more than anyone she had ever met. She would not give up on this as she had given up on so much else in her life – university, modelling, boyfriends, friendships ... the list was endless of everything she had not made a success of.

What she was doing now was going to change all that; she hadn't died in the sea out there and so she could have another stab at life and do it better this time. She could get some proper qualifications, train for a decent, worthwhile job; show all the doubters amongst her friends and family that she was capable of stuff. She had found something out about herself that she would never have believed – that she could be strong, in mind and body. Now she just had to do what was required to convey to the rest of the world that she could be worthwhile, that perhaps, just perhaps, there was a reason she had been put on this planet as the younger of a pair of twins, doomed to always feel second-rate. If she, Edie, could only raise the alarm in time, the *Radomira* might be intercepted and the people rescued and the woman taken to hospital and given whatever treatment it was that she needed. This could happen, if Edie was capable of doing what needed to be done.

And that would be worth more than anything.

***

Over the next hour of walking, Edie began to severely doubt that she was capable of it. She was exhausted, parched, covered in cuts and bruises from the rocks and her foot was getting worse not better, having swollen to twice its normal size and throbbing so hard it was making her feel nauseous. It was still dark from the cloud cover and so hard to see that she kept stumbling and tripping, her feet repeatedly getting caught in the tangled undergrowth. The only hopeful thing was that she was making her way steadily uphill and that meant that when she got to the top, she might reach a road or at least a path. Being high up would give her a vantage point and could show her the way forward. That's what she focused on, anyway.

She had almost reached the brow of the hill when the clouds opened and rain began. It wasn't like British rain, that built up gradually from a few drops – this was a downpour from the very start. In moments she was drenched again, her bikini and shorts that had begun to dry out soaked through. Her wet hair was a ton weight dragging down her back; she had never, ever noticed it feeling so heavy before. But the rain water was fresh and pure and she knelt down on the sandy soil, threw back her head, opened her mouth and let the drops saturate her desiccated lips and tongue.

She stayed like that until the rain stopped, as suddenly as it had started. By then she had begun to shiver uncontrollably. She was freezing, her teeth chattering, her skin covered in goose bumps. She knew she should get up and keep moving, that if she became hypothermic it would be extremely dangerous; they had learnt that on her Duke of Edinburgh training (although she had never done the actual hike, dropping out at the last minute as with so many things).

But all she wanted to do was to curl up in a ball and nurse her poor, swollen, sore foot and wait for it all to be all right. Her head pulsed and her whole body ached with fatigue, every muscle screaming out its protest at what it had been through over the past few hours. Edie was about to give in to the overwhelming desire to sleep that was subsuming her when the faint glimmer of dawn began to colour the horizon gold. It gave her the impetus she needed to get back up and keep going.

The sight that met her eyes when she crested the hill was entirely unexpected. Below her was a precipitous slope created by wholesale excavation of the hillside, the exposed soil pale brown and raw-looking, ripped apart by the bulldozers and excavators that now stood silently by, lined up like a battalion of tanks ready for the next day's battle. Edie knew that there was major construction going on along one of the seafronts; a new town complete with harbour and marina being developed for the high-class, high-spending tourists that the country was trying to attract. This must be where the stone was coming from to build it all, wrenched out of the countryside, leaving a scarred and decimated landscape behind. And then it occurred to her that finding the quarry was good news as, if she were right, it meant that she was still on the peninsula that extended westwards from the resort and therefore that she was not far from civilisation.

Standing still and trying to focus her eyes in the half-light was making her feel light-headed and giddy; she had not eaten properly for many, many hours and although revived somewhat by the rainwater, she was finding it harder and harder to stop her head from spinning. She needed to circumvent the quarry and find the road that the dump trucks were using; this would undoubtedly soon lead to one of the many small villages that dotted the peninsula. The ground was sodden now, the grass wet and slippery, the earth beneath slicked like wet clay. She stumbled a couple of times and righted herself, each time having to pause and hold her head in her hands until it had ceased pulsating.

She wondered what time the workmen turned up; perhaps it would not be long and she could hail one of them and ask for a lift. She wasn't sure if she could make it much further. Her damaged foot shrieked every time it took her weight, her legs felt hollow, weak and empty from lack of food and rest. Something far below, down in the quarry, caught her eye – a lightning flash like the rising sun on a car windscreen – and she turned to look at it, raising both arms above her head in a desperate wave that begged someone to notice. As she did so, the heel of her foot slid on a clump of wet grass, her body flailed madly back and forth and for a few seconds she teetered on the edge of the precipice.

And then fell.

She bounced and rolled down the side of the cliff, unable to do anything to stop herself. There was nothing to grab hold of, not the tiniest clump of grass, not a single tenacious shrub. So this is it, this is how it ends, I've fallen at the last hurdle and let that poor woman down – The wailing in her head subsided suddenly to emptiness. Her mind switched off. Everything went black.

THIRTY-SIX

Edie

The sound was insistent, constant. It droned on and on. It seemed to be coming from nearby but, drowsy from the painkillers and whatever else was being pumped into her through the tube in her hand, Edie couldn't immediately identify it. She wished it would stop, would go away so that she could sleep. She was so tired, and she knew there was a reason for such unprecedented exhaustion but couldn't, at that moment, think what it was or fathom exactly where she was lying. It was all too confusing and the noise was irritating her too much to think about anything else. She lay on her back, staring at the white ceiling, trying to block out the sound. She couldn't. This was unbearable; she'd have to find out what it was and ask someone to please sort it out.

She turned her head in the direction of the noise. There was a bed next to hers, and another one further on, beyond a window with a blind drawn down over it. Slowly, it dawned on Edie that she was in hospital. On the nearest bed was a humped shape, completely covered with bedclothes. No body part was visible, but the shape was heaving gently up and down. Edie listened carefully. The sound that she had been unable to discern the origin of earlier was of someone sobbing their heart out, weeping, keening, and it was coming from the featureless figure whose face was buried and invisible.

Edie turned her head back to staring straight upwards again. Every movement hurt. Her temples throbbed. She wanted to call out *shut up*. But something stopped her. This was no ordinary crying; this was gut-wrenching grief that spoke, wordlessly, of unimaginable sorrow and utter hopelessness.

She must have dropped back off to sleep. The next thing she was aware of, through the woolliness that constituted her brain, was a nurse who came and took her blood pressure and checked her temperature. My vital signs, thought Edie. Is that what they call them? Nothing felt very vital at that moment; on the contrary, she was feeling distinctly second-hand.

'Why am I here?' she asked the nurse. The smile she received in return was charming, kind. But the words the nurse spoke were incomprehensible.

The day drifted on. The crying had stopped and, at some point, the curtains had been drawn around the bed next to hers. Perhaps the woman had died. There was absolute silence from that direction now. If she was on a ward with dead people, did that mean she would die too? Edie thought that intensive care wards were where people generally died and this didn't seem to be like intensive care, at least not how it was depicted on TV programmes, all beeping noises and flashing lights and professionally urgent doctors and nurses. But on the other hand, perhaps she was beyond all that and already halfway to some nether world. This might explain why it was all so white and quiet like an antechamber of heaven ...

Edie slept. When next she opened her eyes it was to be greeted by a dark figure looming over her. The Grim Reaper? The tight grip of fear sent heat rushing through her body. She screamed.

But it was just the doctor, a doctor who spoke English.

'I'm sorry I frightened you,' he said. He had a low, gruff voice that seemed to rumble up from somewhere deep within his chest. 'You're doing fine but you need to get as much sleep as you can. Your parents will be here soon; they're on their way.'

Sleep. That sounded good. Edie was sure she needed sleep. But she had a question to ask.

'Who is the person who is crying?' Her eyes flicked towards the bed next to hers to indicate who she meant.

'We put you in here, with the other girl. It seemed the best thing to do.'

Something about the way he spoke implied that Edie knew who this was, this 'other girl'.

The doctor moved away, towards the other bed, before she could ask for clarification. He disappeared behind the curtains. Edie could hear him talking to its occupant so she couldn't be dead after all. Neither of them was dead. That was a relief. And he'd called her a girl so presumably she wasn't dissimilar in age to Edie. That was good, as it would be a shame to die when still young enough to be classed a 'girl'.

Now that she knew she was definitely alive, and that her neighbour was too, she tried to remember what the doctor had just said. She was sure it had been something important but it had already slipped away, out of reach. It was like the hugest hangover she'd ever had, one of those that gets worse, not better, throughout the day and when tiny snippets of things that happened during the drunken evening keep coming back over the next hours and weeks.

'When will they come?'

The question came from the next bed, but as soon as she heard it, Edie realised her stupidity. The doctor had said her parents were on their way and the next-door voice's question was the one she should have asked them. She wondered who might be coming to visit the sad woman, for it had been a female voice, who she was asking about, but then decided it didn't matter. Sleeping was the only thing that seemed to matter right now. But sleep evaded her.

Fatima

Since the fever had lifted, she had tried to piece together all the bits of what had happened from the moment Ali's money and the documents had arrived. It had been easy, she remembered, with cash and ID papers, to get the ferry off the island they had arrived at. It would take them to another island, not the first one they got to but further along that particular chain. There were so many islands belonging to that country, each one more picture-perfect than the last, and lots of people, locals and tourists, especially young back-packers, touring from one to another. 'Island hopping' they called it, Fatima recalled from some article she'd read once, long ago. Jumping on a boat with a carefree spirit, the sun and the scent of the sea one's constant companions, taking off to explore the black sand beaches or coral coves or sparkling sponge-hunters' bays. But of course that had not been what she and Ehsan and the children had been doing; far from it.

They were fleeing for their lives and how much rather she would have been at home in the courtyard house, the way it had been before this terrible war, she could not put into words.

At least now, for them, with the rediscovery of Ali, life seemed to have taken a turn for the better. For those left behind in the stinking makeshift camp, sleeping on the hard ground, surrounded by the stench of piss and faeces, consigned to grindingly awful day after grindingly awful day, waiting – to be registered, to get papers, for food, for water – Fatima could not bear to think what the future held.

When we get to Europe, she promised herself. *When we get there, and we get settled, and I've paid Ali back all the money he's spent on us, I'll do something to help.* Promises like that are easy to make when they are so remote that the whys and wherefores do not need to be dwelt on, but she knew she meant it.

It was ironic that it was on their journey to rescue, funded by Ali, that things had taken a turn for the worse. The excoriating wind and the sea-sickness combined with the dreadful, agonising labour pains that heralded a birth happening far too soon, a baby that, in these circumstances, could not possibly survive, meant that the rest of their peregrinations were jumbled and unclear, the details too opaque to catch hold of. She had a vague recollection of being taken to a hut on a hill, of Ali begging for her to see a doctor but his friends – the smugglers (yet more smugglers, on top of all those they had encountered along the journey) – refusing. They had said that it was too dangerous, that Fatima would be immediately detained, that their chances of getting into the EU would be over.

Fatima had been vaguely aware, even as the infection took over her body, poisoning her blood and addling her mind, that this was not the reason they wouldn't entertain the idea of fetching medical help. The real reason was that they were frightened – of the consequences of being caught, of losing both their freedom and their illegitimate income.

She was musing on that thought, on how close she had come to an ignominious death, perhaps buried at sea along with her son, when the doctor arrived by her bedside. After checking her notes and consulting with the nurse at his shoulder, he pronounced himself pleased with her progress. Fatima smiled, weakly. He told her that Ali would bring the children to see her soon. She had not even begun to process the loss of the baby. She felt the tragedy of it at the same time as feeling totally removed from it, as if it had happened to someone else. When someone mentioned her children, she thought only of Marwa and Maryam as if there had never been even the shadow of another one. She knew she had been crying, a lot, because her eyes were red and sore. But whether it was for him, her lost boy, or for her twins, or for Fayed and all the hundreds and thousands of dead and millions displaced of her country, she did not know.

She only had one question to ask the doctor, the only one that mattered.

'When will they come?'

Edie

'Soon,' Edie heard the doctor answer. Did it apply to her, to her parents' arrival? She felt too tired to ask.

The nurse drew back the curtains around the bed and Edie saw, for the first time, the woman who had wept so eloquently for so long. Even though her face was etched with pain and loss, her eyes red and sore from weeping, her skin dull and grey, she was beautiful. Beautiful and young, with long black hair that was thick and glossy despite whatever was wrong with her. There was something vaguely familiar about her but Edie couldn't think what it was. She looks the same age as me, she thought. And we're both waiting for people to arrive, so we've got that in common, too. I need to find out what she's doing here. What's made her so sad.

'What's your name?' she asked, when the doctor and the nurse had carried on down the row to the next bed.

The woman looked at Edie. Edie wondered why she thought of her as a woman although she always saw herself as still a girl. There was something about her eyes, the way she regarded Edie now, that spoke of experiences out of Edie's knowledge, of things that should never have been seen.

'My name is Fatima.' She spoke very slowly, as if having to consider each word carefully. Her English was excellent. She was sitting up on the edge of her bed as if about to go somewhere, but she didn't leave.

'Hi, Fatima.' Edie tried a smile but it hurt too much. She had been propping herself up on her elbows but now let herself fall back down. It was too much effort.

'What were you crying about earlier?'

The question was far too abrupt, too direct, for one complete stranger to ask another. But Edie wanted to know and was too weary to work out how to broach the subject tactfully.

Fatima raised her tired, swollen eyes from the floor to Edie. 'It is a long story and at the same time a very short one. Do you really want to hear it?'

'I wouldn't have asked if I didn't.'

In the silence that followed Edie realised that her answer had perhaps not been the most sensitive.

'Sorry, I didn't mean that to sound rude. I'm not feeling a hundred per cent myself.'

As she spoke, Edie realised how much she ached all over, how the pain in every muscle when she shifted the tiniest micro-millimetre was greater than she had ever felt before. But none of it could be as bad as what Fatima had experienced, judging from the gut-wrenching crying of earlier.

'I got an infection.' Fatima was talking again. 'The baby came too early. It – he – died and I lost a lot of blood. It was very dirty everywhere, there was no doctor and no medicine and I became very ill. An infection —' Her voice trailed off. Her eyes searched the room, her expression distraught.

Edie watched as tears welled up in Fatima's eyes. She dropped her head and buried it in her hands as if not seeing could take the pain away.

'I'm sorry,' she continued, lifting up her head and forcing back the sobs. 'I'm not crying for myself. Nobody from my country cries for themselves anymore. We cry only for the children.' Fatima tightened her hands into fists and ground them into her lap. 'How many more children will we lose, how many more will die, before it's over? What will it take for the world to help?'

Edie lay in her bed, watching the agony crossing Fatima's face like storm clouds in a fierce wind. She had absolutely no idea what Fatima was talking about.

The ring of high-pitched voices cut through the white calm of the ward. Fatima turned towards the source of the noise and Edie saw her face transform, the darkness swept away and replaced by sunshine that spread across her countenance like the first rays of light after the storm.

Two tiny girls arrived at her bedside, so similar to Fatima with their glossy black hair and shiny black eyes, calling and shouting in another language. Fatima flung herself off the bed and onto her knees where she gathered the children in her arms and smothered them with kisses. She got into the chair that stood by the bed and pulled them on top of her, love masking the exhaustion that Edie could see threatened to engulf her. The outpouring of emotion equalled the grief of the morning. Edie knew she should not stare but could not stop.

Fatima was fumbling with something, awkwardly raising her hands above her head, trying to move without dislodging the children from her lap. She kept glancing down the long corridor of the ward; there must be someone else coming. Edie saw that she was twisting a headscarf over her hair, fixing it into place without a mirror, her hands following patterns they knew by heart and long habit.

The children were snuggled into her lap, oblivious to their mother's actions. The two of them were complete, indivisible, two halves of a whole, one split egg making a perfect pair. Edie took in their every detail. They were obviously twins, identical Edie was sure. They're just like me and Laura, thought Edie. Panic surged through her veins. Laura. Something had happened to Laura. These two girls still had each other but she didn't have Laura. The aching void of loneliness left by her absent twin opened wide once more, threatening to pull her in and devour her.

Fatima had the scarf in place now, just in time; the footsteps had been fast approaching and now the visitors came into view. Edie closed her eyes then, because it was nothing to do with her and Fatima deserved some privacy. And as she did so, it all came flooding back to her. Fatima was familiar because she was the woman on the boat, the girls the two poor mites who had watched everything with their fearful gaze. She, Edie, had discovered them, had uncovered Vuk and Vlad's evil enterprise, all because she was looking for Laura. Were she and Fatima safe now? Where were the guards, the police, to make sure that no one came in the night to murder them in their beds?

Edie tried to calm her racing pulse and pumping heart. If Fatima had been found it must mean the boat had been intercepted. Did that mean that Vuk and Vlad were under lock and key? She could not even think of Vuk, of how he had deceived her. What about Fatima? She'd never get to Europe now, she'd probably be deported. Her and the girls, the twins. If only she, Edie, were well, perhaps she could help them? Sneak them across the border in the boot of a car; it would hardly be difficult, the border officials didn't search anyone European driving a rental car. She'd take them to the capital, or no, even better, drive them further north, across more borders, take them to one of the countries that was accepting refugees, Germany or Sweden. No, Sweden was too far, but Germany, that would be perfect, and once in Germany and established and a citizen with a passport and all that, Fatima could go where she wanted and it would all be fine; perhaps she'd choose to settle in

England, which would be nice because then Edie could visit her, assuming Edie herself went back to live in England which seemed unlikely but then, where else would she go?

Edie's head spun and she leant out of the bed and threw up on the floor, the spattering sound of her vomit hitting the cold tiles appalling and disgusting her. A nurse hurried over and admonished her in their indecipherable language, giving her a plastic tray in case she did it again. Someone came to clear up the sick. Edie couldn't work out if the stench of the detergent was worse than that of the contents of her stomach. She must be going mad, truly, properly mad, to be thinking these things about facilitating Fatima's escape.

In all honesty, what could she do to help? She didn't even know how to drive, for Christ's sake.

THIRTY-SEVEN

Edie

Edie must have dozed because when she woke up, Fatima and the girls weren't there.

'You have visitors,' a nurse was saying.

It was much darker now; it must be getting late. Evening visiting hours. That was nice, that someone had come to see her. Then realisation dawned. She sat bolt upright.

'My parents?' It was unbelievable how happy she felt that they were here, euphoric even. Or maybe it was just that the drugs were good and strong.

'No. Some other people. Do you want to see them?'

The jubilation deserted her in an instant. Maybe the drugs weren't so great after all. She nodded, listlessly.

She looked towards the door of the ward to see who appeared. Two men were walking along the aisle between the beds. For a heart-stopping moment, Edie thought it was Vuk and Vlad. Her hands involuntarily clutched at the sheet as if holding on tight to it would prevent them from getting her.

Then she saw the men more clearly and it wasn't Vuk and Vlad. It was Patrick and, of all people, Zayn.

'What are you doing here?'

'Hi, Edie, it's lovely to see you, too.' Patrick's freckled face was very smiley but Edie could sense anxiety behind his grin. He sat down in the plastic chair next to the bed. Zayn hovered awkwardly beside him.

'You can sit on the bed, Zayn,' Edie suggested.

Zayn perched nervously on the corner furthest from Edie.

'You stood me up,' Patrick said, still answering Edie's original question. 'We arranged to meet for coffee in the morning – a couple of days ago now, you've been unconscious. Maybe you don't remember, but when you didn't show, I got a bit worried about you, mainly because of the state you were in when I encountered you in the bay.'

Edie searched her memory. She did recall something about planning a breakfast rendezvous, but she was mostly too taken aback by the passage of time to concentrate on remembering exactly what had been agreed. It felt like months had passed since she'd been on the *Radomira*.

'How did you find me?' she asked. She had a vague recollection of a long swim followed by a long walk that had ended – she didn't know how.

Patrick leant forward towards the bed. He patted the back of her hand gently as he spoke.

'It wasn't me who found you. You narrowly missed being scooped out of a quarry like a lump of stone and dumped in a truck with a whole lot of boulders on top of you.'

Patrick paused.

'Oh.' It was the only response Edie could think of.

'Fortunately, the foreman was checking the site to see where to excavate next and he spotted you in the nick of time. He called the police and an ambulance – and the rest is history.'

Edie rolled her eyes. 'What a troublemaker I am.'

'No!' Zayn interjected. 'You are a good person, Edie.'

Edie sighed. 'It was a joke,' she explained, weakly. It was kind of Zayn to come to visit her. Come to think of it though – why *had* he come?

'Why are you here?' she asked, as soon as the thought had occurred to her. And then she shook her head and turned it sideways to look at Patrick. 'I mean, sorry, Patrick, you haven't finished your story yet. How did you know I was here?'

'I already had the police out looking for you,' he replied, softly. 'They were fairly reluctant, I think they had you down as … well, as a fantasist, someone not to be taken too seriously.'

Edie digested this information. It was only what she had known to be the case. But still – the truth can hurt. And what hurt the most was that it was probably the reason nothing had been done to find Laura.

'They didn't believe that Laura was in danger, just that she was a bit unreliable. Like how they saw you.'

Patrick wasn't pulling his punches. It was probably better that way, better than being lied to and given false reassurances anyway.

'I knew that the police were going to do jack shit,' Edie said, blankly. 'That's why I asked Vuk to help – with the posters and – why I confided in him.' The idea that Vuk would be her saviour was not even funny anymore; it was horrific.

Zayn shuffled down the bed to get closer to Edie. 'Vuk had no intention of helping you.' He swallowed hard as if choking back anger. 'I kept one of the posters you made, that you asked him to translate. It didn't say anything about a missing person. Do you know what the writing said?'

Edie shook her head dumbly. She couldn't imagine. 'Kill this girl?' No, even Vuk wouldn't be that blatant.

'He wrote, "Happy Birthday to Laura from England. Many congratulations and have a great year".' The outrage in Zayn's voice was plain to hear.

Edie's disbelieving snort of laughter sent arrows of pain through her body. 'Well, at least we didn't waste the time in putting them up.' She reached out for Zayn's arm and touched it lightly. 'Thanks to you realising how pointless it was.'

There was silence for a moment. Edie could almost hear her brain whirring. There were still so many parts of the puzzle missing.

'But why had you already called the police, Patrick? Didn't you just think I was unreliable, too? You can hardly have been surprised when such a lightweight as me didn't make it for breakfast.' Edie's tone of voice was mocking, of herself and how she was perceived.

Patrick grinned. 'I believed you from the outset. And when I met you in the bay and you told me what was going on – well, I started to wonder if it had any connection to what I was investigating.'

'Investigating? I thought you were on holiday.' Edie wasn't sure whether to take Patrick seriously or not.

'So did I. But I noticed a few things that didn't seem quite right and once my suspicions had been roused I'm afraid the old news hound in me took over. The papers were full of reports of the "new" Balkan route that refugees were following to get to Europe but there's never only one path. I called up some old acquaintances, did a bit of digging – and put two and two together.'

Edie was listening intently. 'Carry on,' she urged him, impatiently. 'What happened when you did the maths and got four?'

'It's quite complicated and I haven't got all the elements straight myself yet. I'll make sure you're the first to see my article when it's published. But in essence, your friends Vlad and Vuk were part of a sophisticated, multi-country people-smuggling ring that extended throughout Greece and the Balkans. They charged top prices to ship refugees as far into the EU as they could and gave them false identities so that they didn't have to undergo the usual procedures for asylum seekers. It was extremely lucrative for them. That's why they had that super-lux boat – they needed to look the part, to fit in as members of the rich, international yachting community flitting around the islands of the Adriatic and across to Italy. But they were ruthless and if anything went wrong, if the money wasn't right or the refugees caused trouble – they were not above robbing them blind and dumping them.'

Edie contemplated this information in silence. It was as she had thought, exactly what she had also deduced by putting two and two together, although perhaps would not have been able to articulate quite as elegantly as Patrick.

Patrick was rubbing his stubbly chin with his hand, allowing her time to take it all in. 'I realised that you were in big trouble. By investigating Laura's disappearance you had exposed Vuk, Vlad, and the resort that provided their cover to a level of scrutiny that was unwelcome, to put it mildly. Remember their reaction to the police search? I didn't think the danger was imminent at first – but when you didn't turn up this morning I went to your room, and when I didn't find you there, I looked everywhere else I could think of. I noticed that the *Radomira* was absent from the harbour. I went to the resort office saying I'd arrived too late for a trip I'd booked and wanted a refund and they told me categorically that there was no trip today. And then I knew where you were.'

Edie wondered if she'd inadvertently walked into a film set or a parallel life of some kind. This was all insane, nonsensical.

'I can't believe it,' was all she managed to say.

'Well, believe it, Edie – it's a miracle that you survived. These people – not just Vlad and Vuk but the whole gang – are utterly ruthless and they weren't going to let a young girl come between them and the money they were making.'

The cruelty in Vlad's mocking laugh as he'd plotted her demise came back to Edie in a red-hot flush of fear. She looked around her anxiously, imagining him appearing from under her bed and stabbing her in the heart. 'Where are they?' she asked, terrified.

'Under lock and key.' A smile of self-satisfaction curled around Patrick's mouth. 'Nothing to worry about now.'

Edie lay back on her pillows, letting this knowledge sink in.

'So the hut on the hill – it was one of the transit points for the refugees,' she asked, working it out as she spoke. 'Nothing to do with Laura.'

There was a tiny, almost imperceptible pause. She snapped her gaze to Patrick who shifted awkwardly under it. What did he know about Laura that he wasn't telling?

'No, nothing,' he replied, quietly.

'And the scarf I found, that disappeared from my room the day the police came? Not Laura's?'

'Dropped by someone else. It may have been used as a hijab. The point is that it would have had scent on it that the dogs might have identified. That's why your room was broken into and the scarf taken, to make sure the police didn't find it. Zayn was asked to get rid of it.'

'Oh.'

There was a long silence while Edie tried to digest all this information. Eventually, Zayn shifted his position on the bed and she remembered his presence.

'But what's any of this got to do with you?' she demanded of him. 'I mean – sorry, I don't mean to be rude ... and of course it's lovely to see you. But I'm wondering how you fit in.'

Zayn nodded as if he'd been expecting such a question. 'It's very simple,' he answered in his soft, gentle voice.

'Fatima, who you rescued, whose life you saved, is my sister.'

THIRTY-EIGHT

Fatima

If it wasn't for Ali, Fatima wasn't sure how she would be coping now, laid up in hospital. She remembered how she had broken the ice on their first call by teasing him about his adopted name.

'Zayn? Do you think you're in a boy band or something?' she had asked, trying to keep the tone light, trying not to pour out all her anguish and distress, to keep her hopes of a lifeline hidden. If he couldn't help it wouldn't be his fault. He mustn't feel obliged, cornered. But he had fallen over himself to offer to do what he could, to work out how he could assist them and bring them to safety. No matter that it was this help that had led them all into the hands of the people-smugglers whose pitilessness might have killed them. He could not have predicted such an outcome.

And now, he had taken on the care of the twins while she was getting better. Ehsan and Youssef were detained for 'processing'; what on earth that meant and what would be the outcome of it Fatima did not want to contemplate. It was ironic that after all of it, all the weeks of travelling, the stench and the flies and the hunger and the degradation – they hadn't even properly got to Europe, had not reached the perceived sanctuary that arrival in the European Union would provide. It was hard not to see the whole venture as a complete disaster, except of course that they had all survived.

All except the baby. Thinking of the birth, weeks too soon, at sea, in boats that baked in the forty degree heat, Fatima bowed her head and felt her eyes grow hot and the tears begin to fall once more. The smugglers had dumped his body at sea without her even seeing him. She imagined him reborn as a water nymph, plump and cherubic, forever happily splashing in his underwater home. It was the only way to cope.

She did not know that Edie had been on the final yacht until Edie told her. And until Ali explained it to her, she had not realised that it was Edie who had saved their lives, her disappearance that had led to the authorities being notified, the boat intercepted and urgent medical treatment sought for Fatima.

She wanted to thank this girl, who seemed somehow lost, vulnerable, despite her fortunate position as someone with a legal status and a valid passport, a right to be here, or anywhere she chose. People like this did not have to so much as envisage the life of the stateless. But how to thank her adequately? She practised in her head:

'Don't you remember, Edie? You saved my life. If we hadn't been found I would have died from the infection, my body would have joined my son's in the sea. My girls would have been orphans. Whatever happens from now on, at least I am still here, alive, a mother. You are the one I have to thank for that.'

The girls were running and playing in the hospital forecourt where Fatima had taken them so they would not disturb the other patients. The fresh air, free from the smell of disinfectant and body odours, was delicious. It was cooler, now, in the evenings, as the long days of high summer drew to a close. She wondered where they would be, when winter came, her and the twins, Ehsan and Youssef. It was more than possible that they could be deported, sent back to where they had come from. Fatima could not even summon the energy to shed a tear at the thought. Nothing was worth thinking about anymore but the present, each day at a time, one by one. The future was out of her hands.

She called the twins to her, scooped them up, covered them with kisses and led them inside, back to the ward where Ali and the strange, pale English man were talking to Edie. The girls were fascinated, and slightly frightened, by this man's ginger hair, the like of which they had never seen before, and his mottled skin – freckles, Fatima knew they were called, but Marwa insisted on naming them spots. Ali, on the other hand, they had adored from the first moment of meeting. Blood is thicker than water, as the saying goes, and it seemed as though they had sensed their kinship without even being told of it.

Edie

Fatima came back with the twin girls just as Zayn had revealed that he was her brother. Edie was surprised, as surprised as she could muster the energy to be about anything right now. Zayn had always seemed so insular, such a lost soul wandering alone on a planet he didn't seem to truly understand. Now she knew why, for he had briefly explained his banishment from the family home for some undisclosed disobedience, followed by his exile, never to return. She was glad he had a sister, nieces, a family. That was nice for him.

'We're going now, Edie.' Patrick's voice cut into her thoughts. 'You need to rest as much as you can. Your parents will be here in the morning.'

'In the morning!' Edie could not prevent the high-pitched shriek that emanated from somewhere deep in her throat. 'I thought they were coming now?'

'They'll be here first thing. Nine o'clock, as soon as the hospital doors open to visitors.' Patrick's tone was reassuring, placatory.

'Right.' There was no point in fighting it. Acceptance; that was what Edie was all about these days. It was the best way. Then she remembered and sat bolt upright in her bed.

'But what will I tell them about Laura?' Her voice was like a wail now, pleading, despairing.

She caught the look that flashed between Patrick and Zayn.

'What?' They definitely knew something that they weren't telling her. 'What is it?'

Patrick patted her shoulder. 'Nothing. Everything's fine. You get some sleep.'

It was quiet once Patrick and Zayn had gone, Zayn tugging the two little girls along with him, one in each hand. They cried to leave their mother but Edie saw that the tears had gone by the time they reached the end of the ward and exited through the doors, urged on by promises of ice-cream.

'Thank you, Edie.'

The words took Edie by surprise. She didn't know what she had done that she deserved to be thanked for.

'You saved my life,' Fatima continued.

'Oh.' Edie couldn't think of anything to say in reply. Saving a life was undoubtedly an achievement but she wasn't quite sure how she'd done it. Still, Fatima thought she had and that was good, good that she, useless Edie who never quite achieved her potential, had done something so worthwhile. Pity she hadn't accomplished the same for Laura.

Fatima was still talking, saying more about what Edie had supposedly done, but Edie didn't really want to hear it, it made her uncomfortable. Anyway, the important thing now that Fatima was alive and likely to stay that way was where she would go next, what she would do.

'Would you like to go home? Don't you miss it?' Edie's question cut across Fatima's words of thanks.

Fatima shrugged. 'Of course I miss my country. But there is no country left to love, or to miss. My country no longer exists.' She looked at Edie and sighed.

'I need to find a new country.'

Edie

The night passed. Edie felt as if she didn't sleep at all but realised that she must have. Even so, at six am she was wide awake. So much had happened, apparently she was some kind of hero. But the one thing she had set out to do – finding Laura – she had not achieved. She had gone through all of this and still not found Laura. She rang the bell and asked a nurse to help her wash and get her dressed. She couldn't stand just lying there like an invalid anymore.

The delight that should have been her only emotion when her parents arrived was dissipated by Edie's preoccupation with Laura. They came clattering through the ward, tanned from their travels but faces etched with worry. Her mother Sophia's brown hair, greying now, was tied in a familiar plait. Her father Alex, who was half-Viennese, bore himself with his characteristic middle-European elegance. James was with them, tousled haired, looking as if he'd just stepped off the bus from Nepal or Ghana or wherever it was he'd been that eluded her now. She had not expected to see her brother. Her and Fatima both, reunited with a much-loved sibling. Tears overcame her, pouring down her cheeks, drowning her words.

Her mother engulfed her in her arms. 'It's okay,' she repeated, over and over again. 'Everything's going to be okay.'

Her father and brother stood awkwardly by the bed like two sentinels, austere, unsure of how to react to such a display of raw emotion.

'We're so proud of you, Edie. So very, very proud.' Her mother said the words and finally they sank in. 'You saved a life. Several lives. You were strong and brave and you didn't give in. You can take that with you, what you have achieved, for the rest of your life.'

She wished people would stop going on about her saving lives. The only life that mattered – Laura's – was still far from safe, or saved.

Her mother had her hands around Edie's head now, her cool palms against Edie's hot cheeks.

'We love you so much. More than the sun and the moon and the stars and the sky.'

Edie choked. These were the words her mother had always said, when it was bedtime, or at any parting. They were etched into her memory, woven into the fabric of her history.

'I've let you down, though,' she sobbed, when she could finally get the words out. 'I did all that, I did what you said. But I couldn't find Laura, I don't know what has happened to her. It's all my fault.'

There was a long silence, punctuated only by her mother's continued reassurances.

Finally, when she was calmer, Sophia relinquished her head from where she had clasped it against her bosom and took hold of Edie's hands in hers.

'Listen to me carefully now.' She paused to check that Edie was doing as instructed. 'You've been so courageous and so clever ... we all love you so much ...'

'Not courageous and clever enough to help Laura, though!' she burst out.

Sophia's grip tightened around her fingers. Edie knew what was coming but could hardly believe it. She felt herself shrivel up inside, her spirit broken.

'You haven't found Laura, have you? Tell me the truth, please.'

Out of the corner of her eye, Edie saw her father shift awkwardly from foot to foot. James coughed. He'd probably caught a cold on the plane; air travel was notorious for it. There was a long pause in which nobody spoke. And then her mother's voice again, calm and low.

'No, Edie, we haven't found her.'

Very, very slowly Sophia shut her eyes and then opened them again, taking a deep breath as she did so. She made sure that she had Edie's full attention before continuing.

'And we never will find her. She's gone.'

Fatima

Ali came to take Fatima from the hospital when the doctors pronounced her better, the infection beaten. He paid for it all as well; it was obvious that she couldn't. So many debts incurred now, so much to repay.

'You can apply for asylum here,' Ali told her.

'But it's not the European Union,' Fatima replied, without thinking of what she was saying, and then was immediately overcome with remorse. How could she be so ungrateful? What did the EU matter? No one was dropping barrel bombs here, no political dissenters were being beheaded in the streets. Polio was well and truly eradicated with no sign of the return that it was making in her country and in the camps where so many had sought refuge, crammed together in conditions that made the world's most feared diseases rub their hands with glee. She took a deep breath and tried to get a grip on herself.

'It's not the EU, no,' agreed Ali, thoughtfully. 'But it's a nice place and anyway, it will be part of the club – eventually. We hope. It's only a matter of time.'

Time. She had lots of that, now. No house to keep, no

husband to care for, no garden to tend, no work to do. No baby, with all a newborn's needs and demands.

'You can get in before the rush.' Ali's attempt at a joke was endearingly well meant.

Fatima smiled. 'Yes.' And then she thought about the resort on which he had been working, the money he had given to his bosses for their passage and documents – all his savings from over ten years' hard graft gone now, and more besides that he still owed them, and no European citizenship and no documents at the end of it all. She didn't want them now anyway, didn't want to be illegal, illegitimate. It would be much better to follow the due process of the law, to be somewhere properly.

'But what will we live on? *Where* will we live?' She presumed Ali's job would be over now, now that the resort's sordid underbelly had been revealed.

'There's nothing to worry about, Fatima.' Ali's smile was so wide and so proud that Fatima had to choke back tears. 'Vuk and Vlad – the smugglers – don't own the place. The actual owner is a foreign investor, he had no idea what was going on. He's clean as clean so the resort can carry on. And so it will – with me as general manager! I get one of the big cabins, there's plenty of room for you and the girls – you can have the bedroom and I'll sleep on the sofa. Plus I'll have a much bigger salary. Ivana – you don't know her but you'll meet her soon – she'll be the finance and business manager ... And you can work with me, earn your own money.'

Fatima could hardly believe it. Surely after so much pain the solution could not be this easy. There had to be a problem somewhere.

'What about Ehsan and Youssef?' That was the problem.

Ali shrugged. 'They have the right to apply to stay, too. But I think they won't. They want to make it to Germany.'

Weariness overcame Fatima. She didn't want to lose Youssef

but she understood Ehsan's desire to press on – which would also mean that she never had to lay eyes on him again if she didn't want to. She considered whether she'd ever tell anyone about the rape, about the humiliation and horror he had meted out to her. Probably not. She would rather bury it with all the other nightmares. As for heading north – Ehsan had always been one to follow the herd. That herd had its nose turned towards northern Europe and Ehsan and Youssef would become part of their number. At least the danger had passed now; the worst of the journey was over. They would make it alive, for sure. For Ehsan, Fatima didn't care. But for dear, sweet Youssef, she did. She said a silent prayer for him.

She turned to Ali. 'Let's go.' The girls were playing on Ali's phone, absorbed in a game he'd found for them. 'Marwa, Maryam, come on. We're going home.'

Edie

Edie thought that, on hearing such news she would scream and shout and cry and wail, keen like you saw women from ancient tribes on educative TV programmes do. But she didn't. Not at first anyway. But then it dawned on her, exactly what her mother was saying and the world collapsed around her.

'So – so she's ... she's ...' Edie faltered, unable to finish the sentence. And then anger filled her and she was screeching, 'And you've all been making small talk and not telling me! Hiding it from me, lying to me.' She threw herself onto the bed and buried her face in the pillow. The tears that streamed down her cheeks fell onto the sheets and were absorbed, leaving dark patches on their crisp whiteness. 'She came here and we went out and then she got lost and now she's gone and nobody ever seemed to take it seriously except me – but now look! And it's all my fault.'

Sophia fiddled distractedly with the corner of the sheet she was clutching. She had taken hold of it when Edie had snatched her hands away, seeming to need to grasp onto something.

'Edie, listen. Laura didn't come, she was never here.'

Blah, blah blah. Edie stuck her fingers in her ears to avoid hearing but it didn't work because she still could.

Sophia paused, her eyes imploring, her grip on the sheet tightening.

'There is no Laura, Edie,' she said, slowly and firmly, her voice never wavering.

Blah. Blah. Blah.

'Laura doesn't exist. You know that. You've always known it.'

A deep silence descended on the hospital ward. Her mother's voice broke through it once more.

'There is no Laura.'

EPILOGUE

'How did the session go?'

Edie shrugged and looked out of the window. It was October and Brighton gleamed in the golden glow of the muted autumn sunshine. A few trees had turned colour and even begun to shed their leaves but most still wore the mantle of summer. The U2 song in which Bono sings of the October trees being bare came to Edie's mind. It wasn't true, she realised for the first time now. Unless the seasons worked differently in Ireland. Perhaps they did. Or maybe it was the effects of climate change since the song was written. Who knew?

'Edie?' Her mother's voice intruded on her thoughts once more. 'I asked how the session went. Did you – was it useful? Do you think?'

Sophia's questions were so tentative, so beseeching.

Come on, Edie, she muttered to herself under her breath. *Remember, it's the new Edie now. The mature, grown-up, responsible one.*

She flicked through her phone and alighted on the photos Fatima had sent her of her and the twins splashing in the sea, the sunlight sending bright flares shooting from the blue.

She put the phone down and took a deep breath.

'I think it went well.' She paused and looked around her, as if seeking inspiration from the mundane surroundings of the family kitchen, complete with the detritus of daily life; the heaps of mail piled on a corner of the table, the half-emptied bag of shopping on the counter. 'It felt – *I* felt – that I've made some progress. That I've begun to understand why I feel the way I do and why I can believe something so strongly that I know isn't true.'

The last words came out in a rush, tumbling on top of each other like her piled up memories that were constantly threatening to cascade downwards and drown her. Except that she was finally beginning to understand that they weren't memories at all, just the febrile imaginings of her damaged mind. This was what she was seeing the shrink to sort out.

'That's good, Edie. Really good.'

Sophia's relief, her desperation for it to be true was so evident in her voice, despite her obvious attempts to hide it, that Edie felt guilt subsume her as it so often had before. She knew how much it mattered to her mother that she should conquer her 'illness'.

Lost Twin Syndrome.

Edie knew, had known all her life, that her twin sister had been stillborn, dying shortly before or during birth; the doctors had never been quite sure exactly when she had passed away. Edie had been introduced to the name of the condition known as Lost Twin Syndrome as a young teenager, when the symptoms had reached new heights – or should that be depths?

The precise way in which she was affected varied over time, but the central point was always the absolute certainty that Laura was there beside her, only for her to disappear, for the illusion to implode so that Edie was left utterly bereft and alone again. She was locked into an endless cycle of constantly searching for a soulmate, for the person who should be Laura, then finding they weren't Laura and having to begin all over again. The last time she had been really bad had been when she was at university. In the end she'd dropped out, unable to cope with the blackness, the desperate sense of loss that pervaded her soul, the constant feeling of something missing, of a part of herself that was incomplete, all of which symptoms manifested themselves in paranoia, psychosis and obsessions.

She'd had some therapy and it had improved a bit but then, on a whim, she'd chucked it all in, packed her bags and headed for the sun. All her mother and father's anguished pleading had not brought her back and in the end, urged on by James who told them they couldn't put their lives on hold indefinitely because of Edie, they'd gone to the Andes for their trip of a lifetime. Edie, defiantly sticking it out, too proud to give in, had spiralled downwards. Her fixation on Vuk, so dangerous, so nearly deadly, had been part of it all.

Edie sensed her mother passing behind her chair. Sophia knelt down beside her, as you do with little children so that you are on their level, and met her gaze.

'I know how hard this is for you. I've spent all your life trying to make the fact that your twin died at birth OK, for you and for me.'

Edie's hands were clenched into fists on the table and Sophia placed her hands on top of them.

'At the time, we were advised to tell you that you had been a twin, not to keep secrets. I've always wondered if that was the right thing to do.'

Sophia's beautiful eyes, creased at the corners with the beginnings of the signs of age, were damp with tears. Edie looked away. She wanted to shout out 'NO', to refuse to listen, to ignore anything that was said to her about Laura's death. This is what she had done so many times in the past.

But things were different now. The realisation came as a revelation. The experiences of the summer, that had culminated in the rescue of Fatima and her daughters, seemed to have brought Edie to her senses, forcing her to take responsibility for herself and her future in a way she never had before. And perhaps seeing little Marwa and Maryam, a real pair of identical twins, had enabled her to understand that that had never been her and Laura. Her childhood with Laura had only ever existed in her imagination – albeit more strongly, more convincingly, more compellingly than anything else she had experienced whilst growing up.

Her mother had always blamed herself, for Laura's stillbirth, which couldn't possibly be her fault, and for not handling the issue properly, for not saying the right things to Edie when she was little and therefore leaving her susceptible to LTS and all its attendant problems – which may or may not be her fault. Perhaps the biggest thing that Edie had learnt that summer, or started to see clearly, was that it didn't matter who was to blame; whose responsibility it was. The person who had to make the effort to sort it was herself.

'It's not your fault, Mum,' replied Edie, her voice calm. 'It's not anyone's fault, as far as I can see. It's just something that has happened and needs dealing with.'

She wiped her hand across her face. She hadn't realised she had started to cry until she felt her nose running.

Sophia passed her daughter a tissue.

'Sometimes,' she said, Edie's hands once more held firmly between hers, 'when you were tiny, I used to think I could hear another baby crying. I was so sure of it, I'd go and check the nursery. But of course there was no baby but you.'

Sophia gave a long sniff. Her voice cracked as she continued.

'I believed that I needed to find the other baby and feed it before I dealt with you. I don't mean that baby was more important, just that I knew where you were and that you were fine and well-fed, but the other baby was hidden somewhere, needing me, but I wasn't there for her.'

'I think it's you who needs the tissues,' said Edie in as light-hearted a manner as possible, trying to lighten the atmosphere that had suddenly grown as heavy as lead. Sophia had never told her this before. Edie had always thought she was the only one who had suffered from Laura's loss. How could she have been so self-absorbed, so selfish, as to not realise what her mother must have gone through, losing a baby?

Edie thought of Fatima, who had so tragically had the same experience.

The memories made her even more determined that she would beat this thing, whatever it was, this time. Some twins make it; little Marwa and Maryam, for example, so scrumptious, their cuteness quite unreasonably beguiling to Edie, who couldn't stand children normally. Some twins don't make it. The human mother is not really designed for multiple births. There are those who believe that the dead twin attaches its soul to the surviving twin. She would take Laura's soul and join it with her own, and together, they would learn the cure, for good and all.

It would take time. Lots of time. She had tried and failed to overcome so many times before. But now she knew that she had reserves she had never imagined. She had uncovered a people-smuggling ring, albeit unwittingly, and been instrumental in its downfall. She had swum the Adriatic Sea, she had climbed a mountain (it had felt like that, anyway), she had fallen into a flipping quarry – and she had survived. Surely she could deal with this? If she were ever to move on, she would have to.

'The woman you saved ...' Sophia had a faraway look in her eye as she began to speak again. 'Fatima ...'

Perhaps they were telepathic, because her mother was thinking of Fatima, too. Edie noticed how she called her a woman, whereas Edie always thought of herself as a girl. She needed to develop that maturity, she told herself. Bloody hell, twenty-three was old enough to have some gravitas about one, after all.

'Poor Fatima. I lost Laura and she has lost her baby boy. I hope her grief is not too great for her to cope with.'

Edie recalled Fatima's seemingly indomitable strength. Yet

Fatima had told her once, when they were in the hospital together, how she hadn't used to be like that, how previously, in her former life, she had been utterly dependent on her husband. She had had to learn to be strong overnight, after their house was bombed and her life destroyed.

Finally letting go of Laura felt to Edie like a task of similar magnitude but of course it wasn't. Any fool could see that. And whether it was or it wasn't, Fatima's fortitude and courage, her resilience, would be her inspiration.

'I'm so sad her baby died.'

It was all Edie could think of to say.

Thinking of the little boy seemed to have set Sophia off on another course of memory.

'When James came along, you used to tell him that he was your twin, and you used to want me to dress him in girls' clothes so that he could be like you.'

Edie contemplated this for a moment. 'Poor bastard,' she sighed, remembering the way she had tormented and smothered him. 'No wonder he goes to all these far-flung places whenever he gets a chance. Desperate to be rid of me.'

'Certainly not!' Sophia sat up straight and, with one last, surreptitious sniff, regained her usual composure. 'He loved you, he was besotted with you. I think he just always felt that he wasn't good enough. That you'd never love him as much as he did you because he wasn't Laura.'

Edie prodded at the wooden table-top, trying to dislodge a crumb that had got caught in one of its ridges. 'Oh dear,' she replied, inadequately. It was hard to know what to say to undo all the injuries of the past. 'I probably damaged him for life.'

'No, Edie!' Sophia's mouth was a round O of horror. 'I don't think he suffered through it, he accepted it. He had so many friends of his own, and girlfriends – how many girlfriends! – he never wanted for adoration. I said that because I wanted you to know that he understands. We all do,' she concluded, firmly. She cupped her hands around Edie's cheeks and kissed her nose the way she used to when Edie was small. 'We just want you to get better.'

Edie nodded.

'And when you are, remember that we promised Fatima we'd go and visit her, have a holiday on the resort. Or nearby, if that has too many bad memories,' Sophia added hastily. 'No working this time – just relaxing. You could practise your free-diving some more. Perfect your skills.'

Sophia attempted a laugh and then faltered as if not sure whether Edie would find it a laughing matter.

Edie smiled. 'Mum, you don't have to tread so carefully. I'm not an eggshell.'

She thought of the resort, of the blazing summer sun and the blue, blue sea glittering beneath it, and smiled again, albeit wanly.

'I'd love to see Fatima and the twins. And Zayn.' She gave a snort of resigned disbelief at the sound of his name. How could she have been so wrong, been such a bad judge of character? She'd dismissed him as weak and ineffectual, as not virile and manly like Vuk. She'd even believed him to be a baddie, just like Vlad – and Vuk – when in fact he'd been doing everything he could to rescue his sister from a fate that was, quite possibly, worse than death. As for Vuk – how terribly she had misjudged him. God, she was rubbish sometimes.

'Patrick and Debs are going at Easter,' Sophia said, as if suddenly remembering something she'd been told a long time ago. 'Patrick rang while you were out and told me – which reminds me that he asked you to call back sometime so that you can tell him how you are.'

The way Sophia mentioned the phone call made it sound as if it already belonged to the distant past. Their chat, more honest and open than they had had in years, seemed to have altered time. Edie acknowledged to herself now that she had never allowed such talk, had shut down any such conversation. But sharing was good, she understood in an instant of self-realisation.

'So don't forget to call Patrick later, will you.'

Edie felt her cheeks redden as she remembered how she had mocked him and Debs, had been so critical and judgemental, especially of Debs. Her dismissive attitude towards others was yet one more bad trait that must be quashed; she had to stop that behaviour, to grow up. Live and let live would be her new motto.

'I will,' Edie assured her mother, and meant it.

'And the holiday? Any initial thoughts?'

Edie watched the sunlight shafting through the tree branches in the garden and casting dapples of light on the window panes. They needed cleaning.

'Perhaps we can go next summer, as soon as swimming season starts again?'

It would be good to go, like getting back on a horse when you've taken a bad fall. Restorative.

Sophia nodded. 'That sounds perfect. But,' she paused and made sure Edie was looking at her before continuing. 'only if you are well. Because in all honesty Edie, that's the only thing any of us truly wants.'

Edie bit her lip and twizzled her phone around on the table before replying.

'Yes,' she finally said, as firmly as possible though she could feel her voice wavering.

'That's what I want, too. To get better. And I promise that I will.' She looked up and met her mother's gaze full on.

'It's time I let Laura's ghost go, to rest in peace.'

AUTHOR'S NOTE

LOST TWIN SYNDROME

Lost Twin Syndrome is one name for a phenomenon in which a surviving twin experiences feelings of loneliness, loss and longing for the twin who didn't make it. It seems that these emotions may be felt particularly strongly when a twin dies at birth or shortly before or after, and they can last a lifetime. There are many possible symptoms, some of which are similar to depression or other mental illnesses, and can involve eating disorders and other destructive behaviours. Sufferers also report experiencing such things as low self-esteem, a tendency to remain involved in unhealthy relationships and the need for a partner to be a perfect soulmate.

KILLER READS

DISCOVER THE BEST
IN CRIME AND THRILLER

Follow us on social media to get to know the team behind the books, enter exclusive giveaways, learn about the latest competitions, hear from our authors, and lots more:

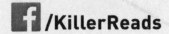 /KillerReads   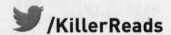 /KillerReads

Printed by RR Donnelley at Glasgow, UK